About the Author

Susan was born in the 60s. She grew up on a council estate in Hertfordshire and has been creating stories in her head since she was a child. Although poor school attendance meant she left with minimal writing skills, her hunger for knowledge drove her to return to education as a mature student, where she achieved three A levels and a degree with Hons at university. Susan now manages a charity. She is passionate about writing and is on her fifth novel. This book is her second.

All proceeds from the sale of this book will be donated to The Scratching Post (Cat Rescue).

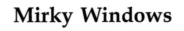

Mirky Windows

Susan Delaney

Mirky Windows

Olympia Publishers
London

www.olympiapublishers.com
OLYMPIA PAPERBACK EDITION

A CIP catalogue record for this title is
available from the British Library.

ISBN: 978-1-78830-232-6

This is a work of fiction.
Names, characters, places and incidents originate from the writer's imagination.
Any resemblance to actual persons, living or dead, is purely coincidental.

First Published in 2020

Olympia Publishers
Tallis House
2 Tallis Street
London
EC4Y 0AB
Printed in Great Britain

Chapter One

'Bliss, no school,' Jane thought, not for the first time that day. Stooping, she pulled off her smelly pumps, wrinkling her nose against the pungent smell of her own feet. The grass felt cool and refreshing against her skin. Heading through the park entrance, Jane was careful not to tread on any sharp objects or dog packages.

The sun was warm, making her skin feel clammy. She headed towards her favourite spot amongst a clump of trees, hoping the canopies would offer protection against the heat.

Being a Saturday made little difference to Jane; she hardly ever attended school anyway. It just meant she did not have to risk being seen and gaining detention for 'bunking off'. How she hated school and longed for the six-week holidays, which were still a whole month away.

'A month!' she sighed to herself. 'That may as well be a whole year.'

Reaching the trees Jane found a spot under a large oak tree and sank down. With her back against its massive trunk, she closed her eyes. A small breeze rippled lightly over her face, tickling her damp skin. Sighing, she allowed her mind to drift back to last night's peculiar dream.

The dream was not unfamiliar to her; it had haunted her most nights for as far back as she could remember. Last night it had been slightly different though. Jane had been standing in the most beautiful garden she had ever seen. At least she did not remember seeing one like it before. Except in her dreams.

The array of flowers had been amazing. Their dazzling glow had even caused her to avert her eyes from the brilliance of colours. The sun was so bright and enormous, it seemed possible it could fall down and crash into the earth. How odd that she could even feel the heat on her skin. 'How could that be?' she marvelled; a dream was not real.

A soft, warm breeze had rippled over the velvet petals of the flowers; they danced, highlighting their glory and wondrous beauty. Their texture was solid on her fingertips as she gently caressed the delicate frames.

In the dream Jane had felt safe, as though she belonged there.

The garden was not unfamiliar, she realised; she had seen it before, but as hard as she tried Jane could never remember where. Maybe in a film or magazine?

Looking down she had been surprised to find her hand clasping the arm of a pink teddy bear. Holding it up, Jane studied the unblinking, brown eyes. It was pristine, obviously new, and never played with or loved by a child. Even the yellow ribbon tied around its neck was a perfect bow, stiff and unwrinkled.

'Isabella,' a lady's voice had called, 'Isabella!'

Jane turned to see whom the voice belonged to, but there was no one there.

She had woken with a start and sat up in bed, staring bewildered around the dismal, dark bedroom. The dream was so real, Jane honestly believed she had been in the garden. Even the teddy had felt firm in her hand, so much so she had searched the bed looking for it.

It was strange, because in the dream and just as she woke, Jane had recognised the lady's voice. As her mind came back to reality, she could not quite grasp who she was.

Pondering all these thoughts she became aware that the sun, despite the tree's shade, was burning the top of her head. Jane could almost swear she smelled singed hair. An image popped into her mind of her standing in front of a big rectangular mirror. Her blue eyes widened with horror at the sight of her long blond hair burned into a frizzled lump. It stood straight in the air and out to each side. Grabbing for a large pair of scissors she began to hack away at the unruly mess. Big clumps fell to the floor, leaving a scalp of bald patches edged by wonky lumps of dull, tangled and singed tufts all sticking out of a very sore scalp.

Jane put her hand to her head just to check her vision was not real. Gratefully, although her head was hot, her hair was intact. It was still smooth, scraped back into a ponytail with an elastic band to secure it. How she hated her hair, as it always got in the way and was forever full of tangles. Trying hard to keep it tidy was a trial and usually resulted in handfuls falling out.

Jane smiled to herself; her vivid imagination had saved her from many a scrape in her thirteen years. She was able to reel off the best, most feasible story in an instant. To Jane they were not lies but survival; her quick-thinking mind saved her from not only many a beating but also from insanity. 'Surrealism,' she told herself; an escape from reality.

Jane felt pleased with herself, as she rarely went to school and knew very little of anything much. But on one occasion she had learned about surrealism in her art lesson. Now her daydreams were her own surrealism and her only happiness away from her dull, lonely life.

She stood up and begun to walk aimlessly through the park. The June heat was exceptionally warm today, making her skin feel damp. She was sure her armpits must smell dreadful and tried a few times to sniff at them. How she wished for something cooler to wear instead of the almost threadbare jumper.

Grabbing at a handful of leaves from a nearby shrub, she took great satisfaction in crushing them in her palm, then felt a little guilty, looking back at the now bare branch wobbling back into place in the bountiful leafy bush. Forgetting her guilt, she picked another and begun shredding it carefully along the thin veins. So far, she had never completed the task without breaking one or two of the fine stalks.

Lost in another daydream, Jane was suddenly amongst a group of imaginary friends and her name wasn't dull Jane. It was something far more interesting; it was Isabella, from her dreams.

The pretend Isabella was posh, clever and ever so pretty. At first, she had long red hair and lots of freckles on her smiley, cheeky face. But, soon becoming bored with this, she now had short black hair with piercing blue eyes and olive skin. Of course, all the boys fancied her and hung around her constantly, desperate for a date.

Along with Isabella was an imaginary group of blurry friends, yet to be created. They loved their beautiful leader intently, hanging on her every word and laughing at the very funny jokes she reeled off.

Isabella was popular and the envy of everyone. Well respected, not only by her peers, but also by adults.

Her clothes, which Jane imagined in fine detail, were not so much modern as unusual, always coordinated, yet with wild and eccentric colours that were so outstanding people would talk about them long after they were discarded for others equally as stylish.

It had taken Jane hour after hour to put these colours and fabrics together to come up with the outstanding outfits. Long winter months spent trawling different clothes shops to decide. Or, when it was too wet and cold, sitting in the library flicking through magazines and books. It was difficult to be original and think of amazing outfits that no one else had already thought of. Then there was jewellery, which always caused more issues, more hours walking aimlessly around shops to find suitable finery to match.

Other girls were envious of Isabella; they tried to copy her. But she was too quick to change her style and ideas, so no one could ever compete. When she was tired of creating outfits, Jane had invented a best friend for Isabella. Her name was first Harriet, but that soon became stuffy and pompous. Now she was Lizzy. Like Isabella she was very pretty; not as pretty as her, though. Her hair was blonde and her eyes large and brown. The two of them were so close they were inseparable; always seen walking arm in arm, whispering secrets to each other.

Dressing Lizzy was a hard task and sometimes tiring; besides, Jane did not want to take any thunder from Isabella. So, most of the time Lizzy just wore jeans and a blurry top.

Discarding the ruined leaf, Jane began to walk again. She was stuck today with what Isobel was wearing. Summer clothes were far more difficult than winter. It was hard to be the height of fashion when it was so hot. Even under the shady trees it was difficult to breathe. As she described it, 'like breathing in air from a hair dryer'. Anything she wore today would make her feel like screaming, tearing it off and running naked through the park. Jane grinned to herself, imagining people's faces if she did that. Staring down dismally at her clothes, she flapped the bottom of her jumper to allow some air under.

On hearing nearby voices, she stopped; her heart sank and she quickly dodged behind the closest tree. Thankfully, the trunk hid her small frame. Jane peered around one side and fixed her eyes on the small gang of girls sitting a short distance away, next to the tennis courts.

Desperate to remain hidden, Jane sank down onto the moss that surrounded the trunk. She pulled at a clump of grass, trying to calm herself. They were sitting in view of Frank's bench. Her friend Mrs Flanagan was not there yet. Either she had been and gone or she was still shopping. But even if she did appear and took her usual breather on the bench, Jane could not go and see her. Not with Lucy Ellis and her friends sitting so close by.

All the children at school hated Jane, but Lucy hated her the most. How she wished she were Isobel and not just drab, ugly Jane.

Lucy was popular and pretty and most boys fancied her, 'hanging round her like flies round a honey pot' — one of her mother's more sober expressions — or 'flies round dog shit', when she had had a few.

Hearing the voices moving closer, Jane quickly stood and poked her head around the side of the tree again. The little gang were heading her way. Her heart began to pound and her clenched palms started to sweat. In her panic she darted to the left of the large trunk to avoid them. It was the wrong way; Jane was right in the sight path of Naomi Harris.

'Oh my God, look what we have here then, it's plain, ugly Jane,' Naomi laughed spitefully.

Jane's heart missed a beat before it began thumping so hard it vibrated in her ears, her breath coming in small, tight gasps. The girls were around her in a flash.

'God, you stink,' Lucy spat at her, the pretty blue eyes glazing with delight and spite.

The others, all five of them, began to laugh as Lucy's hand reached out and grabbed Jane's ponytail.

'Don't touch it, Lucy, it's probably diseased — or at least full of nits.' Emma, one of the other girls, wrinkled her nose in disgust.

'You stink of piss. You need to learn how to keep yourself clean. You're so disgusting,' Lucy advised, sounding the more expert, as she wiggled her hips and pulled at Jane's hair more.

'Yes, she makes me feel sick. It should not be allowed. It stinks the class out,' Emma said again.

'Let's give it a wash then.' Lucy's eyes glistened with fun. 'There's a hose on the tap near the toilets, or better still, let's flush her head down the loo, it smells as bad as her.'

They laughed again as Lucy, loving her new game, began pulling Jane in the direction of the toilets.

'Please, let me go,' Jane pleaded, her voice little more than a whisper, some of her words disappearing in mid-sentence as her voice faded with fear.

'What was that?' Lucy, still holding her hair with one hand, put the other to her ear.

'Please, Lucy, let me go,' Jane begged, feeling tears pricking the back of her eyelids.

'Oh bless, it's going to cry,' Emma laughed gleefully, enjoying the game that alleviated the boredom of the day.

Lucy yanked at Jane's hair so hard it ripped, a handful detaching itself from her scalp. She lifted the clump and smelled it.

'God, that is disgusting,' she spat and shook her hand to rid herself of the contaminated hair, making a big show of flicking it away.

Jane's heart sank even further as Alan McKenzie and Stuart Reamer wandered towards the little gang. Alan put an arm round Lucy. The two of them had been an item for a few months now. Most girls fancied him; not Jane though, she hated him more than she did Lucy.

'What you lot up to?' he asked, although it was obvious.

'We're just gonna go and wash this filthy cow. Doing it a favour cos she needs to learn how to clean herself,' Lucy told him, her expression pensive.

'Good idea, let's give her a drink first, bet she never had one before.' Alan thrust forward a bottle of cider and wobbled it with glee, giving a wide, wicked grin.

Jane tried hard to fight as they pulled her to the ground. Alan sat astride her chest and Lucy squeezed her nose so she could not breathe without opening her mouth. They unscrewed the bottle and laughed as they poured the cider down her throat. Jane gagged and spluttered, trying to turn her head away. But it was firmly clasped between Lucy's knees. The liquid was foul as it flooded into her nose. Jane gasped, trying to breathe, panic gripping her that she would die, either by suffocation or drowning.

'Come on, you lot,' Kelly Morris said. She stood at the back and looked a little awkward. 'Leave her alone, let's go.'

Jane felt grateful to Kelly; she was the nicest of them all.

Suddenly, much to his surprise, something hit Alan around the head, knocking him sideways.

'What the fuck?' he shouted, grasping the injury.

It was Mrs Flanagan. 'Get away from her, you evil bastard,' the elderly lady spat.

So engrossed were they in their game, no one had seen her walking up behind them. She swung her bag again, hitting the shocked Alan even harder. The bag contained two tins and a frozen lamb chop, so it must have hurt.

'Get off her!' the elderly lady demanded again, her old, watery eyes blazing with anger at what they were doing to her young friend.

They did. Alan jumped up, mumbling and the gang walked off down the path to the park entrance, with Alan still clutching his throbbing head. Lucy stuck one finger rudely up at Mrs Flanagan as they swaggered out of the entrance.

'Next time you won't have an old corpse to save you!' she shouted back.

Jane was sobbing as Mrs Flanagan helped her to her feet, allowing the tears to fall onto her welcome shoulder. She was a tiny woman, who could not have been more than 5 feet in height.

'Ahhh, come on dear, don't cry, they've gone now,' she cooed. 'Nasty little sods. I've a good mind to be on to the school about them. I know that Lucy's mother. 'Orrible woman.' Her voice shook with anger.

'Oh, please don't. It'll be worse for me if they find out,' Jane sobbed.

How sad, Mrs Flanagan felt, that bullies got away with it, because children were too afraid to speak out. How many girls and boys had actually committed suicide due to bullying?

'Come on, love, let's go and take a breather.'

Wiggling one hand free, Mrs Flanagan reached into her large grey bag and pulled out a tissue. She handed it to Jane as they walked to the bench.

It was the bench Mrs Flanagan sat on every day in nice weather. The one where her Frank had proposed and she had conceived her first baby. Jane had gone very red when she had giggled while she confessed this.

Jane knew all about sex, most of it learned when she overheard the girls at school talking.

'Don't worry about losing your virginity, Jane; you stink too much for any boy to come near you,' Lucy had called one day, when she spotted her listening to their explicit conversation.

'Do they always pick on you, dear?' Mrs Flanagan gently asked.

'No,' she lied, 'it's not too bad.'

She never told anyone how miserable her life at school really was. The walks home when she was pelted with stones, a small gang waiting almost every night at the top of Farley Hill. When boys were there too she sometimes got kicked or punched. But it wasn't surprising. Jane was terribly ugly, and they were right, she did smell bad. Her clothes were old-fashioned, and dirty, and either too big or small. She never had modern shoes like the other girls. Jane was always in trouble with the teachers for wearing pumps to school. How silly she looked in her once white socks, now grey, when all the other girls wore tights. How she cringed when they laughed at her. Often, she had no knickers, and, at almost fourteen, she should be wearing a bra by now. All the other girls her age wore them.

One of her worst days was when two of the boys grabbed her and pulled up her jumper. All the class had burst out laughing.

'She ain't even got a bra on,' Naomi scoffed, through her hysterics.

'Don't worry, ugly, no one gonna touch your tits,' Terry Lewis had laughed, squeezing spitefully at her small breasts.

Jane wriggled free and ran out of the classroom and school, still hearing the laughter in her head, even though she was a distance away. Finally, she sat down in an alley near home and burst into uncontrollable sobs. Many times, she had considered killing herself, but could never think of a way that would not hurt too much. That night she had swallowed a packet of her mother's headache tablets and waited to die. Eventually she fell asleep, waking sadly the next day. She had vowed never to go to school again, until the school truant officer had been around the flat threatening to prosecute her mother. After a firm slapping, Jane had no choice but to go back.

'Jane, darling,' Mrs Flanagan's voice broke into her thoughts.

She looked up at the kind, wrinkled face with the watery blue eyes that smiled at her.

'Have you no pretty dresses or something … Well, more modern?'

Jane felt her face redden and looked down at the jumper; it was black and bobbly, with a big hole in the elbow. Her jeans, far too big, were her mother's cast-offs, held up with a belt. They bunched around her waist and hips. The bottoms rolled up to stop them dragging on the floor, revealing the dreaded pumps she wore to school.

'No,' Jane whispered.

Mrs Flanagan was at a loss what to say next, at least without hurting Jane's delicate feelings. She did smell dreadful, and looked terrible, with her clothes hanging on her tiny body. Even the child's hair was dull and unwashed. A certain target for bullies, she reckoned.

'Don't your mum and dad help you?'

Jane cringed as she thought of Dan, her mother's boyfriend who lived with them. He had been there for about a year now, not like the rest. They had all left after a few months of being with her mum. Dan was pleasant enough but Jane did not like him. For some reason he made her skin crawl. When they were alone, he tried to pull her onto his lap. Then, grabbing handfuls of her hair, which he would rub between his fingers, he'd burst out laughing as Jane scrambled free and ran from the room, which only made him do it more.

'I haven't got a dad and my mum's got no money,' Jane told her.

'Well, I don't think I can help much; my clothes are a bit old and frumpy for you.'

They sat in silence, lost in their own thoughts.

Finally, Mrs Flanagan spoke. 'Meet me here tomorrow, dear, I have an idea.'

She stood up, grabbed Jane's hand and squeezed it reassuringly, leaving a mint humbug behind in her palm.

'But it's Sunday tomorrow; you don't usually come out on a Sunday.'

'Well, I am tomorrow. In this lovely weather I can come out every day.'

Jane watched her walk back along the path to the entrance of the park.

Mrs Flanagan was tired. It was almost time for her nap, plus Mr Tibbles, her old cat, would be worried. But she turned the other way and headed back towards the town.

'You back again, dear?' the lady in the charity shop smiled.

'Yes, I want some clothes for my granddaughter. Can you help me?'

The lady pulled out a chair and Mrs Flanagan flopped gratefully down.

'You sit there and I'll have a look. What size?'

'She's small, about 13 or 14 years. I don't know what's modern for young people.'

The lady disappeared behind a round rail and could be heard sliding along metal hangers before holding up a T-shirt.

'That looks nice. You sure it's modern?'

'It's what my granddaughter would wear.'

Disappearing again, she then popped up again, first with a flowery skirt, then some cotton trousers, and finally another two T-shirts.

Mrs Flanagan handed over her purse to the lady, who took out a twenty-pound note and rang it up on the till.

'See you soon!' she shouted as Mrs Flanagan made for the door, with a smile on her face.

Chapter Two

After the elderly lady left, Jane walked further through the park. All summer and on mild winter days when she was bunking from school, she waited for Mrs Flanagan. They had been meeting for over a year now and both looked forward to their little chats. Jane loved the stories about the war and how she had met 'her Frank'. He was long since dead, as the elderly lady was ancient. They'd had five children and now she had eight grandchildren and seven great grandchildren.

Jane, being very shy, had not spoken to her for a long time, just a 'Hello', when they saw each other. Until one day Mrs Flanagan, who had always been nosy, finally asked why a young girl like her was in the park at school time.

'Bunking off? You'll get yourself in trouble,' she had gently chastised and then laughed. 'Still, when I was young, I bunked off all the time too. Hated school,' she confessed.

Jane had laughed too and admitted, 'Me too.'

Now they met most days, except during cold weather when the 'old arthritis', as Mrs Flanagan called it, got the better of her.

It was almost dark when Jane arrived at the block of flats where she lived. Climbing up the stone steps, which today smelt even more strongly of urine, to the paint-peeled blue front door with its cracked frosted glass panel, Jane took the key from the gas meter cupboard and unlocked the door. The smell of rotting food, stale cigarette smoke and damp wafted out as she pushed it open and replaced the key.

No one was home, so she went into the kitchen and made herself a cup of tea. She looked in the fridge, hoping to find something to eat. Pulling out a loaf of bread, she put four slices into the toaster. Changing her mind, as there wasn't much bread left, she took two out and replaced the rest back in the fridge. With her tea and toast, Jane went into the small living room and switched on the television. Curling her legs under her, she ate her dinner.

The next morning, Jane woke early to the sun streaming through the window, promising another very warm day. She pulled on the dreaded black jumper and baggy jeans, splashed some water on her face and was outside of the dreary front door by 8 am. Not even bothering to search for money as she could hear her mother and Dan stirring already, she carefully closed the door behind her.

There were a few early morning dogwalkers already on their way home when she reached the park. One or two, knowing her well, ran over for a welcome pat. She bent down to Chilly, the black Labrador, who wagged his tail in greeting. Mr Reynolds who lived in the next block of flats to Jane waved and smiled.

'Hello, Chilly,' she bent to plant a big kiss on his wide black head.

Delighted with the attention, the dog responded with a big wet kiss of his own. Jane laughed as she wiped the saliva from her face and mouth, trying to fight off the onslaught of tongue. Dutifully Chilly bounded off to his owner's whistle.

Watching him go, she carried on walking around the park. It seemed all the other dogs she usually greeted had already been and gone. The threat of a heatwave caused people to rush for the safety of their own shady homes. Heading for her favourite bush, Jane pulled at a leaf and picked away at the fine paper skin as she had done the day before. It would be some time before Mrs Flanagan appeared, so there were a lot of hours yet to waste. She sat down under a large oak tree, closed her eyes, and began to chat to Lizzy and the little gang.

Hearing a slight rustle nearby, her eyes sprang open. From the edge of her sight she spotted a little, scruffy brown dog sniffing at a nearby bin. She knew most of the park dogs by now, but this one she did not recognise. There did not seem to be an owner nearby, so Jane got up and walked over, calling a greeting. Spotting her the dog jumped, its eyes wide with suspicion. It ran backwards and barked, then disappeared amongst the trees. Shrugging, Jane picked up a chewed discarded stick ready to throw for any other passing dog.

'It's a hot day,' Mrs Jilly called over, giving Jane a wave.

She puffed her way up the path with Cooper, a fat Jack Russell, on his lead.

'It's true, dogs do look like their owners,' Jane thought, waving back as she scrutinised the over-large lady and dog, who was named Cooper because his owner was called Jilly. Apparently, Jilly Cooper was her favourite author.

'Thought I would get out and home early before I cook in the heat,' she told Jane, having a little rest.

'You're out early.'

'Yes, it's such a lovely day, too nice to lie in bed,' Jane told her.

'It certainly is that. Aren't you hot in that jumper?' Mrs Jilly smiled, wiping a stream of sweat from her face with a tissue.

'No,' she lied, and watched as Mrs Jilly huffed her way back up the path.

Mrs Flanagan arrived at 11 o'clock, just as Jane was trying to decide on Isobel's food consumption for the day. Hunger diverted her to the finer details of an enormous fantasy picnic. So far, there were sandwiches, all with different mouth-watering fillings and cut into delicate little quarters. Large sausage rolls were sticking over the sides of a little blue plate. To one side sat big clumps of cheese and a warm, crusty loaf of bread with fresh butter. For dessert was an enormous cream sponge and a massive trifle that glittered in the sunlight, but did not melt with the heat. There were so many bottles of fizzy drink it was hard to choose. An enormous pink blanket had been laid on the ground for the food to be served. The friends all sat cross-legged around the edge, with cushions.

Jane's stomach hurt with the thoughts of the food. She was holding it to ease the pain of hunger when she spotted the old lady.

In one hand she was clasping a large bag, along with the usual grey shopping bag. There was an excited twinkle in her eyes as she instructed Jane to sit on Frank's bench. Sinking down beside her, she opened the bag.

'I remembered these clothes,' she lied. 'I thought they might do you a turn.'

She lifted out the blue T-shirt and held it up.

'Oh, wow,' Jane grabbed the T-shirt and stood up, holding it to her. It was a little big but she did not notice.

Mrs Flanagan reached into the bag again and pulled out two others. One was yellow with writing on and the other pink, with a glittery picture. Grinning, she then produced the flowery skirt and white cotton trousers.

Jane cringed at the flowery skirt as she took it from her. 'Thank you so much, they're lovely,' she breathed.

'My granddaughter had grown out of them.' Mrs Flanagan smiled, feeling really pleased with herself.

'Listen, dear, why don't you go home and wash your hair, then put on some new clothes?' she advised gently. 'Then those little bastards won't pick on you again.'

Jane grinned and kissed Mrs Flanagan on the cheek, she grabbed the bag, and despite the heat, ran all the way home.

'See you tomorrow!' she called back.

'You get to school tomorrow!' Mrs Flanagan shouted, laughing.

Her mum was sitting at the kitchen table when she arrived home. A cigarette dangled from her lips and her hands clasped a half-empty cup of cold tea. The table in front of her was piled with dirty crockery and overfull ashtrays.

Jane guessed her mum had a hangover by the moody look on her face. This was not unusual for Toni Watts, who was in a constant bad mood; a hangover just made it ten times worse. Except when Dan was in the room, then her mother giggled like a young girl and even sometimes spoke nicely to Jane, which she rarely ever did.

'I guess there are some advantages of having him around,' Jane glumly thought.

'Where the fucking hell you been?' her mother growled.

'Over the park, Mum. Do you want a cup of tea?'

Toni nodded as she blew out a long stream of smoke.

'Mucking about with boys no doubt. What's in the bag?'

'Nothing, just some clothes an old lady gave me.'

'You better not have nicked them,' Toni grumped.

'No, Mum, honest. They were a present.' Jane held her breath and steeled herself to approach her mum. Now was probably not the right time, but then there never really was a right time.

'Mum, could I have some new clothes for school, please? I need a bra; all the other girls have them.'

'What! You think I'm made of fucking money, do you?'

'No, Mum, it's just the other kids laugh at me and...'

'Shut up!' her mum shouted, holding her head. 'I've got one of me 'eads and it ain't 'elping with you moaning.'

'Sorry, Mum.' Jane put down the tea and, grabbing the bag, went into her bedroom.

Opening her wardrobe, she moved aside the hangers as she had done many times before. Nothing had changed; her clothes were scruffy, either too big or too small. Oh well, at least she had some tops now.

Pulling off the hateful jumper and throwing it onto the floor, Jane chose the pink T-shirt and hung the rest up.

Afterwards, she quietly opened her door and looked out. Her mum was still sitting at the kitchen table as she crept down the hallway. Reaching the front door and biting her lip, Jane slowly twisted the lock.

'Where do you think you're going?' Toni called.

'Just back over the park, Mum,' Jane responded and held her breath to wait for an answer.

'So you can come 'ome 'ere pregnant, you little slut? You get in here and tidy this place.'

'But Mum...' she protested.

'I said get the fuck in here and tidy up. Don't backchat me, you little bastard!' Toni screamed, and then held her head dramatically, regretting the overuse of decibels.

The bedroom door opened at that moment and Dan came out in his underpants.

'What's all the noise about?' He walked into the kitchen, scratching his behind. Pulling out the chair opposite Toni he plopped down. 'Make us a cuppa, Jane?'

Jane sighed and shut the front door. Going back into the kitchen, she made him a cup of tea and began tidying up, reboiling the kettle for hot water to wash the dirty dishes. They needed a good soaking as they had been there for over a week.

Thankfully her mum and Dan went to the pub for lunch, as they did most Sundays, so Jane could go out again.

Dan threw her a pound coin before he left for some chips for her dinner. The chip shop was shut on a Sunday and chips were £1.20, so Jane hid the pound under her chest of drawers. Then she made some more toast. She cut the bread into halves and wrapped the toast in a carrier bag, before filling a plastic bottle with water. Then she went back to the park.

It was extremely hot now; the sun was a blazing fireball in the sky. Most people had disappeared to the safety of their homes. A few couples lay on the grass dozing, or kissing and cuddling.

Jane walked past, trying not to look. She found a secluded spot under the trees and opened her bag to eat her lunch. The scruffy dog was there again, lying under a bush.

'Hello,' Jane called, and the dog jumped up, staring wildly at her.

She pulled off the crust from her bread and threw it to the dog.

Thinking it a stone the dog darted into the safety of the overgrowth. Then a few moments later, it came out and sniffed dubiously at the bread. Lifting it carefully with its mouth, the dog disappeared back into the bush.

Sitting and eating her bread, Jane watched absently as the dog appeared again. It looked longingly at the bread and watched as Jane lifted it to her mouth. Picking off another crust she threw it again to the dog.

It dodged the bread, ran back and sniffed again, this time not bothering to take it into hiding.

'You're as hungry as me, little doggie!' Jane laughed and threw it a bit more.

After the feast the dog sat nearby, watching Jane. Then, deciding she was no threat, it lay down, let out a big sigh, and laid its head on its paw. Its suspicious brown eyes did not leave her.

Crawling on her hands and knees, Jane tried to approach it.

It stared back at her with wide eyes, which moved from side to side, fear clouding the dark brown of them. Its body was stiff and ready to bolt if she moved too suddenly. It was slow progress but eventually Jane was near enough to stretch out her hand to allow a sniff of her fingers. The dog's nose twitched, as did its eyes.

'I won't hurt you,' she told it, trying to lean forward enough to pat its head.

'What we got here then?'

The voice made both her and the dog jump. It was Alan again, thankfully without the gang.

Alan and his girlfriend Lucy were a good pair, Jane thought, shrinking, as if to make herself smaller.

The dog made to run as Alan kicked out his foot at it.

His shot hit the middle of the dog's stomach, causing it to yelp in pain.

'Fucking thing's diseased,' he spat.

For the first time ever, the fear left Jane and anger took hold of her. 'Leave it alone, you bastard.' She jumped to her feet with her fists clenched.

He laughed and pushed at her. Jane fell backwards on the grass with a thump. The little dog suddenly lunged at Alan, baring its teeth and growling. It jumped at his leg and sunk its teeth into him.

He kicked out his leg furiously, but the dog had his jeans and did not let go. He waved his leg about, yelling as the dog flapped about, hanging on with all its might. It did not budge until Alan, losing his balance, fell onto his back. The dog, taking advantage, jumped on his chest and bit into his chin.

His fists clenched, Alan yelled louder as he beat it away. Blood began to spurt from the wound, running down his neck onto his white T-shirt.

In a panic Jane jumped up and grabbed at the dog to pull it off. It let go and Alan, clenching his chin, leapt to his feet. Running backwards he made for the entrance of the park.

'I'm gonna have that fucking thing destroyed for this!' he screamed at Jane.

'Oh no,' she cried, 'what have you done? You'll be put to sleep now.'

Still holding the scruff of the dog's neck, Jane took off her belt and looped it around its neck, hanging desperately on to her jeans so they did not fall down without the belt to secure them.

The big brown eyes stared up at her, a look of pleasure in them.

'I know what you mean,' Jane told the dog. 'I've wanted to do that for years. But we've got to hide you. They'll come looking for you. But where?'

Heading for home, clutching her trousers, Jane crept along the streets with the dog at her side. Finally, climbing the stone steps to the third floor, she let herself indoors. Luckily her mum and Dan were still out. Going into the kitchen, Jane rooted through the cupboard. She found a tin of tuna and dished it into a saucer.

'I'm going to die for opening this.' She put it onto the floor and the dog fell on it.

Within seconds the saucer was licked clean, then licked again and again. The dog looked up expectantly, hoping for more.

Pulling out a chair, Jane sat down. Putting her hand forward she patted the dog, which in turn licked at her fingers.

'As I think you are a girl, I'm going to call you Molly,' she decided, and began calling the name.

Molly responded by giving a slight wag of her tail.

'Well, Molly, I think you like your new name,' Jane laughed.

Her mum and Dan were still out when she went to bed that night. Jane did wonder if she dared put on the immersion heater and wash her hair as Mrs Flanagan had advised. But she decided she had better not take the chance of being found out. Her mum would be angry at the waste of electricity.

The dog jumped onto the bed beside her and they were asleep within minutes, the draining heat exhausting them both.

Molly woke her a few hours later with a low growl.

'Shush,' Jane hushed, reaching out her hand and patting the dirty coat. 'You'll get me into trouble.'

The dog's coat was rough, gritty and smelt bad. Little lumpy scabs lay under the rough brown fur. Molly seemed to understand she needed to be quiet, laying her head back down. They both fell asleep again.

The same dream haunted her; this time a man was calling Isabella. He was laughing and standing outside a little white cottage, with lovely flowers and shrubs in the front garden. Jane could not see his face or the face of the woman that came out of the front door. She just knew they were happy, as he held out his arms.

In one of his hands was the same pink teddy bear, which he held out to her. Then all of a sudden, out of the dream came a woman's voice, so loud and clear it woke Jane up. Startled, she sat up in bed and looked around, positive the woman was in her room. There was no one there, but the words still rang in her ears: 'We must find Isabella.'

Getting out of bed at 7.30 the next morning, with no intention of going to school, Jane went into the kitchen with Molly close at her side. It was safe, as her mother and Dan would not be up for hours yet. Dan's jacket lay discarded over the back of the kitchen chair. Jane fumbled in the pockets, hopeful to find some loose change. There was none; dare she chance the bedroom? She had done this, many times before, to buy food. After a night of drinking, the two usually slept soundly. Luckily, they had not woken yet and caught her. They were probably so drunk the night before they would not remember how much they had spent.

'You stay here,' Jane whispered in Molly's ear, and the dog seemed to understand, sitting down and staring up at her with wide, intelligent eyes.

Going to the bedroom, Jane held her breath while slowly moving the handle. The door squeaked slightly as she pushed it gently open. The smell of stale beer wafted out, causing her to wrinkle her nose. One or the other was snoring loudly, so the squeak was masked. Luckily Dan's jeans were on the floor at the end of the bed. Pushing the door closed behind her, Jane sank to her knees. Rifling through the pockets, her fingers curled around a heap of change. Careful not to take too much, she dropped the trousers and crawled to the door. Jane hesitated before going back and taking a few more coins. Her fingers felt expertly for pound coins. Finally, back in the kitchen, she counted out the money.

'Wow, £7,' she told Molly, who looked just as excited. 'We'll be stuffed today,' she grinned.

Chapter Three

The little minimart a few streets away was expensive, but she did not fancy heading for the larger supermarket and risking being seen with Molly. Tying the little dog up securely outside, Jane brought some cheese, a loaf of bread and two tins of dog food.

Again, the sun blazed as they sat by the river, enjoying a welcome breakfast. Jane, lost in thought, absently watched two swans float past with a little clutch of cygnets. Molly stared, fascinated, sitting by her side, trying to decide which was more interesting; the birds or the piece of bread her new mistress was eating.

Jane was trying to imagine what Isobel would be wearing on such a hot day. She settled for silky, blue wrap-around trousers and a lime green long shirt that she had seen on television recently. The shirt was beautifully embroidered around the neckline with tiny coloured flowers. Around Isabella's waist hung a loose belt with little blue crystals that sat on her slim hips. On her head was a big floppy sun hat with a massive blue rose pinned on the side. Lots of different coloured beads adorned Isabella's neck, giving the outfit an exclusive finish. Shoes were always a big problem, especially with the wrap-around trousers.

'It's not good,' Jane told Molly, who twisted her head on one side wondering what was going on. 'The outfit is all wrong.'

Sighing, Jane patted Molly on the head and the dog responded with a big lick up her arm.

Packing away the remnants of breakfast in a carrier bag, they set off for a walk. They both felt fuller than they had for a long time. Molly sniffed at the borders of the path, trying to size up any dog that had been through the area recently.

Jane, lost in her own thoughts, stood patiently waiting while she worked out their budget. Benefit day was not until Friday; her mother's one week and Dan's the following. Figuring they still had some money, they would probably be back in the pub tonight.

Jane was too scared to go back to the park for fear she was now being hunted down. 'I don't know what I'm going to do with you, Molly. My mum will never let me keep you and it's going to be so hard to hide you. Tomorrow they'll be skint, so indoors the rest of the week.'

Molly looked up at her, trying to understand the problem. Dismissing it, she poked her nose back into the dandelions she had been engrossed with. Then, turning round, she pushed her bottom over the clump to relieve herself. Satisfied, Molly kicked her back legs at the patch before giving the area one final sniff and moving to the next clump of greenery.

'I know,' Jane suddenly blurted out, throwing Molly off course. 'Maybe Mrs Flanagan would take you home for me. I could see you almost every day then at the park.'

Feeling pleased with herself, Jane decided to chance going there after all.

At one o'clock Mrs Flanagan was sitting on Frank's bench.

'Hello, dear,' she greeted Jane, as she bobbed out from behind the oak tree, pleased to see Jane was wearing the new T-shirt and not the usual scruffy jumper. 'Who's this?' She looked down at Molly, who stared dolefully up at her.

Jane gave a garbled version of how she had adopted the dog and how it had attacked Alan.

Mrs Flanagan stared at her, trying to keep up.

'Please will you look after her for me? She's very well behaved,' Jane told her with earnest eyes. 'My mum'll kill me if she sees her,' she pleaded.

'Oh dear, I would, but I'm 85 and I couldn't possibly take on a dog at my age. Besides, my Mr Tibbles would have a nervous breakdown if he saw a dog. His old arthritis is getting bad nowadays. He can't run like he used to.'

Jane had forgotten about the old cat Mrs Flanagan adored. Frank had brought him as a kitten for her birthday many years before. The cat was as ancient as its owner. Although he annoyed Mrs Flanagan at times when he peed on her chair, she would never part with Mr Tibbles.

'But it's only till I sort something out; maybe Molly could be kept in another room to Mr Tibbles? Please, Mrs Flanagan?'

'I'm sorry, dear. I just couldn't.'

Jane's face fell. What on earth was she going to do?

When she went home that night, her mum and Dan were already out. There was still a tin of dog food and some bread from earlier so Jane prepared them dinner.

'Eat more slowly, Molly, or you'll be sick.'

It was too late as the dog had already scoffed greedily at the food. She licked her lips and looked around for more. She gave a small belch and drank some of the water from the bowl Jane had put on the floor for her. There was a knock at the door, and Molly began to growl.

'Shush,' Jane hushed, and peeped around the kitchen and down the hallway.

Through the cracked glass she could see a policeman standing there. He knocked again, and Jane bobbed back into the kitchen. Calling Molly, she crouched on the floor by the sink in case the man looked through the window. He banged again, more urgently this time. Jane bit her lip and got up. Standing in the hallway, she called from the other side, 'Who is it?'

'It's the police; we are looking for Miss Jane Watts. Can you open the door?'

Jane felt the panic rise in her stomach and grip the inside of her throat. 'No, my mum's out and I don't open the door to strangers.' Her voice shook as she spoke.

'We want to talk to you about an incident in the park yesterday. Apparently, your dog bit a Mr Alan McKenzie.'

'I haven't got a dog and I didn't see anything.' Her body shook, especially her hands.

'So, you didn't see the attack?'

'There was a stray dog in the park yesterday but I didn't see it bite anyone,' Jane lied, biting hard on the inside of her cheek.

'OK, when will your mother be home? We still need to talk to you,' the officer told her.

'I don't know. She's visiting my gran,' Jane lied again.

Thankfully, the policeman left, with a promise to be back soon. Jane felt so panicky she went into the living room and sat on the sofa. Molly jumped up beside her and licked her hand.

'Oh Molly, they'll take you away and destroy you. Where are we gonna hide you?'

She racked her brains for a solution but fell asleep before thinking of an answer. The front door opening sometime later caused both her and Molly to jump. Luckily, her mother and Dan stumbled into the kitchen, leaving Jane enough time to dart into her bedroom with Molly at her heels.

'I've got it,' Jane sprung up from the bed, making Molly jump so much, she almost fell off. 'The river, there's an old war bunker on the other side; we can hide you there.'

It was still dark as she quickly dressed and went into the kitchen. Having filled a bottle with water, Jane searched Dan's coat. As before there was no money in the pockets; she braved the main bedroom again. Dan's pockets were empty too, so Jane tried her mum's bag and found some change in the bottom. Back in the kitchen, she counted five pounds, thirty-five pence over a cup of tea. Once the supermarket opened at half past seven, Jane went and brought more dog food and two pies.

When they arrived at the river, the sun was up and already very warm. It must have rained during the night because the grass was damp. The heat was fast drying the fine droplets of water that still scattered the growth.

Once reaching the bank they sat in the same spot to have breakfast. An early riverboat sailed past with a large dog standing on the back end. Spotting Molly, it let out a ream of deep barks. Molly, dancing about, began to yap back excitedly. She ran a little way up the river to follow the boat so she could have the last bark. Then slowly she ambled back, sniffing the edge of the bank. After many concentrated sniffs, a suitable place was found to relieve herself. Kicking at the earth again with her hind legs she ran back to Jane.

The sun glistened on the water casting a magical, silver glow as it rippled from the riverboat's wake. It was hypnotic to Jane, who began to imagine a magical castle below the water's surface. In her mind she had fallen into the water along with Molly and the two of them sank to the bottom. Amazingly they could breathe easily. The castle that shimmered in front of them was made of gold, which heightened the intense glow of its walls. The bottom of the river sparkled with a mass of blazing colours. Beautiful mermaids lived in little rock houses around the castle; they swam around them, studying the human intruders. A loud splash dissolved Jane's daydream, as she spotted the tail of a large fish disappearing below the water's surface.

'Goodness, Molly, maybe there really are mermaids,' she smiled. 'Come on, we've a long walk,' she told the dog, who was intently studying the water for the fish.

The bunker that stood on the other side of the river had long since been deserted. No one ever ventured over that side, not even keen fishermen. Jane often went over by crossing a little bridge, finding peace in the seclusion. She never went far through the overgrown path though. Fear prevented her, as the place was rumoured to be haunted. Soldiers from the war were said to have died there, their lost souls hovering, still searching for Germans. She had asked Mrs Flanagan about it once and the old lady had laughed at her.

'It was a lookout place, dear. I don't think anyone was actually bombed or died there. It's just some silly tale invented to scare you youngsters.'

Jane was not convinced; the place was so desolate she was sure it must be haunted.

'My Frank, who was in the war told me it has secret underground rooms,' Mrs Flanagan had told her.

Jane thought that really exciting as there may be treasure left behind. But even her curiosity was not strong enough to make her explore the bunker.

Finding a long stick, she tried to beat away the tall nettles and brambles that hid the narrow pathway. It was almost impossible, because in parts they were taller than Jane. But determinedly she managed to make slow progress.

Molly dubiously stayed safely behind her, gingerly picking her way through Jane's treads. The deeper they went, the spookier and more silent the thickness became. Jane shivered as they progressed; the nearer they got to the bunker, the colder the air seemed. Not for the first time, she wondered if there was a better place to hide Molly.

Her arms were tingling and throbbing with nettle stings, and she was badly scratched by the time they reached the entrance of the site. Jane finally put her hand on the big sign which warned people to stay away; the structure was not safe. A large concrete plinth had broken away and slid down the bank into a lake on the other side. They were old gravel pits, which had long since been deserted. The area was converted into a conservation area. The concrete stuck out of the water, rejected and of no use to anyone, except the two ducks perching on the razor edge, quaking in protest of the human and dog intrusion. Molly, spotting the ducks, began to bark in excitement, sending them flapping disgruntledly across the lake.

Broken debris and large stones littered the rest of the path to the building that stood looking lost and dejected.

'Apparently, years ago, this was a lookout place,' Jane told the uninterested, worried dog. A long trail of brambles and twigs stuck to Molly's coat.

'It will be a bit dismal living here, Molly, but we have no choice.'

The dog looked up at her and yapped in agreement as Jane tried to clear the array of vegetation from her tangled coat.

They began clambering over the ruins until they reached the core of the building. Jane shuddered again and looked behind her.

'I hope Mrs Flanagan is right and there are no ghosts here,' she told Molly, feeling a little better for having the dog's company. To ease the isolation, she visualised her little group of imaginary friends were with her.

The building, which was a cube of concrete slabs, still had stairs that led to a flat roof. The two of them climbed the worn steps. Arriving at the top, Jane was able to see over to the livelier side of the river. This must have been where soldiers stood on duty watching for enemy planes, she thought. The sun was extremely hot by now and Jane could feel her arms and head burning.

Molly ran around and sniffed; she looked over the edge to the ground below, deciding it was too high to jump off.

Jane, followed closely by Molly, made her way back down the stairs to a large wooden door on the left side of the building. She pulled at it, trying to heave it open. It would not budge, so she dug her heels into the earth and pulled again, slipping on the dusty ground. The door moved slightly, creaking in protest of being disturbed after all these years. Finally, the gap was big enough for her and Molly to squeeze through. Inside, the dark room smelt dank and stale. It was cool and Jane was pleased with the break from the searing heat. There were little slit windows, which offered a dim light.

'It's not much of a home, Molly,' she told the little dog.

The room was empty, only a few discarded rusty cans and old wrappers littered the floor, showing that people had been there in more recent times. They went back outside and tried to walk around the building, climbing over large rocks and pushing aside weeds with the stick that Jane still held.

Finding a little clearing on the other side of the bunker, they sat down to have a rest. Jane gave Molly the remains of the tin of dog food and finished the last of her pies. Then she poured water into the foil pie tray and Molly drank thirstily, her pink tongue hanging out as she panted in relief. Jane also gulped at the water, feeling a little better after. Her head was pounding with the heat and she felt sleepy. They both lay down on the warm grass and promptly fell asleep.

When she woke up an hour later, Jane jumped up and screamed. A large spider was walking across her hair and ants seemed to be crawling all over her body. She danced about, brushing herself down, while Molly, thinking it a game, danced with her, yapping at her feet.

They stayed there all day exploring the area and looking for the entrance to the secret rooms. There was no sign of them, so Jane decided it was just another made-up story, feeling disappointed that there would be no treasure after all. They climbed back up to the roof and looked over to the other side of the river again.

A few fishermen sat meditatively, with their rods in the water, unperturbed by the heat. Most had small tent shelters, which offered some protection.

Jane imagined her friends sitting and laughing with them, which helped ease the seclusion of the bunker again. They had a party on the roof, the bottle of water was wine, and they became tiddly and fell about laughing. That was difficult, because Jane could not think of anything funny that they could laugh at. Still at least they could keep her company on the way home.

All too soon it was time to go. Jane felt dreadful as she shut the door behind Molly, worried she may bark and alert someone of being locked in there. The little dog, confused, whined and scratched at the door. Jane stood on the other side and tried to explain she had no choice. She left the foil pie packet filled with water for her, and her black jumper for a bed.

'I'll be back first thing tomorrow, Molly, I promise.' She turned away, feeling terrible and cruel.

A short distance down the path, Jane stopped and listened. There was no noise from Molly; she must have settled down.

When she arrived home, it was almost dark. Toni was in the kitchen, sitting at the cluttered table. She sprung from her seat when she heard the door.

'Where the fucking hell have you been?' she screeched, meeting Jane at the door.

She flicked out her hand and slapped the young girl hard around the face, knocking her sideways.

Jane was bewildered as she put the palm of her hand on the side of her smarting skin. 'I've been at school, Mum,' she defended.

Toni lifted her hand again and this time clenched her fist.

'You fucking liar!' She brought the fist down and punched Jane in the face with such force, she fell back into the closed front door.

The woman pounced on her daughter and begun pounding harder at the girl.

Jane sunk to the floor and pulled her arms over her head for protection, crying out with each blow.

'You're a fucking lying bastard!' Toni screamed between punches.

Dan, hearing the commotion, ran out from the toilet with his trousers still undone. He jumped onto Toni and grabbed at her arms.

'For fuck's sake, what the hell's going on?' he cried.

'This fucking little whore's been at the boys again,' Toni screamed, trying to wiggle free of the arms that restricted her. Not getting satisfaction, she kicked out her foot, finding Jane's stomach.

Jane cried out with pain as the foot kicked violently into her again and again.

'I've had the fucking school inspector round again and the police!' she shouted. 'Little bastard's been bunking off and is in big trouble.'

Dan dragged Toni into the kitchen and pushed her into the room. Tears fell down Jane's face as she tried to crawl from the floor.

'You stupid cow!' Dan was shouting. Then he lowered his voice, 'You know I've got the boys coming later; I can't have all this happening with them here, can I?' he hissed, before the impact of Toni's words sunk in. 'Police? What do you mean, police?'

Calming down, Toni sunk into a chair.

'I dunno, something to do with a dog biting someone. I told them we ain't got no dog.'

Dan breathed a sigh of relief and went to the cupboard. Bringing out a bottle of cider, he plonked it in front of Toni. He went back to the hall where Jane crouched, sobbing.

'Get yourself to bed.' He flicked his head towards her room.

Jane looked up at him, her face wet and swollen. She pulled herself to her feet and ran into the room. Shutting the door behind her, she threw herself onto the bed and curled her legs into her aching stomach. Why did her mum hate her so much? She cried, allowing the tears to fall freely.

Chapter Four

It was a few hours later that Jane woke with a start; it was the same dream again. Except this time, it was not a beautiful garden, it was a dark room where she could not see anything. She grasped around the edges, trying to find a doorway out. The furniture she bumped into was solid; she could feel its outline in the darkness. Someone else was in the room with her, and she was frightened. The hairs on her neck prickled and goosebumps rose on her arms.

'Isabella,' the lady called from outside the room, directing her to the exit. The voice was soft and gentle, calming and safe; it sounded elderly.

Jane's body ached all over and her face was throbbing and swollen. Blood had dried on her chin, from where her tooth had punctured her lip. She climbed stiffly from the bed and switched on her light, squinting as the beam blinded her.

She could hear faint voices coming from the living room. Quietly opening her bedroom door, she stuck out her head and listened. It was men talking; they must have visitors. She was surprised; they never had people visit. Creeping closer to the door, she stood and listened.

'That's it, Friday week then?' a man's voice was saying. It was not Dan's.

'OK, one more time.' It was Dan's voice this time.

'We leave the van down Boggard Road and jump in the Astra. We drive to the river car park and hide the money up the old war bunker till the dust settles. Then we dish out the readies, and fuck me, we're out of here. After months of planning we're finally gonna do it.' His voice shook with either excitement or nerves.

'I dunno,' another man's voice chipped in. 'I don't think Boggard Road is good enough. I think go for the original and use Duke Street. And the war shelter isn't safe. What if someone finds it? There must be somewhere else we can hide it?'

'You prick, do you never fucking listen? There are too many cameras there. Boggard's clean.' It was Dan again. 'And no one has been near that shelter for years. It's dangerous for a start. No one even knows about the underground rooms. There's nowhere else to hide it. If the police are onto us, they would never in a million years suspect there.'

'Then how do you know about the rooms? If you do, then so do others.'

'I used to go there with my granddad when I was a kid. He was stationed there during the war, that's how. Even the entrance to the rooms is hidden. Not many people still alive even know they exist,' Dan explained, his own voice sounding impatient.

They are planning some sort of robbery, Jane realised. Her eyes widened. She knew Dan was notorious for crime. The kids at school reminded her regularly that her slag of a mother was knobbing a criminal; but a robbery?

'This time next week we'll be millionaires,' another voice piped up, mimicking Del Trotter.

There was much laughter after that and lots of talking all at once. Jane could no longer catch what they were saying. A few ring-pull sounds made it obvious they were drinking beer. 'They are hiding the money at the war shelter,' Jane thought. 'Oh no, what about Molly, what am I going to do?' Feeling shaken by the robbery as well as the pain of her body, she went into the kitchen.

Her mother still sat there, a stream of smoke blowing slowly from her mouth. Jane cringed as she saw her, recoiling at the thoughts of earlier. It was usual; her mum always hit her when she had no money. Benefit day was her 'good mood' day, Mondays and the days after 'the bad'. Her mother did not even look up as she went in.

'Like your no-good father,' Toni slurred.

Jane had heard this many times; constantly reminded of her no-good father. She did not remember him. According to her mum, he left when she was a baby. He did not want her so ran off with another woman, leaving Toni destitute, and having to bring up an ungrateful little cow on her own.

'Worked my fingers to the bone for you.' Jane was continually reminded. 'Ugly little bitch,' she raved. Lifting the almost empty cider bottle she gulped at the contents and threw the plastic bottle towards the bin.

'Did he really leave cos of me?' Jane had asked one day when her mum was in a better mood.

Toni had smiled, a cruel nasty one that did not reach the coldness of her eyes. 'Yeah, he hated you at first sight. Loved him, I did, and what did he do, fuck off cos of you and cos of 'er.' Toni had begun to sob uncontrollably. 'I made 'er pay though; by Christ did she pay for it. They both did.'

Jane had no idea who ''er' was, but shuddered to think how she'd paid for upsetting Toni.

Jane thought her dad must have loved her mum before her birth, because he had written her letters. She had seen them bundled in an old suitcase on top of her mother's wardrobe. She knew they were from her father because Toni had showed her one day when drunk. Jane longed to know what they said, but she could not read enough to decipher the scrambled array of secret codes. She could only write a few words and only understand basic ones and her name.

Moved to the bottom classes, teachers despaired with the unruly pupils to contend with. No one took any notice of the shy, timid Jane, who sat on her own at the back. The other children laughed when, on rare occasions, she was asked to read out work. Jane made it up as she went. The teacher would shake her head and tell her to 'sit down!' and flick her eyes with annoyance at the child's stupidity. Then everyone would laugh at her yet again. She would sit cringing, her face burning so much it threatened to burst into flames.

Turning on the tap, Jane filled a glass with water. She drank greedily and placed the glass on the drainer. Then she went to go back to her room.

'Who the fuck is that?' someone hissed from the living room as she passed.

The door sprang open, and Jane froze like a rabbit caught in headlights. Dan was staring at her with a look of hostility on his face;

Jane stared dumbly back at him. His face relaxed when he saw it was her, and he slammed the door again.

'It's OK, it's only the kid,' she heard him say.

'What if she heard?' the other voice piped up.

'Na, she's a bit thick, she wouldn't understand.'

Jane tried to listen again but the voices became whispers. So she went back into her bedroom and lay in the dark, trying to digest what she had overheard.

Every day Jane got up extra early and headed for the bunker. It took a long time to get there and back in time for school. The first day had been the worst. Poor Molly was distraught; she jumped about yelping and whining for ages when Jane arrived. She constantly apologised to the little dog, feeling sick with guilt for leaving her. Molly was so depressed when Jane shut the door and walked away. Her tail hung between her legs and her head drooped dejectedly. The image and the whimpering stayed in Jane's head all night. She just did not know what else to do. It was also hard to find food for them both. Even knowing there was nothing edible in the kitchen cupboard, Jane still looked in hope.

She had no choice but to face school each day. The fear of another beating was far greater than leaving Molly alone. The teacher, Mrs Small, had asked how Jane had bruised and cut her face. But once she explained a nasty fall down some stairs, no one asked again.

Now she had the little dog that loved her dearly and with so much trust, the children at school did not bother her so much. They still taunted her, and at lunchtime would run into her. Or throw punches or kicks as they passed her in the corridor and even in the classroom. But Jane always tried to find a spot away from them. At least there were free school dinners, half of which were saved for Molly.

Lucy Ellis and Alan Eldridge were her worst fear. They picked on Jane even more than ever. Alan had a nasty wound on his chin and his leg, as he showed everyone in class.

'I've tablets too, cos the dog was so diseased I got infected. Or was it her that was diseased?' He nodded his head towards Jane and everyone laughed.

They even began daring each other to touch her. Wrinkling their noses in disgust when a brave one did. The others in the gang cringed and ran away, giggling from the now infected person.

'You're gonna die for what you did,' Alan threatened, every time he spotted her.

'Yeah,' Lucy jibbed, 'and I'm gonna help him. We're gonna kill you, bitch,' she threatened, poking a finger under Jane's chin and snarling at her.

Jane's mouth went dry and her eyes clouded with fear.

Each night after school she headed back to the river and bunker. Thankfully it was a different way from Farley Hill. If they waited, Jane did not know.

Since hearing about the robbery, she was careful not to make too much of an obvious pathway as she headed for the bunker. If Dan realised someone used it, he may not hide the money there. On every visit she looked for the entrance to the underground rooms, but so far could not find one.

Molly was always so relieved to see Jane, jumping up at her legs and whining for the food she brought. It was dreadful leaving her each night, so Jane tried to stay till almost dusk.

Thank goodness when Friday came at last and there were two whole days away from school. Soon it would be the six-week holidays, which Jane lived for. She missed Mrs Flanagan, who must be wondering what had happened to her. But with Molly to care for, there was no time to spare.

That night, Jane brought Molly home with her, knowing it was Dan's benefit day and him and her mother would be down the pub. The little dog was elated not to be left alone in the dark room anymore. She skipped and bounced alongside Jane all the way, no longer fretful of the brambles.

The following morning, Jane dressed early and raided Dan's pockets, where she found ten pounds. It was risky taking so much, but this time she took the chance. They had been very drunk last night, singing and laughing well after midnight.

'We're getting out of here soon,' Toni had chanted, staggering around the kitchen, banging into chairs and knocking a few bits of crockery off the work surface.

Dan had crept into Jane's bedroom later in the early hours and asked if she was asleep. He had done that a few times recently. Holding the growling Molly firmly under the bedclothes, Jane pretended she was.

'You're still a bit young. But I'm gonna show you a good time soon,' he had laughed and went out again, leaving Jane cringing and feeling a sickness in the pit of her stomach.

Leaving the flat early the next morning, she brought supplies at the mini mart and headed for the bunker. It had rained heavily most of the night and the grass was still very wet. Jane stared in wonder at the rainbow colours that reflected through the gulps of water, as the sun's beams hit them. Soon she became lost in a fairyland that existed beneath the grass, so tiny it could not be seen by humans. She and Molly had accidentally stepped onto a porthole and shrunk so small that even the grass blades towered above them. They were so tall it was hard to see the top. Monster ants and spiders chased them through the forest and they ran down a hole, which was more of a cave, to escape. After a long, dark passageway the pair of them burst out into a massive room, so large they could not see the other side. The room was another world, filled with spirals of colour, prisms of reds, blues, mauves and oranges. So many colours they had to avert their eyes against the brightness.

Little fairy people gathered in groups, chatting and laughing. Some carried baskets filled with peculiar looking foods. They welcomed Molly and Jane, placing beautiful garlands of crystals around their necks. They invited them to a fantastic picnic lunch. An enormous blue cover was laid onto the soft ground with different coloured cushions. Then white shimmery plates with pink, yellow and green sandwiches were placed in the centre. Other plates were bought out with delicious cakes in every imaginable colour and strange liquids for drinks that tasted so fantastic they could not drink enough.

The rumbling of Jane's stomach interrupted the amazing picnic. She clenched it with her arm to stop the dull ache of hunger that plagued her constantly. Leaving the fairy world, she concentrated on finding them a dry place to sit and eat.

Sitting on top of the bunker, Jane and Molly polished off two cheese sandwiches and a bottle of fizzy drink. It was a rare luxury as Jane usually only brought tap water with her. But with ten pounds she had decided to splash out. The sandwiches were dull and limp, but they were both so hungry neither noticed. After breakfast Jane decided to find a place on the other side of the bunker, where she could watch without being seen. This way if Dan or his men came, they would be safe.

The path on the other side was far more overgrown than the one before. The wild shrubs, brambles and dense, thick clumps of weeds made it impossible to even see a path. Large rocks and broken concrete stuck up at various points, having tumbled from the bunker.

Jane decided no one had probably ever been through that way before, or at least not for many years. She stumbled, trying gingerly to find a way through. Twice she fell and scraped her hands and knees badly. A thick sticky line of blood ran down her legs and she could see a patch darkening her jeans. Molly, who was not so brave, stood by the bunker wall watching as Jane disappeared into yet another bush. Scrambling to her feet once again with her pumps squelching, Jane stood up and let out a big sigh. She was drenched, as the sun had not yet dried the dense overgrowth. Her hands were bloody and full of splinters. Almost ready to give up, she sat down and put her chin on her knees.

'No, I won't give up,' she told herself out loud, trying to smile, which turned into more of a grimace at Molly, who twisted her head and lifted her ears at the sound of Jane's voice.

It was not in vain. On the other side of the large boulder she had just slid down was a little clearing. The large patch even had short grass and a few wild flowers. It was perfect; from there Jane could see the bunker clearly. Molly looked pensively in her direction. Jane made the arduous journey back again and this time, carrying Molly, climbed back to the small patch, finding an easier way through.

As it was less than a week until the supposed robbery, Jane felt they would be safer to stay in the little clearing.

As Molly ran around exploring and sniffing every inch, Jane watched her despondently. The dog's bald patches and scabby skin looked sore. The skin had rubbed away with the constant scratching, revealing weeping, bloody sores. Jane did not know much about dogs, but it was clear Molly needed to see a vet. How could she possibly pay for it? Vets were expensive and she was sure none would see her for free. Still, if she got some of the robbery money it would be the first thing to do.

Her intuition was right, as late in the afternoon, just as the two of them were dozing off, Molly let out a low growl. It was a low-pitched rumble that alerted Jane to danger. Her eyes sprang open as she stared at Molly, whose nose was pointed towards the bunker. Crouching on her knees, Jane grabbed at the dog to keep her still and quiet.

'Hush, Molly,' she whispered urgently, and the dog obeyed.

Peering through the undergrowth, her mouth went dry as she saw two men at the bunker. Luckily, she and Molly were hidden from sight. Her heart pounded as she watched them pull out a small axe and chop away at the large bush that covered the sidewall, until the now empty space revealed a small wooden door. One of the men pulled with effort at the door, which slowly creaked open. He crouched to avoid hitting his head and disappeared inside. The other picked up one of the two bulky bags they had been carrying and pushed it through, soon following with the other bag and himself.

'Well, I never,' Jane whispered to Molly, still holding the dog firmly. 'That's where the money is to be hidden.'

Excitement and fear rippling through her body, her heart began to pound erratically. Endless possibilities suddenly opened up for Jane. They would run away from this place and never come back. She and Molly would live happily ever after like a queen and princess in their own fairy castle.

Jane was just thinking of all the food she could buy when the men appeared again. They stood talking for a while before pulling the discarded bush back over the doorway. They disguised it with some rubble and branches until satisfied it could not be discovered. Finally, they headed back down the path Jane herself had come down some hours earlier.

They waited in the hidden patch before feeling safe enough to stand up. Leaving enough time for the men to be back on the other side of the bridge, Jane carried Molly and ventured forward. Pulling the bush, branches and rubble away, she exposed the door. With some effort she managed to move back the rusty bolt. The door was stiff; no matter how much she pulled, it would not budge.

'Bollocks,' she called out loud, sweat running down her face.

Out of breath, Jane sunk onto the ground and wiped her brow with her bare arm.

'What now?' she asked Molly, who sat staring at her, offering no answers.

'No, I will open it.' She clenched her fists determinedly and stood up.

Her hands throbbed with pain from her earlier trial. Giving two big puffs and putting her foot against the wall for leverage, Jane, groaning with effort, pulled again. The door budged and opened so quickly, she fell backwards onto Molly, who yelped in surprise.

The hairs on the back of her neck pricked as she stared into the black empty space. Images of evil spirits floating out of the dark abyss flooded Jane's head, sending a cold shiver down her spine.

'You're just being silly,' she berated herself.

Taking a deep breath, she got up and shook away the thoughts. Going to the opening, Jane peered through the hole into the dense blackness. It was impossible to see without a torch, no matter how much straining she did.

Molly, not in the least bit perturbed, went scampering through the doorway and disappeared down some stairs. The little hairs prickled the back of Jane's neck again, this time joined by ones on the back of her hands. What if she does not come back? Her voice was shaky as she called to her. The little dog came bounding out with her pink tongue hanging from the side of her mouth. She sat by Jane and looked questioningly at her.

Diving in her pocket, Jane rattled the few coins and pulled them out despondently. She had bought a good supply of dog food, so spent most of the precious £10. Admitting defeat, she pushed the door shut and secured the rusty bolt. It took some effort again as it did not want to budge. By the time the entrance was covered by the debris, Jane felt exhausted. It was getting late by the time they both headed home, first stopping at the mini mart to buy some matches.

That night, Jane had horrible dreams of being caught down the tunnel by Dan and his mates. They tied her up and left her down there for days without food or water. When Dan finally appeared, he dug a large hole in the centre of a room. Dragging Jane, he pushed her in and buried her alive. No one heard her screaming as the earth was piled on top of her.

She woke sweating; the pillow was damp and cold, and her neck drenched. It must have been the early hours of the morning, but she could hear Toni and Dan in the living room. For once they did not sound drunk and the television was blaring. Jane climbed from the bed and gently opened the door a crack.

'So, what we gonna do with 'er?' her mum was saying.

'I don't know, she's your kid. Don't the dad want her?'

'Oh yea, but he ain't 'aving 'er. I don't even know where he is.'

'What about letting social services take her? You said they threatened a few times.'

'That lot of nosy bastards. I moved last time they were on my back. Shush, what's that?' Toni whispered. 'She's ear wigging.'

Jane quickly shut the door, jumped into bed, pulling Molly under the covers just in time. The door opened and they stood in the doorway. Convinced she was asleep, they quietly closed it again and went back into the living room. Jane lay awake for hours, thinking over what she had heard. So, her dad had wanted her after all; her mother had lied? She remembered social services coming around a few times, but they had moved soon after the visits. At one time, Jane was taken to stay with some people. But Jane could not recall who they were. The new revelation threw a different perspective on her life. She wondered what her father had been like. She never remembered a man in her life, except the boyfriends of her mum. Maybe she could try and find him. It was a risk; if he did not want her, he could send her back to her mother and Dan. Then again, Jane had no idea what his name was or even what he was like.

Chapter Five

At the bunker the next day, Jane made a torch from a fat branch. First, she wove dried and bendy twigs, grass, and shreds of her old jumper around the end. Finding old newspapers discarded around the site, she added this too. The bundle was secured using twine shredded from reeds. It was something she remembered from primary school when they were doing a project on the Stone Age. Although they had not had newspapers in those days, Jane had improvised.

The torch ready and the entrance cleared, she pulled open the stiff doorway. This time it was slightly easier. Lighting the torch with the matches, she bravely but tentatively went down the stairs. She pushed Molly ahead first, as the little dog did not have any qualms about the eeriness.

Thankful to reach the bottom of the stairs, she held up the torch and slowly twisted it, straining her eyes to assess the opening. The large room spread out before her. It was much larger than the building above. The room reminded Jane of her dream the night before. Finding two doorways on the left side of the stairs, she felt spooked again.

'What if bodies were hidden in there?' She looked around with dilated, fear-filled eyes.

Molly did not seem concerned about bodies as she wagged her tail and sniffed at various points on the dirty floor. Moving the torch about helped to dispel some of the spooky shadows that lurked. The large area was empty, except for some discarded rectangular tins with handles at each end and a few odd-shaped lumps of metal here and there. In one corner sat the two bags the men had left the day before.

The torch went out, and in a panic, Jane ran for the stairs, grasping her way back outside. Once through the small doorway she gasped a big lungful of fresh air, grateful to be in the sunlight again and away from the dark, spooky room. She went to work making another torch. This time she did not light it until she was back in the room. Her hair prickled as she walked down the stairs, images in her head of a big hand grabbing her arm.

Jane gasped and staggered backwards when she saw the contents of the first bag.

'Guns,' she breathed, shocked.

Once the shaking had subsided, she counted four of them, plus a small handgun. There were bullets too, lots of boxes full to the top and, thankfully, two working torches. Shutting the bag, she went to one of the rooms. The door was stiff and creaked as she pulled at it. Inside were six bunk beds, still with mattresses, pillows and blankets and a thick layer of dust on each. There was nothing else of interest so she closed it again. The next room was smaller and empty, apart from a few mice or rats that scurried away in different directions. Jane shut the door and made to leave, making sure she left no evidence of being there.

Once the door was covered, they went to the little clearing beyond the shelter so Jane could think. Her head spun and her hands shook.

Late afternoon, she took Molly home with her, for fear the men would come back and find the little dog. It was risky but what else could she do? It was almost dark as they negotiated their way along the path. The journey was difficult, and once Jane slipped and slid down the bank into the river. Grabbing clumps of brambles just saved her from going under the water. With her legs deeply submerged, she caught her breath while a few angry water birds scattered in protest.

With badly bleeding hands, Jane sat on the bank to pour some of the river water from her pumps. Molly looked solemnly on, whimpering and trying to lick the blood away. The splinters in her hands hurt terribly as they continued the journey. Water dripped from Jane's soaked jeans and very soggy pumps. The walk took twice as long, as the dusk quickly turned to a thick blackness, offering no moonlight to illuminate the way. The landscape changed shape without the guidance of daylight. Jane tripped constantly and again fell, this time onto her very sore knees, her hands finding another cluster of brambles and nettles.

'For God's sake!' she cried, tears of frustration running down her face.

Relief flooded her when they eventually reached the bridge without much more drama, Molly dragging her usual line of greenery behind her. There were so many bobbles in her coat it would take ages to remove them. They did look a sorry pair when they reached the gloomy blue front door, thankful they had not bumped into anyone on the journey. The lights inside were out so no one was home, as Jane grasped the door key with one of her sore, swollen hands.

Going into Toni's bedroom to find a pair of tweezers, her eyes rested on the suitcase on top of the wardrobe. She went to the kitchen and bought back a chair to reach it. The case was very heavy as Jane heaved it down and plopped it onto the bed. Inside were piles of papers and a few old photographs. Jane had never looked inside alone before. She had seen her mother rifling through it once or twice, claiming to be looking for something. But, as Jane could not read, she had never bothered to look herself. Maybe one of the letters would tell her who her father was, she thought. She decided not to take them all, as her mother might notice them gone. Randomly choosing one from the middle of the bundle, Jane hoped it contained some clues to lead her to her father. Picking her way through the unruly pile, she dismissed photos of people she did not recognise, until her eyes fell on one in particular. It was of a beautiful, slim girl with long blonde hair holding a baby and smiling. Jane picked it up and studied it closely.

'It's my mum,' she breathed, shocked.

If it were not for the eyes Jane would never have recognised her. Her mum was a lot plumper now, her eyes dull and angry. She kept herself nice still, and despite the alcohol, was still a handsome woman. But nothing like the beautiful woman that stared back from the photo, who looked to be around Jane's age. The baby must be her, she guessed, and turned it over, squinting at the faint writing.

'*I... s... a... bella.*'

Both Jane's heart and head began to pound as she stared at the words. That's where she had heard the name before. But who was Isabella and why was her mum holding the baby? Jane began to look more closely at the other photos until her eyes rested on one in particular. It was of a young Toni again, but this time she was with another girl, the

47

spitting image of her. Their hair was the same golden blonde, the same length and style. Even the clothes were identical, making it impossible to tell the girls apart. Both wore blue T-shirts and jeans. They looked so happy, with their arm around each other, laughing. Jane was shocked; Toni had a twin sister. It did not seem possible her mother had never spoken of a family or sister. She studied it hard but could not decide which one was Toni. Feeling numb with shock she put the photo to one side and scrutinised the others. There were a lot with the two girls at various ages, holding hands or cuddling. She selected a few to keep and began to look at the papers more closely.

None of them made any sense, and most looked official. One said 'Will' at the top, so Jane dismissed it and grabbed at her small pile of photos and letters. Just as she was bundling the contents back, something caught her eye. She picked up two pieces of paper and unfolded them. They both had printed 'birth something' along the top. The first had her name on it, 'Jane Watts'. The second one was almost identical and had Isabella's name on it.

'I... S... ABELLA,' she read out loud — it was all so strange. Adding them to her little pile, Jane closed the case and returned it.

After an hour of pulling thorns from her aching hands, she went into her room with Molly. Opening the letter, Jane tried to make sense of some of the words. Apart from the odd small one, it was impossible. Lifting the official document, she ran her fingers over the word Isabella, puzzled by the coincidence of the name. She felt baffled but excited to know she had more family.

'It's the girl I dream about,' she told Molly, who thumped her tail at the sound of her voice.

Giving up on the papers, Jane hid them away under her chest of drawers with the forgotten pound coin from Dan.

'At least we can buy some sweets tomorrow for our breakfast,' she told the dog, getting into bed beside her.

There had been little to eat for dinner and they were both very hungry. Molly's tummy made rumbling noises and Jane felt bad for her. All there was in the fridge was some mouldy bread and hard cheese. Goodness knows how her mum and Dan survived. When they had money, they went to a local café to eat. But when the money ran out, she had no idea what they did. Her mother never went shopping and never seemed to bother about Jane's food.

'Gets 'er dinner at school,' she had heard her mother tell Dan one day when he had asked.

'If she don't go, she don't eat. Serves the little bleeder right if she goes 'ungry. Stops her playing truant.'

After the very soggy, gloomy sandwich, which Jane shared with the eager dog, they were both still very hungry.

It was the early hours of the morning when Jane was woken from a deep sleep by shouting voices. Bleary-eyed, she sat up and stared at her mum and Dan, who were standing in her room. Her heart sank as she stared at Molly, who was dancing around, growling and making to attack Dan's legs. Jane leapt from the bed and grabbed at the dog just as Dan's leg flew out to kick her.

'No, Molly,' she chastised, fear shaking her voice.

'Where the fucking hell did that ugly thing come from?' Toni spat with her fists clenched ready to lash out. 'Get it out of the flat now, Dan, or I'll kill it.'

'No, Mum, please,' begged Jane, as Dan reached for the snarling dog.

Jane pulled Molly protectively behind her back. 'Please, she's my dog, I'll look after her, you'll never know she's here. Please,' she pleaded, tears running down her face.

Her mother's fist swung for Jane, finding her temple and knocking her sideways. Molly, teeth bared, rushed forward again.

Jane screamed as Dan's boot flew forward and this time kicked into the dog's stomach, throwing her against the wall. Dan moved quickly as he lifted his fist and brought it down onto the crumpled little dog. A pitiful yelp left her body and a pool of urine ran from her. Jane thought she was dead until slowly, with her belly scraping the threadbare, sticky carpet, Molly dragged herself whimpering under the bed.

Jane was hysterical as Dan pushed her aside and pulled out the bed. Grabbing Molly by the scruff, he picked up the whimpering dog and left the room. Jane made to follow, but this time her mother's foot kicked into her chest.

'You fucking whore, how dare you bring that filthy thing into my flat! Get into bed, NOW. Don't you dare let me see you move out of this room or I swear to God, I'll beat you so bad you'll never walk again!'

She turned and slammed the door behind her. Jane sobbed and sobbed, tears of hopelessness and desperation falling down her face. There was nothing but an endless road of misery ahead for her now. She imagined Molly laying somewhere outside in the dark. Confused and in pain and not knowing where to go, now she no longer had Jane to care for her.

Jane sobbed until she saw the daybreak and heard the birds chirping and singing as they awoke. Several times she looked out of her window hoping to see Molly, but there was nothing, just another block of depressed flats behind her own. New tears of misery fell down her cheeks as a moan escaped her throat. Every time she closed her eyes, she saw her little dog crawling on her belly across the floor, whining in pain, her back and legs seemingly broken.

At 8am her mother came into the bedroom, unusually up and awake.

'Get up,' she hissed, 'I'm going to see you to school today.'

Not knowing what else to do, Jane got out of bed and pulled on her clothes. Going into the bathroom, she splashed her face with water and brushed her teeth.

Her mother walked her all the way to school, which caused the other children to smirk. On the route Jane looked out for Molly.

'Forget it,' Toni snapped, 'Dan broke its neck and dumped it in a wheelie bin.' Her mother smiled with satisfaction, showing nicotine-stained teeth.

New tears fell down Jane's face adding to her already swollen eyes.

At the school gate, Toni watched as Jane shuffled down the path, waiting until she disappeared into the building before turning away.

Jane, her head bent and tears still falling, pushed her way along the corridor, through the crowd of children, heaving and pushing their way to different classes. She did not see or hear any of them until she absently walked past Naomi gossiping and giggling with a group of girls.

Spotting Jane, Naomi nudged the girl next to her. 'What, did mummy walk you to school today?' she laughed.

Jane suddenly lost her temper; clenching her hands into fists, she walked up to Naomi and pushed her face into hers.

'Why don't you go fuck yourself, you evil little bitch?' she hissed through gritted teeth.

Quiet descended on the corridor, no one spoke, and everyone stared at the usually timid Jane.

Even children from other years, not knowing Jane, held their breaths in anticipation of a good fight. Naomi's jaw fell open, wobbled up and down a little, trying to find some suitable words. She could not think of any to retaliate; she was shocked and a little scared.

Jane turned away, walked through the gathered crowd and marched right back out of school.

When she reached the block of flats, Jane searched for Molly's body, not wanting to believe her dead. The four big wheelie bins revealed nothing. After two hours of calling, looking under cars and down alleyways, she gave up. It was around 11 am that she saw Dan and her mum go out, walking down the street arm-in-arm towards the town.

Letting herself in the flat, Jane made a cup of tea and sat down. New tears streamed down her face but she hardly felt them.

Suddenly she sprang up, 'The park, maybe Molly has gone there?'

She ran for the door and stopped. Going into her bedroom, Jane took the small bundle of papers from under the chest of drawers. If Mrs Flanagan was there, maybe she could read them for her.

Jane searched every bush and bin she could find, calling and calling to Molly. But there was no sign of her. Cooper trotted over to greet her on his lunchtime walk, followed by Mrs Jilly puffing along way behind.

'Hello, Jane, no school today?' the ample lady asked. 'Glad the weather is slightly cooler.'

'Yes, definitely,' Jane responded, giving Cooper a little pat.

Mrs Jilly puffed off again, waving a farewell. Jane could see Chilly in the distance and then Raspberry the red setter. Their two owners were deep in conversation as they followed the dogs' trail. Jane made her way to Frank's bench, hoping she had not missed Mrs Flanagan.

The old lady appeared twenty minutes later, carrying the usual grey shopping bag.

'Goodness, Jane, I wondered where you were. I've not seen you for ages. I miss our little chats.'

'Sorry, I've been so busy. Mrs Flanagan, would you tell me what these papers say?' Jane pulled the small bundle out of her carrier bag and handed them to her friend.

Mrs Flanagan began to flick through, puzzled. 'Can't you read, Jane?'

'No,' she confessed, her face reddening as she looked down at her filthy, still wet pumps.

Mrs Flanagan tried not to look surprised as she opened the papers. 'Well, there are all sorts here, but I haven't got my reading glasses so I can't tell you properly. There are two birth certificates and a letter.'

'What's a birth certificate?' Jane asked, eager to know.

'Well, it's a document given when a new baby is born.' Mrs Flanagan opened the first and read. 'It's for an Isabella something Lucas. Mother Vicky.'

'I think it was my mum's sister's baby. Does that make the baby my cousin?'

'Yes, it does,' Mrs Flanagan smiled, opening the second certificate. 'This one is yours. Jane Watts, mother, Toni Watts.' Mrs Flanagan looked sad, 'It's very blurry, but I can't see any father on here.'

Jane looked a little deflated. 'I didn't have a father.'

'It's not that you don't have one, Jane. It's just your mum's not recorded who he was.'

'It feels really strange knowing I have an aunt and a cousin. My mum's never mentioned them.'

Mrs Flanagan opened the letter and began to skim the writing. She felt a little uncomfortable prying.

'This is a letter to Vicky from her boyfriend, but I can't see what it says.' She folded the letter, putting it back in the envelope. 'Where did you get all these Jane?'

'They're my mum's. I … took them,' she blushed again with the confession. 'She told me they're from my dad; I thought I could find him if I took it.'

'I'm sorry it's not from him, but I think you should put them back. It doesn't always pay to know things that are private and someone else's business,' she advised, handing them back.

'I guess not. I don't understand why my mum told me they were from my dad, though. Besides, without prying I wouldn't have found I had other family.'

'Has your mum never talked to you about them?'

'No, never.'

'Maybe she died and your mum found it too painful to talk about.'

Jane felt strange inside; she could not explain the feeling of knowing there was more family than just her mum. Also, the strange dreams; maybe she had known Isabella when she was young and was remembering her.

'Is there no address?' Jane asked.

'Sorry, no. The birth was registered in a place called Thornwood Abbey.'

'Where's that?'

'It's not that far. About 14 or so miles from here,' Mrs Flanagan explained. 'It's a pretty place in the country. I went there once with my Frank and the children for a day out. It has a lovely old abbey and is very posh with quaint little houses and shops. I remember going to a little teashop in the abbey grounds. We had cream teas, all homemade, with warm scones and little pots of clotted cream and strawberry jam.'

Jane was only half-listening; she could not stop thinking about Isabella. Then a stone weight hit her tummy as she remembered Molly. She sprang from the bench, startling the old lady.

'I've got to go,' she called as she ran off down the park path towards the river.

Jane walked all the way to the bunker, calling, but there was no sign of Molly. She really must be dead, she thought, as she turned back towards home.

That evening, after finding some bread in the fridge and beans in the cupboard, she went into her bedroom and ate her dinner, staying there all evening. She stared dismally at the patch of wee that Molly had left when Dan beat her.

Chapter Six

The next day hunger pains forced Jane to go to school. Relishing in the dinner, she did not even notice the nasty remarks from Lucy and her gang. It was pointless raiding Dan's pockets because there would be no money to steal. There never was after the weekend and before benefit day.

Every day she looked in vain for Molly, but it was hopeless, there was no sign of her. Eventually, she went to Dan and begged him to tell her where she was.

'I broke its neck and threw it in a bin,' he laughed nastily and so did her mother.

Jane did not cry this time; she just stared at them. A look of hatred appeared on her face and her small hands clenched into fists. With eyes as cold as ice, she looked deep into her mother's.

'I hate you so much. I hope you rot in hell. You forget one day I'll grow up and have my revenge.' Her voice was calm and sinister.

Toni, who was just about to gulp at her bottle of cider, stopped. Her face whitened as she stared back at Jane. The laughter on her face dissolved and a look of disbelief took its place. Hurt and then shock widened her eyes as she stared at her daughter. Jane turned and walked from the room, suddenly feeling in control. No longer could her mother hurt her.

For the rest of the week, Jane went to school. The day of the robbery loomed and the atmosphere at home was electric. Dan was bad-tempered and edgy. Neither Dan nor her mother went out and for the first time there was food around: a half-eaten pizza that Jane finished for breakfast one morning, the remnants of a Chinese takeaway, and cold chips discarded in the bin the next. She'd never eaten so well and felt so full in all her life.

On the Thursday before the robbery, she was having one last despondent look in the bins for Molly's body, when Mrs Jilly puffed past on her way to the park with Cooper. The bin men were due the next day and it would be too late to give Molly a decent burial. If she could find the body, Jane thought, she could bury her under the old oak tree in the park and lay some flowers.

'Jane dear, I've seen you looking in the bin so many times this week. What have you lost?'

Cooper went to her and wagged his fat tail. Jane bent and gave him a big kiss.

'Nothing. It's just … I'm looking for a little dog.'

'Goodness, and you think it's in there?'

'My mum's boyfriend said he put her in the bin.'

Mrs Jilly shuddered; she knew Dan Wallace from old. Not a nice man; she couldn't imagine what Toni saw in him. Still, the woman was not too pleasant herself. Poor Jane, such a lovely gentle girl, goodness knows what she had done to deserve a mother like her.

Mrs Jilly did not know what to say, the child looked so worried. She smiled sympathetically and puffed off, dragging Cooper behind her. Halfway along the road she stopped and turned back.

'Mr Lewis from flat number six found a dog last Monday morning in the river,' she called.

Jane's heart began to pound so hard her chest vibrated.

'It was apparently in a bad way, he said, he thought some kids had got hold of it and beaten it…'

But Jane had run off and did not hear anymore.

Mr Lewis took ages to open his door.

'You've got my dog,' Jane gushed, as the surprised man stared at her. 'It's a scruffy brown little one with bald patches.'

'Yes, I know the dog. So, it belongs to you, does it? Poor little mite, thought it was a stray. I took it to the dog's home down Hill Rise Park road…'

Jane ran off again, leaving Mr Lewis in the middle of a sentence, not stopping until she reached the rescue centre. She knew the place well and had heard many stories of dogs being destroyed after only a week there; too many unwanted, apparently.

She rushed into the reception, startling the young lady who sat at the desk.

'You've got my dog,' Jane blurted out, ignoring a man in mid-conversation with the receptionist.

The receptionist looked through her big, round glasses with distaste at the scruffy girl. 'Wait your turn, please?' she clipped, and turned back to the man.

Jane sat down on the hard, blue chair and waited. Her feet fidgeted and she kept leaping up, thinking the man was going. But he was rooted to the spot for the day, as he talked about all the animals he had owned throughout various stages of his life. Finally, he did leave, after what seemed like, to Jane, hours of listening to his droning voice. She sprang from her chair and rushed to the desk.

'Name?' the receptionist asked tonelessly, pulling out a form and sliding it across the desk.

'Jane Watts; you have my dog, Molly,' she gushed.

The receptionist pushed a pen forward to join the form. Jane reddened as she stared at the squiggles on the sheet.

'Fill this in, and I will get someone to come and see you.'

'Please; you have my dog — can I have her?' Jane garbled.

'We do not hand over dogs without proof of ownership and, of course, payment for their keep. Please, fill out the form.'

'I... I... can't write,' she whispered, looking around to make sure no one was listening. 'And I haven't got any money.'

'Then you can't have your dog.'

Jane stared at her; she did not know what else to do. All sorts of things ran through her mind, begging and pleading being some of them.

'Can you just tell me if she's OK then?' she finally asked, near to tears.

'Not unless you fill out the form,' the receptionist smiled triumphantly, meeting Jane's desperate gaze.

She had met people like this child before. Off the big estate, no doubt, where the parents were all dropouts on benefits, and had loads of kids only for working people like her to keep them. These people always had dogs and cats that suffered the consequences of overbreeding, to make money from the offspring.

She watched Jane turn and walk away, grateful she had solved yet another problem for the day.

'Can I help you?' a lady, who was just locking up her car, asked.

Jane jumped; she had not seen the lady watching her as she walked along the high boundaries of the shelter's fences calling, 'Molly!' and hoping to hear her little bark amongst the bigger ones. She turned quickly and came face-to-face with a middle-aged lady, who had large, gentle eyes and a warm smile.

'My little dog is in there and they won't let me see her or give her back. I don't even know if she's OK.'

Tears welled in her eyes as she sniffed and wiped her nose on her arm.

'Really, who wouldn't let you?' the lady asked, surprised. 'Ahhh, don't tell me, it was the Gestapo?'

Jane didn't know who the Gestapo was but guessed it represented the horrible lady inside.

'My name's Fiona, I'm sure we can sort something out.'

Jane looked down, astonished, at the hand held out to her. She had seen this in films; it was mostly men that shook hands. But never had anyone done this to her. She suddenly felt important and taller than her small height. Taking the hand, she shook it and met the lady's eyes.

'Jane,' she smiled back through her wet eyes and followed Fiona back into the reception.

The young lady at the desk looked up and her eyes narrowed when she spotted the scruffy girl again, with her boss, Fiona.

Jane thought she looked like a beady-eyed moth, with her large glasses.

'Sarah, I understand this young lady is looking for her dog, and has been turned away.' Fiona's nice eyes clouded into a cross look and her voice changed to one of authority.

'Well... I... I... just assumed...' Sarah stammered.

'No, Sarah, we never assume, do we? Young people are our future. We need to educate them, not turn them against us. One day, rights for animals may just change. But it won't be by us, because we are only planting the seeds. It may, if we are lucky, be by young people like Jane here. So, we never assume, we explain.'

This time it was Sarah's face that reddened; she looked down at some papers in front of her and started shuffling them about. 'Sorry, Fiona.'

'I think the apology is for Jane, not me.'

She did apologise but then made a face behind Fiona's back as she led Jane through the doors and into the shelter.

The barking on the other side of the door was overwhelming. Jane was tempted to cover her ears against the onslaught. As Fiona did not do this, she resisted the urge.

Fiona turned to Jane, 'Now can you give me a description of your dog?' she shouted over the racket.

'Molly, her name's Molly. She's scruffy, small and brown with pretty eyes.' Jane then added dismally, 'She has bald patches and sores on her body.'

Fiona frowned. 'Do you know why she has bald patches?'

By the look on the Fiona's face she did know and this was a trick question.

'I... don't know,' Jane stammered, deciding to be honest, 'She needed to go to the vets, but I had no money. I found her in the park. She was very hungry. I've been looking after her ever since.'

'Ahhh,' Fiona smiled, 'that was kind of you, Jane. Come with me. I think I know the dog you're talking about. Molly, you say?'

Jane nodded, not daring to hope too much. Fiona led the way past the five large buildings that lined the edge of the grounds.

'Dinner time,' she explained, grimacing at the noise, and waving to a lady carrying a pile of large food bowls.

Through the open door of one of the buildings, Jane could see it was divided into little sections made of wire. At the back of each were little see-through doors that flapped, allowing each inhabitant to go outside into an enclosure. Jane counted at least ten on each building. All sizes of dogs, some in pairs, either sat looking gloomily out through the wire, or dancing up and down, jumping and barking at other dogs.

'How sad,' Jane said, feeling sorry for them all.

'It's the older ones,' Fiona told her, looking glum. 'Very rarely do people come and offer them a home. We have no option but to destroy them. The younger ones we allow two weeks to find a home. There are so many abandoned, we have no choice but to take their lives. The cats are the same, two weeks and that's it. Black or older cats stand little chance. Only the young and pretty coloured ones are lucky,' Fiona explained, looking as sad as Jane.

Jane looked over to see similar but smaller buildings on the other side. Most of the runs outside contained large cats of various descriptions, all shapes and sizes. Some had little groups of kittens, playing or piled on top of each other sleeping. There was even a large enclosure full of chickens that pecked and scratched at the earth, nonplussed.

'If people did not breed them, there would not be so many deaths. They are so shallow, never seeming to think of the consequences of their actions. They cause the problems and it's people like us that pick up the pieces. They go off, not a care in the world, or even a thought to the trail of suffering and misery they have left behind,' Fiona continued.

Jane looked back at the dog enclosures and searched each run for Molly; she could not see her and began to worry.

Fiona led them to a building which stood alone at the far side of the grounds. They went through the door into a large, clinical white room. A door to one side was slightly ajar, and as they passed, Jane spotted a pile of dead dogs and cats on the floor in one corner. Puppies and kittens, were also amongst the discarded life. Bile rose in her stomach as she gasped and put her hand over her mouth.

Fiona smiled apologetically, her own eyes traumatic. 'I never get used to it. No one wants them, people prefer to go to pet shops and friends, or breed their own. It never enters their head to come to places like this and save a life, except when they get rid of one of course. Then we are the first they call. Or they throw them onto the streets to fend for themselves.'

They walked through another door at the back of the room, where lots of small cages lined the wall. Jane spotted Molly in one and ran over, tears of relief falling from her eyes.

At first, the dog did not see Jane; she sat, dejected, with her head on her paw.

'Oh, Molly!' she cried.

The little dog jumped up, delight flooding her eyes. Putting her paws on the front of the cage, she began whimpering. Her little tail wagged so fast it became a blur of lots of tails. Jane stared in horror at the stitches along the middle of Molly's little tummy. Fiona opened the cage and she leapt out and into Jane's waiting arms. The two cuddled and Molly washed every inch of Jane's half-giggling, half-crying face quickly and precisely with her tongue; she did not forget an inch and then went over the whole area for a second and third time.

'Let's talk,' Fiona said, smiling at the happy reunion.

She sat on a chair and pulled a folding one out for Jane. With Molly cuddled on her lap, the two sat staring expectantly at Fiona.

'A man fished her out of the river. She had been badly beaten and had hypothermia; she would have died if left a few minutes more. She was very badly bruised, but nothing was broken.'

'Was she cut?' Jane cringed, running her fingers gently down the line of stitches.

'No, we spayed her.' Fiona then went on to explain at Jane's puzzled expression. 'It's an operation to stop her having puppies. She was pregnant, so the puppies were removed.'

Jane's eyes widened, showing her shock. Goodness knows how she would have cared for puppies in her predicament, but it seemed so cruel to take them away.

'Oh, poor Molly.'

'Yes, it seems horrible, doesn't it, but as you see there are so many unwanted ones already. The bald patches are a flea allergy, which we are treating with medication. Do you know who beat her, Jane?'

Jane opened her mouth to tell Fiona about Dan and then stopped herself. If Fiona called the police and he was arrested, there would be no robbery. Then there would be no new life for herself and Molly.

'She escaped out of the front door last Sunday night and I couldn't find her. I've been looking all week.'

Fiona knew there was more to the story. The girl was anxious and hiding something. Having dealt with people for too many years, she could read them like a book.

She softened her voice: 'Are you sure, Jane? You can tell me in confidence; I won't do anything about it, but I need to know.'

Jane swallowed; it was a big risk. But this lady was so lovely and kind, she decided to trust her. 'I don't mind something being done; it's just... not until after tomorrow. I'm going to live with my aunty and cousin in Thornwood Abbey. They're very rich and I know will pay you for Molly's treatment.'

Looking at the scruffy girl opposite her, Fiona thought the story a bit fanciful. But her eyes were earnest and honest as they looked pleadingly back at her. 'OK, so what happened to Molly?'

Jane explained about Dan and what he did to Molly. When she finished, she kissed the little dog's head, and gave her a squeeze.

'Bastard, did your mum not stop him?' Fiona tried to hold her temper on hearing the horrible details.

'She doesn't like dogs,' Jane added sadly.

'OK, when your relatives come to collect you tomorrow, we will hand Molly over. As an adult your aunt can sign the forms to become her legal owner. If she agrees to it.'

Jane's heart sank as she grappled for a feasible excuse. 'They are away at the moment, which is why I'm not going until tomorrow. They're due back at 5 pm; I'm getting the train there to meet them.'

'OK, what about if she calls us to clarify?'

Jane's heart sank even further, right into her boots this time. Then, brightening, she had an idea.

'They're abroad so I can't talk to them. But what if I can get my grandmother to come and sign the form?'

Fiona sat thinking, her eyes flicking from one to the other of Jane's. It was obvious the young girl loved the dog dearly and vice versa. Lots of questions ran through her head, like why was Jane so scruffy if her relatives were so rich? But against her better judgement she dismissed them. If an adult could confirm the story, then she had no reason to doubt it.

'What about the treatment for Molly; you did say your aunt would pay? We are a charity that struggle to make ends meet,' Fiona explained as gently as she could.

'My grandma will pay. I know she will and then my aunt can give her it back when she returns. Will Dan be arrested?' she asked, hoping he would be locked up for years for the way he had treated Molly.

'Sadly, no. I will certainly report it though. You just never know, the authorities may treat it as serious.'

After Fiona's agreement, Jane gave Molly a big kiss and promised to return soon. Then she ran off out of the centre, not looking back to see the dog's distraught look as she was left behind and put back into the tiny cage.

It took Jane a lot of begging and pleading to convince Mrs Flanagan to lie for her the next day when they met on Frank's bench.

'Please; Molly and me are going off to find my aunt and cousin. I spoke to my mum last night about finding out and she agreed I could. She has even given me some money and my aunt's address.

Although Mrs Flanagan was shocked about Molly being beaten, she was worried about Jane going off alone.

'I don't like it, Jane. What if you can't find your aunt? Or what if she has a husband who doesn't want you in their life? You can't just go off and turn up out of the blue like that. You could end up sleeping on the streets. A young girl on her own, anything could happen.'

'I'll be fine, honestly. My mum thinks it's OK; she will be glad to get rid of me. Please…' she begged.

'Well, why doesn't she get Molly from the dog's home then?' the old lady queried, again.

'I told you, she doesn't like dogs. Besides, she doesn't want to get Dan in trouble for beating Molly,' Jane explained, grateful once again for her quick-thinking mind.

Mrs Flanagan paused for a long time, weighing up the situation. She felt uneasy about it. 'OK, I'll do it on one condition. You call me every day at 9 am to let me know you're safe.' She did not consider how difficult this would be without Jane owning a mobile phone.

Jane threw her arms around the elderly lady's neck and gave her a big kiss on the cheek. 'Thank you so much. I promise I'll call without fail every day.'

They headed for the home, Jane going over the story again on the way so Mrs Flanagan, who kept getting in a muddle, did not muck everything up. As it was, Sarah did not ask, she just glared at Jane with a look of dislike on her face as she slid over the form. Mrs Flanagan sat on a chair to fill in the details.

Jane whispered to the unresponsive Sarah that she would be back later with the money, as they needed to go to the bank.

'Aren't you getting Molly?' Mrs Flanagan asked, as Jane ushered her outside.

'Not yet, I'm going to get my stuff together first. I don't want Dan to see her.'

They parted at the end of the street, each going in different directions. It was a very teary farewell.

'I'll miss you so much.' Jane flung her arms around her friend, almost knocking her over.

With the phone number in her pocket she waved back at Mrs Flanagan, whose own tears rolled down her wrinkly old cheeks.

Chapter Seven

As the day of the robbery drew near Dan became more on edge. He rowed constantly with Toni over the most stupid things, even worse when they were drinking. He liked a woman with some meat on her, but in his eyes, she was getting too fat and lazy. He told her often enough and she retaliated, saying he needed to look in the mirror before he criticised her.

Dan went to the bedroom mirror and stood naked in front of it. Turning sideways, he put his hands on his stomach, which had grown more in the past two months. It was true he had put on a few pounds; too much junk food and alcohol, he decided. Not at the moment though, as he needed a clear head.

He lay on the bed and lit a cigarette. Would Scott have the nerve? he asked himself. He was only eighteen and a wuss of a kid, always was, even as a child. He had been working as an assistant gardener at the Old Grange for almost six months now. The old fellow who owned the house was a multimillionaire. Colonel Potts, everyone called him behind his back. It was not his real name; it was Lord Anthony Falcon.

Stuck up old sod, his best pal Mick always said. He never gave his 'staff' the time of day. In fact, if he was in the garden, according to Scott, the staff had to hide so as not to be seen. Silly old bastard, Dan thought; he would like to take him down a peg or two, and soon he would.

Colonel Potts owned a chain of supermarkets in and around the area. Now retired, his sons had taken over the businesses, but the old sod still kept his hand in here and there. The sons both lived at the grange; one was married to a snobby cow and had two kids. The other, rumoured to be gay, was single.

This robbery had been carefully planned in Dan's head from the first day Scott had started working there. It had taken a while to convince Mick and the lad it was a good plan. The old bastard would never even miss the money, plus he must have insurance. So he did not know what all the fuss was about.

'My lad has qualifications,' Mick had boasted over a pint in the Queen's Head one night. 'He worked hard to become a gardener; he will go places, that boy.'

'Get a life, Mick,' Dan smirked, 'He's hardly Einstein, is he? He cuts grass and trims daisies.'

'It's more involved than that.' Mick's shoulders stiffened defensively. 'He's a clever lad, my son. You're always putting him down. Just leave off, Dan.'

Mick's wife had run off over seven years ago with another bloke. The marriage had never been great, both always carrying on with other people. Mick was devastated when she did go, leaving him to bring up the boy alone.

'Come on, Mick, if we rob the old geezer we could be made for life. Out of here and sitting on some beach somewhere. You could buy the lad his own bit of land, a farm even. We could fuck off to Spain or France, whatever. The world would be our oyster.'

It had taken even longer to convince yellow-bellied Scott, who was scared of his own shadow. But eventually, with both Dan and Mick chipping away at him, he reluctantly agreed.

The plans for the robbery had been more difficult to put together. According to Scott, there was a safe somewhere in the library. He had often seen a private security van carrying in metal boxes through a patio door, leading to the room.

There would be no way they could possibly break the safe open without the code. The old bloke would give that to them, Dan was sure. 'Of course, with a little persuasion,' he smiled to himself, thinking up various torture methods.

They needed a day when both the sons and the wife were out. The sons were easy enough; they left every day to work at their head office.

'Most Fridays,' Scott informed them, 'the woman goes out around 11 am and don't come home till 4-ish, after she's picked the kids up from school.'

'Where does she go all day?' Mick asked, wondering why it was only on Fridays.

'Not sure,' Scott shrugged. 'Some beauty thing, I think, and shopping, or to see her sister.'

There were also two security guards to contend with. Dan had no qualms on how to deal with those efficiently. Eventually, a plan was pieced together. How to hide whatever they managed to get out was also a big problem. Nowhere in either home would be safe, so after much thought, Dan remembered the underground rooms at the war bunker on the other side of the river. He had never been down them, but when he was a child his granddad had shown him the entrance. He had been billeted there on lookout duty during the war after being injured fighting. He had told Dan that underground were two other rooms, one where they slept and the other where stores were kept. It was perfect, as no one ever went over the other side of the river; even if they did, the entrance was well concealed.

His mate Marc had managed to acquire some sawn-off shotguns – Dan didn't ask where from. It had cost some, and Marc had put up the money and managed to have a small handgun thrown in for good measure.

Marc was now part of the gang, wanting his cut. He was handy though, arranging a delivery of gravel so they could get through the security gates. All was set and now Dan was agitated, sweating and not sleeping.

Nothing must go wrong; he could not face more years in prison. He had just scraped through the last 18 months; this time, if caught he would be banged up for years.

The small gang had met at the flat to finalise details two weeks before the go-ahead.

Dan left the flat about ten o'clock that morning, meeting at Mick's house on Tenants Street. Scott had already left for work extra early that morning.

'How's the kid?' Dan asked. 'He better not let us down.'

'He won't,' Mick assured, 'although poor sods been in the bog all night.'

They drove Mick's car to Boggard Street, where it was locked up, and walked the rest of the way to the gravel yard, where they met Marc.

Dan carried the bag of guns, which had been stored at the bunker. Two sacks of gravel were already loaded on the lorry, ready for delivery when they got there.

Marc sat in the driver's seat, tapping his fingers. Beads of sweat were glistening on his top lip. The gun bag was thrown behind the seats before the two men climbed into the lorry, their latex gloves already on, as were Marc's.

'Just remember,' Dan repeated, 'keep your face away from the security cameras till we're inside. Then we can put on balaclavas. Make sure the gloves don't tear.' He had already thrown some spare to them both.

The other two nodded, being too nervous to argue and tell him he was repeating himself again.

'Are you sure this lorry can't be traced?' Mick asked Marc.

'I told you, I bought it privately, it's still registered to the geezer I got it from. Cost me some, I can tell you.'

They were off, Mick and Dan laying low in the front of the lorry as they approached the large metal gates. Marc, his cap pulled slightly down, kept his face away from the camera in the guise of rolling a cigarette as he rang the buzzer.

'Delivery,' he shouted down the intercom, and the gate slowly creaked open.

'Not that security conscious, are they?' Mick laughed nervously, as Marc clambered back into the driver seat.

'I can see two security guards,' Marc whispered from the corner of his mouth.

'There are only two according to Scott,' Dan replied, pleased they were both in view, making it easier for them.

Scott met them at the drive, looking as nervous as they felt. He directed the lorry round the back of the house to a place that was not covered by the cameras. His body was stiff with tension, and by the expression on his face, he was not at all sure of what was about to happen. It had occurred to him that morning to pack his stuff and run away from home. Then, realising he had no money or anywhere to run, he stayed.

The security guards walked slowly to the lorry, planning to meet it and watch the unloading. Marc climbed out and made to fiddle with the hydraulic crane. Mick and Dan already had their balaclavas pulled over their heads. As the two security men came near, Marc banged the side of the lorry in signal and the two men burst out, with the guns pointed.

'Hands above your head!' shouted Dan.

The confused, shocked security men dutifully complied, along with Scott, who was not supposed to let on he was involved in any way. The old gardener, Pete, suddenly appeared from behind a bush. He dodged back again when he saw what was happening. It was too late; Dan spotted him from the corner of his eye.

Shepherding him out, he joined the others.

'Anyone else?' he asked the nervous group.

'Only the cleaners and cook,' Old Pete answered. He had been with the family since he was a young man, but any loyalty was forgotten while a gun was pointed at him.

'Where are they?' Mick asked, waving the shotgun at Old Pete.

'The cook is in the kitchen. I don't know about the cleaners,' he confessed, his old heart racing so much he was gasping for breath.

Marc had now pulled on his own balaclava and changed his gloves, as the first already had holes in.

Leaving Marc holding the gun, Dan and Mick turned to the house, through the kitchen. The cook screamed and dropped a stack of plates as she saw the men coming in.

Mick grabbed her and put his hand over her mouth. Noting the bolt on a large cupboard, he pushed her towards it and opened the door. It was a larder, full to the ceiling with food. 'How could one family eat so much? Greedy pigs,' he raved. 'Don't scream and you won't get hurt,' he told the terrified woman.

He pulled his hand away and checked her clothes for a mobile phone. Pulling it out of her pocket, he smashed it onto the floor and checked the larder. It was safe to lock her in, he decided, and pushed the sobbing woman through the door.

Dan left him and walked quietly through the house, looking for the cleaners and the old colonel. He was sitting in the library reading The Telegraph. Scott had already explained he was slightly deaf, so he had not noticed anything. He found the two young girls in a large bedroom, chatting away as they cleaned. He burst into the room, surprising them both. Leading them silently down the stairs, he directed them into the kitchen to join the cook. Waiting for Mick to check for mobiles, he pushed them inside the larder and again the door was locked.

'That's it,' Mick said, checking the window to see if Marc was all right.

They headed for the library and went inside. The colonel looked up, thinking it was one of the guards. He started on seeing the two men, and called out.

'Forget it, they're indisposed. Now we need to know your safe code,' Dan told the frightened man.

'Get out of here or... o...' Colonel Potts shouted.

'Now, don't be silly, we can do this the easy way or the hard,' Dan said calmly, grinning under his hood.

'I'll never tell you, so get out.' His hands had begun to shake, but he was determined not to let them see he was afraid.

'Get the others.' Dan nodded his head to Mick, who left and went outside again.

Five minutes later, he came back with the two security men, Old Pete and Scott. He lined them up at the wall and checked the first security man's pockets. Pulling out a phone, he stamped on it. As he turned to the second to check, the man made a grab for Mick. In an instant Dan was over the other side of the room and had pulled the trigger of his gun.

The deafening blast vibrated the walls, shattering glasses that sat on a silver tray. Books from the vast amount of oak cases fell tumbling to the floor. All eyes turned to the head as it exploded into thousands of gooey, bloody chunks, splattering everyone who stood nearby and dripping from the bookcases and even the ceiling. Dan pointed the gun towards the other security guard, who fell to his knees and began to beg, his hands clasped as if in prayer and eyes squeezed tightly, trying to shut out the horror he was facing.

The second blast was as booming as the first, his head also destroyed, leaving a bloody, sagging neck.

'Fucking hell!' Marc shouted, his eyes wide with shock.

Scott began to gag; he fell onto his knees and heaved.

Old Pete stood frozen to the spot, staring at the mess, blood dripping from his face. He was back somewhere in the trenches, the war raging all around him, his fellow solders falling in the same bloody disarray of bits.

'Why?' he cried in disbelief.

'Shut it, old man, or you join them,' Dan spat and walked over to the old colonel who, like Pete sat transfixed to the spot.

'Not so up your arse now, are you?' Dan laughed, enjoying his power over the man.

Mick, like Marc, could not believe what had just happened. He and Dan had been friends since they were toddlers and shared all their lives, good times and bad. When did he change from that snotty-nosed kid to something so evil? he wondered.

'I have nothing here to offer you,' the colonel told them, his voice now croaky and shaking with fear.

'Well, I would like to take a look in your safe just to make sure,' Dan told him, lifting the bottom of his balaclava to reveal a wide smile plastered on his face.

'So if you could just tell us the code, we can get this over and done with quicker. You don't want your snobby bitch of a daughter-in-law or her spawn to come home and join them now, do you?' Dan flicked his gun towards the bodies.

The colonel opened his mouth to speak, but stubbornness flooded his head. He would not give in — why should he? He had worked hard for his money and status.

Dan grew impatient; he grabbed the old man by his collar, and, with adrenaline coursing through his veins, threw him to the floor. He fell with a thud, the wind knocked out of him. Dan fumbled in the bag he had bought with him and produced a funnel and a plastic bottle labelled 'Antifreeze'.

The colonel gasped at the sight of it.

'Now, we are going to be difficult, aren't we?' he waved the bottle at him, smirking, his face sinister. 'Hold him down, Mick.'

Mick hesitated; he did not even imagine the robbery would be like this. He thought, just frighten the old man a bit, grab the money and run. But he complied; they had come too far to turn back now. He lowered his gun and went over, grabbing the old colonel's hands and pulling them above his head.

Dan knelt on the floor and grabbed his head. His false teeth moved as his mouth opened slightly. It was enough room for Dan to push the funnel into the opening, shredding skin from the roof of his mouth.

The colonel flinched and moaned as the pain gripped him. He tried to move his head away, but Dan's grip was too firm. He laughingly pulled the funnel out, dislodging his teeth as he did. Dan took great delight in humiliating him by pulling at the teeth and throwing them across the room. Then he pushed the funnel back into his mouth, cutting his gums this time. He opened the top of the plastic bottle by unscrewing it with his teeth and began to drip the antifreeze slowly into the funnel.

The old man tried to wiggle as the liquid found his throat.

'Still not talking?' Dan asked.

The colonel nodded his head in surrender. He thought he was brave and did not mind dying; he had had a good long life now, what did it matter? But this would be agonising, he knew that, and along with his already painful aches and pains he was not ready to face an excruciating death. Dan pulled out the funnel from his bloody mouth.

The colonel nodded towards one of the bookcases.

Dan went over and pulled at the books, scattering them onto the floor. Finding nothing, he went to the edge of the wood and felt along. His fingers found a release catch and the case sprang open to reveal not a safe, but a vault.

Dan whistled through his teeth, 'Code?'

The colonel couldn't talk, blood trickling down his throat and mingling with the antifreeze. Dan went over and pulled him up by his collar. 'CODE!' he screamed.

Mick had enough sense to grab a piece of paper and pen and thrust it to the elderly man. The colonel's hands shook so much the scrawl was barely legible.

It took Dan a while to get to the end of the long line of numbers and letters. A few times one or two needed clarification, but eventually the wheel turned and the thick steel door eased open.

All three of them stuck their heads in the opening, gasping at what lay inside. All thoughts of the bloodshed were forgotten as their eyes took in not only money, but jewellery, diamonds, strange artefacts and antiques.

'The old bastard,' Dan said. 'He's been dodging taxes, I reckon.'

Marc left them, running out of the house to the lorry and grabbing the ready bags. They had only bought four with them, thinking it would be enough. He threw them into the library, where Dan and Mick began to fill them. Marc ran up the stairs, raiding each bedroom until he found more large bags to fill.

On his way down, he heard a car pulling up the gravel drive. Going to the window, he could see a woman inside with two teenage children in the back. He ran into the library and warned the others of their arrival. The old colonel looked terrified to know his family were now in danger too.

'Please, don't hurt them,' he managed to whisper.

No one heard as the two men smashed the precious antiques in their haste to load the money and jewels.

Old Pete, still standing entranced, turned his head towards his employer. They had known each other since they were both young men. He did not like him, but had the greatest respect. His eyes full of compassion, he nodded slowly in understanding.

Scott still knelt on the floor, staring at the only clean area of carpet he could focus on. He was too afraid to look around and face the slaughter which lay around him. This was his doing; he had never liked Dan and now he had conspired to cause this massacre.

Marc went into the hallway and met the little family from behind the door. The woman cried out and grabbed both her children as the gun was pointed to her head. He led her into the kitchen and unbolted the larder, pushing them inside. He then pulled them out again and checked for phones. He had almost forgotten, which would have been disastrous.

It was so cramped in the larder he had to heave the door shut to squeeze them all in. But at least they were safe from Dan; goodness knows what he would have done to them. He ran back to the library just in time to see the old gardener lifting the phone slowly up. He grabbed it quickly and ripped it from the holder.

'Fool!' he spat. 'Have we not seen enough bloodshed?'

He grabbed two heavy bags and threw them to the door then another two. Nine bags were bursting at the seams with money, some with diamonds and jewellery. Even with the three of them, they were hard to carry. Before they left, Dan shoved old Pete and Scott into the safe. Dragging the colonel roughly from the floor, he pushed him in too. The elderly man staggered and fell, hitting his head on one of the metal shelves. Dan pushed the heavy door shut and locked them in.

'They'll suffocate,' Mick pointed out.

'I'm sure they'll survive a few hours,' Dan told him, as they made for the back door.

'I hope so, that's my son in there.'

The lorry was discarded down Boggart Street and the money transferred to a stolen Astra. Leaving Mick's car there for the time being, they drove to the river car park and made their way down the path to the bunker. It was a difficult journey as the bags were heavy to carry, three each, plus the guns. Really, they needed Scott's help too. But it was best to leave him behind to eliminate any suspicion of his involvement.

They did it: the money was thrown into a corner after filling their pockets with as much cash as they could carry. A large padlock was fitted on the door, and the entrance carefully disguised.

Chapter Eight

When Jane arrived home, her mum was in her usual place in the kitchen. She was unusually quiet and Jane could feel the heavy atmosphere that hung like a lead weight in the flat.

'Why aren't you at school?' Toni snapped, without looking up from her folded hands.

'School broke up today, Mum,' Jane lied, thankful there really was only another week to go. 'Do you want a cuppa?'

Toni nodded her head, and after she made it, Jane went into her room to gather her very few belongings. Afterwards, she sat on the bed feeling as edgy as her mother was, waiting for Dan. Jane was going over and over her plan to steal the money and get away without being seen. She had decided a few days before that she would have to fill carrier bags with it, so she could carry it easily; Jane already had a collection waiting. She would have to be quick as the dog's home closed at 5.30 pm and it was already 3.45 pm.

After a long wait, she could not stand it any longer. Hearing her mother go into the bathroom, she quietly left the bedroom with her belongings and let herself out of the front door. She took a big breath of clean air, eliminating the stale, smelly flat. She would never be back, Jane thought to herself, both scared and excited at the same time.

The clock in the kitchen, as she walked out, told her she had only been waiting an hour, but it was too long. What if the robbery was not going to happen until tonight? She would have to wait until tomorrow to get Molly and then think up another story to satisfy Fiona.

Jane ran all the way to the river, her heart pounding in case she bumped into Dan. Luckily, there was no sign of anyone, even the usual fishermen, who sometimes nodded a familiar greeting to Jane when they saw her.

The other side of the river was, as usual, deserted. A larger path had been trampled now through the overgrowth; Jane guessed by Dan's gang. There was no one at the bunker and the bush was in place, carefully concealing the entrance. She breathed a sigh of relief, suddenly losing her nerve. What if they came while she was in the room? They would kill her, she was sure. It was a hard decision: take a chance or sit longer and just watch. If only Dan was back at the flat, she would have known she was safe. In the end Jane took the plunge and removed the bush and debris from the entrance. She felt sick and her heart pounded in her ears so loudly her head throbbed.

As she exposed the door, her heart sank almost into her pumps. An enormous padlock secured the bolt, which, Jane thought, even an elephant could not budge. She would never be able to get in there now.

Quickly covering the entrance, Jane rushed back down the river to the bridge, scared she was going to run into the men coming the other way. Once back safely on the other side, she found a safe place to sit and recover herself. There was no way she could get Molly now; her dreams of a new life fizzled away into nothing. Her little dog would be destroyed, as who would want a scruffy thing like her?

With no other option, she went home, dragging her feet all the way. First, she hid her bundle of papers and carrier bags in a hedge.

Her mother was still sitting at the kitchen table when she went in. Jane headed straight into her bedroom and closed the door without speaking. It was an hour later when Dan came home. He sounded drunk as she heard her mother squeal and them both dancing around the kitchen.

'Get yourself dressed up, Toni, we're going out,' Dan said to her mother.

Jane went into the passageway and looked in on them.

'Ahhh, young Jane. Get yourself a takeaway; I've had some luck on the horses.' He pulled £20 from his pocket and threw it at her, grinning.

'Thank you,' she took the precious money and crumpled it into her pocket. 'I think I'll go to the chip shop now,' she explained unnecessarily and made for the door.

Dan was no longer listening as he disappeared into the bedroom after Toni.

Jane bolted down the concrete corridor and urine-splashed steps, running all the way to the town. The local hardware shop, although open late on a Friday, was just closing as she burst through the door.

'Please,' she puffed to the man behind the counter. 'I've lost my padlock keys to my bike. How can I get it off?'

'Well now, young lady, let me see.' The man scratched his head with an amused expression at Jane's serious face. 'Bolt cutters would work. But a little thing like you may struggle to use them. Would your dad be able to cut it for you?'

'No, he's away at the moment and I don't know any other men that would help.'

As it was the bolt cutters were far more than £20. Disappointed, Jane went home again. She sat in the living room feeling sick and trying to fight the panic that kept engulfing her stomach.

'A hammer. I will just keep hitting it with a hammer.'

She ran to the kitchen and pulled out the contents of the cupboard under the sink. Right at the back was a small toolbox. The hammer inside was tiny and Jane doubted it would even break a cup, let alone the massive padlock. She found a screwdriver and wondered if she could just undo the screws on the lock. But she decided it was too rusty and it wouldn't be possible. Still, she took the screwdriver and the hammer just in case. As an afterthought, she ran back and grabbed a kitchen knife from the draining board.

Going to her bedroom, she tried to force herself to sleep. It was impossible; there she lay, fidgeting and was still awake when her mother and Dan returned hours later. She must have dozed off at some point, because when she opened her eyes next the sun was rising.

Getting out of bed and dressing, Jane crept into her mother's bedroom. This time, Dan's pockets were bursting with money. She removed a bundle of notes and carried on searching. Excitement flooded Jane's stomach when she found a little key in his wallet. It must be the padlock key, she decided. It would probably be the first thing he checked on waking, so it was chancy taking it, but what choice did she have?

Jane grabbed the key and made hastily for the door. She rushed out of the flat and ran all the way to the river, retrieving her little bundle of possessions on the way.

She held her breath and prayed while pushing the key into the lock. She danced with delight as the lock sprang open.

'Thank you, God,' she cried, pulling at the door, which again opened more easily than the last time. With her makeshift torch she felt her way down the stairs, not lighting it until she reached the bottom. Jane's eyes dilated as she stared agog at the nine enormous bags straining at the seams with money. There was so much that Jane knew in her whole lifetime she could never spend it all. Now her life would change, but how on earth would she carry so much? Trying to lift one bag, she knew there was no way she would carry one, let alone nine. Looking at her pathetic carrier bags, she quickly made a decision and changed her plan. She grabbed a bundle of notes and filled one carrier. Leaving the room and the rest of the money, Jane went back outside and closed the door, making sure she left the padlock open, so she could get back in. She then ran all the way back home.

Creeping back into the bedroom was risky. It was almost time for her mother and Dan to wake up. She put her hands into his trousers and grabbed the wallet. Putting back the key, she left the bedroom just in time. She heard one or the other groaning, and just as she was shutting the front door, the bedroom door sprang open. Outside, Jane let out a big sigh as she ran down the corridor again to the stone steps.

At the dogs' home Jane apologised to a blank Sarah for not coming the day before. Handing over £400, she waited eagerly for Molly to be brought out. There were items for sale in the reception so Jane brought a lovely pink collar with little diamonds and a matching lead. She then thought it may have been a bad idea, in case she bumped into her mum or Dan.

Molly, elated to see her, was springing up and down excitedly in an effort to reach her face for a big lick. After lots of cuddles and kisses back, the two of them left the dogs' home.

'What now, Molly?' Jane asked the dog, who skipped along beside her proudly on her new lead.

Already the bald patches were better, and after an obvious bath and good food, the little dog looked lovely, all soft and fluffy. Jane made for the big supermarket on the edge of town. Leaving Molly tied outside, she bought some food. It was a real feast, with sandwiches, cakes, sausage rolls and lots of sweets and fizzy drinks. Then on second thoughts, she picked up some dog food for Molly, the most expensive she could find. It was such a fantastic feeling.

Going to the homeware section of the supermarket, Jane purchased some bin bags, a large suitcase with wheels, plus an enormous torch with spare batteries.

After retrieving Molly and filling the suitcase with the goodies, they both made for the bunker.

The journey was extra eerie and creepy because of Jane's fear of the gang appearing. Even Molly whined, sounding spooked at every little noise. Many times she stopped and listened, in case she could hear footsteps or voices. The day was warm, made balmier by Jane's nerves. She tried to keep her mind occupied with thoughts of all the things she would buy. Mentally Jane had spent all the money four times over. She purchased lots of fashionable clothes. Both her and Molly ate at the most expensive restaurants they could find. They bought an enormous mansion and hired staff to cook and clean. Then a big boat and seven sport cars, one for every day of the week. Jane giggled at her silliness, because it would be years before she could drive.

Sometime soon was her 14th birthday, but Jane was never sure what day it was exactly. She had never had a card, let alone a present, or even a Christmas present for that matter. But she knew the other children at school usually had celebrations of some sort or went out somewhere nice. They seemed to get lots of presents from relatives and parents. Jane remembered one Italian girl called Anna asking her to a party when she was at primary school. Jane had been so excited until she heard some of the others laughing about her smelling out Anna's house. She had nothing to wear and could not buy a present, so she did not turn up. Anna felt hurt by Jane's rudeness: apparently her mother had cooked a meal and the food was wasted. She had never spoken to Jane again. It was a shame because she had liked Anna and would dearly have loved a friend.

When they arrived at the bunker, Jane and Molly ran up the stone steps. Sitting down, they had some breakfast. At least Molly did; Jane had no appetite because was far too nervous and waves of sickness kept consuming her stomach. For a while, she felt safer watching the footpath from the roof. While staring, she kept expecting to see a trail of men at any minute.

Absently picking up some bread, she threw it over the wall into the river for the ducks. They burst from every direction, quacking and flapping their wings on the water to gain speed. The two majestic swans floated over with five small grey cygnets close by. Jane laughed as Molly bounced up and down, woofing in pretence of catching one of the now hissing swans.

'It's only cos you know you're safe up here.'

All too soon, it was time to tackle the money; Jane must not delay any longer. They went down to the doorway and she cleared the entrance. Dragging the suitcase and using the torch, Jane went clomping down the stairs. She went into the room to the side where the bunk beds were. Careful not to disturb too much dust, she pulled off the blankets and pillows. Then turning over the first mattress and taking the knife, she stabbed into the material. It was thin and old, ripping easily. Inside was straw that had mostly crumbled to dust.

Working quickly, she pulled out the innards and set to work putting the money in bin bags. It took a great deal of effort and time to drag them into the room, and Jane began poking each into the mattresses. After finishing the first mattress she stood back and studied her work. The mattress looked lumpy with rectangular shapes. Realising her mistake, she pulled the money out and started again. This time, she left a layer of straw on the top. Then she carefully turned it over, pulling together the tear as best she could. It took some time to do because the mattresses were very heavy and difficult to turn without the money bunching up one end.

Once the six mattresses were full, there was still two more bags to go. Jane opened the next bag and gasped, her eyes widening and doubling their size.

Inside between the notes were various pieces of jewellery. She held up the first piece carefully, as though it was fragile and would break at her touch. She ran her fingers lightly over the precious stone that glistened in the torchlight, delicately examining each piece that contained either rubies, sapphires or diamonds, plus other stones that she did not know the names of. There were necklaces, earrings, bracelets and even buttons. Jane guessed they were real and, to her, must have belonged to the Queen, because nobody other than royalty could own such finery. The last thing she pulled out was a velvet bag, which was stuffed with large diamonds. Jane, realising it would be a mistake to take the jewellery with her, emptied out some money from one mattress and replaced it with the gems. She then filled the suitcase with so much money she could not have squeezed in even a feather. There was still some left, so she put the rest in two carrier bags.

It was hard to lift the case once full; even harder to pull along.

Molly lay watching, her head on her paws as the blankets were placed back over the beds along with the pillows.

After scattering some dust from the floor over the beds, Jane closed up the room after checking again; it looked exactly as it had before. The extra straw she had piled into bin bags, which would need to be carefully disposed of. It took some effort and patience to negotiate the heavy case up the stairway but Jane persevered, breathing a sigh of relief on reaching the top. Sweat ran down her face and arms with all the effort she had exerted. Thankfully, the case was slightly easier to pull along the path, which she discovered after a practice run. There she hid it in some nettles a short way along before going back for the straw. There were three bin liners full, which she took easily out of the entrance down the other side of the bunker to the clearing she had found. Once the bags were emptied, the task was complete. The bin bags she tucked into her pocket alongside Mrs Flanagan's phone number.

'That's it, we're finished,' she told Molly. 'We can go now and start a new life.'

Jane went down into the room one more time, just to make sure nothing was left behind or disturbed. Satisfied, she was about to leave when Molly crouched low and began to growl towards the entrance. Jane's heart missed a beat and beads of sweat wetted her top lip. There were voices, which were fast becoming louder and angrier — first at the entrance to the room and then coming down the stairs. Panic ran through her as she fought desperately with her pounding head to think what to do. No ideas came; if she hid in one of the rooms, she may well be left in there forever like in her dream. Thinking of nothing better, she ran to the last bag and grabbed at the small handgun. She held it up just in time as three men appeared on the stairs in front of her.

One of them was a very angry Dan, whose face glowed red in the torchlight. By his expression, he was clearly shocked to see Jane holding a gun pointed in his direction.

'Well, I never, it's the kid,' he somehow seemed to smile.

Jane was not sure why, as sweat ran down her face and her hands shook so much the gun moved up and down.

'Fucking hell, the money's gone!' gasped the man just behind Dan as he pushed himself down the stairs.

The other one just stared, looking from Jane to the empty bags and back at Jane again.

'I thought you said she was dumb?'

'Seems I underestimated her,' Dan answered, his voice flat as he controlled the panic in it.

'Now, where's the money, Jane? Come on, there's a good girl. Just tell me and we won't say any more about it.'

Jane could not have told him if she wanted to. She had no voice, as she opened and shut her mouth a few times like a goldfish. 'Get away from the stairs,' she managed to stammer.

Dan began to walk slowly forward. 'Now, don't be silly, I'm sure you're not going to kill three men, are you? If you get one of us, the others here will get you and very slowly torture you until you talk. I can tell you that won't be too pleasant. Come on, hand over the gun and the money and we'll say no more about it.' Dan reached out his arm towards Jane.

'I've not got any money. I... came to the bunker and saw the little door open. I... I came down and found the bag of guns, then you turned up.'

Dan hesitated and glanced at Marc, who was just behind his shoulder. Could it be true? After all, there was no sign of the money and a small girl could not shift it alone. If she did, where could she possibly have hidden it? How would she have got the padlock off?

'Fucking hell, where is the money then?' blurted Mick, whose voice was also shaky.

Dan looked back at her, clearly panic-stricken also. 'So why are you so scared then? Why are you here at this time of day and where did you get that torch? It's not one of ours.'

'The torch was by the door. I've been hiding Molly in the room upstairs so you don't hurt her again.'

Dan's eyes moved down to the dog that hid behind Jane, baring its teeth.

'I come here every day to feed her. And I'm scared because I found the open entrance with a bag of guns inside. Then you turned up. I didn't know who it was. Now you're frightening me by accusing me of taking money.'

Dan hesitated again, trying to think. The story was feasible and as far as he was concerned little Jane was thick; there was no way she could carry all that money, let alone make it disappear.

'OK, kid, I believe you. Now put down the gun.' He held out his hand again.

Jane began to waver; she had convinced them. As she began to lower the gun, the man just behind Dan moved forward and made a grab for her. Molly leapt forward and grabbed his leg with her teeth. The startled man kicked out and Jane, seeing Dan ready to move forward, lifted the gun and pulled the trigger.

Time froze as they stared at the little girl, shocked. Dan and Mick's eyes moved to Marc, who was looking down at his hands that clenched his stomach. He pulled them away and stared at the thick gulps of blood that leaked from the wound. He slowly crumpled to his knees and collapsed face down. A stream of blood slowly spread from beneath his body, clearly visible even in the dim light.

'Fucking hell, she's killed him,' Mick gasped in disbelief.

Dan looked back at Jane, who was trembling so hard her body shook.

She lifted the gun again and pointed it towards him, desperately fighting at the sickness that rose in her stomach and settled in the back of her throat.

'Get away from the stairs,' Jane hissed, sounding more in control than she felt.

The two men lifted their arms above their head and did as she requested, both scared they would meet the same fate as Marc had.

Without turning from them, Jane fumbled in the large bag until she clasped a box of small bullets and the two torches. Guessing the smaller box of bullets was for the handgun, she pulled them out. The sickness was threatening to explode from her throat any moment now.

'If you come out of the door before half an hour passes, I'll shoot you,' she threatened. For all her cleverness, she did not even think about the bag of guns she was leaving behind.

Both she and Molly went carefully to the stairs. Jane walked backwards, and Molly bared her teeth towards one and then the other of the men. Neither took their eyes from Jane and Molly as they kept their hands in the air.

She turned and ran up the stairs, shutting the door behind her and locking it with the bolt and finally the padlock. Collapsing on her knees, she gagged, bringing up the meagre contents of her stomach until there was nothing left.

Pulling herself together, Jane got to her feet, wiped her mouth, scooped up Molly and ran. In record time she jumped over rocks and weeds to the clearing where she had disposed of the straw.

Before she had reached the area, she heard the gun blasting open the door. Just managing to jump into the clearing, they burst out into the sunlight.

The two men ran out of the opening and stared, squinting, down the river. She saw Dan say something to the other man before he turned and went back inside.

Jane could not get her head around the enormity of killing someone. She kept seeing in her mind the body crumpling in front of her and the thick, sticky blood. Now she faced a lifetime in prison; things could not be worse.

Another gunshot sounded, making both of them jump. She grabbed at Molly as the little dog began to whimper.

It was a while before they appeared again, this time with the body over the other man's shoulder. Dan was carrying the bag of guns. Then they went to the lake on the other side of the bunker and dropped both into the water. They left soon after, still carrying one of the guns and a box of bullets.

Chapter Nine

It had taken Dan and Mick a while to find their way to the bunker doorway after Jane had bolted. With the dense, heavy blackness they lost their perspective on direction. Dan flicked a lighter, which was just enough for Mick to grope his way to the gun bag. They both managed to trip over Marc's lifeless body as they fumbled for the stairs. Dan went reeling forward, losing the lighter and falling with a big thud on the floor.

'Fucking bitch will die for this,' he cursed, picking himself up and getting to his hands and knees to feel for the lighter. His fingers found it and he flicked it again.

Mick stood still, not daring to move until the flame let out a faint glow. 'It's a bit creepy,' Mick admitted.

'Don't be an arse,' Dan threw back with a venomous look.

He led the way to the stairs after Mick handed him a gun. Thankfully, there were small blasts of daylight that leaked through cracks in the wooden door to guide him. He pulled the trigger only to find Mick had picked up an empty gun.

'Fucking hell! I'm gonna kill and torture that bitch!' He swore again through bared teeth.

In annoyance Mick grabbed the lighter from Dan and made his way back to the bag and pulled out another gun. Again, he kicked Marc's body, which released a small moan.

'He's still alive!' he shouted up to Dan, leaning forward with the gun so he could reach.

The blast was deafening in the bunker room as it vibrated around the walls. Pieces of debris showered down, one lump hitting Mick on the ear. After he finished cursing and kicking at the lump, he ran outside with Dan and stared, squinting, down the river. There was no sign of the girl as they scoured the area.

'She's legged it down the river, she won't be hard to find,' Dan reassured Mick and himself.

Giving up, they turned and went back inside the underground room. Inside with only the lighter to guide him, Mick pulled Marc onto his shoulder. Fresh blood ran from the gaping hole down his T-shirt. A moan of pain left Marc again as he was jogged and bumped up the stairs and towards the daylight.

'What you doing, idiot!' Dan hissed from behind him.

'Well... I,' Mick stammered.

Dan, in a temper, pulled Marc roughly off Mick's shoulder and kicked at his body. Marc bumped, groaning, down the stairs, leaving a trail of blood that could be seen by the light of the door. Dan followed him down, helping the quickness with his foot. Once at the bottom he lifted the gun, aimed it at Marc's head and pulled the trigger.

'Jesus Christ,' Mick gagged.

'What the fucking hell was we supposed to do with him? One whiff of that shot, and that would be it. Now pull yourself together and get some concrete; we need to dump his body in the lake.'

'What about his wife and kids?' Mick asked, knowing Dan was right.

'We ain't seen him. Far as she's concerned, he took his money and done a runner. The two ain't been getting on for some time. Done 'er a favour, I reckon. We can give her a few grand out of compassion, when we get the money back.'

Mick nodded slowly and went to fill Marc's clothes with concrete, first dragging him to the top of the stairs so he had more light.

After the body and guns were safely at the bottom of the lake, they went off down the path, hoping the gunshots had not drawn any attention. Luckily, there were not too many people about as they reached the car.

'What now?' Mick asked, pulling the car keys from his pocket and starting the ignition.

'How the hell can a thick kid outwit us?' Dan said out loud but more to himself.

'So where do you think she is?' Mick asked, looking in his car mirror to see just how much blood covered his clothes. 'Do you think she's telling the truth? I mean, there is no way she could shift all that money down an overgrown path and hide it in one night, is there?' Mick puzzled.

'Half a day! She was home last night. I don't know. But whatever; she must know more than she's letting on. You go home and dump your clothes. I'm going to have a look round and see if I can find her.' He sounded more confident than he felt. 'She's hiding somewhere, and I think the park is possible.'

Mick drove near the park entrance and stopped to let Dan out, leaving him to go home.

Dan scoured the park pessimistically, looking for Jane. A group of girls about her age were gathered around a bench, chatting. As he walked over to them, one nudged the other and they started to giggle.

'Do you know Jane Watts? She's about your age,' he smiled politely, ignoring their giggles.

'Yea, we know her, what of it?' a pretty blond girl cheekily replied.

'I'm looking for her,' Dan said, wanting to slap the smug, pretty face.

'Probably drowned in her own urine,' another dark-haired girl replied and they all burst out laughing at the joke.

'She sometimes speaks to that old lady,' another replied helpfully. She pointed to a nearby bench.

Dan nodded and walked off, hearing the sound of their laughter fading away.

The old lady sat, lost in her thoughts. She jumped when Dan sat down beside her.

'I understand you know my stepdaughter, Jane,' he smiled politely.

'Jane, yes, I know her.' Mrs Flanagan eyed the young man with suspicion; despite his manners, she did not like him.

'She didn't come home last night and her mother is worried about her. Do you have any idea where she might be?'

Mrs Flanagan felt panicky. 'She's gone to live with a relative. She told me her mum knew.' She regretted the words as soon as she had said them.

'Did she say what relative?' he asked, feeling a little more hopeful.

Mrs Flanagan felt worried. Her instincts prickled, telling her to be careful of this man, whose eyes were as cold as ice.

'No,' she answered, a little too quickly, 'Is she all right? I do miss her. What's going on? You're the one that hurt Jane's dog, aren't you?'

'Goodness, of course not. Not that sweet little thing. Honestly, that Jane and her stories,' he laughed. 'She never turned up at the relative's house. So I'm just checking she's safe. We think the world of little Jane; her mum's in bits over her going missing,' Dan explained.

Mrs Flanagan was in a dilemma: should she mention the aunt and cousin or not, or the story Jane had told her? She began to feel frightened as coldness crept over her. Her gut instinct was to say no more to the man: after all, they never looked after her little friend properly.

Dan noted the dilemma in her eyes. The lady was hiding something, he felt sure.

'I'm sorry, I don't know anything. I hope she's safe; please tell her to come and let me know everything is OK when she turns up.'

Dan thanked her and walked off towards the back of the park, where a small gate led down a path back to the flats.

Mrs Flanagan watched him go before getting up and making for the front entrance of the park.

Toni came into the hall to meet him as he walked through the front door. He brushed past her, went into the kitchen and took a large swig from a bottle of whiskey that sat on the table.

'Dan, what's wrong? You look white as a sheet,' Toni asked, following him.

She sank onto the chair in disbelief as he reeled off the whole story. 'What, not my Jane, she's just a little girl,' she gasped.

'Yes, your fucking stinking daughter,' he spat, lifting the bottle again. 'Obviously she's not just a "little girl!"' He turned towards the kitchen window to look out onto the gloomy square of grass. 'Where would she go? You must know, you're her mother. Who's the relative the old girl spouted on about?' He turned back to Toni, his eyes blazing with temper.

'There are no relatives. At least none that Jane knows about …' She stopped and got up from the chair.

Dan followed her into the bedroom as she dragged the old battered case from the top of the wardrobe. Toni pulled open the lid and poured the contents onto the bed. Everything seemed to be there.

She gasped, 'Where are the birth certificates?'

Dan grabbed her shoulders and twisted her to face him. 'What birth certificates?' he spat, his temper near to explosion.

'Just two birth certificates … It doesn't matter, they aren't important. But they are missing. She may have taken them, or I could have mislaid them.'

Dan began to shake her hard. 'Where is she?' he screamed into her face.

'I… I… don't know,' Toni sobbed, falling onto the bed as he pushed her away.

Going back to the kitchen, Dan took another swig of whiskey. His temper exploded and he threw the bottle at the wall, the glass showering him along with the contents.

The crash made Toni jump and suddenly she felt really scared.

Dan sank into the chair Toni had recently vacated. Putting his head in his hands, he began to sob. 'All that money. What the fuck am I going to do now?' The tears dripped down through his fingers.

Toni, came into the kitchen and put her hand on his wracking shoulders. He shook her away, suddenly hating her and her daughter. After the robbery and once the dust had settled, he had planned to leave. Filthy cow, he thought to himself. He had only used her for a place to stay. The flat was as disgusting as Toni, who was too lazy to clean it. Who would want to stay round a rotten bitch like her? He was no Tom Cruise himself, with his balding head, beer gut that hung over his trousers and fat, bulbous nose. But he was sure with a few quid in his pocket he could do better than a fat drunk like Toni Watts, who came as a package with a scruffy daughter. Despite the grime, Jane was a pretty little thing, just gagging for a good time, ripe and ready for some love. He had planned to show her one before he left; he may have even taken her with him. Now the money was gone and he was not sure if the kid had taken it or not.

They solved nothing that night, waiting in hope for Jane to appear. Toni went to the mini mart and bought more alcohol and cigarettes.

'Have you seen my daughter?' she asked Mr Khan, the shop owner.

'Not for a few days. She bought some matches last time I saw her,' he replied, clarifying with his wife.

'Some matches?' Toni puzzled.

'I saw young Jane in the supermarket in town this morning buying some shopping; she was clonking along with a big suitcase. Thought she was going away somewhere nice,' Mr Lewis laughed as he paid for his tea bags and milk. 'Have you lost her then?'

'No,' Toni lied, her mind reeling at the information.

'I'm glad she got her little dog back, sweet little thing. Can't think how it got in the river,' Mr Lewis added.

'Dog?' Toni stared blankly back at him.

'So, where did she get the money?' she finished, after telling Dan what Mr Lewis had told her.

'I gave her £20,' he answered gloomily, twisting the top of the new bottle of whiskey. 'Why would she buy matches and a suitcase with it, though? And £20, would not buy her a suitcase and shopping.'

Toni went into Jane's bedroom to check nothing was missing. Nothing was, she told Dan as they both sat down and puzzled over the new information. For the rest of the evening they came up with new ideas and plans. These became more bizarre the more they drank. It was clear to Dan that Toni was hiding something and he wanted to know what it was.

'Tell me more about those birth certificates,' he said; they had been niggling him.

'Nothing to tell.' Toni shrugged and went quiet as she stared at her glass of whiskey.

The next day, with a stinking hangover, Dan went back to the bunker to search around for clues. He went into the room at the side and spotted the foil container and some dog faeces. So part of Jane's story was true; she had kept the dog there. As he turned to go back down the path, he caught sight of the entrance to the underground room, staring at it while he contemplated the next step.

After Dan, Mick and Marc had left the premises on the day of the robbery, Scott and the others had waited almost three hours before the return of one of the sons, Lewis. He had worked late at the office, so he told them via a text to his wife. But truth be known, he had been working late entertaining his personal assistant, Nicola. The guilt engulfed him when he arrived home and found the house in total darkness, and unusually quiet. He hesitantly walked through the front door, calling out. The room where his two children sometimes sat watching television was empty too. He went into the library; it took seconds to digest the scene. Two headless bodies lay in grotesque positions on the floor, the blood-splattered bookcases, carpet and ceiling.

'Jesus,' Lewis gasped, recoiling in horror.

His eyes went to the vault, where the case that usually sat concealing it was open. He ran from the room and up the stairs, calling. He stood outside his daughter's bedroom, hesitating slightly as an image of her blood-splattered body flooded his head. Bravely he threw open the door and was both relieved and panic-stricken to find it empty. 'Thank God,' he breathed.

He went both to his son's room and then the master bedroom.

Running down the stairs again, he headed for the kitchen. The image of Mrs Green, the cook, splattered over the cooker, filled his mind. He frantically called out and heard the tapping from the inside of the larder door. He threw back the bolt; out, burst his wife and children, crying hysterically, cramped and pale-faced from being confined in such a small space for so long. Mrs Green came out next, sobbing, followed by the two terrified young cleaners. For a fleeting moment Lewis wondered how they had fitted in such a small space so well. Mrs Green and one of the cleaners were both ample ladies. He picked up his mobile and called the police, instructing no one to move.

'Sit down in here until prints can be taken,' he instructed.

Leaving them sobbing and hysterical, he went to look for his father. Going back into the library, he tried not to look at the gooey massacre. It was difficult as he opened the vault. Out came the young gardener Scott, gasping for air as he fell forward. His father, having collapsed earlier, lay on the floor barely breathing, and Old Pete sat with him, sweat pouring down his face.

The police arrived and shepherded him into the kitchen with the others. No one was allowed to leave until statements and prints were taken and the security cameras checked.

It was some hours later when the two faithful security guards' bodies were removed. Lewis had called his brother, who by now had come home.

'Who is going to tell the families?' Simon, the first-born brother asked. 'Gary has a young family with, I believe, a newborn, just a few months old. Phil had just got engaged and was getting married next year. Who could have done this?'

'I guess the police will break the news,' Lewis answered, knowing the family were now in deep financial trouble. The vault was empty, except for the broken artefacts worth thousands of pounds. Most of the contents were not insured. It was a tax dodge; money accumulated over years. He had warned his father many times that one day they would come unstuck; now they were financially ruined.

When the police got to Scott, he was shaking more than the rest of them. The two older men had seen much bloodshed during their war years. Scott had watched many horror and violent movies in the past. However, nothing could have prepared him for the reality of seeing a body blown apart in real life. He was so traumatised he could not answer any of the questions. Eventually, he was released and a police car took him home, requesting he return to the station the following day.

It did not look good for Lord Falcon; his heart was failing fast.

Dan, who was waiting for his return with Toni, was relieved that Scott had kept his nerve and not grassed them up. He even patted him on the back as he handed him a whiskey to calm him.

'Well done, lad. I didn't think you had it in you,' Dan told him in a rare show of friendliness.

Scott, who rarely drank, threw back the liquid and choked for a while. The burning of it bought him to his senses. 'You fucking bastard,' he ranted at Dan. 'You shot those men; they were good blokes and my friends. I hate you.' He spat, dancing around the floor, then threw the glass at Dan who dodged the missile.

'Now now, we do what we have to do. I had to show we meant business.'

Scott rushed from the room and soon they heard his bedroom door slam shut.

'Leave him,' Mick advised, 'He'll be OK. Good lad, he is.'

'Mmmm,' Dan mumbled, not sure young Scott would withhold the strain.

Mrs Flanagan had indeed been worried about Jane and fretting terribly, not knowing what to do.

'You hear so many horrible things these days happening to young girls,' she told her friend and neighbour Mrs Pomfree, as they sat having a cup of tea the next day in Mrs Flanagan's small living room. 'I didn't like that man who came to see me at all. Gave me the creeps, poor Jane.'

Mrs Pomfree nodded. 'Yes, a bad un, that one. That poor girl was so unkempt, taking herself to school and running wild on the streets at all hours. And...' Mrs Pomfree lent closer and whispered, 'I think they abused her. I heard the girl could often be heard screaming and crying.'

Mrs Flanagan's mouth went dry as anger began boiling in her stomach, threatening to explode from her mouth at any moment. 'What, you know him?' she asked, incredulously. 'I've been spouting on for hours about him, and months about young Jane and you knew them all along?'

'Oh yes, Dan Wallace. A nasty one he is; always in trouble with the police. I knew his parents,' she confessed, and then became flustered when she saw her friend glaring at her.

'So why did no one report it then? If it was well known the child was being abused?' Her hands were shaking so much she had to put her cup on the table.

'Well,' Mrs Pomfree shrugged, 'you don't like to interfere. It's no one's business, is it?' She fell quiet and began picking at her cardigan sleeve.

Mrs Flanagan was so angry with the stupid woman, who up to now she had considered a friend. 'Words fail me.' She shook her head and shakily stood up, ignoring the dirty look from Mr Tibbles as he was unceremoniously removed from her lap. He had been having such a lovely sleep.

Mrs Flanagan walked straight out of her front door, leaving Mrs Pomfree staring bewildered after her. She made her way along the high road and into the police station.

'I want to report a missing girl,' she told the young officer, who stood behind the counter.

'OK, can I ask who it is?'

'Jane Watts, she's a friend of mine. She's only 14 and has been missing since yesterday. I'm so worried. We usually meet in the park and have a chat. But she said she was going away and her mother's boyfriend told me she did not come home last night,' she told him, firmly without pausing for breath.

The young officer did not really know what to say to the older lady, who stood pensively in front of him.

'You know what youngsters are like. She's probably at a friend's house and hasn't told her parents. I bet she's at home right now.'

'No, you don't understand. Apparently, her mum and boyfriend abuse her. She was running away from home. You need to go and check but I'm not sure where she lives. I know it's on the big council estate in one of those blocks of flats.'

The officer excused himself and left the counter. Going into a back room, he asked the help of Sara, who was far better at dealing with these situations than he was.

'Some old girl's outside the front wanting to report a missing girl,' he told her. 'I don't know what to say. Kid's probably round a boyfriend's or something. Can you see her?' he pleaded.

Sara sighed and raised her eyebrows. She looked out of the glass partition, smiled and waved at Mrs Flanagan, whom she had known since she was a child.

'Come and sit down, Dorothy.'

She led her to the waiting area, and gratefully Mrs Flanagan sat on one of the hard, wooden chairs.

'I'm so worried, Sara,' she told her, thankful it was someone she knew who would humour her. Then she went on to explain everything she knew about Jane disappearing, including Dan coming to see her.

Sara's ears pricked up at the mention of Dan Wallace. There was always trouble when his name was mentioned. They were suspicious that he was involved in the robbery at Lord Falcon's place. Two security men had been shot and killed.

'Jane Watts, you say?' Sara asked, taking the elderly lady's worry seriously.

Mrs Flanagan nodded, and Sara squeezed her arm.

'Come with me, I think you need to see someone.'

She led her into a little room, which had a vacant plaque on the door. Sitting her in one of the chairs behind a desk, Sara went to see her sergeant and make a cup of tea.

The police had been unaware that Dan Wallace was living on the council estate with a woman. They were equally interested to hear about the supposed disappearance of the daughter. Mrs Flanagan told them everything she possibly could, including the discovery of Jane's aunt and cousin.

'Will you let me know, Sara, about Jane?' she asked as she left some hours later.

After she had left, Sara turned to the sergeant with a questioning look.

'Sorry, Sara, it's not top priority. Kid's probably off with a boy or partying somewhere, you know what they're like at that age. The mum's not reported her missing. We got nothing on Wallace as yet, although we're suspicious. '

Sara had a gut feeling, though; it was a niggle.

'What if I pass it to social services then? Just so they can check it out.'

'OK, go for it,' he agreed, dismissing Sara by turning to a report he had been writing.

While Dan went searching for Jane the following day, Toni went back to the mini mart to ask if Jane had been in anymore.

'Not seen her today,' the owner told her. He shouted over to his wife who was just topping up tins of sweetcorn and peas.

'No, not today,' she confirmed.

Mr Lewis was in again buying his lottery ticket, when he overheard Jane's name.

'So, is Jane's dog all right now? Did you find out who almost killed it?' he asked. 'I'm glad the dogs' home handed it over.'

Toni walked past, ignoring him. She stopped at the door and went back again.

'What did you say?' she asked Mr Lewis.

'I just wondered if Jane's dog is all right now and the dogs' home handed it over OK,' he repeated, taking an instant dislike to the rude, aggressive woman.

'What dogs' home?'

'The one on Hill Rise.'

Without saying anymore, she turned and walked away.

'Charming.' Mr Lewis flicked his eyes towards Mr Khan.

'Yes, not a nice woman.' he agreed. 'Poor little mite always looks scruffy and underfed. Fancy having a mother like her.' He shook his head sadly.

Toni met Dan at home some hours later. She told him about the dogs' home and he shrugged. 'What of it? We know she had the dog with her. In fact, Toni, you're fucking useless. Your own daughter and you have no idea where she is.'

He felt his temper explode inside; gritting his teeth, he went to her and put his hands on her shoulders. The urge to push his fist into her face was so great it took all his effort to fight it.

'Do you know what, Toni? I hate your fucking guts, you and your stinking daughter. When I find her I'm going to kill her. Until that time, I'm out of here.'

He pushed her from him and walked out of the kitchen to the bedroom. Grabbing a sports bag from beside the wardrobe, he began to pack his clothes and meagre belongings. He could hear Toni crying from the kitchen, her sobs growing louder, until they were big indescribable animal noises. The sound made his temper boil again until he screamed from the doorway.

'SHUT THE FUCK UP!'

The noise went quiet as Dan, leaving the rest of his belongings, bolted for the front door and slammed it behind him. He gave it a hard kick, with great satisfaction, enjoying the release of anger as he imagined it was Toni's head.

Chapter Ten

Jane stayed at the little clearing for hours, staring at the bunker. Even Molly's whimpering did not break into her deep thoughts. The dog gave up, curled herself into a ball and went to sleep.

Jane did not want to move from the spot, where she somehow found peace deep in her mind. To come back to reality would mean facing what she had done, the fear of not only the men, but of herself.

The light began to fade and still Jane sat and stared. Soon it would be almost impossible to negotiate the overgrown area in the black of night, even with a torch. Somehow, deep in her own world, she chastised herself, pulling herself back to reality. Noting the fading light, she jumped up and stretched out her aching limbs.

Molly sprang up with her and began bouncing about, glad to be on the move at last. Dan and the man were long gone; she was sure they were looking for her. Picking up the wriggling Molly, she made her way through the brambles and nettles back to the bunker. Jane shuddered as she walked past the broken bits of door that lay scattered over the ground. Then, having second thoughts, she went back. Picking up as many bits of wood as she could, she threw them into the nettles. There was nothing left of the door, so Jane re-covered the entrance with the bush and broken twigs. The men might not come back, but at least the money was hidden from any other person that might come to the bunker exploring.

It was hard finding the way down the path to the bridge now it was completely dark. If Jane ever thought it was creepy before, it was nothing compared to now. Every little noise was heightened by the dense blackness that had descended. There was no moon to throw even a slight glow; it was hidden behind heavy rain clouds that crowded the night sky. She was too afraid to use the torch in case the beam was spotted. Every little noise sounded like eerie, haunting spirits floating about lost in between two worlds. Even Molly was shaking, picking up on her fear.

Finding the suitcase was difficult in the dense darkness. By the time Jane did find it, her hands tingled from nettle stings and vicious thorny bushes. Several times she had searched the wrong place, groping bravely through a mass of greenery. She was near to tears, as she found, again, it was the wrong area, and she wished desperately she had thought to leave a marker. Relief flooded when at last her hands felt the hard plastic. Grasping the handle and pulling hard to free it, she made her way along the rest of the path until she eventually reached the bridge.

Convinced one of the men was guarding it, Jane hid the case again and crept closer, not making a sound. There did not seem to be anyone there, but as she retrieved the case again, she was still sure someone was going to jump out at her. Jane was too scared to go on to the road or to the station as she had planned. It was a dilemma, however she decided to keep walking along the river. At least, if she arrived at a town it would be safer to catch a train.

Dragging the heavy case down the bumpy gravel path was hard work and very noisy. The case seemed to become heavier and more awkward the more she walked. A few objecting ducks quacked in protest at being disturbed by the rumble of the wheels and by Molly, who kept sticking her nose in their nests. Every time a bird flapped and squawked, Jane jumped and felt sick again. The image of the man she had shot constantly flooded into her mind, seeing the red blood mingling with the dirt of the floor. She began telling herself that maybe he had not been dead after all. He couldn't have been if they had shot the gun again before dumping him in the water. Jane consoled herself with this thought as she walked long into the night.

Jane was so weary she seemed to be staggering; Molly was dragging behind, too tired to walk much more.

When they reached the next bench, she sank gratefully onto it. Picking up Molly, they lay down and both fell into a fitful sleep. The heavy rain clouds made the night air cold, causing Jane to wake constantly throughout the dark times. She shivered and tried to snuggle more into Molly, who did not seem to mind the dampness.

Each time she did wake, her mind drifted over the terrible events. Would her mother guess she had gone looking for her aunt? If she found one of the letters gone, she might do. Hopefully by daytime her thoughts would seem silly, she thought. The dark of the night was causing her mind to be overactive.

The rain began to fall a few hours later; along with it came loud cracks of thunder and jagged streaks of lightning that lit up the whole sky and the river. There was nowhere to run for shelter, except under the bench or a border of bushes. The rain became heavier and harder, hurting as it hit. Big, barbarous gulps fell from the sky, bouncing down on the gravel and river, its force so powerful it bent the branches of bushes, allowing the water to fall through. The noise was deafening, and Jane flattened her palms over her ears. Large puddles formed within minutes and the river looked like its banks would burst with the weight of the water. Molly and Jane were drenched within seconds and both shivering with cold. The dog's usual unruly coat now sat glued to her back, and drips of water poured off her, splashing off her ears and black nose.

Jane laid the suitcase on top of the bench and considered crawling underneath for a small amount of protection. However, a big puddle helped to change her mind.

'It's God paying me back,' Jane shouted to Molly, jumping as another bang of thunder shook the earth, followed by a blaze so bright that it looked like daylight for a few seconds. They both trembled and felt increasingly dismal and despondent.

The rain stopped as quickly as it had started, and the thunder dispelled to a distant rumble as the storm moved away to scare other victims. Jane sat on the bench, no longer worrying about the wet. Her T-shirt and jeans clung to her skin, and water dripped from her hair, rolling down her face and tickling her skin.

Molly shook her coat a few times until it stood up in spiky clumps. They walked on down the river, not knowing what else to do to keep warm.

At first light, Jane marvelled at how the birds could sound so chirpy as they burst into song, when she felt miserable, cold and scared. She was shivering uncontrollably, her clothes still wet through and clinging tightly to her, making her feel more miserable.

Molly did not seem to notice the discomfort too much as she dragged behind on her lead, exhausted. They sat down to rest for a while, and Jane yawned, wishing she had a nice hot cup of tea to warm her.

She pulled up the handle of the case and the two set off again, bumping noisily, down the river path.

She had no idea where she was, having never ventured this far before. After another hour, a few dogs began to appear out with their owners for their morning walk. Having been let off her leash, Molly ran over to them, wagging her tail in greeting. One dog wagged back, and the two walked in a circle, sniffing each other's bottoms.

Jane, grateful for the distraction, wondered why dogs did this. The next dog to arrive growled and bared its teeth at Molly, who quickly skulked away and hid behind Jane, confused by the aggression. The owner seemed as bad-tempered as the dog, as Jane smiled at him. He stared back at the scruffy, damp girl covered in mud and his eyes fixed on the large case she dragged along. Her heart began to pound again as she realised how suspicious she looked, walking down a river wet through with a suitcase this early in the morning.

At the next river exit, Jane walked out and looked around. She was dubious, in case Dan's gang was waiting at the other side.

The entrance led to a road, which was lined with houses each side. Following the road — which seemed very quiet, until she remembered it was a Sunday — led to a main road. There was nothing there, except the odd, uninteresting closed shop and a scant few more houses. Not taking any chances, Jane went back to the river and continued to walk along.

The next entrance that broke the green hedge barrier led to another street and eventually again to the high road. Jane let out a disappointed sigh and turned back.

At the next bench she sank down, kicked off her pumps, which smelled terrible, and rubbed her aching wet feet. The day was gloomy and dark, the sun only appearing for short bursts from behind big grey clouds that hung heavily in the sky and threatened another massive downpour.

A lady rushed past with a scruffy mongrel on its lead and smiled at Jane.

'Think it's going to rain,' she said, looking at the sky.

Jane smiled back and nodded in agreement. 'Is there a train station near here?' she asked, crossing her fingers hopefully.

The lady stopped, and Molly wagged herself over to the dog, that wagged back.

'Yes, Middleton; it's about a mile away down the river.' The lady pointed in the direction they were heading. 'Keep walking and eventually you'll see the station or hear the trains,' she smiled, saying a brief 'hello' to Molly before tugging her dog away.

Jane thanked her and headed off again. The lady was right: although she could not see the station, before long she heard the distinct rumble of a train as it passed. Popping her head through the next opening, she could see the station in the near distance.

'Thank goodness,' she breathed and, putting Molly back on her lead, headed for the station.

The next few minutes, the sky opened and buckets of rain fell, soaking both their already wet bodies again.

Jane and Molly ran into the ticket office. 'I want to go to Thornwood Abbey,' she told the snuffling man who sat behind a glass wall. She shivered, trying to shake off some of the water.

He was obviously full of the cold and in a bad mood, as he glanced at the drenched girl and the little dog that shook muddy water all over the walls.

'Never heard of it,' he grumped and lifted a map to study. You'll have to get a train to Liverpool Street, then from there a train to Burton Ridge. It's the nearest station. I expect there will be a bus from there,' he sniffed again and blew his nose into a large white hanky.

Jane bought the tickets and went to platform number two over the bridge, to wait 20 minutes for the next train to Liverpool Street. She looked for Dan, studying every man that walked onto the platform. Jane was so grateful when the train finally arrived, and Molly, herself and the case, plus the carrier bags containing wet money, were safely wedged into two seats.

Walking along noisy, crowded Liverpool Street was daunting for them both. They had never seen so many people bustling along in one place before. They rudely pushed and shoved; Molly's yelps were ignored as a few trod on her feet. In the end, Jane picked her up and tucked her safely under her arm. This made the trek through the crowds even more arduous.

A ticket office operator pointed the way to the right train, which thankfully was sitting and waiting for people to board. Jane clambered on and sat on the nearest chair. She was worried about knowing when she reached Burton Ridge. Plucking up courage she asked a young couple who sat nearby, explaining she had forgotten her glasses so could not see the station signs.

'We're getting off the stop before,' the young man explained, 'So you need to get off the one after.'

It was a long journey, as the train stopped every few minutes at yet another station. As the young couple left the train at their station, they smiled at Jane, who nodded and waved a thank you.

The town of Burton Ridge was buzzing with noises, colours and bright shops. People bustled everywhere in little groups or alone, oblivious to the suspicious girl, large suitcase and scruffy dog.

Jane's eyes were out on stalks as she stared in colourful windows, thinking she would buy this and that, but then, she realised, with disappointment that she could not carry anymore. Her eyes fell on a hairdresser's, unusually open on a Sunday. Standing outside, Jane wondered if she dared go inside. She looked so messy and dirty, even the new suitcase was muddy. It took her a while to make a decision, walking away and back again a few times. People were beginning to stare, not only at her dishevelled state, but because she was loitering.

'OK, Molly, let's go for it,' Jane pushed open the door and went inside. 'Can you cut my hair, please?' she asked a snooty girl, who looked with distaste at muddy wet Jane and wrinkled her nose at Molly.

She walked away from the desk without speaking and over to an older lady, whispering something to her. The older lady looked over to Jane and smiled.

'Take a seat; I'll be with you in a moment.'

Jane tied Molly's lead to the suitcase and went to sit in a hairdresser's chair. The older lady came over, still smiling, and pulled up chunks of Jane's lank hair with a sigh.

'I want it all cut off into a short, spiky style, please. Then I would like it dyed black.'

'But your hair is beautiful, thick and blonde; lots of girls would give their eye teeth for it. Even if you have somewhat neglected it,' the hairdresser added dismally, looking at the dull mess.

'I fancy a change,' Jane said simply.

It was a weird feeling to see her long, unruly hair piling onto the floor. Her head lightened with each snip. It looked a terrible, uneven mess as Jane was moved to the sink and her hair washed.

'I thought it would be easier to get rid of some of it first,' confessed the hairdresser, whose name turned out to be Vanessa and who had just been through a tricky divorce.

Jane put back her head and enjoyed the luxury of a hair wash. Then Vanessa chopped away again. A young girl brought over a bowl with a brush sticking out. The liquid was painted onto Jane's hair. It smelt horrible and made her eyes sting. After 20 minutes the gunk was washed away, leaving, very clearly, black hair.

'You will need to colour your eyebrows,' explained Vanessa, 'Or you'll look odd with blonde ones.'

'Oh, I never thought of that,' Jane said, scrutinising the strangeness of her hair.

'We have a beauty parlour upstairs if you want them plucked and dyed; they also do piercing and nails too.'

'Oh, please,' Jane gushed.

So, after her hair was blown into shape and hair gel applied, which Jane bought a tub of to maintain the style, Vanessa pointed her upstairs. Dragging her case and Molly with her, she went up.

Her eyebrows were shaped painfully but expertly using a piece of cotton, a technique she soon learned was called threading.

Then, not only were her eyebrows dyed, but also her eyelashes. After, she asked for her ears to be pierced five times. It was so painful she stopped at the third and chose some diamond studs.

Once finished, she could not believe her transformation. She did not even recognise the girl who peered back from the large mirror.

'Do you want your nails done?' the beautician asked. Jane did, and had them painted a shiny red colour. She had been in there three hours when she paid the bill and left.

The next shop that caught Jane's attention was a very expensive clothes shop. She knew the shop well, as a branch was in her own town. The clothes inside were stylish and modern; how she had dreamed so many times of buying from them. She was told Molly was not allowed inside so she went back to the hairdressers and asked if they would keep an eye on her.

'Course, love,' Vanessa agreed, offering Molly a biscuit, which she gobbled.

Jane went back to the shop and tried on a pair of jeans, which were far too big. With the help of an assistant, a smaller size was selected that fitted her snugly. It was impossible to decide which of the four summer tops to buy, so Jane brought them all. Plus, a necklace, red shoes, four bracelets, along with a lovely bag that had sequins sewn on. She went back into the changing room and pulled on the clothes and pretty shoes with a high heel. She put her old clothes into a carrier bag, which she planned to dump in the nearest bin. It felt so good after all this time. When she looked in the mirror, a film star or model stared back at her. Her age dripped away from her; now she could easily pass for 18, she thought.

It was hard to walk in the heels and soon her ankles ached. But persevering, Jane went into a chemist and asked a lady behind the counter what make-up to buy. She was directed to a beautician, who would be the right person to help.

'I can try some out if you like,' the beautician smiled.

Jane sat in a chair where the lady applied red lipstick at her request, eye shadow, eyeliner and some blusher.

'Your skin is really good so you don't need foundation or powder,' the beautician explained as she worked away, transforming the young girl.

Jane was glad, as she did not know what these things were. After buying all the products from the pleased beautician, who was on commission, she left to collect Molly.

The snotty girl in the hairdresser's did a double-take when Jane walked back in wearing the new clothes.

'You look fantastic,' smiled Vanessa, making Jane do a twirl.

'I feel fantastic,' agreed Jane, with the biggest grin that had ever spread across her face. 'Where do I catch a bus to Thornwood Abbey?

'Go to the bus station at the end of the town and they will point you in the right direction,' Vanessa explained, giving Jane a little peck on the cheek for luck. They watched her walk away with Molly bouncing about next to her.

'How can such a young girl afford all that?' the snooty receptionist asked.

'I don't know, but it's none of our business,' Vanessa snapped.

Chapter Eleven

Jane sat at the bus station on a red plastic bench shared by three other people. Molly stood patiently at her feet until she heard the rustle of a paper bag; her sharp sense of smell discovered it contained hot sausage rolls. Her head snapped up expectantly and two big bulbs of dribble rolled from her mouth into her little brown beard.

Laughing, Jane crumbled one up on the bag and placed it next to Molly. They made a terrible mess of crumbs as they ate, much to the pleasure of four pigeons that hopped bravely in and out, grabbing at strays.

A few of the people in the queue gave looks of distaste that Jane did not notice. One of them, a young man, flicked his foot at the group of birds, who bounced into the air to avoid it.

'Bloody vermin,' he snarled in Jane's direction.

A few of the ladies nodded in agreement.

Jane looked up, surprised. 'Come this side Molly, you don't want to catch something,' she said with great emphasis, glaring at the man.

She tugged at Molly's lead, feeling proud that her new wealth gave her confidence. She made a vow to herself never to be bullied and downtrodden again.

It was late in the afternoon when they reached Thornwood Abbey. Both were tired from the long day and the lack of sleep the night before. Jane stood at the bus stop and stared around. The place looked a small town, more of a village, as the bus driver had informed her. To the front was a large square with shops on both sides. A long street led from it, pathed with red bricks and lined with more shops. They looked small and quaint, silent and dark as all were closed. Amongst them was a large supermarket that still buzzed with people.

The abbey stood magnificently in the centre of the town and to one edge of the square. It was illuminated with a calm, blue light. Jane raised her eyes to look up at the bell tower, which seem to shimmer in the faint glow, looking mysterious and almost supernatural.

A few sightseers milled around the vast grounds, taking photos or just sitting absorbing the atmosphere of the ancient building.

A few pubs had small crowds of people, chatting and laughing, or standing isolated and smoking a cigarette. Some of them eyed her with suspicion or interest and Jane felt conspicuous, with her large suitcase and scruffy dog.

She lowered her gaze and walked forward, bumping along the road awkwardly over the little red bricks. Stopping at an estate agent's, Jane noticed a few places for rent. Tomorrow when they were open, she would enquire, but for tonight she needed to find somewhere to sleep.

After exhausting the street of closed shops, they headed for the abbey grounds; both tired, they flopped onto a bench to rest. A few people walked past, staring at her. It was late for a young girl and dog, along with suitcase, to be sitting there at that time of night. The blue lights from the abbey shone down, making them more conspicuous.

Another cold damp night was spent in a secluded spot in the grounds, cuddled on a hard, wooden bench. In the early hours, or Jane supposed it was, the rain fell without mercy again, drenching them both.

'At this rate,' Jane told Molly, 'we'll both get flu.'

Using the torch, she found a corner with a large bush and they crawled under to keep dry. Wet and miserable, neither got much sleep, especially as insects kept making Jane jump about to brush them off. This caused Molly to leap up, ready to play.

The red shoes and jeans were both covered in mud and soggy as Jane stared miserably at them. Finally, the sun began to rise and with it a little warmth. Thank goodness, the rain seemed to have past as the sun burst out of a clear blue sky. Once they had both dried off, which entailed running on the grass for a while, they headed back to the town. A market was beginning to set up, and Jane stood watching, fascinated, as the traders chattered amongst themselves. Metal poles clattered and vans drove onto the brickwork square to unload their wares. It had never occurred to her that the make-up she wore would run like it had. Jane gasped as she caught sight of herself in a mirror. Long lines of black mascara streaked her face, making her look like a sad, wet clown.

'Molly, you could have told me,' she chastised, her face crimson, as well as black-streaked.

Molly looked up and wagged her tail.

'Don't you dare laugh.'

Finding a public toilet, she dodged in and tried to tidy herself, remembering what the cream was for that the beautician had sold to her.

There was an early morning café near the market, which some of the traders gathered to buy hot drinks. Jane found a table outside and ordered the same big breakfasts as two men on the next table were having.

Her eyes widened when the plates arrived, loaded with food. She had never eaten so much in all her life. Most of the food was new to her, as Jane ate some things and pushed others to the side of her plate, winkling her nose at the taste. She had cut up the contents of Molly's plate and put it on the floor. The waitress did not look too pleased, but did not say anything.

By the time breakfast was finished and the bill paid, they set off to explore the town again. Most of the shops were beginning to place open boards outside. Jane headed for the estate agents she had seen the night before. It took a while to gather enough courage to go inside. Taking a few big deep breaths and one large swallow, she pushed open the door.

'I'd like to rent a property,' she told a young man behind a desk.

He looked her up and down, grinned and offered a seat.

'What sort of property do you want?' he asked, flicking the switch on the computer in front of him.

'Something in the town and pretty,' Jane told him, having no idea what to ask for.

'Can you supply references?' he asked.

'What are they?' Jane grimaced, feeling silly not knowing.

'Letters of recommendation to prove who you are and that you are working and, of course, good at paying rent.'

'No, I've just left home and I don't work 'cos I'm rich and don't need to,' she offered haughtily.

'I'm sorry but all property owners will want references.'

'Is there somewhere I could rent a room then, like a hotel?'

'There's a bed and breakfast down the road. It's in the pub called the White Swan.'

Jane thanked him and made to leave.

'Don't suppose you would like to go for a drink later?' the young man smiled cheekily.

Jane's eyes widened and her mouth opened to speak; no words emerged. 'No...' she eventually stammered, rushing for the door.

In her nervousness she got caught in the exit with Molly, the case and her own body. Dropping the handle Jane almost tripped over it; she felt really silly. Taking a backward glance at the laughing young man, she rushed off down the road.

The White Swan was easy to find and was open as she clambered in the doorway. At least getting a room was easier than renting, Jane mused, even though there was some question if dogs were allowed or not.

The manageress agreed as long as Molly was well behaved and did not bark. Jane signed her name in the book, 'Lizzy Ellis', because she could spell both. Then she handed over enough money for two days in advance. She felt proud and grown up to be handed a key and pointed up a staircase to room number three.

A handsome young man even carried her case for her.

Inside was like a palace to Jane. It was furnished with a wardrobe, dressing table, little writing desk and a double bed. There was even a small sofa and a flat screen television that was screwed to the wall. Jane marvelled that there were no leads to make the television work. A little table stood near an armchair, with tea and coffee, plus a kettle, little sugar packets and milk containers. She bounced on the bed, which felt soft and cosy. The bedcover was a beautiful silky orange colour with flashes of lime green, which matched the cushions on the sofa. A doorway near the bed led to a bathroom, which not only had a bath but also a separate shower. Little bottles sat on a glass shelf, which Jane sniffed at.

'Oh, Molly, there's even towels for us to use.'

The second thing Jane did, after turning on the television and making some tea, was run a bath. Taking one of the little bottles, she poured the whole contents in and watched while a burst of small white bubbles covered the surface of the water. Taking off her clothes, she jubilantly climbed in, after placing a hot cup of tea on the side, ready to indulge in luxury. The television blared out from the bedroom as she lay in the warm water, allowing the cold to ease from her damp bones. Jane could not remember when she had last had a bath. She never remembered so much ecstasy in all her life as the hot, scented water covered her body. Picking up the flannel and little soap, she washed her whole body.

'I need more clothes and certainly some underwear,' Jane told the dog before falling into a deep, exhausted sleep.

It was still daylight when she awoke, and looking at the little white clock on the bedside cupboard, she found it was only 2 pm.

'I also need a bra. Now, you must behave while I go shopping.'

Filling the new bag with money, Jane left Molly, who did not seem to mind in the least, curled up on the bed. She did not even seem to notice Jane closing the door behind her.

There were not many clothes shops in Thornwood Abbey so she caught the bus back to Burton Ridge. There, she spent three hours buying every item of clothing she could possibly carry. Plus, more jewellery, some bags, hats and at last the much-needed bra. Jane had never in her life had so much fun. It was the most fantastic feeling she had ever had, to buy exactly what she wanted. As she passed the hairdressers she waved to Vanessa, and even the snooty receptionist smiled and waved back.

Finally, not being able to carry another thing, she headed back and found Molly still asleep on the bed; she lifted one eye, glanced at Jane and closed it again.

Unloading her bags, she relished each item as she hung it in the wardrobe, taking special care to hang matching colours together. Even her new shoes were laid under matching outfits. For so long she had imagined these things; now they were real.

It was dark by the time she finished. Leaving Molly again, she went out and bought fish and chips for their dinner. They spent a lovely evening lying on the bed, watching television while they ate.

The next day, after another luxurious bath, Jane dressed carefully before taking Molly for a walk. It was a difficult choice because she wanted to wear all her new clothes. Eventually she settled for shorts, a cropped white lacy top, lacy white boots and three brightly coloured necklaces.

Back in the abbey grounds, Jane spotted the teashop where Mrs Flanagan must have had cream teas with Frank. She headed for it and found an empty table outside. The abbey's gardens looked glorious in the sunshine, with clusters of different-coloured roses, picnic tables and beautifully tended flowerbeds.

'What can I get you?' the waitress asked.

'Can I have two dinners, please?'

'We don't do dinners on a Tuesday. I guess you could have ham and chips if you like.'

'OK, thanks. I'll have that then.' Jane smiled, feeling fantastic in her new clothes.

When the food arrived, Jane cut Molly's into small pieces. The dog was whimpering as she stared in anticipation at the plate, willing her mistress to hurry. Dribble ran down her beard and onto the ground. A few of the people, who sat at the next table, watched with horror when the plate was placed on the floor for the dog. A few of them gave looks of disgust, while others smiled. Then they all gave her looks of distaste as Molly, caught short in-between her meal, pooed on the floor. Jane was red-faced as she grabbed serviettes and cleaned it up.

'Sorry,' she apologised.

After they finished, Jane poured tea in a saucer and put that on the floor too. Molly, oblivious to the attention she was receiving, lapped gleefully, licking her lips and giving a little burp of glee. Jane giggled when she finally looked up and had bits of food stuck to her whiskers. The few other people at the tables pretended not to notice the young girl's uncouth ways.

One lady on the next table burst out laughing and went over to pat Molly.

'It's such a lovely day, isn't it?' she said to Jane, in an attempt to make conversation. 'I always come here to cheer myself up. You certainly have with your little dog.'

Jane smiled; she liked the lady instantly. She looked jolly and cheerful with her ready smile.

'I've not seen you round here before,' the lady said, grabbing a cup from her own table and sitting down uninvited with Jane.

'No, I only came here yesterday. It looks such a sweet place I thought I'd stay a while.'

'My name's Rose,' the lady told Jane. 'It is such a lovely place. I was born here, but left many years ago when I got married. I came back last year to look after my sister. She recently lost her husband and I was on my own. So, it made sense to share a house.'

Rose looked so sad that Jane felt sorry for her.

'I'm Lizzy and this is Molly. I had a friend who used to live around here somewhere. Her name was Lucinda Watts,' Jane told her. Then wondered how on earth she came up with the name Lucinda.

'Mmmm,' Rose, frowned in an effort to think, 'the only Watts I ever knew were a family on the big council estate, the other side of town. I went to school with Rebecca Pearson; she married George Watts. I remember they had two twin daughters and a son. I left here when I was 18, so I don't know what happened to them.'

Jane's heart began to thump with the news; she fought to keep her voice level, suddenly afraid of drawing attention to her interest in the family. 'Goodness, that was young; it must be hard coming back.'

Rose looked sad again and her eyes clouded over, 'I was not gifted with children; the only family I have is my sister. She's a bit funny though and not much company. It's changed so much here and I don't seem to know anyone. I guess all the people I did have died or moved on,' Rose explained, then leant closer. 'My sister is a bit of a recluse; she seems to prefer being alone to me pottering about the house. I'll ask her if she knows Lucinda Watts if you like,' she brightened.

Jane had already decided not to look for her family. Dan would be looking for her now he thought she had the money. Her aunt may contact her mother and then her life would be in more danger. But she wanted to know more, maybe even find out who her father was. It was also too chancy using the name Watts herself. She would have to be very discreet with her enquiries from now on. She paid the bill and said goodbye, leaving the lady looking disappointed at losing her company.

They walked through the high street to explore more. Between some of the shops was a red brick walkway. It sat hidden, and, unless you knew it was there, was easily missed. Down they walked to explore, but soon found it led to a maze of streets with new houses that all looked the same. Carrying on through the high street, Jane found another walkway and went to explore that one too. This one led to the same housing estate, so it was of no interest as they turned back. They were almost at the end of the row of shops when Jane spotted a last walkway, almost identical to the others. She almost did not bother, but as they had time to waste, Jane led Molly down. She was amazed to find a tiny shop a short way down. It was completely out of view. A rickety table stood outside, piled high with lots of junk, as Jane saw it. The table bowed in the middle, threatening to collapse if even a piece of paper were to land on it. There was old crockery, books, saucepans and lots of things Jane did not recognise. Dismissing the shop that she was sure did not do any business tucked away down an alley, she walked on. A little further down the path lay three very beautiful, white cottages, with their own front garden and little white picket fence around each. The gardens were all well attended and beautiful, with an array of colourful flowers and shrubs.

Jane thought she had never seen anything so lovely and quaint in all her life. It was so much fun exploring, she wondered if her mother had walked the same route when she was younger. Jane suddenly had the feeling that she had been there before. Maybe she could remember this walkway from when she was a baby; her mother may even have pushed her along there in a pram. Then she remembered her dreams: the gardens and cottages were similar.

The first cottage was fairly large, with two windows each side of a black front door. The grass was a little overgrown, with flowers poking randomly through. To one side almost covering the window was an enormous purple flowered shrub. A few coloured butterflies and some bees hovered around it. Jane stood, mesmerised at the differences in the colours of the butterflies, when the cottage door sprang open and a woman carrying a small baby came out.

'Can I help you?' she asked a little haughtily.

Jane reddened. 'I'm sorry to be nosy; it's just such a beautiful cottage.'

The woman smiled forgivingly. 'Yes, it is. I love it here. Next door is empty and up for rent. I'm hoping we don't get bad neighbours or ones that mind my baby crying too much,' she looked apologetic, and the baby, to prove it could, began to bawl loudly. 'She's teething,' the woman grimaced and closed the door.

Jane walked to the next cottage, which was by far the smallest, squashed in between the other ones.

The neighbour was right: it was empty; an advertisement board stuck out of the bushes. Yellow roses grew up the front wall, the heavy heads cascading down and around the tiny window. Jane opened the creaky gate and walked the short distance to the front door. She peered through the letterbox and then the small window, hoping no one lived there, otherwise she would be in trouble. The room inside was tiny, and a stuffy, worn sofa sat next to a door, which she guessed led from the hallway. A faded rug dominated the floor, hiding most of the floorboards that showed around the edges.

'What do you think you are doing?' a grumpy voice snapped.

Jane jumped so much she dropped Molly's lead.

'I… I'm sorry,' she stammered, spinning round.

Her eyes rested on an elderly man, who could just be seen through the mass of shrubbery in the next front garden. He sat in a wheelchair with a blanket draped over his knees. The weather was so warm Jane could not imagine someone feeling cold and needing a blanket.

'I… thought it was empty,' she apologised again.

'It is, but unless you're interested in renting it, you have no right to be looking in the window,' he snapped again, looking suspiciously at the punk girl, who could only mean trouble.

'Can I rent it?' Jane blurted out, without thinking.

'No! we don't want young people here, parties and loud music. Now bugger off before I call the police.'

Jane picked up Molly's lead and scurried back down the path feeling really upset. How unfair it was to be judged because she was young. She returned to the pub and sat at a table with a cup of tea and bowl of water for Molly.

'Cheer up!' shouted one of the men.

But Jane could not find a smile; she felt really miserable at how rude the man had been to her.

Chapter Twelve

The next morning, having stewed all night over the grumpy man's nastiness, Jane woke up feeling cross.

'I've had enough of bullies, Molly. We don't have to take it anymore. Not now we're rich,' she told her, with a morning pat and kiss on her scruffy head.

After having her breakfast and taking some back to the room for Molly, she left the pub and headed back to the cottage, planning to knock on the front door. As it was, the elderly man was sitting in the front garden in his wheelchair, half dozing. At the path of his cottage Jane took a deep breath and, opening the gate, marched in, stopping in front of him. He looked up in surprise, as he had not seen Jane coming.

'Actually, I don't have parties or play loud music and I think you're very rude and vile to talk to me that way,' she gabbled, turning away to stomp off.

The man burst out laughing, so much so he went into a hacking coughing fit. Jane was worried that she had killed him. His blanket fell from his knees and he flopped forward, gasping for air. She ran back up the path and began hitting his back. Reaching for the glass of water perched on a table nearby, she pushed it into his hands. The old man gulped gratefully, tears running down his face. Bending down Jane scooped up the blanket and pulled it back over his legs.

Finally, the man caught his breath. 'I'm sorry young lady, you're right; I was very rude and should never have spoken to you the way I did.'

'No, you shouldn't have done,' Jane agreed, 'and I still want to rent the cottage.'

The man gapped at her in disbelief. 'Well I never,' he laughed. 'It's £500 a month, with a month in advance.'

'OK,' Jane smiled in defeat, 'when can I move in?'

He smiled too, admiring the cheeky youngster; then looked despondently down at Molly.

'I'm not sure about the dog.'

'Oh please, mister. Molly's no trouble,' her smile faded, giving way to pleading eyes.

'You're a bit young to be renting a place on your own. Where's your family?'

'I have none. Molly is all I have and I'm 18 years old.' Jane puffed out her chest.

The man pondered for a while before relenting.

'Well at my age all you youngsters look about 12,' He did not know why but suddenly he felt very sorry for the girl with no family, and he liked her.

'God, I'm a sucker. But if you play up, you're out. No loud music, no parties and no barking from the dog. Plus, I will check you are taking care of the place,' he grumbled, and then called inside the house.

'Margaret, come out here.'

After a few minutes a lady appeared and stared at Jane with instant dislike. The feelings were mutual, as Jane instantly did not like Margaret. Her face was full of anger and her eyes cold as a fridge; she reminded her of her mother, except for the clothes, which were a tweed skirt, bright orange tights, and a red top, complete with blue cardigan. Her hair, which was a cross between grey and brown, was scraped back into a tight bun which sat at the nape of her neck. The whole look was finished off with flat, navy, very sensible shoes. Jane thought she was probably the man's wife. She was shocked to discover Margaret was his daughter.

'This young lady wants to rent the cottage,' he told the sour faced Margaret, who did not smile and scared Jane with her hostility.

'Really, Dad?' she barked, looking with horror at the punk girl.

'I've told her we'll give her a three-month trial,' the man explained. 'Subject to references that is.'

Jane's heart sank, 'I've not got any. I don't work because I want to enrol in college. My mum died a few months ago and I have no father. I'm very rich though, so can afford the rent.'

They both stared at the girl standing so determinedly in front of them. Neither knew what to say. Margaret suddenly felt a little mean at the way she was acting towards her. Without saying anything she turned and went indoors, coming out moments later with a large key.

'What's your name?'

'Lizzy, Lizzy Ellis,' she told her.

'Well, Elizabeth, I'll show you the cottage,' Margaret clipped, and then seemed to notice Molly for the first time. 'I will not have anything chewed, or dogs mess in the garden.'

Jane nodded and promised she would clean up after Molly, who was intently sniffing the orange legs.

'Just show the girl the house, Margaret, and stop scaring her.'

Margaret pushed past Jane and stomped down the path and back up the next one.

'Oh, how beautiful,' Jane breathed, as she poked her head through the black front door into a tiny hallway. A narrow staircase stood facing her with only ten steps to the upstairs. She followed Margaret inside, careful to wipe her feet and not upset her any more than she already seemed. The low ceilings made the hallway look tiny and only fit for small people. There was a doorway to the right of the front door. At the end of the hallway was another door and Jane was dying to see what was behind it. Various brass items hung on the white painted walls and a small picture, which was so covered in dust it was not clear what it was of. Jane opened the cupboard door under the staircase. It contained various cleaning items and a carpet sweeper, which she had never seen before.

'I expect you to keep it clean,' Margaret clipped.

The door to the right led to the small living room, which she had seen from the window. Along the left-hand wall next to the doorway sat the red, stuffy sofa, the colour long since faded with time and sunlight. In the far corner of the room was a small square table with a gold cloth covering it. On top was a large glass bowl, which Jane imagined she could use for fruit.

A very small old-fashioned sideboard with two drawers and two cupboards underneath was under the window. Jane opened one of the doors and found delicate little cups and saucers. One mouthful of tea and the cup would be empty, she thought, but did not say; then made a mental note to buy some mugs. There was also a stack of dinner plates with different patterns: odd sized tea plates and six glasses of various sizes.

'Just some old crockery,' Margaret's voice sounded almost apologetic. 'You don't have to use them.'

'They're lovely, thank you,' Jane smiled.

Molly ran about sniffing every inch and, to Jane's horror, sat down and weed on the rug.

'I'm so, so sorry,' Jane gushed, near to tears as she pulled out a tissue and mopped at the patch.

Margaret's eyes narrowed as she glared from one to the other, the relationship between them now more damaged and fragile.

'I think she's nervous,' Jane tried to excuse the dog and told Molly off by wagging her pointed finger at her.

At the end of the living room was another door, which led into the kitchen. Jane had never seen anything like the big stone oblong sink, with a wooden draining board, that was below a small window. A grey curtain covered the area under the sink. As she pulled it to one side, she found old saucepans and pots. Against one wall were three wooden shelves with tins and more pots. Underneath them was another small table with two chairs, reminding her of her mother's favourite place.

There was a very old-fashioned gas cooker to one side. It was clean and worked perfectly if lit with matches, as Margaret demonstrated. However, there was no kettle or toaster and Jane made another mental note to buy both.

A little door with a latch revealed a surprisingly large pantry with stone shelves, as Margaret explained, to keep things cool.

The door leading back to the hallway was next to the table, as Jane discovered on pulling it open. The window over the sink looked onto a garden. It was so overgrown it was hard to see how big it was. Tall weeds, brambles, and fat shrubs that looked more like trees blocked any view.

'I can tidy the garden; I bet it was really beautiful once, and there's all sorts of secrets hidden out there,' Jane said, forgetting Margaret's dislike of her.

Margaret looked taken aback, a look of concern flashing through her eyes. 'Don't be silly, it's a mess, you'll never manage to clear it on your own.'

Jane turned away from the garden and bravely faced the older woman, 'Please let me live here. I love it so much. I'll take care of it,' she begged.

'It's very tiny and basic; that's why no one has wanted it so far. Upstairs has only one bedroom and a bathroom. The hot water runs on an immersion heater. The heating is a coal fire which has a back burner, so when it's alight it will heat the water and radiators.'

'Oh,' Jane puzzled. She had seen coal fires on TV, but had no idea how to make one. Still, she shrugged, how hard could it be?

At Margaret's suggestion she went up the stairs to look. At the top were two doors. The one in front had a little step up into the bedroom. Inside was a large wardrobe, a double bed, chest of drawers and a dressing table that seemed too big for the room. The two doors opened to a large cupboard and an airing cupboard, which luckily contained some bedding. Again, a large faded rug covered most of the floor. This time it was pink with faded flowers and lots of zigzags around the border. White floorboards showed again around the edges, and white curtains with little blue flowers hung at the small window.

The bathroom was basic with a large metal bath, sink and toilet; the floor was covered in faded yellow lino, with a little blue bath mat surrounding the toilet. The quaint cottage reminded Jane of an old black and white film she had seen once. Margaret waited by the front door, staring blankly, as Jane came down.

'When would you like to move in?' she clipped again, with no emotion in her cold voice.

'Friday, if that's OK,' Jane answered, trying to sound assertive and like a businesswoman.

'Have you got to arrange your belongings to be moved?'

'I haven't got many. I'm staying at a pub so have only a few carrier bags and a suitcase.' Jane answered.

'You may want to get yourself a TV then. I don't have a spare.'

Leading her outside they went back to the front garden where the man sat waiting for them. Jane promised she would be back within an hour to pay her money.

'I prefer a standing order set up with the bank,' Margaret told her, before turning to go back into her own cottage.

Jane stared after her; she had no idea what that was but did not say anything.

'Thank you very much, Margaret,' Jane smiled, in one last attempt to make friends.

'It's Mrs Nugent,' she snapped.

Jane and Molly were back at the cottage within ten minutes with the money. She paid Margaret the £1,000, which was carefully counted in crisp £50 notes.

'I... I'm not sure what a standing order is,' Jane confessed, her face red because she felt silly.

'The bank will help you set one up,' Margaret suggested, her voice slightly softer.

The elderly man felt sorry for the young girl and a little guilty at being so harsh on her. 'Margaret will help you. Won't you, Margaret?'

'If you give me your bank details, I'll do it when I go to the shops.'

'I... I... don't have a bank account,' she stammered, reddening again and finding solace in her white pumps.

They both looked at the white pumps to for a moment and then Margaret suggested she get herself one. Confused, and guessing the young lady had lied about being rich, they worried that the rent may not appear each month, as promised.

'If you take some ID into the bank, they will open an account for you.'

Jane started to shuffle the pumps around a little. She had no ID and did not really know what it was anyway.

'OK, I'll do that,' she lied, hoping they would forget, 'But in the meantime, what if I pay you six months' rent; that way you know I won't let you down.' She brightened, hoping to dispel the puzzled looks of both pairs of eyes that were boring into her.

Margaret nodded slowly, her eyes clouded with suspicion. There was more than meets the eye about his young girl. She hoped they had not been wrong in allowing her to rent the cottage. It was obvious to her the girl was either a drug dealer or a prostitute.

It was agreed; Jane would move in on Friday, after she had arranged for a few needed items.

The next day, with her new address written by Margaret on a piece of paper, she left Molly in the room and took the bus to Burton Ridge again. It was so exciting buying a fridge, kettle and toaster. The television was more difficult as there were so many to choose from. The salesman suggested several high definition ones with built in DVD players. In the end Jane randomly chose one and asked the man to show her how it worked. When he got fed up with trying to demonstrate and Jane getting it all wrong, he suggested that she paid extra to have it installed.

'They will show you how to use it then,' he explained.

She paid in full for the television, with the agreement it would be delivered at the same time as the fridge on the Friday.

Jane left and went off to buy some bedding. Running her fingers over the beautiful floral set with large blue and yellow flowers, she bought it and a spare set, equally as pretty. Her final purchase was two beautiful fluffy dog beds, one in red for upstairs and the other in cream for the living room. They were difficult to carry with all her other purchases. Jane was so excited she barely noticed the discomfort.

Molly was elated when she returned, bouncing up and down, yapping. Jane showed her the dog beds, which she sniffed at dubiously for a few minutes. Then, dismissing them, she jumped back onto the bed, dug the duvet into a heap and flopped down with a sigh as she watched Jane get ready for her bath.

The closer Friday came, the more excited and worried Jane felt. She was dying to go back and ask to view again, but desperate not to upset Margaret further, she dare not. The day could not come quick enough and it felt like weeks until it finally arrived. But on the other hand, she was scared leaving the pub where she now felt safe and at home. People accepted and even liked her.

It had not taken Jane and Molly long to settle in. The people were so friendly towards them, greeting Jane warmly and petting Molly, who wagged her tail with delight. For the first time in her life she had friends. The landlady Samantha fussed over her and was motherly and protective. Well, Jane imagined that is how a mother would be. Checking she was safe and telling the older men to leave her alone if they put their arms around her, or asked her out. Which Jane felt terribly embarrassed about, as her face burned with heat.

The landlady's son Stuart was so good looking and grown up. He must be at least 18 or 19, Jane guessed. He always had a ready smile for her as he worked behind the bar. If on a break, he came over and spent his time with her and Molly, who was allowed in the bar when the food was finished being served. Some of the locals would nudge each other and smile when they talked. Or make comments like, 'Young love' or 'Ahhh ain't it sweet', which again caused Jane to go beetroot red in the face.

If Stuart's girlfriend was about, she would look at Jane with dislike and never spoke to her. Stuart, like most of the regular people in the pub, puzzled over why a girl so young was there. A few of the more nosy ones asked her outright. At first, she fumbled for excuses but decided to use the same story as she told Margaret and her father.

'My mum died so I'm looking for somewhere new to live.'

'Surely you have other family?' Stuart asked.

'No, there's only Molly,' Jane told him and others who were listening.

'Why here?' one lady asked, feeling very sad for one so young to be alone.

'I don't know really,' Jane said trying to think of a valid reason. 'I had a friend who came from here and it sounded so nice I thought I would come and see.'

'What was her name?' Stuart asked. 'We may know her.'

'Lucy Eldridge.' It was all Jane could think of at short notice.

Thankfully no one did seem to know anyone with that name.

Samantha was a bit more shrewd than the rest. She did not believe Jane's story, as she told Stuart when they were alone.

'There's more to her than meets the eye. You mark my words, that girl is running away from something or someone.'

Stuart flicked his eyes with annoyance. His mum was always so suspicious of everything or everyone, ever since his dad left them.

'You be careful Stuart, Jess doesn't like you hanging around her. I can see you fancy her.'

'Mum please!' he blushed.

It was true though; he did like Jane a bit too much. He had been with Jess since school; their relationship was now stale and boring. She was on about getting engaged, and he certainly did not feel ready for such a commitment. For some time now he had considered finishing with her. Until now he had no reason to. He wondered if Jane liked him as much as he liked her.

Most of the time they spent in their room, watching television. Jane spent hours practising with makeup to create different looks. Most she did not like when she scrutinised the end result. Eventually, with a lot of errors and a few times stamping on the box of eyeshadow, she had the application down to a fine art. It was clear that too much makeup did not suit her.

The more subtle it was, the nicer Jane looked, young and fresh. She began to see herself in a different light. The shy scruffy girl was fast becoming a confident, beautiful, young woman. Many hours were also spent trying on the new clothes that were paraded in front of Molly, experimenting with colours and fabrics, like she had done in her daydreams. Molly would sit, dutifully wagging her tail and yapping as Jane, pretending she was on a catwalk, swaggered up and down the room showing off her latest creation. Just like her imaginary Isabella, she began to develop her own style and identity.

'No longer a plain Jane,' she laughed, falling onto the bed and tickling Molly's belly. 'Not even Dan or Mum would recognise me now.'

Not for the first time Jane wondered if they were looking for her, knowing that there was no way they would not be. Did her mother even miss her being around? Jane doubted she had even noticed her gone, she thought, sadly.

Chapter Thirteen

Suzanne Bailey shuffled through the files on her desk, looking despondently at the names.

'Too many,' she sighed; over 40 cases; it would be impossible to get through them all.

'Who's next?' She could not decide, or even arrange them in priority order. They all looked urgent; even if they did not, it did not mean they weren't. How could she tell until she had investigated further? With all the bad press lately, it felt like childcare services had a gun to its head.

She looked up as a shadow clouded her desk. Deep in thought, she had not seen her manager, Marion, heading her way.

Giving an apologetic smile, she thumped another brown file in front of Suzanne. 'This has just been emailed over. It's from the police. Soooorrrrry.'

Suzanne groaned and flicked her eyes at Marion, not daring to speak and, pointlessly, tell her she was already overloaded with work.

'It may be nothing,' Marion grimaced, trying to make light of the pressure she was placing on her.

In all Suzanne's years of experience, one thing she had learned was nothing was never nothing, not when children were involved. She opened the file, turning away from Marion, and began to read.

Jane Watts, D.O.B. 1991.

14-year-old, female.

Attends Highfields Secondary School.

Reported missing by an elderly friend, Mrs Dorothy Flanagan. She claimed Jane had gone to look for an aunt and cousin. Jane had told Dorothy that her mother was aware. However, Mrs Flanagan reports that Jane's mother and partner did not know and are looking for Jane themselves. The police have no clarification of this from the mother, who has not reported Jane as missing herself.

She has not attended school for the past few days. However, this is not unusual for Jane, who constantly plays truant.

Her mother, Toni Watts, is a single parent, who cohabitates with a man named Dan Wallace. He is well known to the police for violence and robbery.

There does not appear to be any other family involvement. No sign of a father.

'ODD!' Suzanne closed the file, went to one of the secretaries, Helena, and laid a piece of paper in front of her with Jane's details.

'Can you find out if this young lady is known to any other borough please?' She grinned guiltily, having only moments before handed her a pile of letters to type.

Helena saluted and flicked her eyes playfully, 'On it.'

Going back to her desk, Suzanne called the school and spoke to the head teacher, Mrs Harris.

'Jane Watts,' the woman snapped in annoyance, 'skinny child, always bottom of the class. Sometimes pops in if she feels like it. Very scruffy and unkempt.'

'Any friends we could contact?' Suzanne asked, wondering why the stupid woman was never concerned about Jane before. Already to her, it screamed something was seriously wrong.

'No, she always sits alone, in class or in the playground. She's not popular amongst the other children.'

'So, you never thought to speak to someone then?' The sarcasm in her voice was clear and Mrs Harris hesitated. Suzanne guessed she had probably fallen off her perch, by the way she began to stammer:

'Well... I... we had no reason to suspect anything.'

'You didn't? Well, maybe you would be more suited to another job then, serving tables or pulling pints springs to mind?'

She slammed down the phone before she said much more. If not so good at her job, she was sure she would have been sacked for rudeness before.

After writing up her notes, Suzanne left the office to visit Mrs Dorothy Flanagan. There were far more urgent cases than this one, but she had such a niggle inside.

The kindly lady was only too pleased and relieved to help her. She made a coffee for them both and sank into her armchair. Suzanne sat down on a chair opposite, disturbing an old tabby cat, which first looked disgruntled at the intrusion and then delighted as he clambered onto her lap. Twisting slowly around three times, he plopped down.

'Oh, please find Jane. I'm so worried about her,' Mrs Flanagan begged. 'She promised to call me every morning at 9 am and I've not heard a word. I feel sick with the thought of what may have happened to her.'

'Have you any idea where she may have gone?' Suzanne asked, releasing the tabby cat's claws from the skin on the top of her leg.

'Thornwood Abbey,' Mrs Flanagan blurted out.

'Really, why?'

'She went to look for her aunt and cousin.'

Mrs Flanagan went on to explain about the birth certificates that Jane had taken without her mother knowing. Mrs Flanagan then told her about Molly and the dogs' home, which she had forgotten to tell the police.

Suzanne left Mrs Flanagan with a promise to keep in touch and let her know when she had found Jane. Just as an afterthought she went to the dogs' home.

The manager, Fiona, was in reception when Suzanne arrived. After flashing her identification, Fiona took her into an office where they could talk in private. She was told about Dan beating the dog and it being found in the river.

Suzanne cringed. 'Bastard.' She looked apologetic for swearing.

'The story did not ring true; Jane told me her aunt was very rich. She paid £400 for Molly,' Fiona told her.

'Where on earth did she get £400?' Suzanne asked, equally as puzzled.

'She said her grandmother, Mrs Flanagan, would pay it and her aunt would refund her.'

'Mmmm, the story gets stranger and stranger.'

Shaking Fiona's hand and leaving her card in case she remembered anything, Suzanne thanked her and left.

Back in the office, she stood shuffling from foot to foot as Helena relayed the trouble she had had, gathering information on Jane Watts. Suzanne's eyes were glazed as her mind drifted. She was adept at spacing out when people talked without drawing breath. Suzanne was still able to add encouraging comments in all the right places.

'Really!' she said, deciding her next visit must be to see Jane's mother and her partner. 'Goodness, you are a treasure,' she told Helena, who glowed with pride. Suzanne patted her on the shoulder and made to escape, but Helena, feeling encouraged by Suzanne's enthusiasm, began again.

'Really!' Suzanne blurted out, looking at her watch, 'I'm sorry, Helena, I've just remembered a phone call.' Grabbing the papers from her, she made a dash to the safety of her desk.

Taking a big sip of her coffee, Suzanne picked up the first referral and began to read:

Islington Child Care Services, 1997.

Jane Watts. six years old, female.

Jane was reported by headmistress, Miss Protherol. Teachers were concerned that Jane attended school smelling of urine. Her clothes were dirty, and at various times she had been covered in unexplainable scratches and bruises.

Jane is a very introverted child. Does not interact with other children and is often the subject of bullying.

Social worker, Cassie Barker, visited the family on a few occasions. It appeared the mother Toni Watts smelled of alcohol and Jane presented as a very frightened, withdrawn child. The plan of action was to remove Jane from her home into foster care. However, the family disappeared with no trace before action was taken. File closed.

Suzanne closed the file and pushed it to one side.

'Poor child,' she blew out her cheeks and picked up the next.

Haringey Child Care Services, 7th July 2000.

Jane Watts, nine years old.

Neighbour, Mrs Prichard, who was concerned about her neglect, reported Jane. Jane's clothes look dirty and worn. Mrs Prichard often hears screaming and crying coming from the neighbouring flat late at night. She has seen Jane with a bloody nose and bruising on many occasions. Additionally, late at night she had been found digging around dustbins for food. On several occasions, Mrs Prichard fed the child herself.

An urgent duty social worker visited the family. She found mother, Toni Watts, to be intoxicated with alcohol and very abusive. Police were called and Jane was removed from home and placed into temporary foster care. She was returned to her mother two days later.

On the next visit, Toni and Jane had moved from the flat and no trace of them was found.

Suzanne closed the file and went outside the office for a cigarette. She took a big drag and blew the smoke out slowly.

'Poor little cow,' she said out loud.

Once back inside, she went to Marion's office and placed the papers on her desk.

'You need to read this.'

Suzanne sat in one of the office chairs and waited for her to finish.

'Jesus Christ,' Marion finally said, looking over at Suzanne.

'So, where is Jane now? Running wild on the streets of London?' She wiped her hand over her mouth and tried to think.

'Do you think this Dan did away with her? Or the mother?'

'I'm just going to go and see her. The politics of this job sometimes makes me sick. Why was nothing done for this child before? Poor little sod.'

Marion stared after Suzanne as she walked from her office. She was a good social worker but always became too involved. If she knew Suzanne, she would not stop until she got to the bottom of it.

Once Dan left her, Toni went into a deep depression, lost in a world of gloom. At first, she thought he would come back after his temper calmed. After a few days, it was clear he would not. She now sat at the kitchen table, plastic bottles of cider lined up — some empty and others still to be consumed. She did not wash, change her clothes or even go out, except to walk the short distance to the mini mart to buy more cigarettes or alcohol. Her weight plummeted, and, drinking on an empty stomach, she was often sick with violent stomach pains. Letters popped through the door each morning and occasionally people knocked.

Toni sat at the kitchen table, or fell into her filthy bed and slept in a drunken stupor. Very soon, she was throwing up blood, and eventually collapsed in her own bloody vomit in the hallway between the living room and toilet.

It was Suzanne who found her after knocking at the door for some time with no answer. Her rapping became more urgent, as she was sure Toni Watts was at home. Eventually, she opened the letterbox to shout through and saw her legs poking out from the short bend of the corridor.

The police were called to break the door down and an ambulance took Toni to a local hospital.

After she had gone, Suzanne looked around the flat with disgust. She had been left to make the place safe and remove any valuables. There were no valuables, at least none that Suzanne could find. Inspecting the kitchen cupboards and fridge, she found a few mouldy items, sour milk and a green loaf of bread. She left the room and looked into the living room, wrinkling her nose, as it smelled as stale and unkempt as the rest of the flat. Old newspapers, dirty crockery and rotting bits of stray food littered a small coffee table and the carpet. She left the room and went into the next, which she assumed was Jane's bedroom. As she crossed the threadbare carpet her shoes stuck to some nondescript, gloopy gunge.

Faded blue wallpaper hung torn in strips that curled into springy circles at various lengths down the wall. The room, like everywhere else in the flat, smelled musty and stale. The bedsheet, that had long ago been white, had a big tear through the middle. It looked like it had not been washed in years. A greasy patch on the pillowcase showed where Jane had once rested her head. Inside the wardrobe were a few scruffy worn clothes. The only thing that was half-decent was a flowery, long skirt and some cotton trousers, plus two T-shirts. Inside the chest of drawers she found a few pairs of grey knickers and some toddlers' vests, bits of paper and some curly old magazines. Nothing gave any clues to Jane's whereabouts and nothing in there suggested it was a teenage girl's room. No posters, old or soft toys, music, computer or television. What sort of life had this child lived with a drunkard mother? she thought, feeling sad at the injustice. Even in this day and age when things should be different, there were still children that suffered so terribly at the hands of adults, slipping through the net of protection that should have kept them safe.

Suzanne went into the next bedroom and looked around; there were not many male items. It was strange, as Dan Wallace was supposedly living there. Maybe he had left, she pondered, spotting the suitcase on top of the wardrobe. Suzanne pulled it down and heaved it on to the bed. Lifting the lid, she rifled through the contents. Flicking through the small bundle of letters, she pulled one out and began to skim read. The letter was from a Vicky Watts, who had poured her heart out to some boy named Jonathan Lucas at university in Oxford many years before. It seemed both young Toni and Vicky were rivals for the same man. She dismissed the letter and pulled out a few more. All the letters were addressed from 49 Crickleworth Road, Thornwood Abbey, the same place Jane was supposedly heading.

Suzanne lifted an official envelope written by a solicitor; it was a Will from a Justine Lucas, leaving a proportion of his estate to his granddaughter, Isabella Lucas.

'So, who is Isabella?' Suzanne said out loud, 'And why would Toni have this Will?'

She wrote down the address and heaved the case back on top of the wardrobe, not having found anything else of interest. Suzanne locked up the flat, keeping the key with the intention of taking it to the hospital.

On the kitchen table, after first clearing a space, she left a note for Dan Wallace and Jane, asking that either call her on their return.

When Suzanne got back to the office, she endured a long conversation with Helena, who poured out the difficulties of gathering more information on her caseload. She gingerly tried to find a convenient pause to ask her to try and find Vicky Watts, or the Lucas family and the mystery Isabella. For once, she was not kept too long after cleverly freeing herself with the excuse of needing the loo urgently. This had involved a lot of exaggerated wiggling and clenching of her thighs, but it was enough for Helena to release her.

Toni Watts was in a critical state following a bleeding ulcer, Suzanne found out on calling the hospital. Her liver was not looking too good either, and she was barely conscious, so it was not worth visiting her just yet.

It did not take Helena long before she came back with news about Vicky Lucas.

'It appeared she died some ten years ago after an overdose,' she relayed to Suzanne.

'The plot thickens. In fact, this started off as a weedy garden; it's now like Sherwood Forest,' Suzanne said, looking down at the note, which told her no more than Helena had.

When Dan had left Toni, he had gone to stay with Mick. It was easier for the time being. It was also risky for them all. So Dan stayed hidden, only venturing out after dark and carefully going over the back fence instead of using the front door.

After Scott's involvement with the robbery, the police were maybe looking for an inside job.

That evening, he had gone to Mick's house to confess he had no idea where Jane was.

Mick was sat in front of the television, waiting for news of the money as he arrived. He told him the truth, and as he finished Mick grabbed Dan by the collar and threw him against the wall. Bringing up his fist, he held it ready to punch into his face.

'You fuckin' idiot,' he snarled, 'the kid overheard that night and you just ignored it.'

Mick seemed to crumple as he let go of Dan.

'How do we know this is not all your doing?' Scott asked, appearing in the doorway when he heard the shouting. He was glad his dad was angry with Dan.

'You, dozy bastard.' Anger flashed in Dan's eyes.

'What, you think I arranged for the kid to wait at the bunker and shoot Marc? Look,' he reasoned, 'give me time to find the girl. She knows something, I'm sure about that. We'll get our money and then get out of here.'

'What about the girl? Even if she hasn't taken the money, she knows too much,' Scott said, dreading the answer before he spoke the words.

Dan sighed. 'She meets the same fate as Marc, I guess.' He thought he could at least have his fun with her first, he smiled to himself.

'I wonder why Jane bought a suitcase and matches. They're odd things to buy.'

'She probably put our money in the case and needed the matches for light in the underground room,' Scott said, simply.

Mick and Dan stared at him in disbelief.

'You really are a tosser,' Mick said angrily. 'Sometimes I wonder how I ever fathered you. How the fucking hell could she fit ten million quid in a suitcase? When we struggled with nine bags? And where was it? Cos there weren't any case when we got there. And how the hell could she see in that room with a match? We struggled with a lighter.'

Mick picked up an ashtray and hurled it at Scott, who dodged the impact. It smashed against the wall, cigarette butts scattering across the floor and the ash bursting forward in a big grey cloud.

'Just keep quiet, dick, or go play somewhere on the motorway. Leave us to think this out,' Dan snarled.

'Still he has a point; why did she buy those things?' Mick said, after Scott made a hasty retreat upstairs.

Dan and Mick racked their brains, trying to imagine where Jane had disappeared to. They came up with loads of ideas, none feasible.

'Her mother has to know something,' Mick repeated again.

'That dozy bitch don't know nothing. Besides, I'm not going to ask 'er again,' Dan told him, with conviction.

They searched everywhere they could possibly think of, even going back and asking the crowd of girls again. At night, they drove around just looking and hoping to bump into her. They questioned people but no one confessed to seeing a young girl of Jane's description with a scruffy brown dog.

'Most likely she would head for the centre of London,' Mick surmised, when they had depleted all other ideas.

'What makes you think that?' Dan asked.

'All kids go to London looking for fun, I guess,' he shrugged, not thinking of anything better.

So, they trawled the London streets just in case.

'I think,' Scott suggested one evening over a can of beer, 'you're looking in the wrong place. You need to go back to the basics. Try the old lady again; she could be hiding there. Also, the dogs' home.'

'Prat,' Dan said scathingly.

'Maybe, but she would have told someone something,' Scott said, not in the least bit perturbed by the insult. He was used to being treated as stupid.

'He has a point,' Mick said. 'We haven't anything better in the pipeline.'

Dan shrugged grudgingly. 'I guess it won't hurt to start again. I did think the old girl was hiding something. Why did you go back that night, Mick, and cover the entrance to the underground room?' he suddenly remembered.

'I didn't go back,' he looked at Dan questioningly.

'So it was her then, she must have still been there, or went back after we left,' Dan pondered in disbelief. 'Or if it weren't 'er then there was someone else there at the time.'

'What, you mean someone knows all about this? And that you shot Marc?'

'All I know is there is no way that bit of a girl did all this on 'er own. Someone helped her,' Dan narrowed his eyes trying to think.

'But why would they cover the entrance up?' Mick puzzled.

'I don't know. Maybe to cover up after the kid. After all, she did shoot Marc first. Whatever; she's the one with the answers.'

Scott and Mick studied him, trying to digest his theory.

'I don't know, nothing makes sense to me. How can a bit of a kid steal ten million pounds, a load of jewellery, shoot a man and disappear into thin air?' Mick finally said.

'Believe me, someone is hiding 'er, little bitch,' Dan spat, his voice now slurred. 'She's got our fucking money and I want it back. That kid's gonna die when we find her.'

'You and Scott go back to the bunker and search again. I'll go to the dogs' home tomorrow. We'll find 'er, so help me God, and our money. The girl will pay for this.' Dan lifted his can to his lips and gulped. For now, he was too drunk to think properly.

When Dan got to the dogs' home the next day, carefully nursing a hangover, it was due to close for lunch. The snooty Sarah looked up as his shadow darkened her desk.

'I understand my daughter, Jane Watts, came in a while back to get a dog.'

'And?' Sarah said sarcastically. 'She's popular; you're the second person to ask after her.'

Dan's eyes narrowed. 'Who else came in?'

'Some social worker,' Sarah told him, sliding a form over the desk.

Dan picked it up and read, noting Mrs Flanagan's address. Then his eyes widened as he saw the bottom of the page. '400 quid paid for a dog?' he said in disgust.

A hand reached around and snatched the form from him. He spun round to face a lady with eyes that were blazing at him.

'Can I ask, Sarah, why this man, whoever he is, is reading one of our confidential forms?' Fiona snapped, not moving her eyes from Dan's.

'I have every right to, I'm trying to find my daughter,' Dan told her, his temper boiling like a kettle at the arrogant, smug woman.

'I don't believe Jane Watts has a father. However, her mother apparently is living with an evil bastard, who beat a little dog senseless and dumped it in the river.' Fiona's voice was calm, but her eyes threatening, daring Dan to retaliate.

Sarah looked fearfully from Fiona to the man, suddenly feeling worried. She would not like to cross Fiona, but then again, she definitely would not like to cross the man who stood in front of the desk either.

'Dunno nothing about that,' Dan smiled, spitefully, feeling like he had one over on her. 'Fucking hate dogs, myself. I'm sure the ugly thing deserved it — whoever did it.'

'Get out of here,' Fiona told him through gritted teeth, pointing to the door.

Dan went to speak, changed his mind, tipped an imaginary hat, grinned and walked out.

'Phew, that was close,' Sarah breathed.

Fiona turned on her, her eyes still blazing; she was furious. 'How dare you hand over confidential paperwork to a complete stranger.'

'But... I...'

'But nothing, Sarah, get your things and go. You have pushed your luck too far this time.'

Sarah gaped at Fiona, and then, noting by her eyes there was no changing her mind, she grabbed her bag and rushed out of the door.

Chapter Fourteen

The Friday of the move had arrived. Jane awoke early and had a long, luxurious bath to prepare. She wanted both Molly and herself to look their best for the big day. After carefully applying her makeup, she changed her clothes three times before feeling satisfied.

Standing in front of the full-length mirror, Jane twisted each way and gave a nod of approval. She felt fantastic in a pair of lacy cream shorts and a pale pink cotton top with embroidered straps. Her pumps were lacy too, with little white fake diamonds lining the edge. On her head she wore a big floppy, dark pink hat. Around her neck hung three strings of beads, with colours that complimented the hat.

After bathing Molly — which she was not best pleased with, especially when she was dried using the hair dryer — Jane fastened a new collar around her neck. It was also deep pink to match her own hat, with a small frill along each side.

'We have got to look our best, Molly,' Jane explained, while using the hair dryer on the dog's unruly coat. 'We must make a good impression, so they like us and let us stay.'

Judging by the disgruntled glare, Molly did not agree.

Jane felt very nervous and a little scared of both Margaret and her father. Both were grumpy and she hoped desperately she did not annoy them enough that Margaret might beat her or Molly.

Eventually, it was time to pack and get ready. Her new clothes would not fit in the suitcase with the money. The duvet and bed-sets, plus kitchen items and Molly's baskets were impossible to carry along with the case.

Sam agreed the room was hers till 12 o'clock, so in the end, Jane took three journeys before all her belongings were in their new home.

Margaret scowled as she handed over the keys to her, and closed the front door without speaking. The elderly man was not in the front garden today as it had been drizzling with rain earlier.

Jane resisted the urge to run round the cottage and look again until all her belongings were there. Leaving Molly to explore by herself, she went back to the pub for the second time, and finally the third. After paying her bill, she said her goodbyes.

Jane gave both Sam and Stuart a big cuddle and thanked them for looking after her.

'I'll miss you both,' she told them.

'You're only going around the corner,' Stuart laughed.

'I hope you'll come back and see us? We want to know how things are going,' Sam smiled.

'Maybe we could go for coffee sometime,' Stuart shouted, as Jane left, waving, ignoring his mum's disapproving glare and going a little pink as he said it. He had already decided to give Jane a few days and pay her a visit.

'Do you think she'll be OK?' Sam said to her son worriedly. 'She seems so young and vulnerable.'

'I thought you didn't like her?' Stuart laughed.

Sam looked affronted. 'I didn't say that. I just think she's hiding something.'

Jane stood in the living room of the cottage, surrounded by a pile of bags. She twirled round, taking in every detail of the small area. She then slowly walked around every room in turn, with Molly close to her side. She had never smiled so much in all her life. The happiness brightened her face, making her eyes twinkle and glow a deep blue.

Twisting the big key in the back door, Jane walked into the garden. Fighting her way through the high weeds, she found a few neglected flowers to one edge. The garden reminded her of a hidden fairy garden and she was sure every night they came to play there. It was a long time since she had visualised a fantasy world. There did not seem enough time lately, she mused.

The garden was lovely: it made her long to invent one. Large plump roses pushed their way out between crowds of overgrown shrubs, adding to the magic.

Molly ran around sniffing and checking every inch before finding a suitable area to squat and relieve herself in the overgrown grass. She disappeared through a leafy bush and came running out again a few minutes later. She was as happy as Jane and seemed to be laughing, with her pink tongue hanging from her open mouth.

Jane knelt down and gave her a massive kiss on the head. 'Oh Molly, we're going to be so happy here. I can feel it.'

The dog licked her face in response, wagging her tail at her mistress's joy. Suddenly Molly's body stiffened and she let out a low growl towards the back door. Startled, Jane twisted round to see the door slowly shut and the black handle twist to secure it; a dark shadow scooted past the kitchen window. She stood up, feeling spooked. Had Margaret come in to check on her? Jane walked to the door and pulled it open.

'Hello!' she called into the kitchen, but there was no answer and no one there. Molly stayed in the garden and continued growling as Jane walked dubiously inside. A chill ran through her, causing goose bumps along her arms. She went through the living room into the hall. There was no one there. Jane swallowed and walked slowly up the stairs to check the bedroom. She pulled open the wardrobe door and looked under the bed, just in case the intruder was hiding. If it were not for Molly growling, she would have thought she had imagined it.

At that moment, there was a sharp knock on the front door, causing Jane's heart to almost leap from her body. Laughing nervously, she realised it was a delivery for either the fridge or television.

It was both arriving, one a few minutes after the other. The fridge was difficult to squash into the kitchen. After much manoeuvring, the helpful deliveryman managed to squeeze it next to the sink, where it somehow fitted snugly.

The television was soon blaring as Jane practiced with the controls.

After they both left, she unpacked her clothes in the wardrobe and neatly folded her underwear in the chest of drawers.

Opening the wardrobe again, Jane moved the hangers backwards and forwards a few times. Her boots and shoes lay neatly at the bottom, some not even worn yet.

She smiled, delighted to have new clothes hanging there. Pulling a bundle into her face, she kissed them and wiggled her body in excitement of her new adventure and life.

After unpacking, she left Molly and went to the supermarket to stock up on food. It was a hard task deciding what to buy; Jane had no idea how to cook. Reading the labels of packets and tins proved impossible, she realised glumly. If Margaret were more pleasant, she would have asked her advice. She settled for simple food that could be either eaten cold or was already cooked. Then, as a final thought, she bought a few tins of beans. She would have to watch a lot of cookery programmes and learn how to cook, she decided; it couldn't be that hard to produce a decent meal.

Jane had almost forgotten about the man she had shot, pushing the horrible thoughts from her mind. There were so many other things to keep her occupied. She had also forgotten about Mrs Flanagan and her promise to call every day. Walking back from the shops with her heavy bags, she stopped and gasped. A few passers-by gave her an odd look as she stood looking tragic. The telephone number had been in the clothes she had thrown into the bin at Burton Ridge.

'Oh no,' she cried and hurried home.

Sitting on the stuffy sofa, she bit her lip and wondered what she should do to remedy the matter. There was nothing she could do, apart from going back home, and there was no way she could risk that.

Grabbing Molly and clipping on her lead, they left the cottage and were soon sitting on a bus to Burton Ridge; Jane praying her clothes were still in the bin. It was a vain hope. She ignored the looks from shoppers and plunged her hands inside, cringing as they brushed a few soggy rotting food items; her clothes were gone.

On her way back to the bus stop, Jane spotted a toy shop, hidden down a side road. The window was jammed with beautifully hand-crafted toys of all sorts, expertly made and painted in bright cheerful colours. Amongst the array of trains, cars, soldiers and boxed games sat the most beautiful doll she had ever seen. Her long hair was wound into blond ringlets with a big red bow to hold them neatly together. The face was china and so exquisitely painted it almost looked real. She had never owned a doll before. When she was small, Jane remembered carrying around Toni's rolling pin for weeks, wrapping it in various bits of cloth and pretending it was a doll. She had even given it a name 'Lou Lou.' Jane giggled at herself for being so silly over a rolling pin.

Making a decision, she went inside and bought the doll and a whole range of little clothes and shoes for her.

'It's for my niece,' she told the shop assistant, handing over the money to pay.

As she went to leave the shop her eyes fell on a drawing pad with coloured pencils. Going back to the counter, Jane brought them too. She had loved drawing at school and was very good at it.

Once home, she carefully dressed and redressed the doll, trying on every outfit before deciding on a pretty velvet blue dress with little purple stones sewn in. On the doll's head she placed a purple hat, and matching shoes on the feet. Satisfied, she stood her on the sideboard, fixing her into the stand that kept her upright.

Taking the pad and dragging one of the kitchen chairs with her, Jane went into the front garden to draw. She would have liked to sit in the back garden but the grass was far too long, and the bushes too overgrown to squeeze in a chair.

The elderly man was sitting outside again. Jane waved and smiled, before sitting down with Molly in a shady spot under a shrub canopy.

The man grunted a greeting in return. He had been pondering about the young girl since she moved in earlier. She seemed far too young to be alone. It saddened him and he regretted being grumpy with her. He did not really know what to say to a young person to make conversation. At that moment, Margaret bustled out, holding his medication and a glass of water. As she rushed off again, she gave a glance to Jane, huffed and walked back indoors. Jane seemed to cringe and shrink when she saw Margaret.

'Scares me too. Just like the missus, sharp as a razor and prickly as a thistle!' he shouted over, exaggeratedly rolling his eyes.

Jane giggled and carried on drawing.

'What are you drawing?' he asked.

'Flowers,' she told him.

'Can I see?'

Jane went to the little white fence and handed over the pad.

'Mmmm. Very good,' he said, handing it back to her.

'Why are you in a wheelchair?' Jane asked.

'I have cancer; the old lungs aren't so good. Nearly my time, but I won't be sorry to leave here. It's been a long, hard life,' he told her.

Jane looked sad. She had never met anyone who was dying before. 'I would be terrified if it was me,' she said.

'Well, you would be, you're still young. You have your whole life ahead. I'm old and have had a good life, so it's not so bad,' he lied. The truth was, he was terrified of facing death too.

The thought of leaving Margaret was the worst. She had spent many years looking after him. When he went, she would be lost, he guessed; she'd wilt and die like a flower. Poor love was still young herself. She still had time to make a new life but he knew she would not; his daughter was so lonely and isolated.

'Have you really no family, young lady?' he asked.

Jane shook her head. 'I have a cousin and aunt but I've never met them. I didn't even know they existed until recently.'

'Goodness, can't you trace them somehow?'

'I don't know how.'

'What area do they live in?'

'I don't know that either.'

'Maybe Margaret can help you; she's good with the computer.'

The two chatted some more before Margaret bustled out and took him in for an afternoon nap. She ignored Jane, so she guessed Margaret probably would not help find her aunt.

Jane was bored of drawing and the heat was making her clammy. Calling Molly, who lay panting under a bush, they went inside where the thick walls made the rooms cool. Jane switched on the television and found the music channel, and then began to dance around the small living room. Molly jumped around, yapping and wagging her tail with her.

Soon, Margaret appeared outside the front door and gave a sharp bang, making her jump.

'Turn the music down now!' she hissed. 'My father is trying to sleep.'

'Oh goodness, I'm sorry. I didn't think,' Jane apologised, shouting without opening the door.

'No, you young people never do!' she grumbled and stomped off down the path again.

'Oh no, Molly, we're not doing very well, are we?'

Molly looked up and wagged her tail.

Jane went into the kitchen to make a sandwich. The fridge door was wide open and food was scattered all over the floor.

'Molly, you naughty girl,' Jane waved her finger at the dog, who was eagerly sniffing at the cheese. She looked up, surprised at her mistress chastising her. Pulling her tail between her bottom, she sloped off behind the sofa.

It was a while since Jane had dreamed of Isabella but that night the dream haunted her again. The same lady kept calling to Isabella over and over. It was like she was lost and the lady was looking for her. In the background, soft music was playing. Haunting music that she didn't recognise. She woke up and turned on the light; she could still hear the music. Going downstairs, she found the television on, playing the tune from her dream on a classical music channel. Jane laughed at herself and went to turn it off. As she foraged for the button on the remote control, a voice spoke over the music:

'Isabella!' the lady called.

Jane flicked the switch off and ran up the stairs three at a time. She flew into her bed, panting and looking wildly around the room. The cupboard door was now open and Molly lay growling at it. It took her a while to pluck up enough courage to look. Chastising herself for being silly, Jane got out of bed and walked slowly to the cupboard. She pulled the door wider and stared into the space. There was nothing inside, except the empty bags she had put there earlier.

'We're going mad,' Jane laughed, her heart thumping.

The next day, feeling very lonely after the events of the night before, Jane watched from the front room window for the elderly man to be wheeled into the garden. It was not until late afternoon when Margaret appeared pushing the chair. Placing his water, tissues, newspaper and glasses on the little table, she went back indoors.

Once she had left and it was safe, Jane and Molly went out.

'Can we sit with you for a while?' she asked him.

'I would love the company of you both,' he smiled warmly.

They sat together and chatted about all sorts of things, like clothes and makeup, and Jane told him enthusiastically about her new doll.

Although he listened politely to the girl's chatter, it worried him. It was not the conversation of an 18-year-old, who surely by now would be more interested in young men than dolls.

'What can I call you?' Jane asked, breaking into his thoughts.

'Most people call me the Major. Goodness knows why because I was never a Major,' he smiled.

'Shall I call you Major, then?'

'Tell you what, you can call me Henry,' he laughed. 'It's my middle name. I never liked my first.'

'What is it?' she asked.

At that moment Margaret appeared and Jane discretely disappeared into her own cottage.

Over the next few days, Jane went out every day to sit with Henry. On each occasion, she would wait for the coast to be clear of Margaret first.

Henry began to look forward to their chats and waited eagerly for her to appear. She would listen intently to his waffle about his army days and the war, which must have bored the young girl stiff, he thought.

'Bless her,' he said, smiling to himself. She was so sweet. Shame Margaret did not take to her; the girl looked like she needed a mother. But now his sour-faced daughter seemed jealous of the pretty young thing.

'Be a bit gentler on the girl, Margaret,' he had asked the night before.

'Per… you're always so taken in. She's trouble, you mark my words,' Margaret scoffed, as she stomped out of the room.

As soon as he was settled in his spot, Jane came out of the cottage. With her she dragged a chair up her front path and along his, plus the dog on its lead. Grinning, she positioned her chair opposite him and sat down with her pad to draw. Yesterday, she had attempted a picture of him. They had both laughed at the portrait.

'Gosh, do I really have wonky eyes?' he chuckled.

'I can't seem to get them right.' Jane bit her lip as she examined the picture.

'I have something to show you. Open my bag on the back of the chair,' Henry said, after she had settled.

Jane sprang up and opened the zip.

'There's a book in there.'

She handed the book to him.

'No, Lizzy, I want you to look on page 13 and read what it says,' he told her.

Jane's heart sank as she looked down at the book; her face begun to burn. She flicked open the pages to no.13 and her heart began to pound as she stared at the jumbled array of letters, running her eyes over the page.

'Thank you,' she smiled as she closed it and handed it back to him.

'No! Read it out. I know what it says but I want you to read it to me.' He flicked his hand to gesture she take it back again.

Jane reddened even more as Henry waited and then sat forward.

'Oh, my goodness, you can't read, can you?' he said incredulously.

Jane dare not meet his eyes as she shook her head slowly.

'Why on earth not? At your age too.' He could not believe it. Surely all young people could read.

'I… I… don't know,' Jane stammered, wanting the floor to open up and swallow her.

Henry took the book from her and opened the page.

'This is an old army book of mine. There are a very few left now; I'm privileged to own it. It was given to me when I was discharged after the war.' He shut the book, making Jane jump. She had not been listening so it was pointless, his thunder lost and words now falling on deaf ears.

'I hardly ever went to school. The children didn't like me much, so I bunked off,' she confessed.

'Did your parents not make you go, or sort out the bullies?' Henry asked, not understanding.

'I've not got a dad, he left when I was a baby and my mum said he hated me. That's why he left. My mum didn't seem to care if I went or not.'

The man stared at her for a while, wondering if she was making the story up. 'No matter, I'll teach you to read,' he brightened.

Jane looked up excitedly. 'Really? That would be fantastic.' She jumped up and went and gave Henry a big cuddle and kiss.

He laughed, delighted and embarrassed at such show of affection. 'We need some children's books. I wonder if Margaret would pick some up from the library for us.'

Margaret was not pleased. 'Can't read, that's terrible,' she exclaimed. 'Do not get involved, Dad, it's nothing to do with you.'

'I have nothing better to do with my time and she's a lovely little thing. I want to help her.' His mouth and eyes showed he would not be dissuaded.

Margaret reluctantly nodded, knowing it was pointless arguing. The next day, after a visit to the local library, she came back with some simple children's books.

Slamming them on the table in front of her father, Margaret gave a begrudging glare and went into the kitchen.

By the end of the next day, Jane had managed a few more simple words.

'You're a bright little thing,' Henry told her.

'Do you really think so? People usually say I'm thick.' Jane was so happy to receive such a compliment. It gave her confidence to try even harder and please Henry more.

'I do, indeed. Now I'm going for my nap, but I want you to sit and practise. By tomorrow, we shall have you reading the whole book,' he laughed.

Jane left and went into her own front garden, while Margaret came and took her father indoors.

'You know, Margaret, something's just not right about that girl.' Henry told his daughter, while she helped him transfer to the bed.

'Dad, why do you get involved? It's nothing to do with us.' But Margaret, intrigued, eventually asked, 'What do you mean?'

'Well, in some ways she seems very grown up. In others, childish, like maybe a six-year-old.'

Margaret looked at him, not understanding.

'It seems to me that part of the girl has been forced to grow up quickly, leaving parts of her behind as a child that never developed. At 18, she should be more interested in young men and dances, or discos as they have nowadays. But she has just bought a dolly for herself and doesn't in the least seem interested in other young people. I mean, why on earth would she want to hang round a grumpy old man like me?'

'Mmmm, I think you think too much.' Margaret gave a rare small smile. Kissing her father on his forehead, she went to the door of his room.

'Thing is, Dad, they don't have discos nowadays. I think they are raves or garage, or some other thumping mind-numbing thing youngsters attend.' She laughed and closed the door.

Chapter Fifteen.

Jane sat in the front garden after Henry went indoors, struggling over the words he had shown her. It was not long before the sun became too hot to enjoy. Jane could feel sweat running down her back from the heat, and she decided to take her books inside.

Molly, grateful to be moving from the heat, ran excitedly ahead. At the living room door, Jane stopped and stared in shock. Her beautiful doll was on the floor and ripped into shreds.

'Oh no,' she cried, 'Molly, how could you?'

The little dog stared at Jane, her tail sinking between her legs. She let her head fall, until her black nose pointed to the rug. Her ears pulled flat to the side of her head, she walked slowly off behind the sofa.

Jane, very upset, went over to her doll and picked it up, noting the pieces of doll were not bitten at all, but cut. Even the pink dress Jane had dressed her in that morning was shredded. The face of the doll lay on the other side of the room. Although china, it seemed to have a perfectly straight cut along the hairline. The fingers of the doll had also been cut off.

Turning the doll over, Jane screamed and dropped it. The middle of the hair had been scraped off, leaving what looked like bits of flesh hanging. Big lumps of gunge ran from the flesh and Jane's hands were covered with the thick, sticky red and grey liquid. She stared at her hands, seeing the man she shot in her mind. Edging backwards from the room until she reached the door, Jane sank to the floor, staring back at the dismantled doll. Had Margaret come in and done this while she was outside just to scare her? But how, unless she had climbed over the back fence and come through the back door?

It was possible; she did not like Jane so maybe wanted to scare her into leaving. What if it was someone from Dan's gang? They had found her and were giving her warnings.

She ran upstairs and washed away the muck. Grabbing the dog lead, she went out to the front garden, and called to Molly. The dog ran from behind the sofa and followed.

Outside, Jane bent down and cuddled her. 'I'm sorry, I know you didn't do it.'

Molly, relieved, wagged her tail and licked Jane's face in forgiveness.

Making for the abbey garden's café, they found a table where Jane ordered two cream teas to make amends with Molly. From nowhere, Rose suddenly appeared, delighted to see them both. Jane was just preparing their scones with fresh clotted cream and strawberry jam, when she rushed up.

'Oh, I'm glad to have seen you. Can I sit down?' she breathed, fidgeting in excitement.

'Of course,' Jane told her, offering one of Molly's scones.

'I asked my sister about the Watts family and thought you would be interested,' Rose told her, almost bursting with gossip. 'She didn't know your friend, though,'

Jane felt the excitement bouncing into her stomach as she leaned forward to listen.

'It's all so tragic, really, I felt so sad for Rebecca Watts, lovely girl she was, always a bit odd, but there you are.'

'What do you mean odd?' Jane asked, intrigued.

'I can't really explain it, she was always a bit of a loner and sometimes claimed to see and talk to ghosts,' Rose told her, dramatically lowering her voice to a whisper.

Jane felt the hairs on the back of her hand prickle. After all that had happened, the strange dreams and the weird thing with her doll, plus the television incident, supernatural things scared her even more than they had before. Rose was still speaking so she paid more attention.

'There was so much tragedy in her life it's terrible.'

Jane stopped eating her scone and looked more intently at Rose, a little worried about what she was going to hear.

'Did I tell you the sisters were identical twins? They were called Antonia and Victoria, or Toni and Vicky, as they liked to be called. Only

Rebecca, the father and the brother, Alex, could tell them apart. The girls were inseparable when they were young, always into mischief as they sometimes swapped identity. The only difference between them was their personality. Vicky was gentle and quiet, preferred to stay at home reading or studying. Toni was the opposite, bubbly and lively, always up for a good party.'

This confused Jane as it did not sound like her mum at all. It was a strange feeling to hear about her in a different life. She never imagined there was any other time than the one she knew. She tried hard to forget Toni was her mother and visualise the beautiful, laughing girl she had seen in the photo.

'Anyway, when they were 15,' Rose continued, 'Toni went with some friends to a party one night. She had too much to drink and, feeling sick and dizzy, decided to go home. On the way a gang of boys met her. They dragged her to an empty building near here. The poor girl was beaten badly and raped. Her mother was frantic when she didn't come home. It was two days before she was found, unconscious. Three months later, she found she was pregnant and gave birth to a little girl … Lizzy, are you OK?'

The colour had drained from Jane's face as she gaped, horrified, back at Rose. Sickness began to engulf her stomach, threatening to spill out at any time. She grabbed Molly's lead, mumbled she had to go, and ran off through the gardens. Finding a secluded spot, Jane sunk onto the grass and burst into uncontrollable sobs. No wonder Toni hated her so much. Her father was a cruel, evil rapist, whoever he was.

It was Molly who comforted Jane, whining and nudging her and patting her with her paw and kissing away her tears.

'Oh Molly, I'm born of bad, evil blood. My poor, poor mother,' she clung to the little dog, fresh tears spilling from her eyes.

It was after dark when they finally left the gardens and went home. Jane, not wanting to face the doll again, went straight up the stairs to bed. When she finally fell asleep, her dreams were dark nightmares. She saw her mother beaten and bleeding, scared and cold, left for dead. Her rejecting the hateful baby that reminded her of the rape. Her mother fizzled away, and Jane found herself standing in the garden of the cottage, holding the pink fluffy teddy bear with the yellow ribbon around its neck.

The garden was not overgrown like it was now, but beautiful and well-tended. Borders of coloured flowers and shrubs lined a brick pathway that curled the full length. At the top was a gate that led to a field, where amongst the grass colourful wild flowers grew. The sun was shining and birds sung; even rabbits hopped about, playing or just dozing in the heat.

All of a sudden, a big black cloud came from nowhere. The rabbits ran in terror and even the flowers seemed to wilt. Jane, frightened, ran into the cottage to get away. Inside, a sinister blackness spread through the kitchen and into the living room. She ran up the stairs, trying to get away but it followed her into the bedroom. There on the bed lay her mother, dead, her body cold and hard, the lifeless eyes staring at nothing physical anymore.

The noise of her own screaming woke her up, breaking the spell of the dream. Molly stood on the bed, staring worriedly at her.

Flicking on the light beside the bed, Jane sat up, trying to calm herself. If it was not for the doll she would go down and make a cup of tea, but after the events of the day it felt too much to deal with at the moment.

Picking up one of the children's books, she tried to focus on the words, but the image of her mother kept flashing onto the pages.

She must have dozed off, because a while later Molly's growling woke her. Jane sat forward and looked at the dog, who was staring at the door. Her ears pricked in the air as her sharp hearing listened.

'What is it?' Jane whispered, feeling the hairs on the back of her neck stiffen. Then she heard the front door slowly creak open and close. Footsteps began coming up the stairs, one step at a time, taking their time to petrify them even more.

Jane held her breath as she listened, fear making a cold sweat form on her top lip. Her eyes widened as she looked towards the bedroom door in anticipation.

The footsteps stopped outside and, after a pause, the black doorknob began to twist and the door slowly opened. Molly sprang and ran for the door, barking, her teeth bared. Jane stayed frozen to the spot, waiting for Dan to appear.

No one did appear; the only sound Jane could hear was her pounding heart and heavy breaths. Her mouth was so dry her tongue had stuck to the roof of it. Images of how badly she would suffer flashed through her head. Would she die like the man she shot? No one would ever know she was missing or even look for her as fish and water creatures slowly ate her decaying body.

They were still waiting five minutes later. Molly's lips were pulled back and little white teeth on show as she continued to point at the door. It took Jane all her energy and courage to get out of bed and look. There was not even a weapon she could use to protect herself. A coat hanger would not do much damage, she thought dismally.

The little landing was empty and so was the bathroom. Calling Molly to follow, Jane went downstairs and pushed the living room door open. The doll still lay on the floor, face down. Stepping over it, she went into the kitchen and looked in the cupboards. The cottage was empty except for her and Molly, who was now hiding behind the sofa.

They did not go back to bed that night. After picking up the bits of doll and emptying it into the rubbish bin, Jane made a cup of tea and turned the television on. The noise helped her to feel better. Molly, now calm, jumped up and sat beside her. How grateful she was when the darkness faded and daylight finally came.

By mid-morning, Jane had decided that it was Margaret trying to frighten her again. It made sense: the doll, the shadow by the kitchen window and now someone coming up the stairs. There had been a few bits disappearing too, all of which Molly had been blamed for. Firstly, her lipstick, which she knew had been in the bedroom on the dressing table. After searching everywhere and almost giving up, it was found in the back garden amongst the long grass. If the sun had not reflected off the gold case making it glimmer, it would have been lost forever.

'Molly, you must not take my make-up,' Jane had chastised.

Secondly, the television remote had been found in the little freezer compartment in the fridge. She knew Molly would not have been able to do that. Thirdly, her hair gel had been found down the toilet, and lastly, the door keys turned up, hanging on the picket fence in the back garden. It had to be Margaret; other than a ghost or Jane going mad, there was no other explanation.

Later in the day, she went out to sit with Henry, grateful for some company.

'Have you no friends of your own age, Lizzy?' he asked.

The more he got to know her the more he was intrigued; nothing made sense, and she must be so lonely.

'No,' she told him sadly. Only make-believe ones, she thought, but refrained from admitting that.

'So, what are you going to do with your life now then?'

Jane looked up at him, surprised by the question. It had not occurred to her before. She had dreams, of course, imagining herself as a fashion designer, or rescuing animals, like Fiona at the dogs' home did. But, because of her age and lack of qualifications, or reading and writing skills, it was impossible.

'I don't know,' she confessed after a long think.

'Well, you have got to do something, you can't spend your life just drawing,' he told her bluntly.

'I'd like to be a fashion designer, but without reading and writing it'd be difficult.'

'That's it then. You're still young enough, you could go to college,' he decided.

'But I can't read properly and I have no exams.'

'Then you must learn quickly and enrol in the college to gain some,' Henry using the same determined look he saved for his daughter, stated.

'Margaret!' he called, leaning over the side of his chair slightly.

It was a few minutes before she bustled out with a duster in her hand. 'What now?'

'We need to get young Lizzy into college. Could you not drive her and find out about courses?'

Margaret raised her eyes in exasperation. 'Really, Dad! You're too much... I'll order a prospectus from the computer in the library.'

Once she had gone, Henry grinned at Jane as she grimaced. 'She's beginning to like you.'

Henry was right: Jane had mastered the whole book after only a few days. Although it was a simple child's book, it was still a great achievement. She even recognised some words now on shop signs.

'Hair,' she said, while walking past a hair salon. 'Vet, paper, news.'

It was so exciting to be able to understand. By the end of one week, she had mastered most of the children's books. Every night practising till late, desperate to please Henry so she could demonstrate her achievements to him the next day.

Margaret agreed to borrow more books from the library, then insisted Jane went with her to register, which she did eagerly. It was a difficult journey as Margaret did not speak and walked so quickly, Jane had to run to keep up. Luckily, the library was not too far away.

Margaret flicked through the talking books to find one suitable and then found the written book to match.

'This will help,' she told Jane briskly. 'Listen to the tape and follow the words in the book,' she instructed.

Jane did this but kept falling asleep to the tape and losing track. The words were too big and complicated.

'Break them down,' Henry advised, 'for instance: com-pli-cat-ed.'

Jane's limited diet soon became boring. It was the only advantage she could think of about school: the dinners. If she could read maybe she could learn how to cook. But for the moment, Jane and Molly ate out every day.

The people at the café soon became used to her. They no longer scowled when she put a plate down for Molly. One of the ladies even found a special plate for the dog.

'That way we won't lose customers,' she told her colleagues.

Henry had not been sitting in the front garden for the past few days and Jane was worried. She considered knocking to ask if he was OK but Margaret scared her too much, so she dared not.

In the end, she spent her time in the back garden, pulling at the weeds. It was exciting as she uncovered a little winding path. She then felt spooked when she remembered it was the same path as the one in her dream.

It was hard with no garden tools, so Jane went and bought some from the local hardware store.

Back in her garden, it was like discovering another world, as a small rockery turned up under some brambles, which Jane scratched her hands on. There were flower beds along each fence, as she knew there would be, and marvelled over this.

'It is like discovering treasure,' she told Molly, who ran about in the clearer space.

Molly's coat was now beginning to grow back and had a lovely shine.

With the new clippers Jane cut back some of the bushes. A pile of discarded weeds began to form in the middle of the garden. Some of them were plants, but she had not known the difference as she threw another bundle on the growing pile.

Standing back, Jane admired the transformation. She could almost see the back of the garden.

'Molly, what are you doing?' she asked, going over to the dog, who was digging a hole at the edge of the fence and frantically pulling at something.

Jane helped her and tugged at the arm of a teddy bear. It was so dirty and rotted, but it reminded her of the one in her dreams. Going indoors, she put it in the sink and gave it a wash. Although the colour was faded, it had most certainly been a pink colour. She knew Margaret could not have made her dream about a teddy bear. Maybe she had owned one similar when she was a child and was just remembering it. Maybe all little girls had pink teddies and this was just a coincidence, she decided, and pegged it onto the line to dry.

After the whole day gardening, Jane was too shattered to make anything to eat, so she settled for toast. After feeding Molly her tin of dog food, she sat on the sofa and watched TV.

Molly's growling woke Jane sometime later. The room was dark, only slightly lit by a small glow from the half-moon that peeped through the window. This made the usually innocent items look sinister and unrecognisable. The television had long since turned itself off for the night, a little red light glowing in one corner.

'What's wrong, Molly?' Jane asked shakily, squinting into the dark corner of the room that Molly was now barking at and feeling that she would like to run from the house and never come back.

Suddenly the door handles of both the kitchen and living room twisted and they both flew crashing open.

Molly leaped from the sofa and disappeared behind it as Jane screamed. A bright light blazed into the room through both doors and Jane stared, horrified. She wanted to run but both entrances were blocked. The lights from both directions came twirling into the room, spinning all around her. They were hypnotic as she stared into them, wanting to turn her head from the brightness, but unable to snap herself from the vision. Her fear suddenly disappeared, leaving her feeling calm and warm as a great sense of love passed through her. Staring into the light, she began to see pictures of people and hear gentle music that was so beautiful she longed to close her eyes to listen. But she could not turn away from the images. People from all different times flashed past her, ladies with long dresses, nipped in at the waist, gentlemen with black jackets, tall hats perched on their heads. Even people dressed in Tudor costumes and beyond. Jane recognised some, and others she had never seen before. Victorian women with dark dresses, some standing with men and children, others alone. Way off in the centre of the light was a woman, becoming larger as she drew closer.

She was smiling and holding her hand out to Jane, her golden blonde hair a halo around her head as it danced about her, waving in an invisible wind. There was no doubt in her mind that the lady was Vicky, the image of her mother. In her arms she held a baby, holding it forward so Jane could see clearly. Its pink outfit showed it was a little girl, not very old.

'Isabella,' she mouthed, and pointed down at the floor.

As if someone had clicked their fingers and made it all come right, it did. The lights were gone and both doors slammed shut. Molly skulked out from behind the sofa and Jane grabbed her, feeling comfort from her warmth.

'What happened there?' Jane said, unusually calm.

'How strange that Vicky was here in this cottage. Her baby Isabella must have died,' she told Molly.

She stood up and flicked on the light switch, throwing reality across the room. The experience now seemed a dream, something she had created, like her imaginary friends. She stood for a while trying to think, fighting the urge to sleep as she still felt so calm and peaceful.

Jane went to the rug and, after moving a few bits of furniture that held the edges, she pulled it back.

Just where Vicky had pointed, was a doorway in the floor. With great effort and determination, she pulled it open, the lid crashing to the floor. Jane looked down to see stone steps leading down to whatever was under there. After all that had happened, she did not have the nerve to face the cellar.

She pulled the lid back over, covering the hole in the hope of forgetting it even existed. Once the rug was back in place, it was easier.

Chapter Sixteen

The bunker had shown nothing more than the last visit had, Mick told Dan when they got back to the house later that day.

'Well, it seems either the girl or the old lady paid £400 for the dog. So, either the old girl is very rich or they paid from our money,' Dan informed him, his eyes twinkling as he felt he had made a breakthrough.

'Time we visited the old lady then,' Mick smiled knowingly.

Scott looked from Dan to his father, his face full of worry. He did not want to be a part of this anymore. He was too involved now, there was no way out for him. Making some excuse, he went off to his room.

Mrs Flanagan was just taking a nap when the doorbell sounded. It took a while to get there and answer the furious knocking. She pulled it open a little, forgetting the chain in her sleepy state. It sprang open, almost knocking her over. Her eyes filled with fear when she saw the two men, who were now standing in the small hallway. When she recognised Dan, her eyes widened.

'Where's Jane and our money?' he snarled, knowing she was terrified and using this to his advantage.

The other man pushed past her and disappeared into the living room. She could hear him opening cupboards and the sound of smashing. A picture flashed in her mind of her precious belongings in pieces. Her and Frank's home being destroyed, the things that were to be her family's after she had gone. Tears filled her eyes as she heard Mr Tibbles cry out.

'I don't know where she is, or any money.'

Dan grabbed her around the throat and held her wobbly body upright. He pushed his face into hers. 'Where is she?' he screamed through clenched teeth.

Coming back to the hallway, Mick shook his head and ran upstairs. Again, she heard banging and crashing, things breaking. All her possessions collected over a lifetime, even her mother's and grandmother's things, broken into pieces. Coming back down, he shook his head again at Dan.

'Get out of here or I'll call the police,' Mrs Flanagan tried to sound fierce but her voice shook with sobs.

Dan brought up his other hand and slapped her around the face, letting go of her throat at the same time.

Mrs Flanagan fell crashing to the floor, gasping for air, her body shaking uncontrollably. As Dan sprang on top of her, she brought up her hand to try and push him pointlessly away. The hand gripped her firmly and was too strong for her frail years.

'Please,' she begged, 'I don't know.'

Dan brought up his fist and made to strike her again.

She was so frightened she felt the warm wetness run from her, feeling ashamed and embarrassed.

'Where is she?' he asked again.

'Thornwood Abbey,' Mrs Flanagan cried.

He let go of her and stood up and stared at the crumpled lady, who seemed to have shrunk even more.

'Why would she go there?' he stammered, more to himself than her.

Mick was now standing at the bottom of the stairs, watching the scene. 'Jesus, Dan, you've killed her!'

'Naaa, she's OK,' he grinned, as they both hurriedly left.

Unable to move, Mrs Flanagan lay there, little gasping sobs escaping her. She tried to get to her feet but it was impossible; if only she could reach the phone. It began to ring; she pulled herself along the floor into the doorway of the living room hoping to reach it. A burning pain in her chest suddenly gripped her, making her gasp and clutch herself to ease it. The pain, like a fist, went reeling into her heart. It was excruciating as it travelled down her arms and even into her hands. One of her arms flopped to her side, falling onto Mr Tibbles, who must have come to her.

'Frank,' she cried out.

Two strong arms reached out and embraced her. The pain disappeared as she fell into a blissful, empty blackness.

Since hearing from Fiona that Dan had visited the dogs' home and seen Mrs Flanagan's address, Suzanne had been telephoning her. By late afternoon, there still was no answer. Just to satisfy herself, she left the office early and drove the short distance to her house. After banging on the door a few times, she looked through the letterbox. She then went to the front room window and peered through the net curtains. It was difficult to see clearly but she was sure there was no one at home.

'Mmmm, she could be out visiting,' Suzanne told herself.

'Can I help you?' Mrs Pomfree asked, just strolling past with her shopping.

Suzanne flashed her identification. 'I can't get any answer and I'm a bit worried. Is Mrs Flanagan out?'

'No, she'll be having her nap about now. But I'll get the key just to check she's OK.'

Mrs Pomfree went into the house next door and came back a short time later. She opened the front door, calling out to alert Mrs Flanagan of the intrusion, before going inside.

They found Mrs Flanagan lying in the front room doorway, the old tabby cat curled next to her — both were dead.

Suzanne called the police and looked dismally around at the ransacked home.

'Who would want to rob her?' Mrs Pomfree cried. 'Poor old thing didn't have two beans to rub together.'

'I don't know, but it's clear they were looking for something,' Suzanne told her, sad and shaken.

The police arrived and confirmed the death was suspicious. Suzanne went to the station and made a statement, telling them everything she knew about Dan Wallace and how he had visited the dogs' home one lunchtime.

'Why would he be interested in Mrs Flanagan?' she finished.

'I don't know,' the detective sergeant pondered, 'but he was looking for something.'

'He was looking for the girl,' Suzanne said, 'but why?'

Suzanne arrived back at the office just before everyone went home, intending to work late. Helena, with her coat on ready to go, came over to see her.

'It seems that Jane Watts died when she was four months old. I can find no trace of another baby born to Toni Watts,' she informed her.

'How odd,' Suzanne said, feeling even more shaken and puzzled.

'None recorded. Only the baby girl. It seems she died of suffocation; it was recorded as cot death but had a big question mark next to the inquiry. Also, the dead Jane Watts was born six years prior to the live Jane Watts.'

'Nothing makes any sense so far.'

'No,' agreed Helena. 'The child you are searching for doesn't even exist.'

Ignoring Helena, Suzanne picked up the phone and dialled the hospital again. 'What about Isabella Lucas?' she asked, while waiting for someone to pick up.

'Not found her yet, I was just looking into it.'

The hospital told Suzanne that Toni was periodically awake but very confused.

'Bugger,' she told the phone mouthpiece and hung up.

'Think I'll still go and visit anyway, just in case.'

Before she left the office, she called the police in Thornwood Abbey and asked them to look out for Jane.

When Suzanne arrived at the hospital, a nurse was sitting by Toni's bed trying to feed her. Toni was turning her head away from the spoon and her flailing arms were knocking the food everywhere. It looked a slow process and Suzanne was sure the nurse had other things to attend to.

'Would you like me to try?' she smiled and took the spoon and yoghurt that was gratefully handed to her.

She sat down on the hard armchair beside the bed. 'Hello, Toni, my name is Suzanne Bailey. I've come to see you as I'm trying to find Jane.'

'Is that you, Vicky?' Toni asked, squinting at Suzanne.

'Do you know where Jane is, Toni?'

Toni sank back on the pillows and promptly fell asleep. Giving up, Suzanne went to the nurse's desk and asked to see someone in charge. After a few minutes, a nurse in a dark blue uniform came over and Suzanne introduced herself.

'It's the lack of kidney function that's making her confused,' she explained. 'She was so dehydrated her kidneys had stopped working. I'm afraid her internal organs are not in good shape.'

'Has anyone been in to see her?' Suzanne asked.

'Not as far as I'm aware. We have tried to reach her next of kin, but so far have not been able to get hold of anyone on the telephone number. The ward administrator has written to them, I believe.'

'Who is the next of kin?'

'Her mother.'

'Could I have her details, please?' Suzanne requested, hoping the nurse was not going to be difficult about confidentiality.

The nurse handed a brown file to her and Suzanne wrote down the address, noting it was the same one as on the letters from Vicky. She left the hospital and headed for Thornwood Abbey. It was getting late and Suzanne was hungry but felt she could not leave this any longer. She was hopeful the grandmother would throw some light on the mystery surrounding Jane.

'It's a good job I've no husband or children to get home to,' she said out loud, then felt sad that she didn't.

When she arrived in Thornwood Abbey using her navigation, she stopped at a shop and ate chips before she headed for Rebecca Watts house. It was late, the sun had now disappeared, and the air had cooled considerably. There were no lights in the house, suggesting no one was at home. Through the glass door, she could see a pile of letters and newspapers; it seemed no one had been home for some time. She knocked at the house next door and waited until someone answered.

'I'm looking for Rebecca Watts, but there's no one there.' She smiled politely to a nonplussed young man, who peered round the door edge. He turned and called to his mother, who came to the door.

'She went into a home after a fall a few months ago,' the mother informed her.

'Have you any idea which one?' Suzanne asked, her heart sinking.

'Yea, Paradise Lane, can't remember what it's called, though. Her son comes sometimes; I can tell him to call you if it helps.'

'Thank you.' Suzanne handed her a business card and left.

There was a residential home down Paradise Lane, she discovered, but it was far too late to visit that night. She turned her car around and drove back to her home.

When Dan got back with Mick to the house, they called Scott, who was in his room. Then, grabbing a can of beer, Dan pulled the ring.

'Cheers,' he lifted it up to Mick, grinning.

'So, when we going?' Mick asked, feeling impatient; the kid may not even be there, he figured.

'Tomorrow, first thing,' Dan told him, lighting a cigarette and flicking the switch on Scott's laptop.

'The old lady said she had gone to find relatives,' Dan explained. 'We need to find these relatives, and hopefully the girl is with them.'

The three of them left for Thornwood Abbey the next morning, getting caught in horrendous traffic works on the way. They were not in the best of moods by the time they arrived, after roasting in a hot car. Splitting up, they went off to search the town for Jane or the family called Watts.

Dan had found little on the computer to help. There were a few 'Watts' in the area, but which ones were related to Toni, he had no idea. She had never talked about her background or any family and he had never asked.

It did not take long to scour the small shopping area between them, meeting in the abbey gardens an hour later and wondering where to search next.

'I guess it's the pubs,' Scott suggested.

'You twat, the kid's 14 years old, she is hardly gonna be 'aving a pint, is she?' Dan grumbled.

'Why don't you go stuff yourself?' Scott retaliated, feeling fed up with the constant jibes.

Dan leapt forward and made a grab for him, but Mick managed to get between them in time.

'Will you two stop it, you're drawing attention,' he growled, pushing them apart. 'Scott's right; she may have been in the pubs. Young kids do try their luck and locals may know the family. The one I passed earlier was a bed and breakfast, it's worth a try.'

Scott stomped off, calling back that he would try one end and they could try the other.

Dan and Mick headed for the English Gentleman and the white Swan, ordering a pint of beer in each pub. Neither brought them any closer to finding Jane. The locals viewed them with suspicion in both pubs, going so far as to stop talking as they walked through the door. Even more suspicion was raised when they asked about the name Watts. No one said a word to lead them in the right direction.

Scott, having dismissed the other pub, walked in the abbey gardens waiting for the other two. Wandering over to the tearooms, he stopped to chat to an elderly lady sitting alone at a table.

'I'm waiting for my niece,' he told her. 'She was supposed to meet me here about an hour ago.' He flicked his eyes in mock annoyance. 'Honestly, youngsters, she's probably forgotten.'

'You're not so old yourself,' Rose laughed, glad to be around another youngster. 'What's her name? Maybe I know her.'

'Jane, she's 14 years old and has a little brown dog.'

'Sorry, lad, but I don't know her. The only youngster with a brown dog I know, is my friend Lizzy, but she's 18.' Rose told him, feeling sorry for the polite young man, and wishing she were more helpful.

Scott laughed. 'How strange, maybe it's fashionable to have small brown dogs amongst young girls.'

'What does she look like?' Rose asked him.

'Well, last time I saw her, she had long, blond hair. But you never know nowadays. I've not seen her for a few years. It's such a shame. I'm only here for a while; it would have been good to catch up.'

'Oh dear, I'm sorry I can't be more help. It's defiantly can't be Lizzy: her hair is short and black. In fact, I was hoping to see her today; poor love is new to the area and doesn't know many people. I would go and see her but I'm not sure which cottage she lives. I know it's just off the high street. I upset her last time we met by telling her stuff about a family called Watts that lives in the area.'

'How strange, my cousin knows the Watts family,' Scott enthused. 'What a coincidence.' He knew now he had the right girl.

'Yes, it's a small world,' agreed Rose, looking thoughtful.

Scott smiled and chatted a little more before taking his leave.

He walked slowly around the town, looking for the cottages where the old lady said Lizzy lived. There were a few houses scattered behind the shops. He walked past, trying to look discreetly in the windows. He did not know what he thought he would find; maybe the girl Lizzy, who was really Jane, just leaving or standing outside, he smiled to himself.

Most seemed empty, as people were probably at work, he guessed. He found an alley and walked down to look; it led to a large housing estate that he dismissed and turned back towards the high street, narrowly missing Jane, who was just heading home. Then, the next alley he found also led to the same estate; he doubted again that he would find cottages down there. Giving up, he went off to meet Mick and Dan, who were just emerging from the door of the White Swan.

'Nothing.' Mick shrugged as they walked back to meet Scott.

'Me neither,' he told them. 'Why don't I hang about why you two go back? I can get a bus and train later,' he suggested.

Mick looked surprised at his son. It was unusual for him to be so helpful. 'Tell you what, there's a café near the abbey, let's get some grub and think about this.'

Dan and Mick decided to drive home, leaving Scott behind to see if he could find any leads to Jane.

'Maybe another youngster wouldn't be so suspicious asking questions,' Dan said.

'True, it doesn't seem she's here, but you never know. Would be good to tie up loose ends and just make sure,' he agreed, handing Scott some money.

'Oh, I think she's here,' Dan told him.

It was late in the afternoon when Suzanne was able to find time to head back to the nursing home. Crossing her fingers, she rang the doorbell to the large old house.

'Yes, Rebecca does live here,' the young carer told her, requesting she sign a visitors' book before leading her to a large living room.

The room smelt of urine and boiled cabbage, and the television blared out to several sleeping residents. There must have been at least 15 hard armchairs lined against the walls. Suzanne was shown to a tiny lady, who was obviously blind and hard of hearing.

'Rebecca!' the young assistant shouted, while clutching the hand of a very frail lady. 'You have a visitor.'

'Is it Alex?' Rebecca asked, raising her hand to feel for a human nearby.

'Hello, Rebecca,' Suzanne shouted, 'my name is Suzanne Bailey, I have come about your daughter.'

'My daughters! They are both dead,' Rebecca informed her.

Suzanne turned to the assistant. 'Could we go somewhere private, please?'

The carer did not look too pleased as she huffed, and without speaking, she went off to find a wheelchair.

They were taken to a little bedroom, which Suzanne assumed was Rebecca's. Once the assistant left, she sat on the bed and touched Rebecca's hand.

'Can you tell me why you said both your daughters are dead? I know you sadly lost Vicky, but what about Toni?' she gently asked.

The old, cloudy blind eyes looked towards her. 'Why do you want to know?'

'I'm looking for your granddaughter Jane, Toni's daughter. I'm a social worker.'

'Toni's daughter Jane is dead, poor little mite. I found her; she was such a beautiful baby, so well behaved and quiet. She was only four months old. Devastated I was.'

'What happened to Toni, do you know?'

'After the baby died, she ran off. I heard she died of a drug overdose about five years ago. All my family is dead except Alex, my son.'

'Can I talk to him?' Suzanne asked hopefully, not wanting to distress the lady any more than she had already.

'He'll be in soon if you want to. But he won't like no social worker poking around, though,' Rebecca told her.

'OK, I'll wait. What time does he come?'

'About three-ish.'

They sat in silence as Rebecca nodded off, snoring gently. She woke with a start ten minutes later and looked towards Suzanne.

'You lost your baby too, didn't you?'

'How did you know that?' she asked, feeling a little odd but accepting the supernatural, as she was a strong believer.

'I know all sorts,' Rebecca answered. 'Just because I'm blind doesn't mean I don't see.'

'Then you must know Toni is not dead,' Suzanne goaded.

'She's dead to me. And I do not think her long for this world anyway. A bad one, her. It's not her fault, though. They did wrong to her, messed her head up. She was such a lovely child too.'

'What do you mean?' Suzanne asked.

'Don't matter.' Rebecca closed her eyes again.

'Do you know where Jane is? Toni's child,' Suzanne asked.

'Yes, I told you dead. You will find out soon.'

'Can I help you?' a man's voice boomed out, startling Suzanne so much she almost fell off the chair. It was clear that he was Toni's brother as he had the same blue eyes with light wavy, brown hair. Where Toni's eyes were cold and hard, this man's were gentle and kind. He was about 37 and certainly looked a lot younger than Toni; the alcohol must have aged her terribly.

Suzanne introduced herself to him and lifted her hand to shake his. He ignored her and walked straight past to kiss his mother on the cheek.

'Is that you, Alex? We've got some social worker poking around.'

'Yes, Mum,' he smiled apologetically at Suzanne.

She laughed and held out her hand again to him, 'Suzanne Bailey.'

He shook it this time 'Tact was never Mum's strong point.'

'I'm sorry to intrude but I'm looking for Jane Watts, Toni's daughter.'

'We heard Toni was dead,' Alex told her, his voice becoming a little defensive at the mention of his sister. 'Mum has had enough people poking about and asking questions over the years, she just wants some peace now in her old age.'

'It's OK, Alex, I think this one will help us,' Rebecca smiled affectionately, putting forward her hand so he could take hers. 'She'll help put ghosts to rest, so I can die in peace.'

'Mum, we've been down this road a thousand times. What's gone is gone. You have to let the past go,' Alex gently chastised.

Rebecca laughed. 'You'll see,' she said, a beaming smile lighting her crinkly, wise face.

Alex sat in a chair next to Rebecca and they both looked towards Suzanne, waiting for her to speak.

'I'm sorry to burst in on you like this. It's a long story but I'll explain as best as I can. Toni Watts is not dead but critically ill in hospital. She has a daughter, Jane Watts, who has gone missing. No one has seen her for a few weeks. We think Jane may have headed here looking for family. So that's why I have come to see you.'

'Toni did have a daughter Jane. She died at four months old. That was almost 20 years ago,' Alex told her, giving his mum's hand a reassuring squeeze. He knew talk of the past still pained her.

'So I understand. We believe she had another child and named her Jane also. However, she never registered the birth. This Jane is 14 years old.'

At first, Alex looked a bit startled and Suzanne got the impression he was about to say something. He changed his mind and did a quick calculation.

'We don't know about another child. Toni ran away from home when she was 16. The only person she kept in touch with was her twin sister, Vicky, who died when she was 25. After that, no one heard from Toni; we never have, until you showed up now.'

'I'm sorry for your loss but none of this makes any sense, does it? Where would Jane go? She told a friend she was coming here,' Suzanne puzzled.

'Yes, it does,' Rebecca added and they both looked at her. 'Go to the cottages.'

'Mum, don't be daft. That was all years ago.'

'Make the woman go to the cottages, Alex,' she demanded.

'What cottage?' Suzanne asked, feeling more puzzled and wishing they would just explain what was going on.

Alex sighed and stood up. 'OK,' he pacified, 'but I really don't think it's going to help going over old ground that has not only been gone over but dug to death,' he objected, but relented to please his mother.

'I'm telling you, Alex, the young girl is there.'

'Mum's always thought she was a mystic,' he smiled apologetically.

Chapter Seventeen

Jane tried to push thoughts of the cellar to the back of her mind. She took Molly out as a distraction, walking around the shops to find something nice to buy and even venturing to the library and borrowing more books. Nothing helped; she had to know if a body was down there.

After running upstairs to grab the torch, which was still in the suitcase, Jane pulled back the rug again. She felt her palms sweat as she visualised all sorts of horrible things jumping out as she lifted the lid.

Molly hung over the edge, sniffing, not brave this time to run down. Using the torch, Jane lowered her hand cautiously into the hole, just in case something grabbed her. It was hopeless: she could not see anything, so she bravely walked down the steps.

It was creepy and her imagination ran away with her. Now wishing she had not watched so many horror films, she gingerly ventured on, flashing the torch around for a quick assessment. There was a light bulb hanging in the middle. She looked around for a switch, seeing one she had passed back at the entrance. The bulb flicked into life and dimly lit the room. It was very small with white painted walls, peeling in places to show red brick underneath. Huge dark cobwebs hung from the ceilings. Around the walls were piles of boxes and bits of old furniture. Most of the items were a child's disused belongings: a pram, a pushchair, a few dolls and dusty soft toys and even some little clothes and a cot. Jane ran her fingers over them gently, wondering why they were stored there. Lifting the lid on a cardboard box, she found other baby things, bottles, bib, babygros and a few dummies.

'Isabella's, maybe?' she said out loud.

The next box she opened contained men's clothes and toiletries. In another box, Jane found women's clothes, jewellery, shoes and bags.

She closed them, not wanting to intrude anymore. Turning to go back upstairs, Jane heard a scraping from the floor below her feet. She froze, her feet glued to the spot.

'It's a grave,' she breathed.

The scrapping turned into a knocking, not just one knocking but loads. She heard the sound of children crying and screaming beneath her. Dropping the torch, she ran all the way upstairs, slamming the hatch and pulling back the rug back into place.

Taking Molly, Jane ran from the cottage with a vow never to return.

'You seem troubled today, Lizzy, is anything wrong?' Henry asked, when they were sitting in the garden.

Jane looked into his eyes, desperate for someone to confide in, but not wanting to trust anyone. He would think her potty, she thought, if she did try and explain about the cottage.

'No. I didn't sleep much last night so am just a bit tired,' she told him.

Henry stayed silent as he studied her face. Lizzy was hiding something; she was jumpy and kept looking nervously behind her.

'Lizzy, please, tell me what's wrong?' Henry tried again.

She opened her mouth to speak and then stopped herself. How could she begin to explain what had happened?

Henry gave up: if Lizzy would not confide him there was nothing he could do. She was such a pretty girl, if it wasn't for all the earrings, he thought to himself. Plus, the strange, spiky hair, but then that was youngsters.

They sat, reading for a while and chatting, before Henry decided to go indoors himself, as he did not feel so good lately and also had not been sleeping.

Jane took Molly for a long walk, allowing herself time to think. Lost deep in her thoughts, she did not notice a young man watching her from the ruins of an old wall in the gardens. As she started to go back to the town, he ran up behind her.

'Jane?'

She turned quickly, coming face to face with Scott, her eyes trying to register who he was and how he knew her by her real name. Molly began to growl and pull towards him with her teeth bared.

He grabbed her arm, trying to dodge the dog and pulled her behind the wall, where he had been watching her. She began to struggle to escape.

'It's OK, I won't hurt you,' Scott reassured, which was difficult as his voice sounded as panicky as she felt. 'I'm trying to help you, not scare you.'

'Why would you do that?' Jane asked, desperately trying to think straight and calm her panic.

'I know you have the money. I don't want Dan to find you and hurt you. They're looking for you and it won't be long before they find you, like I have,' he told her, his eyes looking earnestly into hers.

She felt frightened. 'I don't understand.'

Jane didn't, why would he want to help her?

'It's a long story but I can't bear to see anyone else hurt. Dan is an evil man and my dad is so tangled up with it all and easily led by him. They have done terrible things and I don't want to be a part of it anymore.'

Jane did not know why but for some reason she started to relax. She studied the man, who looked not much older than herself. 'Were you part of the robbery?' she asked.

'They talked me into helping them. I didn't know anyone would get hurt. Dan shot two security men. They were my mates. I just want out of here,' he told her, his voice breaking with the haunting thoughts of all the bloodshed. He could not get his head around how someone could be standing one minute and a mass of gunge the next.

'Why didn't you go to the police?' Jane asked, glad he hadn't because she would not have escaped.

'How could I, after helping them? I'm a part of it and would go to prison.'

Jane sat quiet for a while. She saw him in the same predicament as herself: unhappy and desperate for a way out. So desperate you would do anything to escape. They would both go to prison if the police found them.

'So now what?' she asked.

'If I help you, will you give me some of the money so I can go off and start up on my own? I'm a gardener, almost,' he added. 'I could start my own business somewhere and change my name. They would never find me.' His eyes stared desperately into hers.

Jane stood for a while, contemplating what he had said. 'How do you know I have the money?' she asked after another long pause.

'Because you didn't deny you haven't,' he said simply.

Jane fell quiet again, trying to digest Scott's words and weigh it all up.

'What if you are trying to trick me?'

'Why would I do that? You've already admitted you have the money. I could just run off and tell them I've found you, just as easy as you could agree and disappear again. We'll just have to trust each other.'

'That's true,' Jane admitted. 'OK, it's a deal.'

Scott smiled gratefully to her. 'Give me your mobile number,' he took out his own phone.

'I haven't got one. I had no need of it so didn't bother.'

'Great,' he grimaced, 'this is going to be difficult. Give me some money and I'll go and buy one.'

Jane paused, trying to think. Then making a decision, she handed over three twenty-pound notes.

'Stay here, I'll be back soon.'

Scott was gone for about half an hour. Jane began to worry that he would come back with Dan and she would be found. She kept looking around the corner of the wall to watch for him.

He appeared behind her, holding a small carrier; if Molly had not growled again, she would not have known he was there. Scott gave her a quick lesson on how to use the phone, as luckily the battery was slightly charged. He put in his number and then texted his own phone so he had Jane's number.

'It's safer to text. Don't phone me,' he stressed.

Jane, suddenly aware of how good-looking Scott was, went all coy and could not face telling him she could not write too well.

'Just tell me,' he asked, handing her the phone, 'how did you manage to move and hide all that money?'

Jane looked at the phone, thinking she would never learn to use something so complicated. She did not want to answer him or tell him where the money was.

She looked at him, grinning. 'Thanks, Scott,' she said, taking the opportunity to examine his dark wavy hair and deep, sincere green eyes.

He held his hands up. 'OK, I get the picture.' He grinned back.

He had instantly liked Jane: she was clever and very pretty for a kid. 'I have to go now so I can get back. I'll text to warn you of anything you need to know. Keep the phone charged at all times and keep credit on it. Stay here until I've gone. Just in case anyone sees us together.'

'How much do they know about me?' Jane asked as he turned from her.

'Not much; they think you're here somewhere but so far they have no clues. It won't be long, though; they are looking for your mother's family, thinking you have gone there.'

Jane stayed quiet while she thought about this. She was glad now that she had not told anyone her real name or tried to find them herself. 'I need to move on from here,' she said.

He smiled apologetically. 'I think they are going back to see your mother,' he told her. 'It's the dog that gives you away. But yes, you're right. If you stay here, they'll find you.'

'Can I come with you?' she asked hopefully.

'That would be madness. Look, don't do anything for now. Let me see what I can find out first. I'll warn you when the time's right. Then you will need to leave here.'

Jane had no choice but to return to the cottage. Doubts about Scott kept creeping into her mind. Her heart did a little somersault when she thought of him, trying to remember every detail of what he looked like. She was so glad she had not told him where she lived. But then again, how long had he been following her? He probably already knew. If he was genuine it would be good to have an ally, she thought to herself.

As night-time grew closer and the light began to fade Jane felt really scared. She was so tired from not having much sleep the night before, but was too frightened to go to bed. She went upstairs and pulled the thin cotton curtains, thankful they did not block out the fading light completely. It was a warm night, and the upstairs of the cottage felt airless and oppressive from the hot daytime sun. Lying on top of the bed fully clothed, she tried to sleep. It was hopeless, as her eyes sprang open every few minutes as she checked the room. In the end, she went back downstairs. Pulling the sofa cushions onto the floor, she lay there instead. She felt worse, knowing there was something horrible underneath her. Sleep never came so Jane put the cushions back on the sofa and sat up with the television on. It would be good to leave here, she decided, as there was no way she was going to stay in the cottage another night. She picked up a book and tried to concentrate on the words, all the time looking fearfully around the room.

It was dark when Jane woke with a start to the noise of Molly growling. Fear gripped her as she fumbled for the switch on the bedside lamp and then realised she was downstairs and not up.

As she reached out, a hand grabbed at her own. She felt the definition of fingers and knuckles in the darkness. She screamed and within seconds was off the sofa and standing with her back to the kitchen door, Molly by her side.

Jane stared wide-eyed into the living room, straining to see the silhouette of who was in the room with her. The moon was bright, making it easy with her night vision to see across the room. Nothing was there, so she began to relax slightly, her breath slowing to a steadier pace.

It quickened again as a pinprick of light appeared from the centre of the ceiling. It vibrated in one spot for a while before moving around the room. Other lights began to appear until the ceiling was no longer visible. The pictures on the walls began to shake and the two cushions from the sofa floated upwards. They hovered for a while before flying towards the window and falling on top of the sideboard.

Jane was frozen in terror as something hit her in the face, and she screamed. A plate on the table, which she had earlier eaten toast from, whipped into the air and smashed against the wall. Molly, who had shot behind the sofa, appeared and began barking upwards. Her body was whisked into the air and hovered halfway towards the great white void that was once the ceiling.

The dog whimpered, confused. Jane, suddenly finding strength to move, grabbed at Molly's legs and pulled her to safety. Holding the wiggling dog, she ran through the chaos as everything in the room was now flying in a circle towards the ceiling. Something hit her in the temple and she staggered, almost falling onto the sofa and dropping Molly. Determination kept her upright; grabbing again at the dog, she ran to the living room door, which refused to open as she pulled frantically. A small hand touched the back of her head and Jane, almost hysterical, screamed out. The door sprang open and a white form hovered in the doorway reaching out its hand towards her. It was a woman, whose hair hung long and straight, blowing about with the energy that buzzed in the room. Jane screamed again and recoiled from the hand, frantically not knowing where to turn.

'Elizabeth,' the woman shouted urgently. 'Take my hand!'

Jane realised the apparition was Margaret in her nightdress, her eyes as wide with terror as Jane's. She reached out towards her and gripped the girl's arm, pulling her towards the door. They both ran from the cottage and along the path. Margaret glanced back to see the lights still whirling around the room through the window.

'What the hell…' Margaret started to say as the front door slammed and then reopened. Something flew out and smashed on the path.

Neither stopped to see what it was as they rushed into the house next door, slamming the door behind them.

They couldn't speak: there were no words to explain what had happened next door. They stood dumbly staring at each other, Jane gasping air through hysterical sobs. She sank to the floor against the door.

Margaret was the first to move as she went into the living room; lifting up a crystal decanter, she poured two large brandies with shaking hands, forcing one of the glasses into Jane's.

'Drink,' she commanded.

Jane's own trembling hands shook so much she almost spilt the brandy. Margaret clasped her own over them and helped the glass to her lips. The liquid burned Jane's throat so much she coughed and spluttered.

'What's going on, Margaret?' shouted Henry from the next room.

'Nothing, Dad, it's OK, just the telly being too loud. Go back to sleep,' she said, her voice shaking as much as her body.

Margaret pulled Jane to her feet and ushered her into the living room, gently pushing her onto the sofa. She was still clinging to Molly, who looked just as dazed they both did.

'Deep breaths, Elizabeth,' Margaret instructed.

Jane did as she was told and tried to calm herself.

'What the hell was happening in there?'

'I... don't know. I thought at first it was you trying to scare me, but it's got worse and worse,' Jane told her.

She began to tell Margaret about the strange events, her voice garbled and shocked, making it difficult to follow the story. Margaret felt hairs prickling the back of her neck as Jane spoke.

'But why would you think it me?' she asked once Jane had finished.

'Because you don't like me and Molly,' Jane began to sob again.

Margaret looked horrified; she had been appalling to the young girl, making her think she was so spiteful.

She put her hand on Jane's, 'I'm so sorry. I'm an absolute misery,' she apologised. 'I would never do something so horrible to torment you like that. I... I... was just jealous, I think.'

'Jealous, why?' Jane blinked in disbelief.

'Because you are so young and pretty and I'm old and sour. Dad thinks the world of you.'

'I'm not pretty,' Jane sniffed. 'I'm ugly.'

Margaret laughed and got up to pour herself another large brandy. She took a gulp. 'Elizabeth, you are a beautiful young lady, and so loving and gentle. I was wrong to be so harsh on you. As for the cottage, I don't know what to say. No one has lived there for years. My brother stayed in it for a while about 10 or 11 years ago, but since then, apart from a few people staying here and there a few months at a time, it's been empty.'

Just then the living room door swung open making them both jump, and they stared wide-eyed at it. Jane felt hysterics rising in her stomach and was just about to start screaming when Henry wheeled himself through the doorway.

'Dad, for goodness' sake, you scared us half to death. What are you doing up?' Margaret's voice was shaken again.

'You think I'm silly; I knew something was wrong. What's happened?' Henry said, feeling shaky himself.

Margaret took a deep breath and began to explain, Jane adding bits that she had got wrong.

Henry calmly listened without interrupting. 'Good grief, you're telling me the cottage is haunted?' he burst out at the end of the story. 'We've never had any ghosts in there before. Or anybody reporting them, although I must say people never hung around long.' Henry scratched his balding head. He was not sure he believed in ghosts but both Lizzy and Margaret looked pale and stressed, so something had happened.

Margaret stood up. 'Come on, Dad, back to bed, you know how grumpy you get without your sleep.' She kissed him on the head and twisted around his chair.

'Can Lizzy stay here tonight, Margaret?' he asked, sounding like a child.

'Of course, she can. I certainly wouldn't be evil enough to send her back there now, would I?' she nodded towards the wall that adjoined next door and they all stared glumly at it.

'I'll make a bed up on the sofa,' Margaret announced.

Margaret came back from Henry's room a few minutes later to find Jane sitting outside the door, shaking again.

'Come on, it's OK, I'll make you some hot chocolate,' she said kindly, suddenly feeling motherly towards the vulnerable young girl.

'The three cottages belong to me,' she began to explain, trying to take Jane's mind off the events, which she was also struggling to understand. 'This one is the largest. Your one is the tiniest. My husband and me bought them many years ago. We intended to knock them all into one and make a big house. In fact, I believe many years ago the cottages were one big house.

'Why didn't you do it?' Jane asked, surprised that Margaret had been married.

Sadness clouded her eyes, 'My husband died in a car accident. We had only been married two years. I never bothered when there was only me here. Three years ago, my mother died and Dad was diagnosed with lung cancer. The family home where they lived was too big and too far from the town. So, I bought Dad here to live with me. It's easier to care for him and close to all the shops and doctors. When Dad goes, I'll be on my own, a bitter and twisted old lady, dull and frumpy.' Margaret pulled at her white winceyette nightdress to prove it.

'When we brought the cottages, there was only a small high street. Behind the cottages were fields which led to the abbey gardens, it was so beautiful …' she stopped speaking as Jane was gaping at her, bewildered.

'The field outside the garden led down to a little stream and had wild flowers in the summer,' Jane added, her eyes staring beyond Margaret's to some distant place.

'How did you know that?'

'I saw it in my dreams,' Jane said, amazed and disbelieving. 'Who is Isabella?'

It was Margaret's turn to look surprised at Jane. 'Where did you hear that name? '

'In my dreams again,' Jane told her, eager to hear the long-awaited answer. 'And...' she began, but changed her mind. It was too chancy to tell Margaret the truth.

'And what, Elizabeth?'

'Nothing, just a name I heard in my dreams.'

Margaret looked sad. 'Isabella was a little girl who lived in the cottage once. She died, at least we think she did, no one really knows. It was a long time ago now. Her body was never found.'

Margaret hesitated at telling Jane the story of Isabella. She did not want to frighten her anymore.

'Do… do you think she is buried somewhere in the cottage?' Margaret suddenly asked.

Jane thought for a while. 'I'm not sure. Please let's not talk about it anymore,' she begged, starting to shake again at the thought of a body in the cellar as well as ghosts. 'I think I would feel better if it was daylight.'

Margaret smiled sadly. 'Me too. OK, enough for one night.'

'I was frumpy and dull too,' Jane suddenly said, changing the subject. 'Since coming into money, I went shopping and brought lots of clothes. The hairdressers transformed me,' Jane confessed, fighting for something to brighten the mood, and optimistically thinking she could solve Margaret's problems.

'I don't think there is hope for me,' she smiled. 'You're young and have a life ahead of you still.'

'Well, I think we should go to town and buy you new clothes. Modern ones,' Jane enthused. 'Please?'

Margaret laughed, caught in the young magic, which lightened her miserable life. 'OK. It's a deal. But for now, I think it is bed time.'

She saw Jane shudder. 'Please don't leave me down here on my own.'

Suddenly there was an almighty bang on the wall from next door. Both of them jumped and clung frantically to each other. Molly begun to growl towards the wall.

'Do you mind sharing?' Margaret asked, still clinging to Jane.

Jane shook her head and they both, including Molly, went upstairs together.

Margaret lent Jane a nightdress and they both got into bed together. It felt very strange as Jane had never shared a bed before, but how grateful she was not to be alone. Molly jumped up on the end of the bed and curled up; at first Margaret was going to object, but she changed her mind when she saw Jane's pleading expression.

Chapter Eighteen

Dan and Mick returned to Mick's house after leaving Scott behind.

'What now?' Mick asked, taking a cold lager from the fridge and handing one to Dan.

'I'm going back to the flat to see Toni. She's got to know where the kid is,' Dan answered, taking a gulp from the can.

'How do you know she didn't set us up?' Mick said. 'She could have arranged for the girl to take the money behind your back. She's the only one, other than us, that knew anything.'

Dan sat and thought about this. It was true: she could have and then arranged for Jane to hide at her family's house. He put down the beer, 'Mmmm, maybe you have a point.' Without saying anymore, he walked out of the front door.

Judging by the pile of letters and papers, Toni had not been home for a while. He pondered on Mick's words; he was right: she must have done a bunk with the money.

He walked into the kitchen and spotted Suzanne's note on the table, giving it a vague glance. He went into the bedroom, stepping over the patch of dried, bloody vomit and urine on the floor. He did not fancy ringing some social worker because it was too risky. But then again, they may have taken Jane into care, he pondered, trying to decide what to do. Eventually, he went and asked the neighbour if they knew where Toni was.

'An ambulance took her away. The police were 'ere and everything,' the elderly lady informed him.

'Do you know what hospital?' Dan asked, wondering what had happened.

'No idea, sorry.'

He called the local and was put through to the Records department. They could not help him but suggested a few more he could try. In the end, he found Toni had been taken to St George's.

'It's Toni Watts's husband; can you tell me how my wife is today, please? I've been away and only just found out she's with you.' The lie rolled smoothly from his tongue.

'Goodness,' the nurse exclaimed, 'we didn't know there was a husband. I'm so sorry. She was brought in after collapsing. She's comfortable, but slightly confused. I can't really tell you any more than that. Shall I tell her you send your love or something?'

'Yea, whatever.' He hung up the phone.

It was difficult to decide, but eventually he went to the hospital.

Toni was asleep; three very elderly people occupied other beds in the small unit. None of them looked very coherent and two seemed close to death.

Dan looked at Toni and wondered what he had ever seen in her. She looked so old, her skin ashen with a tinge of yellow. Dark rings circled her eyes and her hair hung down, lank and greasy. She had been fun when he first met her, always ready for a joke and a good drinking pal. In fact, he mused, she could drink him under the table and all his mates put together. With nowhere to live, Dan soon charmed his way into her home. He hadn't bargained on her having a kid, but she was no trouble. Half the time, they didn't know she was there. Half the time, he smiled ironically, she wasn't. In the end, he fancied Jane more than her mother: scruffy and unkempt, but ripe and just ready for a man like Dan.

Toni moaned and mumbled some incoherent words in her sleep, breaking his thoughts. He leant forward and shook her arm.

'Toni,' he whispered as loudly as he dared.

She moaned again and mashed her dry mouth.

'Toni,' he shook her again, and this time her eyes flew open and she stared at him.

'Dan, you came back,' she said, the dullness of her eyes lighting slightly.

'Yes, Toni, what happened to you?'

'It was him who did it,' she nodded her head to the lady in the next bed and Dan looked over. 'He stole my life and he made me kill my baby. I'll never forgive him, Dan.' Her head fell back on the pillow. She looked exhausted from just that small show of emotion.

'Are you saying you killed Jane, Toni?' Dan asked, not understanding what she was talking about.

'Yes, I killed her. I smothered her while she was asleep. Poor little soul.' Toni began to cry.

'Bloody hell, Toni, when did this happen? Did she say where the money was before you done away with her?'

Toni sniffed a few times and turned to him. ''Bout time you showed up,' she said.

Dan could feel his temper boiling again, and he wanted to slap her into talking, but a few nurses were milling about attending the other patients.

'Will you tell me what happened to the money? Please, Toni. We can be out of here then and make a new life for ourselves. Just think of that. Where is the money?'

'What money, Alex?' she asked, looking at him with a screwed-up expression, which annoyed him further.

'Where's Jane and the money?' he asked through gritted teeth.

'Dead, she's dead!'

'Can you tell me more about Toni Watts, please?' Dan asked at the nurse's station. 'She keeps saying she killed her daughter Jane. Is that true?'

The young nurse left and went off to find the right person for him to talk to. She came back a short while later with another nurse.

'I'm afraid she's very confused,' the nurse explained, looking hassled and needing to get on as she was very behind with her workload. 'I'm sure the new drugs will help her soon. Her kidneys were in a very bad state,' she told him, hoping he would not hold her up much longer.

'Has she killed her daughter?' he asked her.

'Goodness, I hope not, we have not had any reports of a dead daughter.'

Dan thanked her and gave one of his biggest smiles. She hurried off, grateful the meeting had not taken too long. Once she had disappeared back into a bay, Dan lent over the desk and flicked through some of the files he could see in a holder. Finding Toni's, he opened the first page and saw the next of kin. So, the old girl was right: there were relatives in Thornwood Abbey, he smiled to himself. He pulled out the page, threw the file on the desk and left the hospital.

Suzanne walked to the nursing home's reception with Alex.

'I've no idea where to head now; any suggestions?' she asked, glumly.

'None whatsoever,' Alex shrugged. 'If I do meet this girl, who you tell me is Toni's daughter, I'll call you,' he reassured her.

'She's in danger. For some reason, Toni's partner is looking for her. He's a dangerous man. He has already killed an elderly friend of Jane's.'

Alex looked shocked. 'But why?' he asked stupidly, as she had already said she did not know.

'I think the police know more than they're letting on and are after him. But why he's interested in Jane, I have no idea.'

'Well, all I can suggest is the cottages that Mum said. But she rambles a lot. Goodness knows why she thinks the child would go there.'

He wrote down the address on a piece of paper from the back of the signing-in book and handed it to Suzanne. She thanked him and left, feeling his eyes on her back as she climbed in her car. She had no choice but to head home for now. It was getting late and she had other work to deal with. There was nothing more she could do to find Jane, other than hope the police spotted her or try the cottage Rebecca had suggested.

'Right, Mick, me old mate, we're going back to Thornwood Abbey. It turns out little Jane has a granny that lives there,' Dan told him, grinning in triumph.

'Well, I never. How did you find that out?'

'Never you mind,' Dan, grinning wider, tapped the side of his nose with his finger. 'Grab us a beer, Scotty.'

Scott, who had arrived home a short time earlier, went to the fridge and threw a can at Dan, hoping it exploded all over his face when he opened it. He then sat in the armchair and flicked the TV over.

'So, when we off?' Mick asked.

'Tomorrow morning, I guess it's a better time than any. I think we'll watch the house for a while this time. Don't want to alert anyone, do we?'

'I'll come with you?' Scott offered. 'If you want, I can do another round of the town?' He was due back at work the next day, but had decided he would rather keep an eye on his dad and Dan. Without them knowing, he had handed in his notice a few days ago. Even without the promise of Jane's money, he had decided to leave. Desperate to not raise suspicion, he did not want to go too quickly. Colonel Potts was still in hospital and not in good health.

'Pneumonia,' Old Pete had told him, with the sort of nod that suggested the old boy would not make it.

More blood on all their hands, Scott thought glumly, his more than the others, as he had helped in the first place. Two new guards had already started to work on the estate. Scott had told Pete he wanted to move on: he no longer felt comfortable working there. The explanation had been accepted, as none of them felt they wanted to be there anymore. A big black cloud now loomed over the place; no one ever smiled or spoke much. There was no light-hearted banter as there was before the robbery, just a dismal depression that overtook them as they walked through the metal gates each morning. Even the children were quiet and not their usual rowdy, cheeky selves.

Now young Scott was leaving and he could not wait to be away from there or his dad, and more so Dan. He had thought a lot about Jane and her asking to go with him. Maybe she was right: with all that money they could buy a house and make a good life together, him being like an older brother.

'You're not even listening, are you? Once that telly is on you're in another world,' Mick was saying.

'Sorry, Dad, I was miles away. What did you say?'

'It seems that nutter Toni may have done away with Jane. We're wondering if the money has been taken back to her family. If all you can do is stare blankly, forget it.'

They both left to go to the pub and Scott used the opportunity to text Jane. After an hour and still no response, he called her.

'The number you have dialled is unavailable, please try again later,' an automated voice told him.

Had she thrown the mobile and done a runner? he wondered. The dreams, which had grown since conspiring with her, began to melt away into a big slushy pool, dried up by the sun and scattered into dust. He tried to tell himself different excuses, like she was out of range, or had forgotten to charge, or even turn on the phone. But his mind drifted back to the same conclusion: Jane had dumped him.

The next day, with still no word from Jane, Scott left with the other two to find Rebecca Watts's house. It was not too difficult, although the numbers of the houses did not seem to be very well organised.

The house was situated on a very monotonous council estate, where they all looked the same. Grey breezeblock buildings, with little courtyard gardens, surrounded by high wooden slatted fencing. If the front doors had not been different colours, they would have thought they were going round in a circle.

Finally, the right address was found and they sat outside for a while to assess any happenings. A few people walked past the car looking in, instantly suspicious at the three men who sat there. It did not take too long until a man came along; using a key, he went into the house.

It was only about ten minutes before he came out, carrying a plastic bag with contents.

'Follow him, Scott,' Dan hissed. 'Carefully though, you know what an idiot you are.'

'Fuck off,' spat Scott, getting out of the car, glad to be away from them.

In another vain attempt, he tried Jane again. The phone was still off, convincing him he was right in his assumption. He felt really disappointed and let down, but, in a funny way, not surprised. Who could blame her? He somehow admired her cleverness and bravery at such a young age.

'There's no one living there,' Dan said to Mick once Scott had gone.

Having noted the man had used a Chubb key to unlock and relock the door, Mick and Dan got out of the car and went around the back of the house. The gate leading to the garden was secured with a large padlock.

'We'll go in after dark,' Dan advised. 'See if there's anything to lead us to Jane.'

'What if she is dead?'

'Hopefully we'll find out either way. She did something with the money and we haven't anywhere else to look. Wonder where she stashed the body?'

'What shall we do till then?' Mick asked.

'Food,' Dan grinned, thumping his friend on the back.

Scott followed Alex out of the estate and into a street, which in turn led to a much nicer road than the council estate they had just left.

Alex turned into a driveway and, unlocking a front door, went inside.

Scott left him and ran back to the car, telling Mick and Dan where the man had gone. They drove to the house, parking a safe distance away and waited.

It was an hour later when Alex came out again, retrieved his car from the adjoining garage, and drove out onto the same main road. After stopping at a garage and filling up with petrol, he drove to a nursing home.

'Bet Granny's in there then,' Dan guessed.

'Now what? Don't seem like the kid's here,' Mick said.

'Let's go back to his house; he must be a son or relative of some sort,' Dan suggested. 'Maybe the girl's in there.'

They went back and continued to watch the house for a while.

'Why don't you knock, see if a dog barks?' Mick suggested.

'Not bad, geezer, not bad.' Dan got out of the car and knocked. It was not long before a young girl answered, wearing pink fluffy pyjamas and a matching dressing gown. At first, he thought it was Jane; she certainly looked like her with the same long blond hair and blue eyes. This girl was older though and by the looks of her had still been in bed.

'Yes?' she asked, annoyed at the disturbance.

In an instant, Dan's hand flew out and grabbed the girl around the throat, pushing her into the hallway and against the wall.

She screamed out in terror as he produced a knife and put it to her throat.

'Where's Jane?' he snarled at her.

Seeing what was happening, both Mick and Scott jumped out of the car and ran into the house.

'Please don't hurt me,' the girl pleaded, her eyes dilated with terror.

Scott guessed her to be about sixteen or seventeen. His own heart began to pound as he imagined Dan slitting the pretty young throat. He had no illusion that he would do just that once he had finished with her.

'Check the house,' Dan commanded, flicking his head at Scott and Mick.

He turned back to the terrified girl. 'Just tell me where she is!'

'Who? I don't know a Jane,' she choked, too afraid to fight back as the knife was cutting into her throat.

She could feel a stream of blood running down her neck, where it had broken the skin.

Scott had not moved, his eyes flicking from Dan to the girl, frozen to the spot, not knowing what to do. He looked around for an object to hit Dan over the head with, but he could see the knife was cutting the girl's skin. If he whacked him, Dan may kill her as a reaction.

'Now tell me where she is and I'll let you go. You seem like a nice, honest girl. Far too young and pretty to die.'

'Please, I don't know who you're talking about. Please, let me go. My dad'll be home soon. Please,' she pleaded, tears rolling down her face.

Dan grinned, his eyes lighting up, a look of excitement spread across his face. He eased his hold on her throat and began to pull the knife slowly over her jugular.

In an instant Scott snapped out of his daze, picked up a heavy glass vase and thrust into Dan's head.

Dan heard the loud, dull thud before he felt it. His eyes lost sight for a moment and all he could see was lots of little pinpricks of light.

Scott hit him again, and Dan fell forward, dropping the knife.

The young girl tried to register what was happening. Her hands went to her throat, covering the wound Dan had carved there.

Scott looked from Dan's crumpled form to the girl, whose startling blue eyes were wide and full of fear and confusion. Then her fingers moved slightly, showing the slit thick red blood began to drip from. The blue eyes grew even wider with disbelief and her mouth opened to scream out.

'It's OK,' Scott told her, grabbing her hand, 'you'll be OK.'

He pulled open the front door and, dragging her, ran into the street.

'Run,' he shouted, pushing her from him.

She did run, screaming, down the path of the next house where she thumped, panic-stricken, on the front door.

Scott ran too, heading the other way and hoping desperately to escape both his dad and Dan, if he had not killed him, and the police, who he was sure would arrive at any moment.

'Jesus Christ,' Mick spluttered, leaping down the stairs as Scott ran out of the house with the girl.

He bent down next to Dan and pulled him over. An enormous swollen bruise had formed on his temple, but he was still alive.

Mick shook him. 'Get up, quick, we've gotta get out of 'ere.'

Dan groaned groggily, lost quite happily in a distant void, where he could hear a faint voice penetrating the darkness.

Mick dragged him to his feet where his legs flopped weakly. 'Dan, quick, we've got to get out of here.'

The voice was louder and closer, Dan thought, and then a throbbing pain shot into his head. He moaned, covering the area with his hand.

'What happened?' he moaned.

Mick dragged him with great effort out of the front door and towards the car. He could see the girl screaming and hammering out of the corner of his eye. He turned quickly to see the front door open and a woman recoiling in horror as she dragged the girl inside.

He reached the car and bundled Dan into the back, which was quicker than the front. He just managed to catch sight of Scott running out of the road and heading to the right.

'What happened?' Dan was now sitting up, squinting his eyes against the searing pain.

'It was Scott, he just whacked you in the head,' Mick told him. 'He's done a runner and so's the girl. No doubt the police'll be here any minute. We've got to get out of here!'

Dan sunk back into the seat, his hand still clasping his temple. He squeezed his eyes tightly shut for a second and opened them. The movement hurt his head more, but it was a vain attempt to focus his blurred sight.

Mick drove the car out of the road in the same direction Scott ran.

'I want out, Dan,' Mick told him his voice shaking. 'This has gone too far now.'

'Don't be an arsehole. We get our money first, and then we're both off.'

'Too many people are getting hurt. Now look, Scott has completely lost it. Can't say I blame him, he thought you were gonna kill that kid, I guess.'

'I was going to. I was gonna slash her throat,' Dan confessed, with no conviction.

'Jesus, Dan. That's it. I've really had it now. I'm out of it and I guess Scott is too.'

It was some time later when Scott stopped running. His lungs burned, his legs ached and his head thumped with the rush of blood pounding in his ears. Despite the discomfort, he never wanted to stop running from his dad, Dan and himself. He was never going back — ever. He glanced over his shoulder and saw their car gaining on him. Both his dad and Dan would kill him after what he just done. Panic set into his chest as he searched for an escape.

People stared at him and cars beeped as he tried to run out into the road to cross. It was the forest that he saw on the other side of the road. If he could reach it he might just lose them. It looked safe there, calm and peaceful, no blood, and no people, and he was not stopping until he was in the safety of those trees. The road was too busy to cross in his haste. His dad's car was getting closer; his only hope was the dense trees, and taking the chance, he ran into the road.

The beeping he heard sounded a long way off. It was an alien noise that he could not even register in his fuddled mind. He heard a loud bang that vibrated through his body. Like the car hooters, he could not acknowledge what it was. His body flew through the air and he did not even feel the thump as he landed with a crack on the hard concrete.

Cars swerved around him, one driving over the other side of the road where an oncoming car hit it. It spun round and back to its own side, facing the wrong way. The next car hit that and the next hit it again. A lorry swerved and another crashed into the side of it. One of the drivers, alongside his wife and two children, were killed instantly as their car went under the side of the lorry, peeling the top from its metal case as easily as butter spreads from a warm knife.

Scott heard none of this as he lay wondering what had happened. He felt himself lift into the air and there he was, looking down from above. He was almost as high as the blue sky, seeing fluffy white clouds just above him.

They looked so serene and peaceful. Casting his view down, he could see a road below him. There were cars piled all over it. People were running in a frenzied panic like ants under attack. He could even see his dad, who had parked clumsily on the kerb side and was running along the road, past the disarray of cars. His eyes followed the line of the road and he saw himself lying on the concrete. He thought how strange his body looked, lost and even vulnerable. One arm was folded behind his back. A man was kneeling beside him with his hand on Scott's chest. Then the man began pounding Scott's chest up and down, before breathing into his mouth. On and on it went until Scott felt the pull, down and down. He fought against it because he did not want to go. He wanted to stay where he was — peaceful and safe. He did not want to face what was down there. But the pull was too strong for him to fight, so down he went, crashing back into his body.

The pain hitting him was like a thunderbolt. Not one bit of his body was not consumed in agony. He felt he would pass out with the enormity of it. Eventually he did, and nothing more was known to him of the crash that day.

Chapter Nineteen

Thankful for the arrival of daylight, Margaret and Jane went back to the cottage the next day. There was little evidence of the previous night's activities. The cushions now sat neatly on the sofa. The pictures on the walls were straight and undisturbed. The ornaments that had whirled round the room looking like threatening missiles the night before, were now back in their usual place. The only sign of the weird happenings was the smashed plate that was scattered in a vast number of pieces across the floor.

Jane begged Margaret to stay outside the bathroom and bedroom door while she changed and brushed her teeth. Margaret felt spooked herself, but tried to be brave for Jane's sake. She felt even worse when Jane went into the bathroom and closed the door behind her, leaving Margaret standing feeling jumpy on the landing.

Chastising herself for her silliness, she went silently downstairs to the kitchen and looked through the window to the garden, feeling very sad when she saw all the work Jane had done to try and recreate its glory. Guilt flooded her again; she could have lent her some garden tools, or even helped. Her mind went back in time and she smiled, remembering how Stephen and she had transformed it from a heap of earth to a beautiful cottage garden.

'Maybe it is time I let you go,' she whispered into the air.

Something in the garden caught her eye. Opening the lock, Margaret went outside. It was a teddy bear, lying on the floor beneath a makeshift washing line. It had long since lost its colour, but she remembered it was pink with a yellow ribbon around its neck.

Jane was standing behind her as she studied the teddy in her hands.

'Where did you find this?' Margaret asked.

'It belonged to Isabella, didn't it?'

Margaret looked shocked at Jane's familiarity with Isabella, then smiled sadly and looked again at the bedraggled bear. 'Yes, it did. She never went anywhere without it. We thought… we thought she had been buried with it.'

'I found it wedged between the two fences. Maybe that's her grave. Or maybe the cellar.'

Margaret shuddered and put the teddy behind her back. 'Come on, I thought we were going shopping.' She smiled in an attempt to cheer Jane up, wondering how she knew about the cellar. It was too much to ask at this moment.

They left Henry in charge of Molly and drove to Burton Ridge around lunchtime, both glad to get away from the troubled cottage for a while.

Henry smiled as he watched them go from the window. He was still not sure about ghosts; there had to be another explanation, he thought. But he could not decide what. 'Out of the dark always comes some light,' he told Molly, who sat staring at the biscuit he was holding.

The first visit was to the hairdressers to see Vanessa, who undid Margaret's tight bun and brushed the hair loose.

'Can you make a beautiful hairdo, like you did mine?' Jane asked hopefully.

'Not too dramatic, and please not cropped and spiky,' objected Margaret, looking dubiously at Jane's hair.

'Well… I think if I cut it to shoulder-length and put in a slight layer it would take years off you,' Vanessa suggested. 'Then you need some colour; I suggest some golden blonde highlights and some red and brown.'

'Oh goodness, I'm not sure.' Margaret did not like the sound of it at all.

'Please, Margaret,' Jane pleaded, until she laughed and nodded.

Jane took a towel and covered up the mirror in front of her so she could not see and possibly object again.

Vanessa laughed at the terror on Margaret's face as she chopped away.

It was two hours later when the towel was removed and the hair blow-dried, and Margaret gasped with shock. There was no longer a severe, angry woman staring back, but a pretty young woman, with sparkling green eyes.

'You look so beautiful,' Jane breathed, in awe.

Jane ushered her upstairs, where her eyebrows were plucked and nails painted. Then they both left to trail around clothes shops, where Jane chose brightly coloured skirts, tops and shoes for her. Then she made Margaret change into one of the outfits. After, Jane dragged Margaret into a coffee shop for refreshments.

Margaret was delighted and kept flicking and patting her new hairdo. She could not believe how she looked, so young and even pretty. She was almost forty, but felt like a girl again; even her step was light and springy.

'What a wonderful time I've had,' she told Jane, a broad smile lighting her face.

'You're beautiful when you smile,' Jane said, the happiness rubbing off onto Margaret. 'I wish you were my mum.'

'What an odd thing to say. Surely you loved your mum?'

Jane shrugged and looked down at her mug of hot chocolate. 'I don't like her much,' she confessed.

'You said she was dead!' Margaret was shocked Elizabeth had lied.

Jane, realising her mistake, reddened and begun to garble an explanation, 'I... I didn't like her before she died.'

But it was too late, she realised, as Margaret was studying her, with her newly plucked eyebrows raised in suspicion.

'Don't you think it's time to tell Dad and me the truth, Elizabeth?'

Jane did not speak; she wanted this moment to end and go away. Margaret got up and went to pay the bill. They walked to the car in silence.

They were both shattered when they arrived home. Molly barked and wagged her tail in delight at their return, spinning round in circles.

'Good gracious!' Henry gaped. 'I cannot believe it's my daughter, you look so... so... lovely.' Tears filled his eyes, remembering her when she was younger: bubbly, always joking and so pretty. The day he gave her away when she married Stephen. Damn evil life, to steal away her happiness like it did, and his daughter. She had never loved anyone except Stephen.

After a cup of tea, Margaret went into the kitchen to prepare dinner for them. Jane followed, eager to help, and Henry smiled. He loved the fact they were now friends; he knew they both needed one.

'It's OK, Elizabeth, you go keep Dad company. I'm OK on my own,' Margaret told her, trying to usher her from the kitchen.

'Please, I want to help you.'

'OK,' she relented, 'you can peel potatoes and then go and sit with Dad. How's that for a compromise?'

Jane smiled, nodding eagerly in agreement.

As Jane chatted, she watched Margaret chopping salad, placing the pieces in a large glass bowl. Taking some eggs and milk from the fridge, she beat them together.

Holding the small knife Jane had been given and the small pile of potatoes, she begun to slice off the skins as she had seen from a television programme. She soon realised it looked far easier than it was.

Margaret, catching sight of the mess in the corner of her eye, laughed.

'Elizabeth, have you never peeled potatoes before?'

Jane felt silly as she confessed, she hadn't.

'Surely at school they taught you to cook?'

'No, I always bunked off that lesson,' she grimaced, embarrassed.

'No wonder you can't read if you played truant.' Margaret took the savaged potato from her and showed Jane how to peel it. Margaret then explained what she was doing, allowing her to grate cheese and cut tomatoes for the flan she was making. While it was cooking, they went into the front room and sat with Henry, who had been dozing on the sofa with Molly next to him.

Over dinner, Henry and Margaret tried to gently question Jane more on her background. So far nothing seemed to add up.

'So, you said you lived in London before coming here Lizzy, whereabouts?' Henry asked.

'We lived all over the place. Mum liked to move a lot.'

'Really? That must have been hard on you,' Margaret sympathised, hoping to prompt more information.

'This dinner is fantastic, the best I've ever tasted,' Jane enthused.

Margaret was pleased. 'Oh, it's nothing, I love cooking.'

'Will you teach me? I would so love to know how to cook.'

'My girl is certainly a fantastic cook.' But Henry had only had a few mouthfuls when he pushed his plate away.

He had begun to deteriorate over the past week. He felt so weak and tired; he knew his time was drawing to an end.

'Dad, please, could you not manage a little more?' Margaret looked so worried.

'I'm sorry, my girl, it's lovely, but I can't get any more down,' he smiled apologetically.

'Can Molly have it then? I left her food next door,' Jane asked, not realising the relevance of his lack of appetite.

Margaret went to get an old bowl from the kitchen, grateful to hide her sadness. When she came back, Jane had put her father's plate of the floor for Molly.

'ELIZABETH!' she screeched, on seeing her best, very expensive plate being slobbered over.

The dog jumped and ran behind the sofa, and Jane flinched, covering her arms over her head and squeezing her eyes tightly shut.

'I'm sorry,' she cried, her body stiff in anticipation of the first blow.

Henry and Margaret gaped at her, horrified.

'You thought I was going to hit you!' Margaret stammered.

Jane opened her forearms and looked from one to the other. They were both staring at her, agog.

Margaret walked back to her chair and sat down, placing the bowl in front of her.

'I would never hit you,' she said with the same gusto as a deflated balloon.

'I think you had better tell us a little more about yourself, Lizzy.' Henry said, gently putting his hand on hers.

Jane looked at the table in front of her and fiddled with her plate.

'I… I ran away from home, but I'm 18 so I can leave home if I want,' she added defensively.

'If your mother hit you then I don't blame you,' Henry smiled reassuringly. 'But how can you afford to live?'

Margaret saved Jane from providing any further explanation. 'I think it has been a long day, let's clear the table. Molly can finish her supper and we'll watch a little TV before bedtime.' She jumped up and begun clearing plates.

She put her hand on Jane's shoulder. 'I would never hit you,' she said tenderly, before adopting her briskness again.

Jane got up and helped her. 'You've both been so kind, but I need to leave. I can't stay at the cottage anymore.'

'I've been thinking about that,' Margaret told them. 'We'll go and see Kordelia; she has a little shop along the high street. She's a clairvoyant, and although I never really believed in all that… stuff, we will see if she has any ideas.'

Henry shrugged as he eased himself from his wheelchair to the sofa. 'Whatever you think. If it makes you both feel better. I'm still not convinced it's a ghost.' He laughed a little uneasily, not wanting to believe but feeling he may have no choice.

Jane and Margaret got up early the next day; they had a lot to do, as they were to visit the clairvoyant. Margaret had explained to Jane in bed what a clairvoyant was. She did not like the sound of talking to the dead at all. But she was excited and intrigued; maybe they would get to the bottom of what lurked in the house, maybe even uncover the lost body of Isabella. Jane shuddered at the thought of a young child being buried there.

At Margaret's request, Jane went off to buy Henry a newspaper and some milk for tea, while Margaret got her father out of bed and dressed. Jane knew it would take over an hour so she decided to have a stroll with Molly first. She walked around the abbey gardens, marvelling at such a lovely day. The sun was warm but thankfully not too hot. She saw Rose sitting at the abbey tearooms and chatting to another lady. Jane was thankful Rose was otherwise engaged and had not noticed her. She did not know why but just did not want to face the woman since being told about the rape. As the other lady walked away, Jane tried to disappear quickly behind one of the old ruins. It was too late; Rose spotted her and beckoned her over.

Jane hesitated, not knowing what to do, but eventually relenting, went to speak to her.

'I'm sorry, love; I upset you last time we met. I didn't mean to. I'm just an old gossip,' Rose apologised sheepishly.

Jane faked a laugh. 'Of course not, I must have eaten something dodgy. I didn't feel too well. It wasn't you.'

She sat down at the table and Rose ordered another cup for tea.

They chatted about the weather for a while, and Jane finally asked, not really wanting to know, 'What happened to Toni after the rape?'

'Well,' Rose looked from side to side and leant forward, 'apparently, she was never the same again, hardly left her bedroom, didn't speak to anyone apart from her twin sister, Vicky. Her mother was worried sick. They tried everything to help her. But she just became more withdrawn and depressed,' Rose whispered sadly, secretly loving a good drama.

'What about the baby? Did she hate it?' Jane asked, already knowing the answer.

'She gave birth to a little girl and called her Jane. The baby died of cot death at four months old. But according to my sister, there were rumours that she suffocated her.'

Jane had gone very cold and began to shiver uncontrollably as she stared back at Rose, no longer seeing her, but a young woman – her mother – with a pillow over her head.

'Old Rebecca and the sister, Vicky, were devastated. Poor little mite,' Rose continued.

Jane's head felt very fuzzy; she thought she would faint. If she could stand, she would run off again. But her legs and hands were trembling too much.

'They buried her at the cemetery up on the hill. Are you OK, dear, you've gone so white? It's a horrible, story isn't it?'

'I'm sorry,' Jane managed. 'I've to go, we're late.'

She got gingerly to her feet and walked dazed back home.

'What's wrong, Elizabeth? You look like you have seen a ghost,' Margaret laughed nervously, realising what she had said.

'Nothing, but after we have seen the clairvoyant, I need to go somewhere.'

They left Henry sitting on the sofa looking after Molly. The clairvoyant's little shop was only a short distance past the end of the alleyway. A bell chinked as they went inside, where they were greeted by a young man at a desk.

'Can we see your mother?' Margaret asked, smiling.

'She's in with someone at the moment, but she should be out in about 20 minutes, if you want to wait.'

They sat in the waiting area and, while Margaret flicked though a magazine, Jane sat thinking about the dead baby. It did not make any sense to her at all, unless her mother had another baby after and called her the same name. She did not even know how old her mother was or how long it was since the baby died. It had not occurred to her to ask Rose or look on the birth certificate that was tucked safely in the suitcase.

A door behind them sprung open and two women came out chatting. It turned out the clairvoyant was the pretty dark-haired lady. Jane had expected her to have big gold earrings and a headscarf, but she looked perfectly normal, not like the ones she had seen on television that spoke with an accent at all.

The lady who had been with her left, and Kordelia came over and shook Margaret and Jane's hand.

'How can I help you, Margaret?' she smiled. 'I didn't think you were into all "this stuff."'

Margaret blustered slightly, 'I didn't believe it until recently.'

'So what's happened to make you a believer?' Kordelia smiled, slightly smugly.

'We have a haunted cottage and wondered if you could come and … well … do something about it?' Margaret looked embarrassed.

Kordelia led them through to the room she had just vacated with the lady. They sat down and Jane was asked to relay the whole story. When she finished, Kordelia looked in amazement at her.

'That sounds like a bad haunting. Someone or something is certainly very disturbed. I can come, but it may be beyond me to clear it. You may need further help,' she explained.

Kordelia left the room and came back a short time later, carrying a diary. She flicked through the pages backwards and forwards and ummed and ahhed a few times.

'I tell you what: the lady I'm seeing this afternoon is a friend. She won't mind if I cancel. What if I come today?' Curiosity was getting the best of her; she was dying to see what was happening.

'That would be fantastic,' Margaret enthused.

'OK, three o'clock.'

Henry looked very dubious when they arrived home and explained.

'I'm not sure I agree with all that mumbo-jumbo,' he grumbled.

'You're just scared, Dad; you're worried about Isabella and finding out what happened to her,' Margaret said, looking sad herself at remembering the child.

Henry looked taken back at the blunt words, but did not disagree.

'I need to pop out for a while,' Jane told them, clipping on Molly's lead, who was still jumping up and down in greeting, and then again in anticipation of a walk.

'I'll be back by half two.' She dashed for the door, leaving them both discussing the supernatural.

It took Jane a while to find the cemetery on top of the hill. Thinking it a short distance, it actually took her almost thirty minutes to get there. Trawling the gravestones looking for Jane Watts's grave was a gruelling, laborious task. Somehow, she had thought it would be easy to find, but there were thousands of stones as far as her eye could see. Many had faded inscriptions, which were impossible to read. She asked a few people, who were attending graves if they knew where the baby might be buried. One man pointed to a wall with lots of little stones decorated all over it, none read Jane Watts. She asked another man cutting the grass; he in turn asked if it was a burial or cremation. Jane had not realised there would be a difference in types and confessed she did not know.

Finally, a lady, who was just putting fresh flowers on a grave, helped.

'I know the Watts family and remember the baby dying,' she told Jane. 'I know Rebecca Watts well. She's blind now, bless her, such a lovely lady and a tragic life. Did you know the baby?' she asked, sympathetically.

'Sort of. I knew Toni Watts,' Jane said, smiling, as the lady was so kind and gentle.

'I'm not sure where the baby is buried but I do know it was with the grandfather and daughter, Vicky.'

'Is Vicky dead too then?' asked Jane, unnecessarily, as she had already known the answer.

'I'm sorry, didn't you know? Yes, she died quite a few years ago now, goodness how time flies. It seems only yesterday. But then again, the older you get the faster it goes,' she smiled thoughtfully back at Jane.

'Oh.' So there was no aunt, cousin or even herself now. There was her grandmother though. If it were not for Dan, maybe she would risk meeting her. She thanked the lady and turned towards home.

Chapter Twenty

Suzanne went back to work the next day and tried to concentrate on some of the other cases. She attended two meetings, one a case conference on a ten-year-old boy who had been throwing stones at an elderly lady. The second was a visit to foster parents of two brothers to assess their progress. All the time, thoughts of Jane flooded her head. She called the police to discuss the case.

'We do have strong suspicions that Dan Wallace was involved in a robbery on someone's house recently,' Detective Sergeant Paul Dodds admitted. 'It turns out that Dan's best friend's son worked as a gardener for the person. We have no evidence yet, but a lot of theories. The young lad seems to have disappeared, and we need him for questioning.'

'But how would that involve a girl of 14?' Suzanne asked him.

He offered no explanation and was as confused as her.

'Why kill an elderly lady? What on earth was her role in all this?' Suzanne suddenly remember the £400. Paid for the dog.

'I don't know, but we have a warrant out for Wallace. So, once we trace him, maybe we'll have more answers.'

Suzanne hung up the phone and pondered on the new revelation. So, Jane had taken some of Dan's money. It was the only explanation. She called the hospital. There was little change with Toni, but the nurse told her, her husband had recently visited.

'There is no husband,' Suzanne told her, shaking her head at Dan Wallace's audacity. 'Look, if he comes again, please call the police straight away. They're looking for him.' She could hear the panic in the nurse's voice as she hung up the phone and called the detective sergeant back again.

Opening the envelope Helena had left in her pigeonhole, Suzanne read the contents. She was off for a few days so did not have to endure any long conversations, allowing more time to work. She briefly read the long note, which explained the trouble acquiring the enclosed information.

Even when she's not here, she gets me, Suzanne grinned to herself putting the note aside. The newspaper article rang a vague bell with her. The more she read, the more she remembered. How silly she was and not her usual bright self; it had never occurred to her to search the name Isabella Lucas on the computer. Why would it when she was not looking for Isabella?

Suzanne read the headline of the newspaper print out:

Missing from her home, four-year-old Isabella Lucas
   Isabella Lucas, 4, was last seen at her home in Thornwood Abbey at 11.45 am on Saturday, September 25th
   Distraught mother Vicky Lucas left Isabella playing in the garden to answer the telephone. When she came back ten minutes later, the child had gone.
   Isabella has long, wavy blonde hair and blue eyes. She was last seen wearing pink shorts, a yellow T-shirt and yellow shoes.
   The Police Forensics team have conducted routine searches of the house. Meanwhile, people in the local area have been conducting a controlled search of parks and countryside for the child.

Suzanne put down the paper and Googled the name. There were many similar reports. The saddest was that Vicky Lucas, who had been suffering from a terminal illness, motor neuron disease, took an overdose and was found dead by her husband two months after the child's disappearance. The child still had not been found.

Suzanne grabbed her bag and left the office to go back to the nursing home. She found Alex just leaving his mother as she went inside.

'Why didn't you tell me about Isabella disappearing?' she asked without even a greeting.

Alex looked surprised and then shrugged. 'Why would I, it was many years ago and the case dead and buried. It's obvious the child was abducted and is most likely dead.'

'How do you know Jane is not Isabella?' Suzanne blurted out with a rush of words.

Alex studied her for a moment. He sat in the reception, and Suzanne sat next to him.

'Well?' she prompted.

'What, you mean it was Toni who abducted her niece ... her sister's child? That's the most ridiculous thing I have ever heard. I mean, why on earth would she do that? I know Toni went off the rails, but to take her niece is unthinkable,' Alex answered incredulously.

'Why not? Her own was dead. Possibly smothered by her. There was obviously some sort of rivalry between the two.'

Alex studied her eyes hard, staring straight through them. 'Rivalry? What makes you say that?' he asked, intrigued with her theory.

'Because they both loved the same man. The father. And he chose Vicky.'

'Well, I don't know about that. We were all kids, we used to play together. Maybe there were a few crushes as we were growing up, but nothing serious. Look, please, don't worry Mum anymore with all this. It's just dragging it all up again.'

Suzanne looked down at her fingernails, noting they needed a good trim. 'OK, I'll leave it for now. Do you know where I can find the Lucas family? Maybe they can help.'

Alex got up and went to the table with the signing-in book and turned to the back page where he had torn the paper from the day before. He scribbled an address and tore the paper out again, handing it to Suzanne without speaking. She looked down and noted the two addresses.

'Try the first one, they may be there,' he told her, having the grace to look a little sheepish.

'So, it's the same address as the cottages you gave me yesterday?' she said, a little annoyed. 'So, the Lucas's live where your mother said I would find Jane.'

Alex smiled apologetically. 'Sorry, Mum is fanciful at times. I guess she thought the girl had gone to the Lucas's. But like Mum, I think they have had enough of people poking around. I don't know why you would think the girl might be there, but I genuinely hope you find this Jane.'

'Anything's worth a try, Alex,' she smiled, grimly.

There was no time now, she decided, looking at her watch. She was due in court as a witness for a child abuse case. Jane Watts would have to wait again, at least for now.

Alex drove home, all the time mulling over what Suzanne had said. It was still ridiculous, when he had covered every angle. The disappearance of Isabella had been a mystery, an unsolved one at that.

He had heard the rumours that circulated amongst the small community. Toni had killed her baby, and his sister Vicky, had killed hers years later. Both sisters were deemed mad. He had lived with the stigma of it himself. People who he had known for years turned away from him after Isabella's disappearance, more so after Vicky's death, because it proved her madness. But Vicky was ill, not mentally, but physically. She was diagnosed soon after Isabella's birth. She was then told she would not live to see her child grow up. She was given eight years at the most before her life would be cut short. Before that happened, she would face the indignity of losing the use of her body. Even her voice would be snatched from her. If she was lucky her eyes could still move side to side, just to let them know she was still with them. How devastated the family were at the news.

When the child, whom the parents adored, disappeared, it had put an end to Vicky's life more quickly. She was already struggling to walk by that time. Her hands were losing their grip and her voice was fading rapidly.

Once the child disappeared, she no longer wanted to live; she had no reason to fight anymore. Vicky had sunk into a depression so deep that no words could reach her.

Toni had already gone, so not even her sister was there to help her, the one person who may have been able to reach her at such a terrible time. He had tried himself desperately to find Toni, to beg her to come back and help Vicky. He was unsuccessful and had just found one weak lead, when Vicky ended her life.

The rumours that she had killed Isabella and buried her somewhere hurt, almost as much as her death. Because her own life had almost ended, she had taken her child to heaven to wait for her. The injustice of it all, the stories circulated like fire on a newspaper — the death of little Jane, the disappearance of Isabella, Vicky's illness and now Vicky's death. It had taken its toll on his mother, who seemed to shrink and grow old all of a sudden. She lost the bounce in her step, the twinkle in her eye and faded as if someone had fed her poison; and they had.

She deteriorated rapidly until her sight disappeared and then her mobility and at times, her facilities. Two months ago, she'd collapsed. He'd found her and called an ambulance. The hospital warned him that she was no longer safe in her own home.

Alex had considered taking her home to live with him many times over the years. But his wife Lorraine had objected. Their marriage had always been tricky and there were many times he regretted that they had ever married at all. He never would have done it if she had not fallen pregnant. They were young and silly, thinking they were in love, never bothering with precautions. Very soon, it became clear their marriage was a big mistake. Only the birth of their daughter kept them together. They survived until Marcia, his daughter, was fifteen, before agreeing to separate. Marcia wanted to stay at the same school where all her friends were. Going through exams, they all decided it was best she stay at the house with Alex. Lorraine moved out, leaving them the family home. They remained friends and the break was amicable enough; once Marcia was 18, next year, and at university, the house was to be sold and the equity split between them. Or if he could afford to buy her out and keep the house, he would.

Alex pulled into the drive of the house he loved so much. He climbed out of the car and unlocked the garage. He guessed Marcia would still be lazing in bed and had not done any of the chores he had asked her to do. Mr Davis, his neighbour, was out cutting his lawn and Alex had the feeling he was waiting for him.

'Noisy old sod,' he smiled to himself, as Mr Davis knew everything that happened both inside and outside people's houses. Alex swore he knew the colour of his underpants. He rushed over, seemingly excited today about some tragedy or other. He fidgeted from foot to foot, eager for Alex to emerge from the garage.

Alex deliberately took his time, just to annoy him. A small retaliation that made him feel better. Not finding much more to fiddle with, he got out of the car.

Mr Davis rushed forward and waited at the edge of the garage. 'It's young Marcie,' Mr Davis shouted, as Alex opened his boot to bring out the shopping he had brought earlier. He looked at Mr Davis with a mock surprised expression, noting the nosy old devil's eyes were dramatic and round.

'Marcie? What has she been up to now? I thought she'd still be in bed.'

When she was young, she had plagued Mr Davis with her little gang of mates, causing a stream of constant complaints.

'Three men came earlier and knocked on your door. They took her hostage, almost killed her, they did.'

'WHAT!' Alex screeched, losing his patience with him and his exaggerated stories.

Mr Davis looked delighted; his news had caused such a good reaction. 'It's true; Mrs Warner next door took her to the hospital. She was trying to call you, but your phone's off,' Mr Davis said, satisfied that he was the one that got to break the news first.

Alex had a terrible feeling as an invisible icy finger froze his spine. He did not wait for any more explanation from his neighbour. He threw the shopping in the car and jumped in himself.

'Have they gone to the General?'

Mr Davis nodded. 'Give her my love.' He waved and went off to find someone else to tell.

He found Lorraine waiting in casualty and looking extremely anxious. She jumped out of her seat and ran forward when she spotted Alex.

'Three men attacked her,' Lorraine told him in one great rush. 'Jesus Christ, Alex, they could have... could have done anything, not least killed her.'

Alex felt anger rise in his stomach and threaten to explode at the idea anyone had even contemplated going near his little girl. 'Did they touch her?'

'Not in that way. One of them held a knife to her throat, threatening to cut it. They did cut her, but not too badly. I think she's more in shock than anything else.'

Lorraine began to lead him through two double doors into a room with curtain cubicles on either side. 'I just went out for a few minutes to pull myself together,' she explained, pulling aside a curtain to the fourth cubicle. 'We're waiting for the police to arrive.'

Marcie burst into tears when she saw her dad.

Alex rushed forward and wrapped his arms around her trembling body while she sobbed into his chest.

Marcie had been his little princess since her mother had first pushed her into the world and he had held her for the first time. The two of them were inseparable; even Lorraine complained that she felt cut out at times.

The little girl had followed him everywhere, even when her legs were still wobbly. He had dried her tears when she cried, laughed with her as he chased her around the garden. Told her off when she was naughty and then felt guilty as she stood looking at him with her bottom lip pushed out. She always knew how to get round her dad.

How proud he had been when she swam her first length of the pool. Passed her spelling tests, won a few trophies for dancing. The rosaries for horse riding that decorated the wall in her bedroom. Passed all her A-levels with high grades. She was going to university; his baby was going to be a journalist.

'Do you want to tell me what happened?' Alex asked gently, once the sobs had subsided slightly.

Marcie tried to relay all the details as she remembered them. 'Who's Jane?' she asked, once she had finished.

'I don't know,' Alex told her, 'or rather, I'm not sure. But whoever she is, these men are intent on finding her.'

The doctor appeared around the curtain, holding a clipboard. 'It seems you can go, Marcie, but we are just waiting for the police so you can give a statement,' he smiled. 'You can sit in the day room if you would like?' he suggested, pointing the way. 'I'm sure they won't be much longer.'

'What about her wound?' Lorraine asked anxiously.

'We've given Marcie a tetanus shot. She'll need to see her doctor in a week to remove the butterfly stitches. I have prescribed a course of antibiotics in case of infection. I would say you are a very lucky girl. A few millimetres deeper and the knife would have cut your jugular.'

The curtain opened and two police officers walked in.

'Miss Marcia Watts? I'm Constable Jason Barter and this is my colleague, Laura Pugh. Are you feeling well enough to talk and tell us what happened?'

Marcia looked anxiously at her dad, who smiled and squeezed her hand.

'It's OK, chicken, your mum and me will stay with you.' He smiled, using the pet name he was usually told off for, now she was a young woman.

'Have you any idea why these men would have attacked you?' Constable Barter asked once they were sat in the day room and Marcie had finished giving an account of what happened.

'I think I can help with that,' Alex offered. He explained about Suzanne and her search for Jane, who Suzanne believes is his niece.

'But why would they be that desperate to find a child?' Lorraine asked.

'I don't know, I only found all this out yesterday. But for them to come here to look, they must be clutching at straws.' Alex handed over Suzanne's card. 'I'm sure she can tell you more.' He turned to Marcie. 'I think until this is sorted out you need to stay with your mum.'

She nodded solemnly, but did not object. 'You're coming too aren't you, Dad?' she asked, worried he was in danger.

'If your mum doesn't mind,' Alex smiled.

Lorraine looked at him, weighing up what to do. 'Of course not, just for a few days.' She did not think for a minute Larry, her partner, would like it, but under the circumstances it could not be helped.

'If it was not for the younger one, that man would have killed me. I owe my life to him.' Marcie was saying.

'We'll need to take fingerprints, if you could let us go to your house before you go into it.'

They left the hospital and Alex followed them in his car to Lorraine's flat. He went in to make sure they were safe before he left. Marcie became panic-stricken when he told her he was going home to retrieve some of her belongings.

'It's OK,' he reassured. 'I'm going to meet the police so they can take their prints. I'll be back soon with your bits.'

'You promise?'

Alex smiled. Despite all her bravado and cheek, she was still a little girl.

'I promise,' he smiled, kissing the top of her head. 'Now you go and get some sleep and I'll be back before you know it.'

As he left, he called Suzanne and told her what had happened. She was as shocked as he was and agreed to meet at his house in a few hours' time.

Mick held Scott's hand in the back of the ambulance. This was his fault; now his boy might die. He closed his eyes and began to pray to a God he had never believed in until that moment. Tears fell down his face as he dared himself to look again at the lifeless body of his son. At that moment, he hated Dan more than anyone he had ever hated in his life before. He had left him and his car at the side of the road, no longer caring what happened to either. He made a deal with God that if his boy lived, he would turn himself in and confess to everything.

Guilt flooded his stomach and mind for the way he had treated Scott in the past. The times he had put him down and called him useless. Given him a thump for not behaving when he was a child. It had been hard for him since Julie had run off. He did not have a clue how to bring up a child. Scott had been such a gentle, loving kid, even crying at cartoons if one of the characters met some tragedy. Mick had been extra hard on him, believing he needed to toughen him up for a life ahead. Calling him a poof and a girl. If God let him live, he would make it up to him. He would make sure Scott was clean and that no one ever knew of his involvement in the robbery. He would let him live his life in peace and hope he did not make a cock-up of it, as his father had.

He heard a moan and opened his eyes, squeezing Scott's hand reassuringly.

'It's OK, son,' he told him, 'you're gonna be all right.' He then added the words he should have told him many times before, 'I love you, son.' His tears ran freely now, seeing Scott's deathly white face and tinged blue lips.

Scott's body jerked and the monitor registering his heart became erratic before it slowed to a long straight line.

Dan knew he had lost both Mick and Scott now. He sat in the driver's seat, his head still throbbing painfully, making one eye stream. He waited for the road to clear so he could drive away. He would not give up on the money or Jane; maybe Toni really had killed her. He vowed to find her dead or alive, whatever it took.

The mess of cars in front of him would take hours to clear, allowing him time to think. The police came up to his car and he wound down the window.

'If you can turn round and find another route it would help. It'll be sometime before we clear this lot,' the officer explained.

Dan nodded in agreement and did a u-turn. He drove back to the grandmother's house, parking up at the back entrance this time. Looking round to make sure there was no one about, Dan jumped over the back gate. He gave sharp kicks to the back door, until it sprang open.

With the curtains drawn, the inside of the house was bathed in a cool, gloomy dimness. The smell of urine caused him to wrinkle his nose. He pulled open the curtains slightly, allowing more light to brighten the room. He opened drawers and cupboards to search for clues, but he found little. There was no evidence that Jane or the dog had ever been there. On finding nothing, Dan cursed several times, kicking a cupboard with his foot to relieve his frustration.

Upstairs were three bedrooms, which, as with the downstairs rooms, gave no clues as to the whereabouts of Jane. He sat down on the bed and lit a cigarette, swearing again as he now had no leads or ideas of where to look next. Each dead end he found made him hate the girl more, swearing that when he did find her, he would make her suffer extra for his inconvenience. His mind raced with various torture methods to make her talk. Even just mentally acting them out helped to ease some of his annoyance.

Opening a chest of drawers, he absently pulled out a photograph album and flicked through. There were all sorts of pictures showing family gatherings, some of them with a happy, laughing Toni. He was amazed at how pretty she was when younger. Much like Jane, he mused, wishing he had known her then. He came to a whole page with photos of two sisters together and realised not all the photos he had seen had been of Toni.

'Well, I never,' he smiled, 'there's two of them.' He pulled at one of the photos and looked at the back.

'Vicky and Toni age 12,' he read.

So, Jane could be hiding with an auntie, he grinned, feeling excited that he had made some progress. He ran downstairs and rifled through the papers he had earlier strewn over the floor. Finding the address book, he remembered seeing, he ripped out the page with Vicky's address and tucked it into his pocket. He left the house by the front door this time.

Chapter Twenty-One

When Jane arrived back at the cottage, Margaret told her that a young man, Stuart, had been asking for her.

'He asked if you would go and see him in the pub. He said it's important.'

Jane could not imagine what he wanted, so she decided to go after the clairvoyant had been. They had some lunch and sat waiting in anticipation. By the time 3 o'clock ticked round, Frank had gone to his room for a nap. They saw Kordelia walk along the garden path and Margaret opened the door before she knocked and made Molly bark, waking her father.

The three of them went to the cottage and Jane began to shake as she opened the door and allowed the other two women inside. Everything was still and as they had left it earlier. Kordelia walked slowly down the short hallway and came back again. Going into the living room, she shut her eyes and began whispering. Jane and Margaret looked at each other nervously, wondering whom she was talking to.

Kordelia opened her eyes and smiled at their anxious faces. 'Just asking my angels to protect us,' she explained, walking towards the kitchen.

'I have Stephen here,' Kordelia said calmly, as though talking to the dead was an everyday occurrence.

Margaret's eyes widened; like her father, she was having trouble believing all this stuff. She had fought with herself to find explanations for what had happened the other night. So far, she had not come up with anything other than some strange supernatural activity. But for Stephen to be here and talking like he was in the same room was too much for her.

'He said hello to you, Margaret. He said to tell you he loves you very much. That will never change, but you must let him go and start to live again. You did not die — he did. It's time for you to move on.'

The words were harsh on Margaret's ears and momentarily she felt hurt before anger flashed into her eyes. It dispelled, and was replaced by sadness; unable to hold them in any longer, tears rolled down her face.

Kordelia put her hand on hers and she smiled gently.

'I know you're a non-believer. But he is real. He never died really, just went to live in another place. It's a beautiful world where he has found happiness. It doesn't mean he's stopped missing and loving you. One day, you'll be together again, but until that day, you must find happiness and let him go.'

Jane stared at Margaret and at the tears pouring down her face. She grabbed her hand and felt the grateful squeeze back.

'Tell him I love him too,' she choked, her voice shaking with emotion.

'He knows. He's giving you primroses and tells me you still have his photo under your pillow. He's going, but he is always there with you, Margaret. There is another for you on this earth; he is waiting to meet you. You must walk forward to allow this new love to blossom.'

'Never!' Margaret said, firmly.

Kordelia closed her eyes again. 'I have a child here. She passed over very young.'

'Isabella,' breathed both Margaret and Jane together.

'She has grown up in the world of spirit. They do if they die as children or babies. She said to tell Jane to keep looking; you'll soon find the answers. But you must be careful as you are in danger.'

Margaret looked at Jane questionably. 'Why did she say Jane?'

'Things are not what they seem. Keep looking. You are very psychic and one day, when you're older, you'll see. Use your intuition more; those little niggles you keep getting are messages. The windows in your life are murky; wipe them and you will see through.'

Jane did not understand; she bit her lip, wondering how she could explain the slip of name. Then had a little panic inside when she had visions of seeing ghosts popping up all over the place when she was older.

'Is it Isabella?' Margaret asked, looking back at Kordelia.

'No, she said her name is Jane.'

'Baby Jane, goodness.'

Jane looked at Margaret: had she known of the baby and even her mother? She bit her lip again, wondering if it was safe to trust her.

'What about the haunting?' Margaret asked.

Kordelia fell silent in concentration. 'There are bodies buried here. They're not at rest. They do not mean any harm. They are trying to tell you they are unhappy.'

They all shivered, Kordelia included.

'What bodies?' Jane asked, her eyes scanning the room in case one was visible. She then remembered the noise from the cellar.

'I... I... don't know,' Kordelia fell silent, and squeezed her eyes shut in concentration. Her eyes flew open but were glazed and no longer seeing the room around her.

'They're buried under the house's foundations. They have been here many long years. The light of the child has brought them to the surface of darkness. They have been lost in a time void. They're attracted to the innocents and youth. They want you to see them and help. They wanted to show you what happened here.'

Suddenly one of the ornaments on the sideboard lifted up and flew against the wall. The loud crash scared them all, even Kordelia whose eyes fast refocused. The table lifted and the three of them ran for the front door, hearing it crash to the floor again.

When they got back, Henry was out of bed but dozing on the sofa. Molly woke him as she jumped from his lap and ran to Jane. Margaret made tea while Jane and Kordelia flopped gratefully on the two armchairs.

'I cannot clear the cottage,' Kordelia confessed, once Margaret came back with four mugs and a plate of biscuits on a tray.

'Something is very wrong. It'll need a rescue group to sit and try and get through and send them on their way,' Kordelia explained, when she saw the look of confusion on Jane's face.

'Sometimes a spirit becomes stuck between two worlds. They're in limbo, not realising they are dead and thinking they are still alive. They need energy generated by a group of people to reach them and convince them to pass over. Does that make some sense to you?'

'I'm not sure. I always thought if someone died, they just went to God,' Jane answered, trying to untangle the mysterious web.

'Not always; if they die suddenly or tragically, they're not always aware they are dead. If you died right now, all of a sudden, you would still be sitting here looking at us. You may even get up and start doing all the things you do normally.'

'But surely as time passes, I would realise.'

'These souls died in a horrible way. They were plunged from living into darkness – into limbo. There is no time in limbo, it could be a minute or a hundred years.'

'Why did they refer to you as Jane?' Margaret suddenly asked.

'I... I... don't know,' Jane reddened and she knew she looked guilty.

'I'll get onto a group of people I know and see if we can arrange a sitting. Maybe we can find out why they are stuck here. There is something more. I was just picking it up. There was a young woman; she was showing me a baby, a little girl dressed in pink.'

'I saw her,' Jane blurted out. 'I think it's Vicky with baby Isabella.'

Henry, who had been listening, trying to absorb what was said and not interrupting, almost spilt his tea.

'How do you know that?' he looked at Jane, almost accusingly, making her suddenly feel very uncomfortable.

'I saw her one night; she held the baby and mouthed "Isabella", and pointed to the cellar.'

She wanted to confess it was possibly her auntie, but could not.

'Isabella was only a toddler and disappeared ten years ago. We believed her to have died. Her mother Vicky killed herself soon after the child disappeared.' Margaret explained to Kordelia, looking worriedly at her father, whose face was more white than usual.

'Yes, I remember. I'm sorry. I don't know who the baby was. For the time being, there's nothing more I can do. The group I know may be able to find the answers. I'll be in touch.' Kordelia stood up and handed her mug to Margaret. 'I must go now.'

After she left, Jane, needing some air, went out with Molly and headed for the pub.

Stuart was taking glasses out of the washer behind the bar when she went inside. He smiled and led Jane to a quiet table in the corner. A few of the regulars waved and said hello to her, then smiled knowingly at the couple.

'Two men came in a few days ago,' Stuart explained.

Jane's mouth went very dry and her heart began to pound.

'They were looking for a 14-year-old girl with long, blonde hair and blue eyes. Apparently, she's a runaway and her mother is looking for her.'

The look of fear on her face told Stuart, as he suspected, it was her they were looking for. 'Of course, the girl was nobody anyone knew, until they mentioned a little brown scruffy dog.'

Jane looked down at her glass of orange juice and twisted it around in her shaking hand.

Stuart watched her and put his hand on hers.

'I thought it was you, Lizzy. But your name isn't Lizzy, is it? It's Jane.'

Her eyes met his and again told him he was right.

'So, wanna tell me the truth?' he asked gently.

'I can't tell you.'

'Those men did not look too good.'

'Did anyone tell them anything?' Jane asked worriedly.

'I don't think they realised. They just told them they never saw any girl, but if they did, they would send her home. I realised though. Don't worry, I didn't say a word. But Lizzy, or Jane, you need to get in touch with your mum.'

'How come you took so long to tell me?' Jane asked, grateful to have stalled for a little time to think. Was Stuart referring to the same day Scott had told her about, or had they come back again?

'I wanted to come and see you but I was going through a bad patch with my girlfriend. She's jealous of you and was watching me constantly. I have been hoping you would pop in so I could tell you.'

He felt really upset knowing Jane was only 14 years old.

'Oh, I'm sorry. Those men are lying; my mum's not looking for me. I stole something from them and they want it back.'

'Money,' Stuart looked dumbfounded, 'you took their money.'

'How did you know?' It was Jane's turn to look amazed.

'Because no 14-year-old I know is able to stay in a room, rent a cottage, and buy all new clothes and stuff.'

'They'll kill me if they find me,' Jane told him dramatically.

Saying her goodbyes to Stuart and then the local pub people, she left. She stalled at the doorway to look around the town, in case Dan was there. Feeling assured he wasn't, Jane walked out of the doorway and into the street.

Stuart watched her, feeling disappointed and let down by Jane's age. He shrugged to himself, grateful he had not got involved with a child thief, who had gangsters after her.

Jane scurried down the street with Molly, wondering why she had not heard from Scott. She had heard nothing since their meeting in the abbey gardens. He could be tricking her, giving her a false sense of security. She dashed for the alleyway, feeling really unsafe, and stood just inside for a while to be sure no one had followed her. She pulled the phone out of her pocket and pushed the button on the side to make it light up. Nothing happened so Jane gave it a shake. All the children at schools had mobiles, but she had no idea how to use one, only the crash course Scott had given her. If he were trying to trick her, surely he would not have bothered with the phone. It was no good; even if he did warn her that Dan was back in Thornwood Abbey it really was time for her to go. She could no longer put Henry and Margaret at risk.

Jane made her way to the cottage and stood outside. How scared she felt to go back inside, knowing there were spirits floating about. But she had no choice; all her stuff was still inside and the money. She gasped big, exaggerated breaths, filling her lungs and letting them out again.

With each breath, she tried to console herself that it was the last time she would ever go in there.

The lady, Christine, from next door came along with her baby in a buggy and waved to Jane. Trying to look as normal as possible, she waved back and pulled the key from her bag. Inserting it in the lock, Jane slowly pushed open the door. She looked down the hallway first to make sure it was quiet. Her eyes darted up the stairs, expecting to see some horrible demon floating at the top.

The house was still and looked as she had seen it that first day, a quaint little cottage. Building up enough courage she rushed up the stairs without looking back. Darting into the bedroom, she quickly pulled a few clothes from the wardrobe. It was soon clear she would be limited in what she could carry as there was still no room in the case.

In no time at all, she had packed a few meagre belongings. Prioritising, she took her makeup from the dressing table and toothbrush and a few toiletries from the bathroom. The case clonked downstairs as she ran into the living room and grabbed a few food items. Shutting the door behind her, she breathed a large sigh of relief before going to face Margaret and Henry.

'But I don't understand.' Henry's voice was angry. 'Why do you have to go?'

'Please, I just do.' Jane was almost in tears. 'I'll miss you both so much. But I have to go. Please do not ask me anymore.'

Her tears fell as she walked over to Margaret and gave her a kiss and cuddle. Then to Henry, who threw his arms around her.

'I've not got long left now. I thought you could be a friend to Margaret for me. Please, Lizzy, stay?' Henry asked, his anger subsiding and his voice pleading.

'It's OK, Dad. If she needs to go you must let her.'

Margaret's looked away, her own eyes filling with tears. 'I had begun to think of you as a daughter, Elizabeth, and even got to like Molly here.'

The dog wagged its tail on hearing her name.

'But you are young and don't want to stay with two old fogeys like us. Please, one day, let us know how you're getting on and keep in touch.'

She put her hand on Jane's shoulder and gave a little push towards the door to allow her freedom to leave without crushing the girl.

Leaving was more difficult than Jane anticipated. It would have been easier in the dark. Margaret watched her from the window and was again puzzled why she seemed to be dodging about and looking around. It was as though Elizabeth was frightened and being followed. She relayed this to Henry, who sat gloomily watching the window.

'Go after her, Margaret, find out what's wrong.'

Margaret looked at him and bit her lip, trying to decide. Then making a rash decision, she ran out of the front door and down the walkway to catch Jane up. Putting her hand on Jane's shoulder, she felt her jump.

'Elizabeth, please, what's wrong? You're hiding from someone, aren't you? You can tell me, I want to help.' She looked into the frightened eyes as if trying to read them.

'Please, Margaret, you don't understand. I must go otherwise I'll put you both in danger.' Jane looked pleadingly at her.

'Danger? Don't be silly; what could be that bad that you are so frightened? Look, if you really are hiding from someone, maybe we can help. You could stay at our family home until we sort out what's wrong.'

Jane hesitated. 'But you've already helped me so much. I can't be more of a burden to you.'

'We can't let you go like this. Come back to the cottage and let us talk.'

Jane relented and went back, much to Henry's delight. His eyes lit up when he saw her, then looked confused as he saw the expressions on both their faces.

'Now sit down and tell us what's wrong,' Margaret insisted.

'OK, I'll tell you, but not now. There are some men after me and if they find me, they'll kill me. Please, I've got to get out of here,' Jane begged.

If it were not for the fear in her eyes, Henry and Margaret would have thought she was exaggerating.

Henry was the first to speak, 'Margaret, call a cab and send Lizzy to the house. She can stay there tonight,' he instructed. Then he changed his

222

mind. 'In fact, no, you drive us there and we can all go and then she can explain once we're there.'

'But, Dad, it's too much for you. You'll make yourself more ill,' Margaret objected.

'I'll be more ill with worry if we send her alone,' he told her determinedly.

Saying no more, she went to her bag and checked her car keys were inside. Then, quickly gathering some overnight items for both herself and her father, she went off to move the car closer.

Jane wheeled Henry the other way down the alley to the car park. It was difficult to negotiate the chair, Molly and the suitcase, but Jane still managed to be waiting by the time Margaret drew up with the car. She was so thankful to finally be inside and, for now, safe, as she slammed the back door. How she wished Margaret would not fluff around checking she had not forgotten anything. Three times she had got out and ran back to the cottage, first for Henry's breathing pump, then his morphine and, finally, just as Jane could feel a scream rising in her throat, his clean underwear.

To take her mind from it, she pulled out the phone again. 'I can't get this phone working,' she told Henry, who sat silently in the front.

'Maybe it needs a new battery,' he suggested, not really interested.

'It's new, though,' Jane told him, giving it another shake and keeping her finger on the button for longer. It flickered slightly, offering her a slight relief, and then it died again.

'Maybe it needs charging then,' Henry offered helpfully, looking back to the cottage to see if Margaret was on her way.

Scott's words flashed in her mind, 'Make sure you keep it charged.' She had dismissed them in the panic of the moment.

'How do I charge it?'

'Honestly, Lizzy, where have you been living – Mars? Even I know you have to plug them in.'

Jane turned the phone over and studied the corners, back and front. She could not see any way of plugging it in. After Henry's comment, she did not have the heart to ask, so popped it back into her pocket.

Margaret appeared again and climbed into the driver's seat. She reeled off an ineligible list of items to herself, ticking off each one with an allocated finger. Turning the ignition, the car thankfully began to move. They stopped at the end of the turning and waited for a gap in the stream of traffic.

'Oh, no!' Margaret blurted out.

Jane's felt her heart fall thorough her body to her knees.

'Oh, for goodness sake, now what have you forgotten!' Henry bawled.

'I forgot my own tablets.' She turned her head as she reversed the car into a space to turn around.

They were finally on their way, relief flooding Jane as she sat low on the back seat, her eyes darting from side to side like a wild dog. Every pedestrian or car they passed was a potential Dan looking for her.

'Lizzy can't get her phone to work,' Henry told Margaret absently, just for something to dispel the heavy silence.

'Mmmm, really,' Margaret murmured, just as blankly.

'Maybe it's out of charge.'

'I can't see anywhere to charge it. Does it have somewhere to put batteries?' Jane asked, cringing in anticipation of another snipe from Henry.

'It should have a charger that plugs in with it,' Margaret answered, then frowned, wondering why someone of Elizabeth's age would be asking such a thing.

Jane leant forward and grabbed at the carrier bag Scott had given her. She was meaning to throw it away but had grabbed it when she collected her bits from Henry and Margaret's. She looked inside the mobile phone's box and found a neatly wound-up wire with a plug on the end. It had a small metal bit on the other end, which after much poking into the phone, found a home.

'Oh!' Jane said.

'Wonder what's happened here?' Henry said, as they slowed to join the long line of traffic in front of them.

They could see blue lights, flashing in the distance.

'A big accident, by the looks of it,' Margaret stuck her head out of her open window to see what was wrong. The curl of the road blocked her vision.

There, they sat without moving for ten minutes before Margaret turned off the ignition. A few people had deserted their cars to walk a distance down the line.

'What's wrong?' Henry called to a man making his way back to his car.

'Massive pile-up. Looks like a lot of people are badly injured. Think we'll be stuck here a while before it's cleared!' he shouted back.

'Poor devils,' Henry said.

Chapter Twenty-Two

Dan reached the cottage just as Margaret's car pulled away, so intent on studying the buildings, he had not noticed Jane sitting in the back. He had already peered through the window and banged at the door of the cottage with the 'For rent sign' in the front garden, to establish no one was at home. He went to the cottage where Henry and Margaret lived, and knocked there too. Cursing again, he went to the last door, knocking despondently, when he heard a baby cry from inside.

The door sprang open and a lady stood, rocking the crying baby in her arms. In his eagerness to find Jane, he had almost forgotten the large bruise on the side of his head. The lady stared at it instantly, suspicious.

'I'm sorry to disturb you; I've just been mugged.' Dan put his hand on the bruise and flinched to prove it hurt. 'I've come to see my daughter, who lives next door with her aunty Vicky. I was hoping to clean up and report what has happened. But there's no answer,' he told her, wincing to show some urgency and gain sympathy.

Christine looked even more suspicious and not quite convinced. 'I don't know any Vicky. There's a young girl living next door, but I don't know her very well,' she told him, patting the baby's back as well as rocking her. This seemed to pacify the baby, who stopped crying and stared at Dan.

'I'm not sure where she is. Maybe out with her dog. Or you could try the other cottage; I've seen her with them so think they're friendly.'

Dan thanked her and walked back down the path. The lady stared after him, then went indoors and locked her front door behind her.

Dan walked back along the path, feeling unsure. This could possibly be where Jane was; the only clue was the dog. There was only one way to find out, he decided. He went back to the middle cottage door and gave it a sharp kick. It sprang open. Looking around to make sure no one had seen him, he dodged inside. It did not take long to walk around the downstairs to clarify there was no one at home. A sharp banging from upstairs sent Dan running into the hallway. He rushed up two steps at a time into the bedroom. Finding nothing, he looked in the cupboard, and finally under the bed. As he went to stand up something flew through the air and hit him clear on the head, right on the bruise. He fell forward onto the floor, making a loud bang.

'Fucking hell,' he swore, feeling sick and sweaty with the pain.

He pulled himself to sitting position and grasped his head again. He could feel the blood running down his face from the wound as he looked around the room to see what or who had hit him. Noting the heavy glass trinket box on the floor, Dan lifted himself onto his knees shakily and sat back on his haunches. His eyes grew wide as he stared at the wall, where he could see a white mist swirling about. He shook his head and stared again. I must have concussion, he decided, looking fascinated as the mist was dancing and making all sorts of shapes. It slowly formed itself into a woman, not just any woman but the young Toni he had seen in the photos. Her mouth moved but he could not decipher the words it formed. He opened his own mouth to scream, but nothing came out as his lips wobbled, and his cheeks seemed to sink in the effort.

It took all his energy to pull himself to his feet as the woman floated closer, reaching out her hands. Dan tried to scream again, as the beautiful face turned into a grotesque man. Blood dripped from the eyes that stared with evilness at Dan. The enormous mouth pulled back, showing pointed, rotting yellow teeth. On the face were big green and yellow puss-filled scabs, which dripped onto the floor.

Dan threw himself from the room and down the stairs. He lost his footing, and clumsily clonked down each step, landing in a heap at the bottom. Dragging himself up, he threw himself towards the front door and tried to pull it open. It was stuck, and no matter how he pulled, it would not budge. Kicking out his foot, he smashed against it, but it stood firm.

Giving up, he ran through the living room to the kitchen. The back door would not open either. Grabbing at a chair, he lifted it up and threw it at the window. It bounced off, narrowly missing his chest.

The room behind him suddenly came alive: pictures were moving, chairs lifting and banged on the floor. Ornaments flew across the room through to the kitchen, where Dan stood paralysed with fear, and crashed against the walls either side of him. He saw the toaster lift from the corner of his eye and wobble from side to side.

'Fucking hell!' he shouted, backing towards the door, staring at the objects moving all around him.

With his back flattened against the door, his legs gave way and he slid slowly down, his body a heap of jelly.

Someone or something grabbed his shoulder; he turned around so quickly he felt dizzy. There was no one there, only the door that he was propped against. Suddenly a broken doll lifted from the bin and flew at his face. He screamed, but only a small squeak escaped him. Covering his head with his arms, Dan began to say the Lord's Prayer, surprised at himself for remembering the words. As he spoke the words the room about him began to quieten. He stayed where he was, repeating the prayer over and over until feeling confident he was safe. He looked up and around him. Various objects had levitated into the air and were floating in a circle around the centre of the kitchen. The table in the living room had lifted a few inches from the floor and was hovering.

Dan sat, transfixed, as lights of all colours flashed around the walls and onto the ceiling. Pulling himself slowly and unsteadily to his feet, he stood, scared that any fast movement would disturb the scene and draw attention to him again. Turning towards the back door, Dan gave one almighty kick. The noise that erupted made his heart thump so hard he feared a heart attack. A child let out an almighty scream and all hell broke loose once again. Ornaments came hurling towards him. Voices were shouting and screaming like some torture was taking place. A child was crying and then also began to scream, a piecing noise that hurt his head once again.

Dan, in a panic, kicked frantically at the door, desperate to escape. It began to smash bit-by-bit. The wood, old and solid, gave way and the large lock buckled, and finally, the door sprang open. He tried to run through the debris as a hand grabbed at him, pulling him back towards the mayhem.

It took all his effort to free himself, as he managed to stagger into the garden, fighting to stay on his feet. He ran to the neighbouring fence leading towards Margaret and Henry's; he jumped in one leap, straight over, falling headfirst into a large shrub.

He did not care that the branches ripped into his skin. Blood ran from the scratches, but he did not feel the pain, as he freed himself and ran to the back door.

He kicked at the door and it gave way without protest. Dan, going into the lounge, spotted a brandy decanter and poured a large amount into a crystal glass. He swallowed the contents in one big gulp and felt slightly better as the liquid hit his throat.

Suzanne met Alex outside his house later in the afternoon. The police milled about, taking prints and putting various objects in plastic bags. Carefully, they picked up the vase that Scott had hit Dan with, claiming it looked like what Marcie had described earlier.

Alex was shaken as he explained to her in more detail than he had on the phone to her earlier. They sat in her car along the road watching as neighbours stood on their front lawns to observe the goings-on.

Mr Davis, the ring leader, was pointing and seemed delighted as he relayed the story to all the nodding and shocked people, flaying his arms to add expression to his words.

Alex, despite his upset, found himself wanting to laugh at the sad, elderly man.

'I still cannot understand why Jane is so important to them,' Suzanne said, a look of bewilderment plastered on her face. 'I believe she may have taken some of the robbery money from them. But surely a small amount missing wouldn't brother them that much?'

'Me neither,' Alex claimed, just as mystified or even more so. He had not even known the mysterious girl existed until recently. 'My daughter was almost murdered because of this girl. Whoever she is.'

'What now?' he asked Suzanne, whose clouded blank expression did not offer any solutions. 'All I can suggest is trying the cottages your mum said? Maybe the Lucas's know something. Or maybe we'll find Jane and she can explain it all. All I can think is she must be a very frightened young lady.'

'OK, let's go.'

Suzanne smiled gratefully as she had not expected him to go with her.

Alex called Lorraine to find out how Marcie was.

'She's asleep,' Lorraine whispered.

'Tell her I'm OK. I'm going to a friend's house so tell her not to worry.'

Hanging up the phone, they left Suzanne's car and Alex drove the short distance through a series of back streets to the cottages.

They walked down the front path of Henry and Margaret's cottage. The curtain twitched but no one answered the door.

'Margaret's a funny old stick,' Alex explained, 'I guess she's ignoring us.'

They went next door to the cottage with the 'to let' sign in the garden. Alex explained it was the cottage his sister had died in ten years earlier.

'Is this where Isabella disappeared from?' she asked, knowing the answer but needing to hear it confirmed.

He did not answer as they both spotted the broken lock at the same time. The hairs on the back of Suzanne's neck prickled, as Alex pushed the door slowly open and called out. There was no reply so they went inside dubiously, imagining Dan suddenly springing out of somewhere. They walked into the living room, where a few ornaments scattered the floor and the three pictures on the wall were very wonky. Absently, Suzanne picked up an ornament of a lady figurine, noting she could remember her grandmother having one just the same. Alex went through to the kitchen and saw the smashed back door.

'It looks like Dan had beaten us to it.' Suzanne said exactly what Alex was thinking. He was cross now that he had not listened to his mother's ramblings and come before.

Suzanne had left the room and gone upstairs. She opened the wardrobe and looked inside and then through the chest of drawers. There were a few items of clothing and toiletries scattered about the room. On the floor against the wall was a dog bed; it was very likely that it was Jane who had been staying there. She went down again and told Alex it seemed a young girl, judging by the clothes, had been living there.

'She also had a dog, so it is a strong possibility it was Jane,' she finished, both pleased she had hopefully solved some of the puzzle and frightened that Dan had reached her first.

Leaving the cottage, they went to the one the other side in hopes someone was home. A young lady opened it, peering out the gap that had a security chain across the door.

'I'm sorry to disturb you, but I'm looking for the person who lives next door,' Suzanne asked, as the woman eyed them suspiciously. She held up her identification, hoping it offered some reassurance to her.

'You're the second person today,' Christine told her. 'A man came earlier. He said he was the girl's father. He had a big bruise on his head and looked ever so rough.'

'Is it a young girl living there and a little dog?' Suzanne asked, wanting to clarify her theory.

'Yes, that's it. She looks very young.'

'Did the man find her?' Suzanne asked, holding her breath in anticipation.

'I don't think so. The people were out in both cottages. Which is unusual. The man, Henry, next door but one, is very ill so never goes anywhere.'

'Have you any idea where they might have gone?' Alex asked, hearing a baby cry in the background.

The woman looked behind her, apologised and went to close the door. 'I'm sorry, I have to go, she's teething.'

'Please, it's urgent I find them. They're in danger from that man,' Suzanne told her, not hiding the panic in her voice.

'I've no idea, sorry.' She shut the door, not wanting to be involved in any foul play.

They walked back to Margaret and Henry's cottage and Alex banged, the front door louder. He lifted the letterbox, shouting, 'Margaret, Henry, it's Alex. Open up!'

They heard a noise from inside and looked at each other. 'Dan!' they both said.

Alex was like a raging bull as anger crossed his face. He shoved the door with his shoulder and was through the wood in seconds. Suzanne ran in after him as he was in the kitchen and out into the back garden in an instant. She saw the back of, a man, she assumed was Dan, as he leapt over the adjoining garden, over the end fence and into the housing estate, with Alex closing on his tail. She grasped for her phone and started to call the police. She then hung up again, deciding to wait for Alex first.

'Lost him,' he told her, coming back 15 minutes later.

'Now what?' she asked Alex, hoping he had a solution.

'Come on. They have another house. We can try there.'

'What about this place?' She looked around despondently.

'Let's call the police and say we were passing the properties and have seen someone trying to break in,' he suggested, suddenly noting what a pretty woman Suzanne actually was. Her long, blonde hair cascaded in little spiral curls in an unruly mess and her intense brown eyes that emanated so much warmth. In the outer corners were slight crinkle lines that suggested she laughed easily. He stared intently at her for a few moments, his own eyes full of expression and lost in his own thoughts. Was she aware her eyes seemed to bare her soul, not hiding anything that she was perhaps trying to? He thought them so sexy and as for those lips, well, he mused, as he smiled at her. He wondered then if she was with someone, as she wore no wedding ring, and then chastised himself — what a time to be thinking he fancied her.

He could hear Marcie's words in his head, 'Get a life, Dad.' Realising he was smiling directly at Suzanne, looking very stupid, he quickly looked away.

She had noticed his intent gaze and blushed, looking down at her phone as a diversion. She too thought Alex a lovely looking man and did feel attracted to him. But she really could not be bothered with the complications of a relationship in her life.

She called the police and reported the break-in, deciding to be honest that they had been to the house to try and find the missing girl. The police officer asked her to meet them there. Looking at Alex, Suzanne bit her lip, trying to decide whether to make an excuse and leave, or wait for the police. Alex flicked his eyes when she decided to wait. He was not pleased at being held up any more than Suzanne was.

Dan, peering through the curtain of Henry and Margaret's cottage, had seen the couple walk up the footpath. He recognised the man but could not think where from, in his fuddled state. He was relieved when they had knocked a few times and left. Pouring himself another brandy, he sat on the sofa to gather himself. His head thumped badly, both from the large swelling bruise and from what he had seen next door. His hands shook as he fought to steady them. Lifting the glass to his lips, he took another big gulp. The brandy began to do its job; he felt light-headed and nicely numb. He had no idea where he should go now to find Jane. Maybe she did live in the cottage and he should wait to see if she appeared. Not that there was any way he would ever go back inside.

He saw the couple come back down the path and stood up. He hid behind the curtain as they thumped at the door again and the man called through the letterbox. Dan remembered: it was the man he had followed, the one he assumed to be Jane's uncle. Smiling to himself, as now he had another lead, Dan waited; he would follow them and hopefully they would lead him to the girl.

In an instant and taking him completely by surprise, the man crashed through the front door. Dan dropped the glass he was holding and fled through the back door, leaping in one swift movement over the fence into the garden next door, and then the end fence, with the man close on his tail. Realising how unfit he was, but adrenaline pumping, he managed with some clever effort to dodge along alleyways and through more gardens, and eventually the pursuer lost him. Hiding behind a large shed, Dan watched as the man gave up and headed back towards the cottages. Smiling to himself at his cleverness, he waited a while before heading back himself.

Climbing into Mick's car, Dan drove through the car park so he had a clear view of the cottages. He felt sure they were still inside; lighting a cigarette, he sat and patiently waited for them to emerge.

'So have you any children?' Alex asked, as Suzanne sat on the sofa to wait for the police.

She wondered what Margaret and Henry would say if they came home at that moment and found them in their home.

'No,' Suzanne answered, a little too sharply, not wanting to elaborate anymore.

Alex took the hint and stayed quiet, looking out of the window, just in case Dan wandered past.

'I did have a daughter. She died,' Suzanne said, after a pause.

'I'm sorry. Trust me to stick my size tens in it.'

Suzanne laughed. 'It's OK.'

'What was her name?' he prompted, his sadness heightened because he could have lost his own daughter today and could imagine how devastating that would be.

'Jade. She was born with brain damage and only lived two months. The loss ended my marriage because after we could not bear to be with each other as a constant reminder of what we both lost.'

'I'm sorry,' Alex said again, not knowing what else he could say, then chastised himself for not finding some more suitable words.

'We're still friends though and occasionally meet up for a chat. He's remarried now and has two children,' she told him, wondering why she was telling Alex this. Suzanne rarely spoke about her personal life. There was not much to speak about as she had so little of one.

'And you?'

Suzanne laughed again, and blushed, knowing why he was asking. 'No, I haven't remarried. I live for my work. There is never time for relationships.'

'But you're so lovely. I can't believe no one has snapped you up.' Alex suddenly felt silly because what he had just said sounded corny and daft.

'Well, thank you. That's very sweet.'

God, she's mocking me now, he cringed and stayed quiet, deciding it was safer.

'Well, it sounds like you've had your own grief to deal with, so I guess you understand.'

Yes, he had, Alex thought. He had had a few relationships since his divorce, but nothing had lasted. Being a single parent had probably not helped much.

Chapter Twenty-Three

Molly began to wiggle on the seat next to her and Jane was worried she would pee. They had not moved now for almost an hour.

'Do you think it would be OK to take Molly for a walk?'

Henry was also wiggling, more through frustration, though.

His tablets were due and Margaret was becoming anxious. 'Yes, go ahead. If we start moving, I'll pull over and wait. But don't be too long, will you?' she told her.

As Jane walked, she could see the fire engines ahead. They were cutting people from cars. Two ambulances had already sped past. They had shuddered, wondering if the victims were badly hurt. Judging by the blue lights that flashed, Henry said they probably were.

Many of the cars in the queue had turned and gone back the other way. But Margaret had told Jane the road where they needed to turn was just ahead. She had suggested going back to the cottage but Jane had a panic attack so it was not an option.

The cars started edging forward just as Jane was in sight of the crash, but not before she saw at least six cars that looked mangled. It didn't seem possible for any passengers to have survived.

'What happened?' she asked the police officer, who stood next to his car, a distance from the accident.

'Seems a young man ran into the road causing the traffic to swerve, and this is the result,' he told her glumly. 'Do not go any nearer, though,' he warned.

'That's horrible,' she shuddered. 'Were many people hurt?'

'We haven't a final count yet. But yes, a few. Ironically, the man who caused it is still alive. Or he was when the ambulance took him away,' he told her.

Receiving a radio signal, he jumped into the police car and pulled to one side to allow one line of traffic through.

Jane ran back to the car, and climbing in, told Margaret and Henry what she had found out.

They arrived at a house in the forest, just minutes after the traffic started moving. Margaret drove down the short gravel drive and parked in front of a country mansion. At least, it seemed that way to Jane.

'Wow,' she breathed, 'how beautiful.'

'Thank you; this was my childhood home, where me and my brother grew up,' Margaret explained.

Although Henry did not weigh much, it was hard work pulling the wheelchair up the two front steps. Between them they managed, and stood before the door, relieved to have reached it.

The door led to a large hallway with an open stairway in front of them. There were doors on each side and Jane was dying to peer in and take a look at all the rooms. Margaret led the way to a door on the left of them, pushing Henry in front of her.

Jane followed and walked into the most beautiful room she had ever seen. Two long, cream sofas, which were each big enough for at least four people, fitted easily into the large, bright lounge. Two matching armchairs sat each side of an enormous fireplace, which Jane imagined alight, with logs burning in the winter months. Fine paintings adorned the walls, and exquisite ornaments and antiques surrounded the solid oak furniture. She walked over to the French windows, which looked out onto a patio and then a magnificent garden, which was so vast it was hard to see where it ended. There was a large fishpond with a female stone figure in the middle. Coloured borders of shrubs and plants lined both edges and a few round flowerbeds were dug into the middle of the vast lawn. Tall fruit trees and vines were scattered about a little wooded area at the back of the garden. Beyond these was a never-ending forest where all sorts of ancient trees grew, towering above the rest. They were far taller than her oak tree at the park.

How she longed to walk free in the gardens and forest and mentally escape into a fantasy world, instead of facing the reality of Dan and somehow explaining to Margaret and Henry her dismal story. Would they call the police and have her taken away? she pondered, not wanting to turn back into the room and face them.

'Oh, how wonderful, it's the most wonderful place I've ever seen, even in a film,' Jane gasped, dreamily.

'Yes, my brother stays here when he's in England. But apart from that the house is empty most of the time,' Margaret explained. 'Now, Elizabeth, please do sit down and tell us what is going on.'

Jane sighed and walked to one of the armchairs near Henry. She ungraciously plopped down and Molly jumped onto her lap. Taking a big breath, she began to explain as best she could. 'I stole some money from the men and now they have come looking for it.'

'How much money?' asked Henry, intrigued.

'I don't know how much there was. But about nine big bags of fifty-pound notes worth.'

Jane looked down at Molly's coat, finding it easier than looking into the eyes that bore into her own.

Neither Margaret nor Henry spoke, as they fought to find suitable words and digest Jane's.

Suddenly the door sprang open and the three of them, including Molly, jumped.

'My God, I thought we were being burgled,' a man who entered said.

He was about 37 years old, with brown scruffy hair and blue laughing eyes. Jane thought him very handsome and went all shy.

'Jonathan,' Margaret smiled, going over and kissing him on the cheek. 'I didn't know you were here.'

'Is that you, Margaret?' he laughed, holding her at arm's length and studying the new look.

Margaret laughed, delighted. 'It is me, thanks to Elizabeth here.'

Jonathan walked over to his father and patted his shoulder. 'How are you feeling, Dad?' he asked, before going over and shaking Jane's hand.

'Not so bad, son. Good to see you back again.'

Jane could see the twinkle of delight in Henry's eye and smiled.

'I'm over for a few weeks; I only arrived late last night. I was coming over to see you both later as a surprise,' he explained.

'Jonathan lives and works in Italy, but he's in England on business regularly,' explained Henry, looking very proud of his son.

Jonathan went to a decanter and poured a large brandy. 'Anyone else?' he offered.

They all declined and Margaret went off to make them tea instead. Even Henry, who at first nodded and, seeing Margaret's looks of disapproval, then refused.

Jane felt bored as Jonathan and Henry talked about business, which she had no idea about. When they paused, she asked if they minded if she took Molly into the garden. She went through the patio doors and walked down the stone steps to the fishpond. She could see orange and black fish basking in the sun.

'Look, Molly, they're sunbathing,' she marvelled.

Much to Jane's horror, the little dog, seeing the fish, leapt in the middle of the pond to catch one.

'So, who's she?' Jonathan asked, once Jane was out of hearing reach.

'She was a lodger in the cottage next door,' Margaret answered, negotiating herself through the living room door with a balanced tray.

'Oh,' Jonathan's eyes clouded over and Henry wished his daughter had not mentioned the cottage to him.

'So, why's she here? She looks a bit young to be on her own,' he said, flopping onto one of the large sofas.

Both Margaret and Henry began to explain as much of the story as they knew and Jonathan listened intently. He laughed when Margaret told him the cottage was haunted. He then looked shocked and disbelieving when she told him what she herself had experienced, and then about the clairvoyant's visit. When they got to the bit about the men who were after Elizabeth, Jonathan looked both angry and worried.

'So, you both put yourself in danger for a young girl, who you know nothing about,' he ranted, getting up from the sofa and stomping to the window to watch Jane, who was now at the end of the garden near the woods. 'You're both soft touches; have you not got enough to worry about without this?' He walked out through the doors towards Jane.

The way he strode, Henry and Margaret could tell he was cross. They waited as he asked Jane to come back and explain to them what was going on. They watched as they both walked back, Jane's shoulders hunched as she dragged her feet.

'Right, sit, young lady, and explain to us about these men and the money you stole.'

Jonathan pointed to the armchair, and, head hung low, Jane sat down.

She looked up at the three pairs of eyes that now stared in her direction. 'I don't know where to start.'

'From the beginning will do.' Jonathan poured another brandy and stood with his back to the fireplace. 'It seems you have put my family in danger, so I want to know why.'

'I was so unhappy at home and school. When I heard my mum's boyfriend saying he was going to do a robbery, I waited for him to do it and stole the money and… and ran away, with Molly,' she finished hoping that was enough information.

'School! School!' Jonathan ranted, his face reddening and almost spilling his brandy. 'How old are you, Elizabeth?'

Jane's heart sank as she had not meant to mention school but with her fear she had blurted it out.

'Fourteen,' she whispered.

Jonathan choked on his gulp of brandy. 'How old?' he wanted to know, not believing what he had just heard.

Margaret stood up and went to Jane, who was now looking terrified.

'Stop it, you're scaring her.' She bent down in front of Jane. 'It's OK, he is all bark, he won't hurt you,' she consoled.

Henry was gaping, lost for words; he knew she seemed younger than 18, but she was just a little girl.

'I'm in so much trouble, I'm going to prison,' Jane said, covering her face from the burning eyes and beginning to cry.

'Hush, it's OK, but we need to know more. What's your real name for a start; it's not Elizabeth, is it?'

'No,' Jane confessed, looking up red-eyed to peer at the angry Jonathan and make sure he was a safe distance away.

'It's Jane. Jane Watts.'

Henry gasped, and Jonathan dropped his glass, splattering splinters everywhere.

Jane jumped and looked terrified through her red, swollen eyes.

'What's your mother's name?' Jonathan asked hastily.

'Toni, Toni Watts,' Jane was terrified of the man.

They were silent, gaping at Jane, until Margaret asked, 'What made you come here Eliz... Jane?'

'Well, I... I found some photos in my mother's suitcase. They were of her and a sister. I never knew she had one. I found a birth certificate of an Isabella. So, I thought I would come and find my aunt and cousin. But then I was too scared to look cos of Dan being after me. Then I found out Isabella was dead and you knew her. So, I was too afraid to admit I may be related. Then Vicky turned out to be dead too so there was no point, anyway. Then I kept dreaming of her and ...'

Jonathan walked across the room to Jane; pushing Margaret to one side, he grabbed her shoulders.

Jane was even more terrified that he was going to hit her; she flinched and sunk further into the chair.

He lifted her head and bore his eyes into her large blue ones, darting from one to the other trying to recognise the child.

'No, Jonathan, it's not possible,' Margaret gasped.

'Yes, it is,' he said with passion. 'That bitch took my daughter, it makes perfect sense. Look at her, she's just like her. Toni did not have a baby fourteen years ago. She kept in close contact with Vicky; we would have known. Toni was bitter and jealous, and wanted to make us suffer.'

Jane, feeling more confused, looked at Henry, who was staring like a statue with his mouth open. He was fighting for words, but the look of shock in his eyes prevented any from coming. She stood up, shaking Jonathan, who seemed quite mad to her, off her.

'Leave me alone!' she shouted, feeling the need to get out of this house.

'It's OK,' Margaret said, trying to calm her down.

'Jonathan thinks you may be his lost daughter, Isabella.'

Jane did not know what to do or say. She was Jane, always had been and now this man was thinking she was her cousin, Isabella.

'Your daughter was Isabella?' she asked in disbelief.

'What is your birth date, Jane?' Henry finally managed to ask.

'I... I don't know. It's July sometime. I've a birth certificate somewhere in my case, shall I look?'

'Where's your case? I'll go and get it.'

Without waiting for an answer, Jonathan snatched Margaret's keys from the table and went outside. He was back in an instant and Jane shakily unzipped a pocket in the front. She handed the two certificates to Jonathan with trembling hands.

He opened the first; it was for baby Jane who had died. The second was for Isabella, his daughter. He held it out for them all to see.

'Where did you get these, Jane?' Margaret asked.

'I took them from my mother.'

Margaret's face had drained of blood as she handed the certificates back to Jane. Look at the birth dates, Eliz... Jane.'

Jane stared down at them, confused, until Margaret explained. 'If you were Jane you would be 19 years old. Isabella has recently turned 14 years old and was born in July.'

Jane's face went ashen as she stared at the dates. She looked up at Jonathan and back at the certificates again.

'It does not 100 percent prove it though, does it?' Henry said, his face a very pale grey.

'But my mum is Toni,' Jane stammered, feeling more confused and now a little sick inside. She needed to get away from all of them to think. Her hands trembled so badly she put the certificates on her lap.

Margaret was the first to hear the car draw up, breaking the silence. She looked out of the window, 'It's Alex.'

'Mmm, what a beautiful house,' Suzanne said, as Alex manoeuvred his car behind Margaret's.

A man opened the door to them and shook Alex's hand. He introduced Suzanne and explained she was looking for a missing girl named Jane.

'You'd better come in, then.' Jonathan opened the door wider and stood to one side.

He led them into the living room, where Molly ran up and barked at their legs. Suzanne smiled and bent to pat the little dog.

'You must be Molly,' she said to the dog.

'This is Suzanne Bailey,' Jonathan told them, from behind her shoulder.

Suzanne walked towards Jane, who sat, looking terrified, in a large armchair that was too big for her small frame.

'Hello, Jane, you have certainly given me the run around,' Suzanne smiled to try to reassure her and held out her hand.

Ignoring the hand, Jane began to tremble again.

'It's OK you've done nothing wrong. I just want to talk to you. Well, after all this chasing about, I don't quite know where to begin myself. First of all, I want to tell Jane that her mother, Toni Watts, is very sick and in hospital.'

'It's not her mother, though, is it?' Jonathan spat, anger blazing in his eyes.

Suzanne smiled nervously, not wanting to build his hopes up. 'I'm not sure, but no, I don't think it is. I believe you may be the missing child, Isabella Lucas.'

'But I don't understand,' Jane stammered, wanting to run from these people who started talking all at once. She began to feel faint; nothing in her life made any sense. 'Please, do you mind if I take Molly outside for some air?'

No one heard her; Suzanne was talking to Jonathan, and Margaret to all of them at once. Henry was trying to shout above the noise to be heard, and Alex stood awkwardly in the background, looking just as confused as Jane. It sounded like a loud parrot cage that Jane had been into on a school trip once.

She crept to the French doors, which were still open, and Molly, also feeling overpowered by noise, followed her. They ran through the garden, climbed over the back fence, and into the woods, where Jane sank down, needing to just stare into nothing.

Little Molly started whining and nudged her with her nose. Jane put her hand on Molly's head, feeling some comfort as the warm tongue licked at her face. Jane got up and, with Molly just behind her, began to run again. It felt good to be free and away from the stifling people where she could think properly.

Dan sat at the end of the drive, watching them going into the house. Pulling his car to one edge, he crept through the trees that lined the driveway entrance until he was at the back garden. He looked through the edge of the French doors and, to his delight, saw Jane. At first, he did not recognise her: the clothes she wore, the make-up and the new black hair. As she turned her head, he knew it was her: mannerisms (like a scared rabbit) and the burning blue eyes. At that moment she stood up, coming towards the back doors.

He dodged behind the side of the house and watched her run down the garden.

'Perfect,' he whispered to himself.

She was too far away for him to follow her on foot, so he ran back to his car and drove to the other side of the wood. Parking up on the edge, he ran out through the dense woods to find her.

Jane had stopped running and sunk onto a welcome mossy clearing. She heard footsteps nearby, just as Molly began to growl, baring her little white teeth. Not feeling ready to face the crowd of people yet, Jane stood up. She began to run through the trees again. The road was not too far away; she could see the cars flashing in a blur through the growth.

Having reached the edge of the forest, she stood, feeling emotional and not knowing what to do. Molly sensing her sadness, stood and looked up, wanting to comfort her mistress again. From where Jane stood, she could see the skid marks from the earlier accident. The wrecked cars had been removed, leaving the road clear. She spotted something on the curb a little way down and walked the short distance to pick it up. It was a cap, the one Scott had worn the day she had met him.

Jane turned to go back into the woods and screamed as she came face to face with Dan. Because of the noise of the traffic, neither Molly nor herself had heard him approach. She tried to run, but he was too quick. Wrapping his arms around her chest, Dan easily lifted her from the ground. Molly, teeth bared, jumped up and bit hard into his leg. Dan swore and kicked his leg. The movement making him lose his grip on

Jane, who quickly darted away. He grabbed the dog by the scruff and threw her hurtling into the cars speeding past.

Jane stopped and screamed hysterically as she saw Molly fly through the air, landing in front of the traffic.

There was just one loud yelp from the dog as a car thumped into her little body.

Dan was back on her in an instance, grabbing her arm as Jane stood screaming. He pulled back his fist and hit her hard in her jaw. She lost consciousness immediately and Dan, throwing her slight body over his shoulder, ran back to the car. He piled her into the back and was soon heading back to their hometown.

Chapter Twenty-Four

It took a while before the room hushed; they were all burnt out with questions and no answers.

'Where's Jane?' Margaret snapped, noting the empty armchair.

'In the loo?' Suzanne suggested.

Jonathan ran out of the room, calling. There was no answer as he ran upstairs and came down again shaking his head.

'I'm not surprised,' Henry announced, once they congregated again. 'You scared her witless, all talking at once. Telling her she doesn't exist. Tact is not anyone in this room's strong point is it?' he grumped.

'He's right,' Suzanne looked shame-faced; she should have known better. 'Poor child.'

Jonathan ran into the garden, calling her, and Alex followed. They searched the garden, quickly noting she was not there.

'The woods,' Alex suggested: they both ran forward and soon disappeared from sight amongst the trees.

Margaret sank into the chair beside her father who looked very white and tired. 'Come on Dad, do you think you need to have a rest?' she gingerly suggested, knowing the answer before the words were out of her mouth.

'Rest! Are you mad Margaret? How the hell can I rest?' he screeched, going into a wracking coughing fit.

Margaret grabbed for his pump from her bag and held it until he had the strength to breathe it into his failing lungs.

'Get me a brandy please,' he asked, when he felt more in control.

'Dad! No.'

'Please, I need something to calm me,' he begged and she relented; it had been quite a day.

'Did Jane or Isabella have a good life with Toni?' Henry asked, once he could breathe again, thankful of the brandy that felt so good after all this time. Even one sip went straight to his head, sending his senses into a blissful fog.

She hesitated, not wanting to make things worse.

'Tell us the truth please. I need to know,' he pleaded, again knowing the answer by the look on her face.

'No, I'm afraid not. She's going to need a lot of help I think to get over her past and adjust.'

'Oh no!' Margaret cried, feeling even more horrible for the way she had treated the child when she first met her.

'Toni had no time for her. She neglected her badly.'

'What about the money?' asked Margaret, feeling as overwhelmed as her father.

'Jane said there are men looking for her because she stole their money. She was just beginning to tell us when all this happened. Apparently, it was her mum's boyfriend. He stole the money and Isabella or Lizzy stole it from him,' Henry replied.

'Oh my god,' Suzanne blurted out, 'I knew she had stolen some of the money, but all of it? No wonder they are looking for her. But how. There was millions….'

Jonathan and Alex reached the edge of the forest just in time to see Dan throw Jane into the car and drive off. Jonathan called out to her but the noise of the traffic diluted his voice in an instant. They both ran towards the car, knowing it was hopeless as they were too far away.

'NOOO!' Jonathan shouted, like a wounded animal.

Alex grabbed him by the arm and pulled him away.

Snapping quickly out of his grief, Jonathan turned to follow Alex back into the woods. As he did, he spotted the dog laying near the centre of the road, the traffic just managing to avoid the body as they swerved around her. He saw the blood all around her mouth. Scooping up the body he held her to his chest. Drivers seeing him holding the dog took pity and began to slow down, allowing him to run across again. Blood from the dog's body ran down his shirt; she was clearly dead.

They ran through the trees and back into the garden and into the living room. Margaret rushed forward and grabbed Molly's from Jonathan.

'He got her... the man,' Jonathan looked dramatically at Suzanne hoping she would offer some magic answer to where they would have gone.

Not waiting for any more explanation, Suzanne grasped her phone and called the police, thankfully being put straight through to Paul, the Detective Sergeant. The fear and panic in her eyes matched that of both Jonathan and Alex.

'It was Dan Wallace who took the money; he has abducted the young girl Jane Watts, believing she has stolen it. I don't know what he'll do to her.' Her voice was anxious, her social work training and usual calm dissolving.

Jonathan snatched the phone and told them the number plate of the car and handed it back to Suzanne.

'Did she say where the money is?' Jonathan asked, trying to calm himself and keep focused.

'She didn't have a chance, so many people talking all at once. Lizzy never spoke at all,' Henry snapped, angrily, fear flooding his body.

'We have a trace on Dan Wallace, we're just about to check it out,' Paul told Suzanne, who now had the phone again.

'Strange though, Michael Collins' son Scott, who we think helped with the robbery, is now in hospital. He was hit by a car earlier today, causing a mass pile up in Thornwood Abbey'.

'What hospital?' Suzanne asked, thinking he may know where Dan would take Jane.

Cutting off the phone she relayed the story to the eager family. Jonathan did not wait for her to finish before running for the front door.

'Come on!' he shouted at Suzanne and Alex.

Margaret laid Molly's body on a towel, wondering what she should do with the little dog. Eliz... Isabella will be devastated, she thought and then realised they may never see her again.

'Oh, my goodness,' she looked sadly at Henry, 'the dog's still breathing. I'd better get to a vet and have her put to sleep. Poor little mite must be suffering.'

'I don't really think you'll make it before she goes,' Henry said, equally as sad. 'We owe it to the little dog to put her out of her misery, and to our girl who the dog cared for. She adored her. Maybe you could get her ashes in a casket or something. I've heard they do that sort of thing for dogs. We could bury her in the garden.'

Margaret nodded; what else could they do? At least they were doing something.

The journey to the hospital was a long, slow one. It was the same hospital where Toni was. When they finally arrived, Scott was in the operating theatre, the casualty department told them. When he came out, he would be unconscious for quite a while.

'We'll wait,' Jonathan told them, not knowing what else to do.

At his request, Suzanne led them to the ward where Toni was.

Toni was not much help as she was still confused. Jonathan wanted to strangle her as soon as he saw her. Alex was amazed at how old and withered his sister looked after all this time.

'You bitch,' Jonathan spat, years of pent up anger bubbling to the surface.

Suzanne hushed him with her eyes. 'Toni,' she said gently, deciding it may be the better approach, 'Dan has taken Jane. He'll kill her. Do you know where he would have taken her? Please, it's important.' She was tempted, like Jonathan, to shake the woman to make her speak, but it would not look too good.

'Jonathan,' Toni suddenly said, focusing her eyes on him.

Suzanne turned to see a look of pure hatred on both their faces. Toni burst out laughing so much she became hysterical.

'You evil bitch,' Jonathan spat, his hands going for her throat again.

Alex pulled him away, 'No!' he hissed.

'Why did you take my daughter, why?'

'Because I loved you.' Unusually coherent, Toni's eyes blazed with anger. 'She had everything and you loved her and not me. I hated her for that, and you.' She began to cry, great, wracking sobs.

'You're a twisted up evil bitch, Toni. How could anyone love you? You took my daughter just to spite me and killed your sister, who loved you deeply. You've got a lot to answer for on the other side. May God send you to hell to burn,' he cursed.

Toni stopped crying and looked at him again. 'And you with me,' she hissed and begun to laugh again. A blood curling hysterical laugh, which soon died as she began to garble nonsense once again.

Jonathan sunk onto a chair, his shoulders sagging in defeat. 'We all grew up together. Alex and me, plus his two younger sisters, Vicky and Toni. The girls were only a year and a half younger. The four of us would hang out together. Much to my parent's disgust, he gave a slight grin towards Alex. They were rough estate kids and I was supposed to be a budding gentleman. When Toni was 15, we got together; young sweethearts,' he gave an ironic laugh. 'We... we had sex, it was her idea not mine. I kept telling her we were too young. We only did it once and she became pregnant.' He looked at Alex apologetically, who was looking back at Jonathan in shock. 'I didn't know what to do; my dad would have killed me. Because I was scared and out of fear of my father, I rejected her. It was my fault she went off to a party and got drunk. She left the party alone and was trying to make her way home. She never came home that night or the next. We all searched for her and eventually some children playing in a ruined warehouse found her. She had been badly beaten up and raped; she'd been missing for three days. Toni was unconscious for weeks and no one ever thought she would live. They found out she was pregnant and amazingly the baby was unharmed. I was consumed with guilt, but still never confessed it was my child.

When she woke up, I was terrified she would tell people the baby was mine, but she didn't. She gave birth to a little girl and called her Jane.' Jonathan put his head in his hands.

Suzanne put her hand on his arm and gave it a squeeze.

'It's OK, Jonathan,' she looked around at Alex to see his reaction to his best mate's confession. He looked so shocked, a mixture of emotions passing over his features.

Jonathan looked up again, tears of pain in his eyes. 'She came to me and begged me to own up. But I was a coward. Four months after the birth, the baby was found dead by Toni's mother.'

Alex sat on the edge of the bed, grateful to give his shaking legs a break.

Jonathan stared off into space as he spoke, 'Toni was so screwed up after the rape. We all suspected she had killed the baby, but somehow it was covered up because of her mental state. We all tried to help her. Vicky and Toni had always been so close, she was beside herself with worry for her. Nothing we did made any difference. Toni started drinking heavily and taking drugs. Hanging out with bad gangs of kids and always in trouble. In the end I guess we gave up on her.'

'But what about you and Vicky?' Suzanne asked. 'Did she know about baby Jane?'

'No, she never knew that baby was mine. I never told anyone until now. Years later I fell in love with Vicky and we got married. Toni hated us for it, she was so bitter and twisted. Soon after the wedding she disappeared. We brought a little house near my parents that needed renovating. While we were doing it up, we moved into a cottage owned by Margaret. Her husband had recently died. Vicky became pregnant; we never planned it. No one really heard from Toni but she still kept in touch with Vicky. She gave birth to our little girl, Isabella. What a beautiful child she was from the start. We adored her, so did my family. It seemed to buck Margaret up, who was full of grief. When Isabella was born Vicky became ill and was diagnosed with motor neurone disease. We were devastated that she was going to die. I promised her I would care for our daughter. Then Isabella disappeared while playing in the garden. Vicky couldn't take anymore. She took a massive overdose. And that's the whole sorry story. I've not seen or heard from Toni until now.'

What a horrible, tragic story, Suzanne thought, feeling tears pricking her eyelids. She put her hand on Jonathan's and gave a little squeeze. Jonathan looked to Alex; it was clear he wanted his forgiveness. But Alex did not speak; so Jonathan looked away from his gaze and back towards his sister who lay motionless in the bed, staring from one to the other.

'Now I have lost my little girl again,' Jonathan said, meeting Toni's eyes.

'Let's go to the flat and see if we can find anything to lead us to Dan,' Suzanne suggested. 'It's clear Scott will take a while to wake up and we may find something'

Both Jonathan and Alex nodded in agreement, grateful to be doing something practical.

They drove to the estate and Jonathan looked dismally at the grey dull flats.

'My little girl, living in this dump,' he said sadly.

It got worse for him as Suzanne opened the front door and the smell of rotting and damp hit their nostrils. Jonathan walked dismally around the rooms, feeling the disgust rise within him. He wanted to murder Toni even more now. He pushed open the door of Jane's bedroom, not wanting to see it, but needing to.

'Jesus Christ!' he cried, with horror.

Alex walked in behind him, appalled that anyone could let a child live that way.

'Smart Isabella,' Alex finally said.

Suzanne, who had joined them, and Jonathan looked at him in surprise.

'She worked it all out. She stole that money from gangsters to start a new life. Taking a risk of death, but being so desperate, she still took a chance.'

Jonathan smiled dismally, 'That's my girl.'

Suzanne nodded solemnly, taking on board the enormity of Alex's words.

'She certainly has guts,' she agreed.

Suzanne searched the post and found nothing to help them. She dragged down the suitcase from the wardrobe and tipped it untidily onto the bed. Jonathan picked up the bundle of letters.

'They're Vicky's and mine. We wrote them while I was at university. Why would Toni have these?' he asked incredulously. Taking the letters, he put them into his pocket. Next, he lifted up the Will.

'This is my father's, leaving some of his estate to Isabella. He wrote it when she was born. Maybe she was going to blackmail us after my father's death. Maybe that's why she took this stuff.' He took that too and flicked through various photos for pictures of Vicky.

'I have something,' Suzanne called, having wandered in from the hallway.

Jonathan dashed out of the bedroom, holding a small yellow T-shirt he had found in the case, and found her clasping an address book.

'There is Dan's old address, before he lived here. Maybe he's taken Jane back there,' Suzanne stopped talking and looked at the child's top in Jonathan's hands. Alex, standing in the kitchen doorway, looked too.

'It's Isabella's, isn't it? The one she was wearing the day she disappeared?' Alex said.

'I think that's all the proof we need, isn't it?' Jonathan looked to Suzanne for clarification.

She reached forward and put her hand on Jonathan's shoulder. How hard this is going to be for Jane and Jonathan, she thought. So many wasted years.

'Come on,' Alex said, snapping them both out of their trance. 'We've got no better plans, so let's try his place.'

The flat was close by and had new occupants.

'We're looking for Dan Wallace,' Suzanne said, 'do you know him?'

'Yea, what of it?' the undesirable man said and went to slam the door.

'Please,' Suzanne said desperately, 'his sister's dying and there's not much time. We need to find him.'

'Didn't know he had a sister. Try his mates Mick and Marc, they're usually together. They drink down the Queens Head,' he slammed the door, not waiting for a reaction.

'I know the Queens Head,' Suzanne panted, as they ran off to the car again. 'Let me go in, they may feel more comfortable with a woman,' she suggested.

She ran to the bar. Acting had never been her strong point until now.

'Please, can you help me?' she asked the bar maid, 'I need to find Mick and Dan Wallace, his sister's dying and she wants to see him now.'

'Oh no, how terrible. Try his girlfriend, Toni.'

'I've tried, he isn't there. I think he's at his one of his mate's houses.' Suzanne's face was traumatised, and if the situation were not so serious, she would have put herself forward for an Oscar.

The barmaid hesitated and, seeing how frantic the woman was, picked up a beer mat. Tearing off the print, she wrote an address on the cream cardboard. 'This is Mick's, I use to date him. I don't know Marc, but it's a start.'

Suzanne grabbed at it, a look of gratitude in her eyes. She thanked her and ran out of the door.

Suzanne frantically banged at the front door of Mick's house, while Jonathan left them and went round to the back. There was no reply. Alex ran to the front room window and stared through the dirty glass, putting his hand to the edge of his eyes to shield them from the setting sun.

Jonathan ran through an alleyway by the side of the house. There was a tall gate blocking his way to the garden. It was locked. He lifted his leg and kicked twice with the bottom of his foot. It buckled under the onslaught and sprang open. He then kicked at the back door until that too sprang open. Running through the house, he checked every room; no one was there. He opened the front door and shook his head at the other two.

They despondently headed back to the hospital.

'The lad saved my daughter's life,' Alex said, suddenly remembering what Marcie had told the police.

'So hopefully when he wakes up, he'll help us.' Suzanne tried to be positive.

Scott was out of theatre when they arrived, but unconscious and in the intensive care unit. They were refused entrance by the doctor, who sat at a desk outside his room. They could see him through a glass window, lying white and listless in the bed. When the doctor walked away, Jonathan rushed in and tried to wake him.

Suzanne pulled him away, 'You're too emotional, let me try.' She glanced over her shoulder to make sure the doctor had not returned.

'Scott please, we need your help. We're trying to find Jane. Dan has her and will kill her if we don't find her soon.'

The doctor returned and was horrified to see them both at Scott's bedside.

'Out, now!' She pointed her finger to the door like they were naughty children and they sloped off, feeling like they were.

As they walked away a man approached them looking angry. 'What do you want with my son?' he snapped.

'Michael?' Suzanne asked, surprised.

Alex sprang forward and Jonathan quickly grabbed his arms to stop him.

'Please, you've got to help us? Dan has Jane, he'll kill her.'

Mick laughed, causing Alex to try frantically to twist away from Jonathan.

'You bastard, you were one of the men who hurt my daughter,' he snarled, wanting to kill him.

'Not here,' Mick said simply, looking back at the angry doctor, who had lifted a phone to call security.

He turned away and they followed him to a corridor just outside the ward.

'It was my son that saved your daughter's life,' Mick told Alex, almost proudly. 'Now he's paying with his own. I lost him earlier; he died in front of my eyes. My boy, who without even realising it I adore.' Mick looked away to hide the grief and torment in his eyes. 'Even now he might not make it. They've just managed to stem the internal bleeding. He has a broken collarbone, four broken ribs, a broken arm and leg. A lot of poor bastards died today in that accident, and do you know what? It's all our fault. Not that lad's in there.'

'Where would Dan have taken Jane?' Alex asked, not absorbing the enormity of the earlier accident.

Mick looked at him as if surprised he was there. 'I don't know. Maybe the old war bunker where the money was hidden. Apart from that, I've no idea.'

At that moment two police offers walked through the swing doors ready to arrest Mick, who calmly turned to face them, ready to be taken. He would have liked to have been there if Scott woke up, but the best he could do was to clear his son's name from the robbery. If he lived, Mick would make sure he was free to have a life now. He was better off without his dad in it. He hoped he lived his life well and would be happy.

Suzanne nodded her head as a signal to Alex and Jonathan to move quickly; the last thing they needed at the moment was to be tied up with the police again.

They walked past just in time to hear them read Mick his rights.

'Where's the old war bunker?' Jonathan asked Suzanne.

'I've no idea,' she furrowed her brow, trying to think quickly.

Her office was shut by now so there was no one to help her. Who could she ring?

Chapter Twenty-Five

When Jane woke, her head was throbbing. She couldn't work out what had happened or where she was. Her mouth was covered and something scratchy was over her head. She was lying on a hard, damp floor, with her hands and ankles tied to something, so she could not move. At first, she fought to remember what had happening. The pieces began falling into place. The last memory was of Molly being thrown into the road. She visualised her body crashing into one car after another until not much was left of her. Hysteria rose through her body, making her feel she was suffocating. She could not see anything through the dense material. Squeezing her eyes tightly shut, she tried to blot out the fear and memories of Molly.

'So, young Jane.'

Dan's voice was close and she jumped at the sound of it. She could see a white light that splayed through gaps in the material.

'I'm glad you're awake at last. I was just about to throw some water on you.'

He lent forward and put his hand on her head, feeling Jane jump and squirm. He pulled the cover from her head. Her eyes were blurry as she squinted, trying to focus. The room was dark and cold; she guessed she was in the bunker.

He shone the torch in her face, making her close her eyes to the sudden brightness.

'I want to know where the money is. Now I'm going to undo your gag. If you scream, I'll beat you until you stop. Now nod if you're going to behave.'

She nodded slowly.

Dan undid the knot and Jane gasped in a lungful of dusty air.

'So, where's the money?' he hissed, dying to beat the girl into talking.

If she confessed, Jane knew she would follow the same fate as the man they had dumped into the water. If she hung on a while it would prolong her death a while longer. Either way, she was going to die.

'You killed Molly,' she blurted out, her voice full of hatred.

'Fuck the dog, I want my money,' he snarled, his face close to hers. 'Then I'll let you go to live your life and you'll never see me again,' Dan told her, fighting to keep the explosion of temper contained.

'I don't know about any money,' she bravely replied.

'So, do you think if I beat you, you'll suddenly know about the money?' He grabbed her throat and squeezed a little.

Jane squealed in terror, trying to swallow from her already dry throat.

'You paid £400 to get that dog back and before you tell me that old girl, who incidentally I killed, paid the money, forget it.'

Jane gasped, and let out a sob. 'You killed Molly and Mrs Flanagan. You're so evil, I hate you!' she cried.

Dan grabbed her throat again and Jane started to scream, making him wince. He struck her across the face hard. Jane head banged against the metal bed frame, to which she was tied. She heard the rustle of plastic before she lost consciousness again.

Dan got up, swearing at his own stupidity of knocking her out again. He went outside of the bunker and lit a cigarette. It was dark by the river but he welcomed the air. It had been a long journey carrying her all this way. He berated himself because she was out cold and, he figured, it would be some time before she came to again. He threw away his cigarette and went back into the bunker room.

Shining a torch in her face confirmed she was still unconscious. He cursed himself again as he tied her mouth and pulled the sack over her head. He would have great satisfaction killing her after all the trouble she had caused. He planned to have lots of fun with her first. The thought whet his appetite, which he fought to control. He decided to leave her for a while until she came to. It would hopefully scare her enough to talk. He would find Mick and try and make amends with him. Once he knew he had found the girl, he might come round and help.

'I'm pretty sure after a night in here you'll talk. All you've got to do is tell me and it'll all go away,' he said, hoping she heard him from the depths of her darkness.

Outside in the night air, he barricaded the entrance as best he could and left to face the river path.

Jane woke groggily an hour later. No amount of wiggling would free her. The knots on the rope tightened the more she struggled, stopping the blood flow on her already numb, painful wrists. She could hardly breathe and felt cold in only a cotton top and shorts. She began to shiver uncontrollably, due to a mixture of shock and cold that soaked through to her bones. Just like her dream, Dan was going to kill her and no one would ever know she was here.

Suzanne sat trying to think while Alex drove; she had never heard of any war bunkers that would still be standing this long.

'Stop!' she shouted, startling Alex, who slammed on his breaks.

He was none too pleased as a driver behind him began flailing his arms and mouthing a stream of swear words towards Alex. It was hardly surprising as the driver had almost crashed into them. Other angry drivers began to hoot from the convoy that was now forming along the high street.

'I'm going in the British Legion, it's just over the road there,' Suzanne pointed. 'They must know where the bunker is.'

She leapt from the car, leaving Alex to deal with the road rage and find a parking place. Jonathan jumped out the car and ran after her.

By the time he reached Suzanne, she was already talking to a man at a table in a small lobby. Judging by the raised voices, it was not going well.

'I just want some information,' Suzanne was saying. 'Are there any war bunkers in this area?'

'I've already told you, you need to be a member to come in,' the man grumped, obviously taking his job very seriously. 'Or if you know anyone inside, maybe they could sign you in,' he added helpfully.

'You, silly old sod!' Suzanne shouted in frustration, again forgetting her training.

She turned hopelessly to Jonathan, whose eyes were darting about frantically.

'The river,' the man suddenly piped up.

'Sorry?' Jonathan asked.

'There's three down the River Lea, close to here. On the other side, one on the right and two on the left. I think the furthest on the right is a crumpled ruin. The other two are condemned and dangerous.'

'Thank you!' Jonathan called back as they rushed out of the door.

As an afterthought, Suzanne ran back and apologised for being rude.

She directed Alex to the river, and then changed her mind. There were a few accesses to the river.

'Turn around,' she commanded.

'Yes, Mum,' Alex smirked, half amused and half fed up with causing disruption on the road.

'I just thought; there's an entrance to the river close to the flats where Jane lived.'

So Alex swung the car around and drove the other way under Suzanne's instruction.

'Torches!' she shouted.

'I have a large one in the boot,' Alex assured them.

'There are three bunkers though, so we all need torches,' she snapped impatiently, pointing towards the supermarket.

They stopped in the car park and Jonathan ran into the shop, coming out a short time later with two torches, plus batteries. As they put them in, Alex made his way, again with directions from Suzanne, to the river.

There were a few night fishermen that sat on the bank with small tents in the dark, the full-moon light illuminating their silhouettes.

'Have you seen anyone crossing the river tonight, mate?' Alex asked.

'Not seen anyone, really, there was a man about an hour ago who came across. Don't think he was fishing though, unless he left his stuff behind. No one usually goes over there,' one of the fishermen told them.

'Did he have a girl with him?' Jonathan asked.

'No, mate, he was on his own.'

'Where is the bridge to cross?' he asked and the man pointed the way.

They crossed the bridge and stood staring into the dark gloom. Both ways looked equally dismal.

'We could be on a wild goose chase,' Jonathan said, deflated.

'Come on, we can't give up now. I'll go left, you two go right,' suggested Alex.

Not waiting for an agreement, he walked a little way forward, then came back. 'On second thoughts, let's all go right.'

The path on the left was so overgrown that there was little doubt anyone had been through there for many years.

They would have liked to run down the path, but it was so treacherous they daren't. They carefully picked their way gingerly through to avoid tripping or cutting themselves too much. It was a long dark journey that was never ending. All three of them wondered if there was some mistake and the bunkers did not exist anymore. Suzanne constantly reminded herself that a man had been seen coming from this side of the river earlier. But then again, he could have been a fisherman and not Dan.

It took a while for Dan to trace Scott at the hospital. He had not expected to find him in intensive care. Having slipped by the nurse and doctor, he stood at the end of the bed staring down at Scott. He certainly did not look too good as a heart monitor bleeped away.

'Can I help you?' a voice asked from behind him.

Dan turned to see a female doctor, who looked too young to be in charge.

'I'm looking for the boy's dad,' Dan told her, not taking his eyes from the grey face of Scott.

'He was taken away by the police earlier,' the doctor informed him, in a matter-of-fact tone. 'I'll have to ask you to leave. Only close family are allowed in here.'

Dan turned away, found a chair in the corridor, and sat down to think. Would Mick grass him up? He did not think so, but did not want to take chances. He needed to get away from the area tonight.

Dan left the hospital and made for Mick's house. His passport and clothes were there. When he arrived, he watched the house for a while before feeling brave enough to go inside and collect his belongings. He took the shotgun from the boot of the car first, just in case. Dan was in and out of the house within minutes, noting the broken back door. He drove back to the bunker, his mind full of thoughts of how he would make Jane talk, and quickly. She was a stubborn little thing, he smiled to himself. Dan decided to drive as far as possible before daring to attempt an airport, possibly Scotland; he would ditch Mick's old car somewhere and buy another to get him there. Maybe he should take Jane with him, and she could entertain him while he made plans to leave Britain. He smiled to himself, lost in wonderful thoughts of the fun he could have with her before he left.

Suzanne sunk to her knees again and swore as the thorns from a particularly prickly bush sunk into her hands and knees. She felt like crying as this could all be pointless and Jane could already be dead. They had been walking for ages and still no bunker. They did not even know if they were in the right place. The bunkers could be anywhere along the river, miles even.

Alex bent down and, grabbing her arm, eased her to her feet, as he did the time before.

'You OK?' he asked, his voice full of concern.

Not daring herself to speak, in case she burst into tears, she nodded and turned away.

'It's creepy down here,' Alex smirked, making Suzanne smile.

Jonathan was well ahead of them by now. 'I think we're almost there,' he called back, as the light from his torch settled on a 'Danger' sign.

They stood beside him and stared at the creepy, isolated building that seemed ghostly and eerie.

'Poor Jane, if she's here,' Suzanne said and wished she hadn't as she noted the look of anxiety on Jonathan's face.

They agreed to split up in order to search all the areas of the bunker quickly. Jonathan went up the steps and found nothing but a roof lookout.

Alex pulled open the doorway that led to Molly's hideout. Suzanne attempted a circle around the bunker. She swore as she fell over a concrete bolder and cut her hand on something the sharp.

'Bollocks!' she said, sitting up and clasping the wound to her stomach as the pain took her breath away.

Alex flashed his light on her and knelt down. 'You OK?'

'No, actually, I'm not,' she said through gritted teeth, wanting to slap him because her hand hurt.

Jonathan joined them. 'It's no good, there's nothing here.'

'Now what?' Alex sat down beside Suzanne.

'Go back and let the police try and find Jane, I guess,' Suzanne half-heartedly suggested, feeling any hope for Jane being alive leaving her.

Jonathan sunk down beside them both. They sat in silence, lost in their own thoughts and trying to come up with some other plan of what to do. None of them wanted to give up on Jane, but it was hopeless and she could be anywhere.

Alex was the first to speak and offer the solution they had all been considering. 'Let's get out of here,' he stood up, and grabbed the torch.

'Shush,' Suzanne hissed, 'there's someone coming.'

They listened and, sure enough, they heard twigs cracking by heavy footsteps. Turning off their torches, they scrambled to the edge of the bunker. They could see the light from a torch getting closer to them. It was hard to be sure in the dim light, but the silhouette was the same build as Dan.

The man went to the wall of the bunker close to where they were standing. Jonathan stood on a branch and it gave a loud crack. The man stopped and shone his torch in their direction. They shimmied carefully out of sight around the wall edge. Standing perfectly still, they held their breath and waited. They could hear movement of some kind as the person cleared the entrance and pulled the ruins of the door away from the gap and disappeared through the hole.

Once they were sure the coast was clear, Alex stuck his head round.

'He's gone,' he hissed.

He walked out from behind the wall to see where Dan had disappeared. Jonathan turned on his torch, holding his hand over the front so only a small amount of light showed.

'There's a doorway,' he whispered.

Jane's hearing, heightened by the silence, heard someone outside, long before the door opened. She had no idea how long she had been in there. It must be the next day, she thought, as the fear gripped her insides. Now she will die or be buried alive, like her dream. She felt beads of sweat running down her neck and tickling her back. The door of the room opened and she could see a beam of torchlight through the cloth covering her head again. She squeezed her eyes shut against the burst of the sudden light. Dan kicked out his foot into Jane's stomach and she let out a muffled scream. Pulling the sack from her face, he shone the torch in her eyes and watched her squirm. He put his hand around her throat and she let out another muffled scream.

'Right, you little bitch, you will tell me where the money is or so help me...'

Dan's full weight fell forward on top of Jane, knocking the wind out of her. Within seconds, his weight was pulled from her and someone was untying the ropes. Her cramped limbs ached and her numb hands and feet throbbed with pain. The pain became worse as the ropes were released and the blood began to flow.

Now she was to be buried alive. Jane could not see anything as she was still blinded by the torchlight. She became hysterical when her gag was taken off.

'Please, don't hurt me,' she pleaded through her hysteria. 'I'll tell you where it is. Please let me go.'

She felt arms wrap around her.

'It's OK, Jane, you're safe.'

It was a woman's voice and Jane did not know who it was.

'Hush, you're safe from Dan now, he can't hurt you anymore,' the voice cooed, as a hand stroked her hair in an attempt to calm her.

Jane still did not know who it was, but the arms were so good to feel, she began to sob, great wracking pent-up tears of relief and pain for Mrs

Flanagan and her beautiful Molly, whose body was just a bloody mess on the road somewhere.

The lady continued to stroke her hair, allowing her to cry, offering words of comfort, and telling her everything would be all right. But it would never be all right. Not ever, now that her best and only friend was dead.

Jonathan and Alex, by torchlight, tied up Dan's hands and, just to be on the safe side, his feet too. He was waking up but very groggy as he groaned.

'Well, I never,' Jonathan said, shining his torch towards the bed where Jane had been tied. On the floor beneath them was a diamond necklace and a large wedge of fifty-pound notes. From where Jane had been tied, she had jogged the frame so much, some had fallen through the tear in the mattress. Hanging through the metal bedsprings was part of a plastic sack, the opening showing more precious jewels and more money. Alex went forward and lifted the mattress. Out came carefully packed bin bags full of money.

Dan, now awake, was staring in disbelief as Jonathan pulled apart the tear in the next mattress and pulled out more bin liners full of money.

Jonathan grinned at Dan. 'Outfoxed by a little girl.' He burst out laughing at the shocked look on Dan's face. 'That's my girl.'

'Let's get her out of here and call the police,' Alex suggested.

She tried to get Jane to her feet, but her legs were weak and painful.

'Come on, sweetheart, we need to get you out of here,' Suzanne coaxed gently, trying again to help her up.

In the end, Jonathan scooped up her small frame and carried her up the stairs, through the opening to the outside. Jane gasped greedily at a lungful of fresh air.

'When is the last time you had a piggy back?' he asked her,

'At school,' she croaked, through a very dry throat.

He crouched down and, recognising his body language, Jane climbed on to his back. It was a slow journey, until Suzanne could gain a signal on her mobile. She called the police and told them about the stolen money and Dan at the bunker.

Reaching the car, they climbed warily in. They dropped Suzanne back at her car at Alex's house. She promised to come the following day to see them.

'You're not taking my daughter away, are you? I've got her back and am never going to lose her again,' Jonathan told her, slightly aggressive and not offering any negotiation.

'There are a lot of things that need sorting out, Jonathan. I'm sorry, but there's so much… "red tape" at the moment. But I wouldn't dream of doing that. I've a feeling you'll have a hard task on your hands, though. Jane has been through a lot, it's not going to be easy,' she explained, giving him a gentle warning.

'My life has never been easy since I lost my beautiful wife. But it's my problem, not yours. My daughter will be OK. I'll make sure of it.'

He slammed the door, leaving Suzanne feeling hurt, as she stood watching the car drive away.

'Thanks a lot, too,' she said out loud and sadly turned to her own car. She was shattered, aching and still bleeding from her wound.

Chapter Twenty-Six

Jane opened her eyes the next morning, not knowing where she was. She put her hand out to feel for Molly, but the spot was empty. Her head felt fuzzy and her wrists sore as she tried to sit on the edge of the bed. Every part of her body was painful. Her jaw and head, which were swollen and throbbing, felt worse.

Her wrists and feet had electric shocks shooting down them. She rubbed at them, staring, bewildered, at the angry welts. The sun was streaming through a crack in the heavy dark curtains as she stared around at the room. It was enormous, as was the bed, which swamped her small body. The vision that hit her head made her cry out, as she saw again the cars hitting Molly's body. The door sprang open and Jonathan ran in, grabbing her in his arms; Jane hit him with her small fists to him to push him away. Margaret came in after him and rushed to the other side of the bed. She pulled Jane away from Jonathan and into her arms.

'It's OK,' she cooed, smothering Jane as Suzanne had done.

'Leave us,' she mouthed to her brother, who was looking so sad that his daughter did not want him near her. 'It's too soon. Give her time.'

'My little Molly's dead!' Jane cried.

'I know, sweetheart, I'm so sorry! I know how much you loved her.'

Jonathan stood at the doorway, his fists clenched. He wanted to kill Dan for hurting her so bad. Then he wanted to kill Toni for what she had done to them all. He turned away, his own tears now silently falling. He heard his father calling from the makeshift bedroom downstairs. Ignoring him, he went into the lounge, pouring himself a large brandy, downing the liquid in one gulp. He could still hear his daughter's sobs and each one was like a stab in his heart. The life she had led, living with Toni in that disgusting flat: he would never really know how much she had suffered at the hands of that evil woman.

Jane stopped crying and had gone very silent.

'Why don't you lay back and sleep a little more? It's still early and we gave you something to help you rest,' Margaret advised her.

Jane lay back and stared at the wall. Her eyes soon shut and she was breathing deeply as Margaret stood up and tiptoed from the room, leaving the door ajar in case Jane woke again. She went down to find Jonathan, who was staring out the French doors into the garden.

'I'm going to take her to Italy with me,' he told his sister, not turning round, but guessing it was her.

She walked over and put her hand on his shoulder in a rare show of affection.

'Do you think that's wise? It'll be so alien to her. We've just got her back. She needs schooling and...'

'A family,' he finished.

'Well, yes: Dad, me and you. In a strange country with just you, she'll be lost.'

He sighed. 'You're probably right, but I never want to leave her again. I'll take some leave until I decide.'

Margaret smiled; he was a good, kind man, but so hot-headed. Leaving Jonathan, she went to her father, who was demanding to see Isabella.

'You mustn't call her that yet, Dad. She's so confused and overwhelmed, we must call her Jane for now,' she told him gently.

It was clear he was elated to have his granddaughter home again. How he had adored little Isabella; they all had. The little soul who had bought so much lightness to their sad, tragic lives.

'What about the dog? We can't break her heart with that yet,' Henry said, looking like he was about to cry for the child's sadness.

'She knows, Dad. That's why she was crying. When we get the casket back, we can have a burial, maybe that'll help ease a small amount of pain for her. Maybe later, when she feels better, we can get her another dog.'

'Damn tragic, I say,' Henry said. 'She loved that scruffy thing. Must say I got fond of her myself. Poor child has been through enough. Now the police may want to punish her as well. Did you look into her case?'

'No, I didn't have the heart. But maybe we should when you're up.'

It was ten o'clock in the morning when Suzanne arrived. Jane was still in bed, Margaret told her. The four of them sat in silence, each lost in their own thoughts, until Henry suggested they open the case. Jonathan wheeled it into the centre of the room and undid the zip. Inside was packed with money and a few items of clothing. He gathered them up and Margaret took them from him.

'I'll take them up for when she wakes up.'

His eyes spotted the gun at the same time as Suzanne. They all looked up guiltily as they spotted Jane in the doorway, her eyes red from more weeping and her face badly bruised. Margaret had wanted to take her to hospital the night before. But, fearing the authorities taking Jane away, they refrained from doing so. An emergency doctor had been called and advised she went the next day. Now she stood there, looking horrified to see they had found the gun and money.

Jonathan went to her and put his hand on her shoulder. 'It's OK, we'll get rid of the gun so you don't get into more trouble.'

'I shot a man, I'll go to prison,' Jane confessed, as it did not seem to matter any longer.

They all looked to Suzanne, as she was the authority and would have to play by the rules.

'Who did you shoot, Jane, can you tell us about it?

Jane walked to the armchair, remembering that just the day before Molly had sat squashed on her lap. She sank down and told them from the beginning what had happened: how horrible school was, Lucy Ellis, her friend, Mrs Flanagan, the robbery, how she and Molly had hidden at the bunker in a patch of ground nearby, how she had hidden the money, when she got caught by Dan and how she had shot one of the men with him, and finally, how Dan and the other man had dumped the body in the river. They listened intently, without interrupting, except at parts when Jane got stuck or began to cry again about Molly. At the end, she stopped speaking and the room fell silent.

'Right,' Suzanne said, breaking the silence, 'we need a plan to protect Jane. How about something like: you hid Molly at the war bunker; you discovered the entrance to the underground room; you found the money and hid it in the mattresses. You knew nothing of the robbery. Forget about the man you shot, you know nothing about it. Do not even mention it,' she finished, pondering for a while, realising her story had many open gaps. 'We can of course perfect the details between us. Jonathan can get rid of the gun in some river.'

'But I thought as a social worker, you wouldn't lie?' Margaret said.

'I'm a social worker to protect children, not to harm them. Jane has been through enough in her life. It wouldn't benefit her for the truth to come out.' She turned to Jane. 'What do you think?'

'Well... I... will it work?' she asked, amazed that these people were going to protect her.

'It needs some tidying up but I think it will. If I speak to them,' Suzanne told her, smiling.

'What about the case full of money?' Henry asked.

'It's not ours, it's Jane's. Compared to the rest of it, that's probably a pittance.' Suzanne looked at Jane, whose face looked so relieved.

'It's a police car,' Margaret panicked, as she looked through the front window.

Suzanne went quickly to Jane, who had started to shake. 'Now you're going to have to be brave and stick to the story. I'll get rid of them for now. But soon you'll have to face them.'

Jane nodded and Suzanne went to the front door.

She came back a while later. 'They've gone. I said Jane was ill, but as soon as she's better we'll go to the station and make a statement. It gives us time to get our stories straight.

As the police car drove away, they passed Alex on his way to them. Suzanne blushed as his eyes lingered a little too long when he greeted her. Jonathan saw the look that passed between them and grinned cheekily, making Suzanne blush even more.

They told him the plan and he helpfully added bits to tie up loose ends.

'Isabella.' Alex saw Margaret shake her head from the corner of his eye.

'We have still got to have DNA tests to prove it,' Suzanne interrupted.

'Sorry, I mean, Jane. Would you come and visit my mother when you feel better? She was devastated at losing both Vicky and Toni. It would be fantastic if she could rest in peace now after meeting her beautiful granddaughter.'

'No!' Jonathan objected. 'It's too soon.'

'I would like to meet her.' The determination in Jane's voice put him in his place and reminded him he was not accepted as her father.

Suzanne smiled and made her apology: she really had to get back to work. But she promised to come back later that night. Alex walked her to the door.

'Would you let me buy you dinner after you have finished here later?' he asked, feeling his own face grow hot.

'I don't think it's a good idea, Alex.' She saw the hurt look in his eyes and tried to soften the blow. 'It's not that I don't like you, it's just...' Suzanne looked at the ground, fumbling for the right words.

'It's just what?' Alex prompted. 'You're scared? What harm would dinner do?'

Suzanne smiled and met his eyes. 'Oh, what the hell! OK then, as long as I pay my half.'

He laughed, delighted. 'You're on.'

After she left, Margaret showed Jane where the bathroom was so she could have a long soak and ease some of her aches.

Jane thought she had never seen anything as grand as she walked into the room. There was a separate shower unit, and a large bath that was oval and had gold coloured taps. She walked to the bidet that was next to the toilet and looked puzzled, thinking it odd to have two toilets next to each other.

Margaret explained, and Jane looked amazed and then giggled. One wall was lined with small cupboards and drawers, which Margaret opened, pulling out a clean towel and some sweet-smelling bath salts.

The bath was luxurious and Jane lay in it for almost an hour, going over the events that had happened in the last few weeks. How her life had changed and how muddled she felt, not even knowing who she really was. It still did not seem possible that she was really the missing Isabella. Everyone seemed so certain, except her. She closed her eyes and fought to remember her earliest memory. There was nothing she could remember but being in various different flats with Toni and her many different boyfriends. They had moved a few times and she remembered changing schools. At one time, a woman and the police came and took her away. She had spent two nights with a lady and a man at their house. They had been so nice, but Jane had felt strange and cried constantly to go home. There was nothing else, no memories of a life before her mother.

After the bath, Jane went to the bedroom where she had slept. The curtains had been pulled back and the windows opened. Like the bathroom, the room was enormous, and the grandest Jane had ever seen. The large double bed was so high she had to climb on and felt worried about rolling out and hurting herself. A long blue sofa filled the space under the large window. Gold brocade lined the edge with small tassels that hung down. Scattered on the top were various cushions. The window filled almost the whole wall. It certainly stretched almost from floor to ceiling. The two doors were the same as those of the living room and were open wide, revealing a grid metal railing halfway up.

Jane stood by them looking out, deciding they were for preventing anyone falling from the window. The view looked over the garden and into the forest. A large double wardrobe of dark, carved wood stood opposite the bed. To match was a large dressing table and chest of drawers next to it. She marvelled that there was even a table with two chairs around it, guessing that maybe ladies took tea in their room at one time.

On the wall hung wallpaper decorated with large yellow sunflowers with big green leaves. The room was beautiful, bright and airy. Jane sat on the sofa, reluctant to go down and face Jonathan again. She was not sure she liked him and could not accept the idea of him being her father at all. As it was, when she finally did venture downstairs, he had borrowed Margaret's car and gone to fix new locks on the cottages and try to repair the back door. Henry was having a lie down, the recent events making him feel depleted. Margaret came into the living room smiling, bringing with her a glass filled with orange juice and a sandwich, as she figured Jane would be hungry.

'I've just heard from Kordelia. She's arranged with the group of people to meet at the cottage this evening to try and 'cleanse it' as she put it. She asked when we were free. But I told her we were tied up and to go ahead without us,' she told Jane, sitting beside her on the large sofa.

'I'd like to go,' Jane said, her mouth full of cheese sandwich.

'Don't you think it would be too much on top of everything else? Especially after all the spooky happenings? Besides, we need to go to the hospital yet and get you checked over.'

'I'd like to help the lost souls.'

'Well, I'm not sure I fancy it, especially when it's dark. Kordelia said the supernatural beings are more active at night. Shot the wind up me last time,' Margaret admitted, giving a big shudder.

'I could go without you,' Jane replied. 'What time?'

'I wouldn't dream of letting you go alone. They suggest ten o'clock because of the light evenings.'

When Jonathan came back carrying a tool kit, he strongly objected to Jane and Margaret going to the cottage. This made Jane more determined, as she did not feel he had a right to tell her what to do.

'Well, I'm going, and you can't stop me,' she told him, noting the look of hurt on his face as though she had slapped him.

'OK then. I'll go with you,' he relented.

It was agreed they would all go, except Henry, who like Jonathan, was totally against it.

'I think we've all had enough drama,' he grumbled, and then wondered if he dared ask Margaret if he could have another brandy and risk a telling-off. He decided not to ask but wait until they had left and help himself.

The hospital, after an X-ray, declared Jane was OK. She was to rest but should return if she experienced any blurred vision or headaches. Suzanne returned around six o'clock and they talked more about what Jane would say to the police. She looked lovely and had made a special effort with her make-up and hair. Jonathan smirked again, knowing the effort was for Alex, who appeared an hour later.

At 10 o'clock, they met the group of four people at the cottage door. Both Jane and Margaret lingered outside, not wanting to face what may be lurking inside.

Jonathan unlocked the door using the new key. They walked solemnly inside. Margaret gathered chairs and the group sat in a little circle in the living room. It was very cramped with so many of them. The head of the group introduced herself as Lucinda. It was clear from the clipped way she spoke that she was in charge. The tones of her voice let them know she demanded respect and would not tolerate any nonsense. Jane felt a little nervous of her, reminding her of the first time she had met Margaret. Lucinda was explaining that there could be some disturbance, which might frighten them a little.

'That may be an understatement,' Kordelia said, realising that the group may not have ever been exposed to anything like this before. She wondered if this might even be beyond them.

Jonathan raised his eyes and smirked, dismissing it as mumbo jumbo. He behaved himself once Margaret gave him a prod in the ribs and a warning look. She herself felt shaky and did not want to be there at all.

'OK!' Lucinda gave an authoritative snap. 'We need to begin. I want you to close your eyes and visualise a yellow circle of protection around us all. I'll do the talking. No one else is to speak. I want you to visualise a white light on the ceiling and the souls going towards it. Mr Lucas, do you think you should be here if you cannot be serious and not mock our work?' Lucinda snapped, noting his wide smirk.

Jonathan looked at all the eyes boring into him and felt very embarrassed. 'Sorry,' he stammered.

It was Jane's turn to smirk when she saw his face redden.

'All join hands,' Lucinda clipped, holding up her own to clasp Kordelia's and a man to the left of her.

Lucinda closed her eyes, as did everyone in the circle. Jane kept having a sneaky peek just in case something was happening. She saw Jonathan was doing the same and felt a giggle boiling up inside when his one eye met her one eye.

Lucinda's voice was loud and penetrating, making it clear she was not only in charge but demanded her orders were adhered to. She breathed in a few loud, deep breaths, before she spoke again, 'I ask my guides to come forward, to protect us. I ask God to bless us and offer healing to all of those present. I ask the archangel Michael to come forward and help us rescue the souls that linger around this house. I place a quartz crystal in the middle of this group to send out its light and help those lost to draw near,' Lucinda bawled in a matter-of-fact, toneless voice that suggested she had learned the words off by heart, but did not have any emotion left to speak them.

'Lost souls, we know you are here and we have come to help you. You must trust in us so we can show you the light, you need to pass over where your loved ones are waiting for you ...'

Jane was having another peek, feeling nervous; she could not see a crystal in the centre of the group.

Dismissing it, she closed her eyes again. There was a loud bang and she felt Margaret and Kordelia, who held her hands either side of her, jump. Her eyes sprang open and everyone except Lucinda was staring nervously around the room. One of the pictures on the wall had fallen off, its edge sticking out the back of the sofa. Jonathan burst out laughing and Margaret thumped him on the arm.

'Mr Lucas?' Lucinda chastised, very cross. She turned to Kordelia. 'I really do think this is a waste of time if these people cannot be serious,' she snapped, and Kordelia apologised, also giving Jonathan a chastising look.

'Well, I'm sorry but this is ridiculous. A bunch of grown people having a séance.'

'Jonathan!' Margaret said, annoyed with her brother. 'You weren't here, you didn't see it.'

Lucinda stood up. 'I'm sorry, but I'm not prepared to sit here with a disruptive man like him.' She pointed an accusing finger at Jonathan and waggled it a little.

The little group nodded and mumbled in agreement and, before any other pacifying could be done, they stood and scurried out of the door.

'She's a difficult woman,' Kordelia admitted, after she closed the door to the group, again offering a sincere apology. 'But you really shouldn't make fun of them, Mr Lucas. It was good of them to come all this way.'

'I'm sorry, but I lived here and I didn't see any ghosts or headless demons.' He shrugged, glad to be rid of the vile woman.

Kordelia smiled at him. 'I'm being told you will laugh on the other side of your face before the night ends.'

After she left, Jonathan received another telling-off from Margaret. It was Jane's turn to smirk, especially as Jonathan kept pulling faces as Margaret looked away.

They went out of the door into the front garden with Jonathan still being heavily chastised. Jane ran back inside, deciding if there was not going to be anything untoward happening, she would gather a few more of her belongings. She dashed upstairs and ran into the bedroom. Jonathan and Margaret, still engrossed in their argument, did not see the front door silently close behind her.

Chapter Twenty-Seven

Pulling open the wardrobe door, Jane dragged out some of her clothes and piled them onto the bed. As there was nothing to pack them in she ran back down to the kitchen to get some carrier bags. Grabbing a handful she ran back into the living room, surprised and shocked to see the rug pulled back and the cellar wide open, exposing the black hole. She ground to a halt and backed, terrified, into the kitchen. Her back hit something and she turned quickly to find she was against a little girl. Jane screamed and tried to run as the girl's hand grabbed at her.

Jonathan and Margaret heard the scream and ran back to the door, but it was locked. Jonathan fumbled in his pocket to find the key. Even when it was fitted into the lock, the door would not open. He shoved his shoulder against it, but it stubbornly would not budge. Margaret ran to the window and looked in. She could see the room was alive with lights, just as it was, the night she had rescued Jane. Pictures shook on the walls and ornaments twirled around in a circle in the centre. The ceiling was a blaze of colour and the blue lampshade that hung there was no longer visible. Thinking quickly, she picked up a rock and threw it at the window. It bounced off, narrowly missing her head.

Jonathan was still shoving the front door with his shoulder and then kicking the bottom with his foot. It crashed and thumped under his force but stayed tightly shut. A young boy's face appeared at the window and laughed at Margaret. She screamed and clasped her hand over her mouth. Jonathan looked over at her and caught sight of the face. His own eyes widened with a mixture of shock, disbelief and terror. He brought back his foot again and kicked with all his force. It gave a slight movement, weakening the new lock. Feeling encouraged, he tried again and again until finally it shot open. Both Margaret and Jonathan hesitated, neither wanting to go inside. Then remembering Jane, they rushed through the opening, calling to her. A blaze of light greeted them from the stairs.

Colours drifted into each other, forming glorious patterns that transfixed them both. They were so bright they hurt their eyes, but neither could turn away. The shapes changed into the silhouettes of small humans.

'Children!' Margaret shouted.

Not knowing where Jane was in the cottage, Jonathan tried to run up the stairs through the lights. A hidden force prevented him, as it pushed him almost back out the front door. Margaret ran into the living room, all the time calling Jane's name.

She could just see her at the other side of the room, her back against the kitchen wall.

'Jane!' she shouted.

Jonathan, hearing his sister, ran into the living room. He was across the room in an instant and grabbed Jane, who seemed mesmerised and not aware he was there. He threw her over his shoulder and ran back out, grasping at Margaret's hand on the way. Outside the front door, he put Jane down on the path, trying to catch his breath.

'What the hell happened in there?' he panted.

'Let's just get out of here!' Margaret shouted and, ignoring him, ran to the gate and pulled it open.

The blaze of lights could still be seen through the window.

'Are you a believer now?' Margaret asked Jonathan, when they were safely in the car and driving along the road towards home.

He looked at her, his face white with shock and disbelief, but he did not answer.

'Are you OK, Jane?' Margaret asked.

'They showed me, Kordelia told me they would.'

'Showed you what?' Margaret was intrigued.

But Jane said no more, lost in her own thoughts and Margaret did not push her, assuming she was in shock.

When they got home, Henry was waiting for them.

'Dad, you are bad. I left you in bed and thought you would be asleep by now.' Margaret wagged a finger at him like he was a naughty child.

'Well, what happened?' he urged, ignoring his daughter and hoping she did not spot the used brandy glass. He had enjoyed two large ones while they had been gone and felt nicely calm. He could not believe what

Jonathan told him and even Henry had to admit to ghosts being real after he finished explaining.

'So, Jane, what happened?' Henry asked, and they all looked to where she sat silently, staring into some distant place beyond the room.

Jane looked at them like she was surprised they were there. She had heard none of the conversation.

'It's children that haunt the cottage,' she told them, her eyes filled with trauma. 'They showed me.'

'Go on,' Margaret prompted.

'I saw them, there were about twenty, of all ages from babies upwards. I was at the kitchen door and a child grabbed me. Then there were lots of them all around the room. The room filled with light, and scared them; they suddenly disappeared. I saw a place where these children had lived. It was like some sort of children's home. They were terrified of a man who ran the place. He lived in there, but it was not like the cottage. It was a large gloomy house. He was some sort of doctor who used them for experiments. He would cut them up and sew bits back on,' Jane shuddered as she recalled the horror.

'One little girl had her fingers cut off and they were sewn back on to another girl. She was only about four years old, and died from the injuries. Others, he cut into their brain to see what would happen if he took parts away. One little boy had a head from another boy sewn onto his neck. They were strapped to a table so they could not move and part of their throats cut so they could not scream. If they misbehaved, he would lock them in a cellar under the building with the rotting bodies of the dead children that had died from the horrific experiments, sometimes for days without food and water. They were too terrified to try and escape because there was nowhere to run. People would not listen to children. Or they would think they were making it up. But one little boy was brave enough to get away. He ran to a policeman. It took some persuading but eventually the policeman came to the place and discovered what was happening. The man was found guilty and hung. What had happened was kept very quiet, so the bodies were left under the floor and the room boarded up. The authorities did not want people to know what had happened. The children have been hiding in darkness for years, too afraid to make themselves known. Like Kordelia said, they did not understand they were dead.

'When I moved in, they thought they could trust me, so tried to make themselves known,' Jane finished, and looked at them.

Margaret had her hand over her mouth. Jonathan and Henry were cringing and shocked at what they had heard.

'Just think; that sort of atrocity still happens today and people ignore it still,' Margaret said.

They looked her way, horrified.

'What on earth do you mean by that, Margaret?' Jonathan asked.

'It's what research laboratories do to animals,' she told them.

'Don't be silly, Margaret,' Henry snapped, dismissing the statement. 'They're only animals, it doesn't matter about them.' He then realised what he had said, because he knew how much Jane had loved her little dog.

'Like it did not matter about the children, I guess. But I know my Molly felt pain and it would kill me to think of her cut open like those children were,' Jane said, angry at Henry for what he had just said.

'What can we do?' Jonathan asked, trying to change the subject.

'I don't know. I guess like the animals, there is nothing we can do,' Jane told them, feeling really despondent.

'We could find them and give them a burial,' Margaret offered, feeling a little brighter at having an answer.

'But how?' Jonathan asked, still struggling with the whole episode.

'Their bodies may still be there, in the room under the cellar,' Jane told them. 'I think I know where it is.'

'Bits of the cottage date back to the 16th century. Jane is right, there was thought to be a children's home there once. They dug up the foundations when they built the housing estate. I assumed the cottages were part of that, probably where the keepers lived,' Margaret told them, remembering the research she and Stephen had done on the area some years before. 'There is a drawing of the large building in the museum. Have you any idea how long ago all this happened, Jane?'

Jane shook her head. She was never very good at history, so could not even begin to guess.

'What sort of clothes did they wear?' Margaret asked.

'Greyish dresses that looked very rough,' Jane replied.

'Well, that doesn't help,' Jonathan added.

They went to bed that night; no one could sleep for thinking of the atrocities that had happened all those years ago. Jane in particular could still see the little girl with no fingers, blond wavy hair and a beautiful face, as she held up her hand to Jane to show her the wounds. The little boy with only half a head and another little girl who had her skin cut away and put onto another child. Jane's nightmares were so bad she got up at 4 am and went to the kitchen to make some tea.

It was not long before Margaret joined her.

'You too, ehh?' Margaret smiled, miserably.

'I can't stop thinking about the children,' Jane told her, making Margaret a cup too.

'Me neither. I think I'll go and see Kordelia again,' she suggested. 'Maybe she'll know what to do.'

'Can I come?' Jane asked.

Kordelia did not seem surprised to see them the next day as she invited them into her room.

'So, your brother is now a believer?' she smiled knowingly.

How shocked she was when Jane told her the story of what she had seen.

'I know the local historian Simon Douglas; I'll see what I can find out about the area. Is there any chance we could dig the cellar up?'

'I'll ask Jonathan, I think he's keen to solve the mystery now,' Margaret replied.

'I think we owe it to the children to give them a burial and let them rest in peace. As for you, Jane, I think one day you'll be a fantastic clairvoyant.'

Jane looked horrified. 'Not me; I couldn't bear to keep seeing ghosts.'

Kordelia laughed. 'You'll change your mind when you're older.'

Jonathan, still very shaken by the experience at the cottage, did agree. He spoke to Alex who, after going very quiet when Jonathan told him, decided he would help. He relayed it to Suzanne, whom he'd had a lovely evening with, and was already planning another.

She was intrigued and wanted to come too. They agreed on the following Saturday to meet at the cottage early, before dark.

Jane, with much prompting from Margaret, Suzanne and the police, finally went to the station to make her statement. Suzanne and Jonathan took her and she relayed the carefully perfected story. The police were very kind and gentle as they questioned her. Both Suzanne and Jonathan were allowed to stay during the interview. Luckily, they were more interested in her being the missing child, Isabella. They took a DNA sample and told them it would be seven days before the results were confirmed.

The confusion for Jane had now developed into a fog. She felt very lost inside herself and tried not to think about it, as her mind could not cope with anymore. She had lost her identity and did not know who she was. Although Jonathan tried hard to befriend her, she could not accept him as her father. If he was then why had he not looked harder for her and rescued her from Toni? Nothing made any sense in her life. She missed Molly, her only true friend, dreadfully. When alone in bed at night, Jane cried herself to sleep. Her dreams were full of nightmares of being down the bunker cold and in the dark, and then being buried alive, like some of the children at the cottage had been.

Margaret had tried to console Jane by telling her that when the ashes of Molly were returned, they would have a proper funeral and bury her in a place in the garden. It was Jane's choice of where, and so far, she had changed her mind several times. She decided on a spot under a beautiful tree where she could be alone with her dog, but deciding which tree was a problem for her. Once Molly had a grave, at least she could visit and lay flowers for her, Jane reasoned. She could also chat to her and tell her how she lonely she felt, even with people around her.

The Saturday arrived and they were all very nervous as they headed for the cottage. Henry was left in the living room for the day with a flask

281

and sandwiches. He was as nervous as they were. How he wished he could go too, but it was out of the question, Margaret told him.

Kordelia gave Jonathan a knowing look when she arrived outside where they all congregated. He thought how pretty she was when looking smug. No one was confident enough to go inside until they were all present.

'Why now?' Alex asked, as Jonathan, who had fitted another new lock, opened the front door.

He pushed it open slowly and nervously poked his head around it.

'What do you mean?' Margaret asked him.

'This cottage has been here for years, so how come nothing happened before?' Alex queried.

'I think,' Kordelia answered, 'it's because Jane here is psychic and young. The children have been hiding in darkness, too afraid to come out. Her pure light or soul glowed and sent out a beacon to them that they latched onto.'

'But Jane has lived here before,' Jonathan said, equally puzzled, then added quickly, when he saw Jane glare at him. 'We think. Although, I remember, Isabella did have imaginary friends. She kept changing their names, so maybe she did see the children. But there was certainly not all the stuff happening that we saw the other night.'

'Well, I don't know,' Kordelia told him truthfully. 'Something has disturbed them. Do you know, Jane?'

Jane shook her head, only half-listening as she felt nervous. 'Maybe they were frightened?' was all she offered.

The cottage was silent, with no hint of what had happened the other night. The cellar entrance was closed and the rug pulled back in its place. Margaret went into the kitchen and made tea, feeling braver with more people around. Jane went down into the cellar with Jonathan and Alex, while Suzanne and Kordelia helped Margaret.

'Where do we start digging?' Alex asked, thinking they were all slightly potty, but he was broad-minded, as he had told Suzanne earlier, especially after growing up with a mother who claimed to have second-sight.

Jane walked over to a spot and pointed. 'It's here.'

Jonathan was not listening as he stared dismally at the pile of Vicky's and his daughter's belongings. He could see a piece of blue dress sticking out of one of the boxes. Lifting the lid, he pulled it out and held it to his face. He could still smell her scent on it. In his mind, he saw her wearing the dress, laughing as they sat in the living room talking, with little Isabella already asleep in the bedroom upstairs. They were due to move to the new house the following week, the building work now completed.

Someone put their hand on Jonathan's arm, snapping him from his dream. He turned to see Kordelia smiling at him.

'I'm so sorry for what you've been through.' The sympathy in her eyes reflected the words, making them more meaningful.

Jonathan felt choked and, to hide his emotions, he folded the dress and tucked it back in the box. He really needed to sort this stuff and get rid of it.

Alex had already gathered tools to complete the job of digging up the floor.

Jonathan grabbed a crow bar. 'Let's get going then.'

He wedged it under one of the boards covering the floor and levered it out. Underneath was a dirt floor, which was compact with the amount of time it had sat there undisturbed. Alex picked up a pickaxe and chipped away at it, while Jonathan dug, regretting that he had not covered the pile of boxes to save them getting dirty. He then decided they were already dirty from the years stored in an old cellar.

Margaret called them for tea so they took a break.

'So how come this is the only cottage that's haunted?' Alex asked.

'Cos that's where the bodies are buried and where it all happened,' Jane told him simply.

'But in those days the three cottages were one big house,' Margaret added.

'Maybe,' Kordelia offered, 'this was the place the children were kept and the experiments done.'

None of them felt they wanted to expand on that theory.

It was only about thirty minutes later that Alex's pickaxe hit something wooden. He looked to the others, who were crowded in the small cellar.

'A coffin?' he said, feeling a chill run down his spine.

Jonathan cleared the area that revealed more boards, which he levered up with the crow bar again. Underneath lay a large hatch. It took both men a lot of effort to prise it open. Jonathan shone a torch into the dark gap.

'It looks the same size as this cellar,' he told them.

'There's something down there, but I can't see what it is. I'm going down.'

'No, Jonathan!' Margaret warned. 'Let's call in experts?'

He ignored her and lowered himself into the hole.

'Jesus Christ!' they heard him exclaim.

'What is it?' Alex called, pointing in his own torch.

'Jane's right: it's full of small skeletons and other things.'

Alex dropped into the hole after Jonathan and gave the same reaction. He shone his torch around, exposing various tools that had been dumped into the hole.

'It does look like medical stuff,' Alex said, 'or rather instruments of torture.' He cringed at large plier like contraptions, saws and various sizes of knives.

A heap of disjointed bones were piled into one corner, of all sizes. Alex felt the sadness as he noted some were tiny, probably babies and children of various ages. He felt sick as he examined the tools more closely. They both scrambled up to the cellar again and re-laid what was down there.

Kordelia said a prayer for the children, asking God and the angels to show them the light. She took out her phone and called the local historian Simon; on hearing what they had discovered, he dropped whatever he was doing and turned up within the hour. With him, he brought a professor, Robert Neilson.

'There are very vague records about the children's home around here,' Simon told them, fascinated, after going down himself to look.

'The foundations were dug up when the housing estate was built. As far as we know, this was part of the abbey. This is an incredible find.'

'What about the bodies?' Jane asked. 'Can we bury them now?'

He laughed and patted her head patronisingly. 'I'm afraid, young lady, it's not that easy. We need to research this; the bodies will be taken away, and a full investigation needs to be undertaken.'

Jane was not pleased at being treated like a child and scowled at him. She had promised the children she would help them. Now they were going to be cut up even more. She looked at Kordelia, who seemed to understand by virtue of a small reassuring smile.

'They need to be buried,' Jane said stubbornly, 'they've suffered enough and want to be free.'

Simon ignored her as he turned to Margaret. 'I understand the cottage belongs to you?'

'Yes, and I agree with Jane: the bodies need to be buried and put to rest,' she used her snappiest, sharpest voice.

'I'm sorry for the distress this has caused to you all. Of course, I do understand your shock at what is hidden down there. But this is an enormous discovery. It could change the history of the area. We need to know why these children have been left in an area we believed to be part of the abbey. The decision will be taken out of your hands. I have already informed the authorities. This area needs to be cordoned off for investigation. I suggest you gather any belongings you need,' he advised.

Margaret looked affronted and very upset, but she slowly nodded and tried not to meet Jane's eager, pleading eyes.

Simon disappeared down the cellar hole again, where Alex was still studying the discovery in disbelief.

'Come on, Jane, let me help you pack some of your things,' Jonathan said, putting his hand on her shoulder.

Jane ignored him and turned to where Kordelia was sat with Suzanne.

'Come and sit down, Jane,' Kordelia patted the seat next to her.

'I know what you're feeling and how sad you are about all this. It's OK. We'll do our own service and help the children pass over. We don't need their bodies to do this.'

'But how?' Jane asked.

'If you agree to be part of it, we'll wait until Simon leaves and begin. Suzanne has already agreed to help us. I think Margaret will as well and hopefully Jonathan and Alex.'

'Will it work?' Jane's voice was full of hope.

'We can certainly try.'

Simon emerged from the cellar, still talking excitedly, followed by Alex.

'How long do we have to move out of here?' Kordelia asked Simon. 'We would like to say prayers for the children, before we go.'

Simon was not a religious man. But he could understand the enormity of the find and the distress. He nodded his head in understanding. 'A couple of hours, would that be OK?'

'Yes, thank you. Could you leave us then?' She smiled, showing it was a demand rather than a request.

Simon smiled back. 'As long as you can assure me you will not interfere with the cellar.'

He left them, promising to return in two hours. Kordelia told the rest she planned to do a service for the children. No one argued with her or objected, even Alex, who had doubted the haunting.

'Then you will help me? No mocking?' She directed her words towards Jonathan, who looked sheepish and nodded.

At Kordelia's request, Margaret went next door and gathered some candles. When she came back, a circle of chairs had been placed around the centre of the living room. Kordelia had pulled the curtains together, creating a soft dim light. They sat around expectantly as she pointed to the chairs. Lighting the candles, she put them in the centre of the circle.

Kordelia looked at Alex. 'Would you go down the cellar and get something from the room where the bodies are?'

He suddenly looked very nervous. 'What, me?'

Jane smirked and so did Jonathan. 'I'll come with you,' Jonathan offered.

Alex stiffened his shoulders and straightened his back. 'Don't be silly.'

Then at the cellar door he looked nervously back, seeing big smiles spread across all their faces.

Jonathan got up and went with him.

They were both back in record time with a piece of cloth.

Kordelia took it from him. 'It belonged to a little boy.'

'I... I... don't know, I just grabbed it,' Alex confessed with a shudder.

'William.' They looked at Kordelia questioningly. 'The little boy was William. He died at the age of seven. He wants his mummy.' Kordelia closed her eyes and began to speak to him. 'It's OK, William, we're going to find your mummy for you. But I need you to bring the other children with you. We need to find their parents and loved ones too.'

The room was silent, and Alex looked around, expecting to see William standing somewhere nearby.

'Please, all join hands,' Kordelia instructed, and no one argued. She felt nervous too and totally out of her depth with it. But she did not let on to the others.

'I call upon my guides to protect us and place a light of healing around this circle and the lost souls that are present here. I call upon the Angels Michael and Gabriel, Ariel and Rafael to stand within the four corners of this house and keep us safe. I ask God to send healing and light to help the souls pass to your kingdom,' Kordelia chanted, with passion in her voice.

Margaret thought, at least she had more enthusiasm than Lucinda.

'William, are you here?' Kordelia was asking.

Nothing happened, so she repeated her words several times. It was hopeless, the room was silent.

'Jane, you must try, they trust you. It seems they are afraid to show themselves to adults.'

Jane did not want to try: she was too embarrassed in front of so many people. But remembering the faces of the children, she nodded. 'What do I say?'

'Tell them they're safe, we won't hurt them. You spoke to them before.'

Jane looked nervously around at the others. Margaret and Jonathan smiled encouragingly.

She swallowed and shut her eyes. 'It's OK, William, we won't hurt you. These people have come to help you find your parents. Cora, are you there? Please, show yourself, we're going to take you from the darkness and you will go to a place where you can be happy. Where your fingers will be back and you can cuddle your dolly again,' Jane's voice was strong, but gentle with the compassion she felt inside.

Kordelia looked at Jane with amazement; she knew she was right, that one day she would be a fantastic healer, who would have great empathy for both animals and humans.

The candles began to flicker and a vase lifted into the air and flew across the room, smashing into the fireplace and making all of them jump.

'Keep holding hands,' Kordelia instructed, feeling the hands she held either side of her, tense and begin to tremble. 'They won't hurt you.'

'Isabella?' a little girl's voice called. It was distant, but they all heard it.

'Isabella, you said you would help us.' The voice became clear, but sounded like it was speaking through a large tube.

'Speak to her, Jane,' Kordelia told her, confused as to why the voice spoke to an Isabella.

Jane was shaking so much she could not find her voice. Both Margaret and Jonathan either side of her squeezed her hands.

'Tell her again you're trying to help her find her mother,' Kordelia instructed.

'It's OK,' Jane said, 'we're trying to help you.'

The noise in the room became loud as ornaments began moving, the pictures on the wall started vibrating and bits of furniture scraped across the floor.

'It's OK,' shouted Kordelia above the commotion. 'We're here to help you. I call upon the Angel Michael to hold out your hands to these children, show them the light and the pathway to the other world.'

Jane's eyes were wide with terror, as she stared around the room along with the rest of them. She stood up, still holding onto Jonathan and Margaret.

'You must look for the light; your loved ones are waiting for you. Look for the light!' she shouted with the same passion as Kordelia had.

They saw the light from the ceiling growing bigger and bigger. It twirled and grew, forming shapes of all colours, just as it had when Jonathan and Margaret saw it on the stairs. The shapes came together and formed into people, some holding out their hands. They could see the silhouettes of the children, who cowered near the darkened window.

One of the children — a little boy — bravely broke away and came forward, his arms wide spread. A lady from the light came forward and met him as he reached out to her.

'It's his mother,' whispered Kordelia.

None of them were nervous now they felt too overwhelmed by joy for the little boy who found his mother. He disappeared behind the crowd. The other children watched as two other people came forward. A girl of about five moved slowly towards them. She was unsure as she was trying to decide if she should run back or continue.

'It's OK,' Jane called to her, 'go to them.'

Two hands stretched out towards her and she reached forward, seeming to recognise them. The hand of a man grasped her and scooped her up, cuddling her close. The couple were laughing as the man swung her round. The other children watched with great interest and then one after the other they came forward. Each was met by one or two people who took them away.

Jane looked around, and the little girl with no hands was there. She stood looking at Jane. In her arms she held a baby boy. She smiled and Jane smiled back.

The girl turned and, with her baby brother, went to the last of the waiting people.

One lady remained, and Jonathan gasped when he saw her. He stood, let go of Margaret's hand, and reached out his to the lady.

'Vicky,' he breathed.

'You've found our Isabella,' she smiled, her eyes filled with love for both her husband and her daughter.

'You can now rest in peace,' Kordelia said, from behind Jonathan. 'Your daughter is now safe.'

The light began to fade, and with it, Vicky, her arms still outstretched to them. Her image turned to a shape and then a bright blue colour, which faded back to the ceiling and finally disappeared.

The room was silent as Jonathan, rooted to the spot, stared at the ceiling. Kordelia stood and put her hand on his.

'She's at peace now, Jonathan. Let her go.'

He turned to her, his eyes tormented and tragic. He sat, without speaking.

Kordelia sat too and said some prayers, thanking the angels and the people who had come, taking the children. Once she had finished, they sat in silence for some time, trying to understand the enormity of what had happened.

Chapter Twenty-Eight

None of them spoke of what had happened at the cottage after that day. No one would have ever believed them if they could have found the words to explain it. They all felt overwhelmed, and life for them all took on a different perspective and meaning.

Margaret had given a brief description to Henry, who was still struggling to come to terms with it. The historian Simon had kept in contact with Margaret and the two of them were becoming good friends. She kept them up to date with developments of the progress. It was slow as the bodies had been a great revelation.

Soon after the discovery, Margaret cooked a special dinner one evening. She invited Suzanne and Alex to join them. The two were fast becoming an item. Although Suzanne had not yet met Marcia, Margaret felt it would not be long before she did. She had waited until the dinner had ended and they were all enjoying a coffee, before she informed them of the latest developments.

'Apparently, the cottage was indeed part of the monastery. One monk was training to become a doctor. He was allowed to live in the cottage to study. He was found guilty of experiments on the children and animals. Because it was a monastery, the discovery of his crimes was kept very quiet.'

'But where did the children come from?' Jane asked.

'There are many different theories, but they're not really sure. Simon thinks they were either sold because families were so poor and had so many children, or kidnapped, or of course, some came from the children's home. But goodness knows,' Margaret told them.

'Seems you and Simon are quite pally,' Jonathan said, with a suggestive nod towards Alex, who grinned back.

Margaret blushed and looked at her napkin. 'Don't be silly, Jonathan,' she snapped.

'I have some news too,' Suzanne announced, trying to rescue Margaret from the embarrassment. She held up an envelope. 'It's from the police and I asked if I could bring it to you, Jonathan and Jane. It's the DNA results.'

Jane's heart begun to thump and she felt sick.

'Well?' Henry prompted, eager to know.

'We already know,' Jonathan said, a wide grin plastered on his face.

'Clarification is always good, though,' Suzanne smiled, before noting the apprehension on Jane's face. 'I don't know if you wish to look at it in private or with us here.'

'I think everyone needs to hear the results,' Jonathan told her, his mouth suddenly going very dry, because, despite his bravado, he could be wrong. 'Jane?'

She nodded reluctantly, not wanting to be here and hear the results at all.

'Jane is indeed your lost daughter, Isabella,' Suzanne told them, her eyes not leaving Jane's.

Margaret seemed to sense how Jane was feeling on hearing the news. She clasped her hand. 'At least you know now.'

Jane stood up, anger blazing in her eyes as she looked at Jonathan. 'Then why didn't you come looking for me? Why did you let me live like I did?' she screamed and ran from the room.

Jonathan seemed to crumple and shrink at the words that stung him so badly. He did not know what to do or say.

'Give her time,' Suzanne reassured.

'She hates me.'

'No, she doesn't, she's just confused,' Margaret said gently.

She pushed back her chair and followed Jane to her bedroom. Margaret found her lying on her bed sobbing. She sat down on the edge and put her hand on Jane's head, waiting for the tears to subside a little.

'He did look for you, Jane. He never stopped looking or believing one day he would find his little girl. Why do you think he never married again? Oh, he had plenty of female followers. He's a handsome man. But all he has ever lived for was his little girl coming home. You've been through so much. Much more than most people live in a whole lifetime. Now it's time for you to be happy.'

'I'll never accept he's my father,' Jane said with conviction, 'I don't even like him.'

'You don't know him yet. Give him a chance to prove to you what he's really like. He loves you, Jane.'

Margaret sat in silence, and eventually Jane fell asleep. Pulling the duvet over, she went back downstairs. Jonathan was looking mortified, and Henry sat there, looking miserable for both his son and his granddaughter.

'How is she?' asked Suzanne.

'It's such a lot for her to take in,' Margaret told her. 'But I think she'll come round.'

The next few days passed in a blur for Jane; most of the time she stayed in her room, away from Jonathan. At meal times, she answered questions with short answers or stayed silent.

Alex tried to offer a solution. 'Let me take Jane to meet her grandmother.'

'I don't know, it may be too much overload. We expect so much from her. She just needs time to come to terms with it,' Margaret advised.

'The story will leak to the papers soon. The Isabella story will be plastered everywhere. The police have held off, wanting to give the family time, but they won't do that forever,' Alex warned. 'Soon, young Isabella will be swamped and not know which way to turn.'

'He's right,' Jonathan said. 'Maybe it's worth a try.'

So later that afternoon, with Jane's agreement, Jonathan took her to meet Rebecca Watts. Alex stood in the reception, eagerly waiting for them.

'Mum's in her room,' he explained and led the way down a long corridor.

Jane felt nervous meeting the lady who was her grandmother, which felt so odd: first having no relatives and now having lots of them. She still had to meet Marcia, Alex's daughter, whom, Alex told Jane, she would get on well with. They stopped at a door and Jane hesitated. Alex knocked and opened it. Jane stood and stared in at a tiny lady sitting in an armchair by a window. She knew instantly that they had met before, but Jane could not think where. At last, she must be having memories of her childhood.

'Mum, this is Jane,' Alex said, not daring to use the name Isabella and upset Jane more.

He held his hand out and gently ushered Jane into the room to stand before the blind, elderly lady.

Rebecca reached out her hand towards Jane. 'Isabella.'

Jane gasped as she suddenly realised, she did recognise her.

'You're the image of Vicky, except the hair,' Rebecca laughed.

'It's dyed black. I thought you were ...' Jane stammered.

'Blind? Yes, I am, but it don't mean I don't see,' she repeated, as she had to Suzanne, her voice stronger than her body looked. 'I knew you'd come home one day. I never doubted you were alive,' Rebecca told her.

'But I'm so confused. I don't know who I am,' Jane confided to this woman she trusted instantly.

'Course, you do. You're Isabella. I called to you often enough and you heard me, didn't you?'

'Yes,' Jane admitted, 'you're the voice in my dreams.'

Jonathan and Alex looked at each other, both feeling a creepy shiver ripple down their spines.

'Yes, darling, it was your old Gran. And your teddy, you found it, didn't you? I hid it in the garden so one day when you came home, it would be waiting for you and you'd know your old Gran left it there for you.'

'But how did you know?' Jane asked, in disbelief.

'I told you, cos I'm your Gran. You're a part of me. You have the sight too. I always knew you had.'

'You knew Toni took her?' Jonathan asked, not wanting to believe she was a part of it all.

'No, son, I didn't know it was Toni. Or I didn't want to believe a daughter of mine would do such a thing. She was so bitter and twisted after what happened to her. I didn't know who took Isabella, just that she was not dead. I felt it in here.' Rebecca hit her chest with surprising force. 'Now, child or should I say young lady, you have a father here who loves you very much. He's missed you every day since you've been gone and has lost ten years of being a part of your life. He's a good man; now you must let him make up for that time and not reject him anymore. You're not that grown up yet that you don't need a dad.'

'But I...' Jane stammered, looking round at Jonathan.

'But nothing, you've both suffered the cruel consequences of one of my daughters. Now, you must go forward and be happy. Life is hard enough without bitterness to add to it.'

Jane turned round and looked at Jonathan and he smiled sadly at her.

'Dad,' she said quietly.

His eyes welled as he held out his arms to his little girl.

She went to him and buried her face in his shoulder. Rebecca smiled and so did Alex.

Jonathan decided to take a year break from work to spend time with Isabella, or rather Bella, as she now insisted on being called.

'Jane is dead,' she announced at dinner that night, smiling warmly at her father.

'Oh goodness,' Margaret laughed. 'Not another name to remember. You've had so many I keep getting muddled.'

For the next few weeks life became hectic for Bella. The story of her turning up unexpectedly hit the newspapers and became front page news. The story was even on the news, and reporters plagued their home. It was difficult to avoid them, so in the end Suzanne talked them into doing a press release, where Isabella could be asked a stream of questions. This was on the condition that the media then left them in peace to get on with their lives.

Bella agreed and the story was printed, leaving Toni's name out of it for now. Once she returned to health, she would be arrested and face years in prison for child abduction and abuse, only if Bella would testify.

Bella could not decide what to do about testifying. But she did insist on going to see her mother, or aunt, as Jonathan kept reminding her, at the hospital.

In the past few days, Toni's health had improved and she was apparently now coherent. She had liver damage and was warned if she ever drank again, she would be dead within a year.

Jonathan was not happy about Isabella going to see her but relented, understanding that his daughter needed to close chapters in her life in order to move forward.

They walked in together, and Toni looked with daggers when she saw them.

Bella held her head up as she walked over to the bed. 'Hello, Toni,' she said, blatantly and coldly.

Toni was shocked; she did not even recognise the young lady that stood in front of her. She was so upright, confident and grown up. She never imagined ever facing Jane again.

'Hello, Jane, how are you?' she managed to stammer, guilt clear on her face.

'I'm good, thank you. As you can see, I found that father who never wanted me and rejected me from birth.'

Toni laughed nervously, the guilt deepening. She did not want to look into the face that showed her how she had destroyed so many lives.

'It's his fault, he fucked my life up,' she nodded towards Jonathan, who was trying to restrain himself from leaping forward and strangling her.

'He made me pregnant and walked away. He made me go through a birth on my own. Too cowardly to own up and admit he had fucked me and got me up the duff. Then he went off with my sister, leaving me to rot. I loved him with all my heart.'
Jonathan could not contain himself anymore. 'I was 16-years-old, you... evil cow! Just a kid!'

Jane looked at her father, not really understanding the significance of what was between them.

She looked back at Toni. 'So, you took it out on me? Made my life hell. Beat me, punished me and hated me. You took me away from my life because you wanted to make my father suffer?' she said, with conviction.

Toni looked away from her, not wanting to look into her accusing eyes.

'My mother killed herself because of you. Your own sister. I want to hate you, but all I do is pity you. You're the one that'll go to prison for a long time and suffer the prison that you put me in.'

Both Jonathan and Toni stared at Bella — so many grown up words from a young mouth. She turned from Toni and walked away.

'I'm sorry,' Toni called.

Bella never heard the words that were too weak to give her back what had been stolen from her.

Next, she asked for Jonathan to take her to see Scott, who was now out of danger. Suzanne had told her how he had saved her cousin's life.

He was sitting up talking to a man in the next bed when she walked into the ward. He looked surprised to see her, but smiled dubiously.

'I thought you'd done a runner with the money,' he told her.

Jane blushed while she explained about the phone. Jonathan had shown her how to charge it and they had read his warning messages.

'What'll happen to you now?' she asked him.

'I don't know. I've got no family and nowhere to go,' he shrugged. 'My dad will go to prison for a long time and our house was rented. I won't be able to keep it on. But I guess I'll survive. At least, I won't go to prison, or you, I hope.'

Jane smiled. 'I've a present for you.' She reached into her bag and bought out a carefully wrapped parcel.

'I think we owe you a great deal,' Jonathan told him. 'When you get out of here, come and see me. We might be able to sort something out.' He held out his hand and Scott shook it.

'You didn't kill the man down the bunker that day. You know that don't you? Dan did,' Scott said, knowing she was probably wracked with guilt.

After they left, he opened the parcel; inside the wrapping was a bag packed with fifty-pound notes.

Jonathan drove Bella, at her request, to a florist where she brought a big bunch of yellow roses. They walked through the entrance of the park to 'Frank's bench.'

'I'm so sorry,' Bella said, her eyes filled with tears as she laid them down. 'These are for you, Mrs Flanagan and Mr Tibbles.'

A little group of young people sat by the tennis courts. At first, Bella cringed and her immediate thought was to hide. She chastised herself, and holding up her head, she walked to the middle of them.

'Remember me?' she asked, as they looked blankly at her. 'It's Jane, you know, the girl whose life you made so miserable I wanted to kill myself.'

Lucy Ellis gasped, as she stared at the smart girl with designer clothes.

'There will be times in your life when things are so bad and unbearable for you too. When they are, I want you to remember me. Remember how terrible you made my life and relish how hell feels. You may even feel like taking your own life, just like I did. There will be a difference with the bad times you face. Because the times you hurt me and made me feel so terrible were inflicted by you.'

No one spoke as she walked away.

'Better?' Jonathan smiled.

'Not really,' Bella confessed.

He put his arm around her and led her back to the car. 'When did a little girl become so grown up? You sometimes seem older than your old dad.'

Bella laughed.

The dogs' home was next, where Jonathan took the suitcase from the boot of the car. They went into the reception and a lady looked up from the desk and smiled.

'I want to leave this case for Fiona,' Bella told the lady. 'Can you tell her it's a big thank you from Jane Watts, please?'

As Bella and Jonathan left, they watched from the car as Fiona opened the case. They could see her face as a look of disbelief, confusion, and then delight crossed her features. The case was full of money. She looked out of the window and saw Jane in the car. They both smiled and Fiona mouthed a big, tearful, 'Thank you.'

'Margaret just phoned,' Jonathan told her. 'There's a surprise for you at home.'

'Really, what?'

'I'm not telling you,' he laughed. Despite her begging all the way, he did not give in, although he was dying to see her face if he did.

When they pulled down the drive, both Henry, in his chair, and Margaret came out to meet them. Jane gasped and burst into tears. She opened the door and jumped out of the car almost while it was still moving.

In Margaret's arms sat a wiggling Molly.

Jane ran up and grabbed her from Margaret, sinking her wet face into her scruffy brown coat. The dog in turn licked the tears with her pink tongue.

'How?' asked Jonathan, putting his arm around his sister.

'It wasn't cheap. When I told the veterinary college how Bella loved the dog that night, they felt sorry for her; they fought to save her. Apparently, it was touch and go, but eventually through willpower and love of her mistress, the dog fought back. I didn't know at first, and then I never told anyone in case Molly died and we broke Bella's heart all over again.

'How much?' Jonathan asked, smiling and kissing his sister's cheek.

'You don't want to know, Jonathan, but I did say you were paying,' Margaret laughed.

'It's worth every penny,' he smiled, glowing, as his daughter did, with happiness.